Joanna Trollope began writing w̶h̶e̶n̶ ̶s̶h̶e̶ was first pregnant, and working as a te̶a̶c̶h̶e̶r̶.̶ ̶F̶o̶r̶ ̶y̶e̶a̶r̶s̶, she combined both careers, writi̶n̶g̶ ̶i̶n̶ ̶t̶h̶e̶ ̶m̶o̶r̶n̶i̶ngs 'to fill the spaces after the chil̶d̶r̶e̶n̶ ̶h̶a̶d̶ ̶g̶o̶n̶e̶ ̶to bed'.

She has written e̶l̶e̶v̶e̶n̶ bestselling novels, whose common theme is the nature of modern relationships, especially within families. Her own family is extremely important to her. She is the eldest of three, has two daughters, two stepsons and nine grandchildren.

Joanna was appointed OBE for services to literature in 1996. She lives in London.

Visit her website at www.joannatrollope.com

www.transworldbooks.co.uk

Also by Joanna Trollope

THE CHOIR
A VILLAGE AFFAIR
A PASSIONATE MAN
THE RECTOR'S WIFE
THE MEN AND THE GIRLS
A SPANISH LOVER
THE BEST OF FRIENDS
NEXT OF KIN
OTHER PEOPLE'S CHILDREN
MARRYING THE MISTRESS
GIRL FROM THE SOUTH
BROTHER & SISTER
SECOND HONEYMOON
FRIDAY NIGHTS
THE OTHER FAMILY
DAUGHTERS-IN-LAW
THE SOLDIER'S WIFE

and published by Black Swan

Balancing Act

JOANNA TROLLOPE

BLACK SWAN

TRANSWORLD PUBLISHERS
61–63 Uxbridge Road, London W5 5SA
A Random House Group Company
www.transworldbooks.co.uk

BALANCING ACT
A BLACK SWAN BOOK: 9780552778558 (B format)
9780552778565 (A format)

First published in Great Britain
in 2014 by Doubleday
an imprint of Transworld Publishers
Black Swan edition published 2014

Addresses for Random House Group Ltd companies outside the UK
can be found at: www.randomhouse.co.uk
The Random House Group Reg. No. 954009

The Random House Group Limited supports the Forest Stewardship
Council® (FSC®), the leading international forest-certification organisation.
Our books carrying the FSC label are printed on FSC®-certified paper.
FSC is the only forest-certification scheme supported by the leading
environmental organisations, including Greenpeace. Our paper procurement
policy can be found at www.randomhouse.co.uk/environment

Typeset in 11/16pt Giovanni Book by
Kestrel Data, Exeter, Devon
Printed and bound in Great Britain by
CPI Group (UK) Ltd, Croydon, CR0 4YY

2 4 6 8 10 9 7 5 3 1

MIX
Paper from
responsible sources
FSC® C016897

To everyone at Eastwood Pottery, Stoke-on-Trent,
with my love and grateful thanks.

Balancing Act

CHAPTER ONE

'What *is* all this?' Cara Moran said loudly to her youngest sister over the telephone. 'What's all this about Ma buying another house?'

In the design studio of the factory, Grace Moran sat with her eyes closed and her phone held a few inches away from her ear. She counted to five and then she said, deliberately non-committal, 'I don't know.'

'Yes, you do!'

'Car, I don't know any more than you do.'

There was an expression of disgusted impatience from the London end of the telephone line. Cara would be at her desk, Grace thought, in the new office suite that the company had acquired only a year ago, wearing an expression Grace remembered keenly from their childhood and which never boded well.

'You must know,' Cara said crossly. 'Of course you know. You're in Staffordshire, aren't you? How can I know from London what nonsense Ma is getting up to in Staffordshire?'

Grace opened her eyes and glanced down at the sketchbook in front of her. A whole page of drawings of jugs. Jug after jug. Tiny modifications in each sketch, so that what her mother liked as a design idea would also work in production.

'I want a pinched spout,' Susie had said. 'I want that cosy, domestic, traditional look. A Dutch jug.'

Grace had not sought support from her two young design colleagues, who had remained steadfastly staring at their computer screens. She had said to her mother patiently, 'You can't have a pinched spout on that, Ma. It'll be different every time they cast it, and then it might crack in the firing.'

Now she said to her sister, in the same patient tone, 'Ma's allowed to buy a house, you know. It's her company, after all.'

Cara gave a little yelp of mocking laughter. 'Don't we know it!'

'And this isn't an expensive house—'

'Since when was half a million not expensive?'

Grace picked up a pencil and added a daisy motif to one of the jugs. She said calmly, 'So you *do* know about it.'

There was a short pause.

Then Cara said in a different tone, 'Ashley and I Googled it at lunchtime.'

'Ah.'

'It looks like a sweet house.'

'It's where her great-grandfather worked. The one who was a dairyman.'

'I know.'

'The Parlour House. It's a cottage, really.'

'In Barlaston.'

'She was born in Barlaston,' Grace said.

'Gracie, I know. I get all that. But she hasn't got time to live in it. She's got a perfectly good house in London, and she's busy. Flat-out busy. Anyway, what about Pa?'

'I don't know.'

'Has she even told him?'

Grace sighed. 'He won't mind. He never minds.'

'Well, there's the money.'

'I suppose the house would be an asset—'

'Not if it's for her private use. You know how it works – how it's always been. We're all salaried and then the company gives Ma and Pa what they need. But finding an extra million before tax—'

'She's not extravagant—'

'That's not the point.'

'So you and Ashley and Dan have already discussed it?'

Cara said firmly, 'Just Ashley and me.'

'Why are you ringing me? You never ask my opinion on anything to do with money. You don't think I have any aptitude for it. You think I only just understand that a cash machine isn't a kind of money box—'

'Rubbish, Gracie.'

Grace threw her pencil down. It clattered lightly along the central table and then fell on to the wooden floor and rolled gently under a desk.

'Grace?' Cara said. 'Are you still there?'

'I'm here.'

'Will you go and see her?'

'What?'

'Will you,' Cara said, enunciating deliberately as if speaking to someone hard of hearing, 'see Ma tonight and explain to her that buying another house might not be the most practical use of her time or energy, and that property of any kind really has to be seen as an investment asset for all of us?'

'Why me?'

'Because, Grace, you are in Stoke, and Ma is staying out at Barlaston tonight, and we are all in London.'

Grace got up and crossed the studio to retrieve the pencil. She said, stooping, 'But I'm not here tonight. It's Friday.'

'I know it's Friday. Why aren't you there?'

Grace straightened up. It was a nice pencil. The lead didn't break all the time when you sharpened it. She said, 'I'm going to Edinburgh tonight.'

'Edinburgh? Why?'

12

'Jeff's got a friend doing a gig up there. We're going to support him.'

'But—'

'I'm allowed time off!' Grace cried. 'I've been here since eight o'clock this morning!'

'It's not that.'

'It's Jeff, isn't it?' Grace said. 'You don't want me doing anything with Jeff.'

Cara said carefully, 'Well, I am just not wild about relationships made online.'

'Everybody does it now,' said Grace. 'It's what we all do.'

'Okcupid,' Cara said with distaste. 'Luvstruck.com.'

'You don't like Jeff.'

'No, I don't like Jeff. I don't think he's good enough for you. But that's beside the point. The point is that Ma needs to be talked to before she hands over a deposit.'

Grace dropped the pencil into the mug – the mug made in the factory – that held all her pens and pencils. She said, slightly defiantly, 'Sorry. Anyway it's Friday. No money will get transferred till Monday.'

'We need to talk to her.'

'*You* talk.'

'Grace, I always have to do the talking.'

'You're the eldest.'

'And you're the youngest, so you never get to do any-thing difficult.'

Grace wanted to say that sometimes being the youngest made every single thing difficult. Instead she said as levelly as she could, 'I'll call Ma on my way to Edinburgh.'

'You really are going to Edinburgh?'

Grace's private phone, lying on the desk beside her sketchbook, flashed again. 'Jeff,' said the screen. Grace picked it up.

'Yes,' she said to her sister. 'Yes, I am.'

Ashley Robbins, née Moran, let herself into her car in the underground car park and dropped her handbag and workbag – indistinguishable in size or weight – into the footwell of the passenger seat beside her. The footwell already contained several empty, dented juice cartons, a half-drunk bottle of one of Leo's irritatingly boastful energy drinks and a drift of crumbs. The latter would, of course, now adhere to the bottom of her bags and she would forget that they were there until, like last week, they transferred themselves shamingly to the immaculate desktop of the chinaware buyer of a big chain of department stores, who might – or, now, might not – put in a substantial order for a wide range of Susie Sullivan pottery. The buyer had behaved as if her desk had not just been smeared with crushed crisps, so Ashley spent much of the meeting surreptitiously trying to remove the mess with wet wipes, which filled the room with an insistent aroma of synthetic lemon. There had, as yet, been no confirmation of the order.

Ashley buckled on her seatbelt, started the engine and turned on the headlights. The car radio, bursting into life with the engine, announced that it was three minutes to six and the weekend weather would be mild and unsettled with slow-moving bands of rain advancing from the west. Rain which would, in turn, curtail visits to the playground – some mothers took towels to dry off the slides and swing seats, but Ashley was not one of them – and prevent Leo from making progress in the stretch of mud and broken concrete that he assured her would one day be a garden. She had tried not to say, 'When the children are too old to use it,' and failed. Leo had drawn a beautiful plan of the projected garden and pinned it up in the kitchen. When it had been there a month, Ashley suggested that they get quotes from a few garden companies to put the plan into practice. Leo had looked deeply wounded.

'I can do it, Ash. I'm good at that sort of thing. You know I am. I want to do it myself for the children.'

The western end of the King's Road was solid with Friday-evening traffic, and a light, persistent drizzle was making the windscreen look as if it had been daubed with oil. She ought to have walked. The office was only a twenty-minute walk from home, in Fulham, and perfectly walkable, but it had been threatening to rain that morning, and she was late, and there were her bags to carry and the car was at the kerb outside. So she had succumbed to the car, and now she was jammed behind a number 22 bus, with another car almost touching her back bumper. Leo would have taken over from the nanny by now – not a wildly satisfactory nanny, this new girl, either, but then nobody had been, since Nicky left to get married and moved to Australia – so there wasn't the frantic rush there might have been. But frantic seemed to be her default mode at the moment, and wherever she was, at work or at home, felt somehow wrong. The guilt that stalked her seemed to have no respect for the number of simultaneous roles she was required to fill. Mothering? You should be at work. In the office again? You should be at home. Friendships? Don't even bother going there.

At least Leo never said that. He never reproached her about work or the fact that working in a family company meant that the lines between work and home were not so much blurred as irrevocably tangled. Leo didn't seem to share the urgency that surged in Ashley's bloodstream; he didn't seem to feel driven, or impelled, or even much obliged to do anything beyond the most immediate requirement. He would sit on the floor with Fred, building an unhurried Lego tower, and giving no indication that his mind was on anything other than helping Fred's small fat hands to slot a blue brick on

16

top of a red one. And when Maisie hurled herself at him in one of her three-year-old turbulences, he would just catch her and hold her, until some kind of inner resolution eventually enabled her to stop thrashing about like a pinned firework and be set down again.

If she was honest, he'd had that effect on Ashley, too, at the beginning. She'd thought, after university, that the last thing she wanted was to join the family firm. Her older sister was determinedly gaining merchandising experience in a household-name company, her younger sister was doing a graphics course at art school, and the comfortable assumption was that both of them would join Susie Sullivan pottery at a significant level in due course. But Ashley said she didn't want that. Ashley said she wanted an academic career. Then she said she wanted to go travelling. Then she said she thought she'd try property development, at which point Leo Robbins, whom she'd known vaguely at university, showed up at the party of a mutual friend and indicated to her, largely by what he left unsaid, that it was a pity to waste her cleverness by behaving like an airhead trustafarian.

She started going out with Leo and she got an unremarkable job in the marketing department of a major newsagent chain. It was a horrible job, mostly consisting of cold-calling advertisers and cosseting tiresome customer accounts, but it had a revelatory side. Within three months, Ashley was as hooked on marketing as she was on Leo. Marketing was, of course, largely common sense, but it was also analytical. Leo, gazing at her shining face, never said *I told you so*, but he took real pleasure in her enthusiasm and aptitude. His own job, as a Media Studies supply teacher in the Greater London area, seemed not to be a matter of huge concern to him. Sometimes he worked, sometimes he didn't. He was amiable, capable, practical, and devoid of Ashley's compelling energy.

'He's a great foil for you,' Ashley's father said.

'Is that a compliment?'

He shrugged. 'It's an observation.'

So here she now was, marketing director of Susie Sullivan, married for six years to Leo Robbins, with two small children and a shabby house in Fulham, sitting in her car on a Friday night in a traffic jam in the rain, lining up in her mind all the things she would need to do once she got home. One of which was to ring her mother. About this house.

It was quiet in the office, with the kind of Friday-night hush which presages a prolonged period of inactivity. The desks were all tidy, and in the so-called boardroom – only Susie could have insisted on a boardroom which resembled nothing so much as a pretty kitchen – the alternate red- and duck-egg-blue-painted chairs were neatly arranged around the blond wooden table. The table itself bore nothing except a Susie Sullivan jug of scarlet and royal-blue anemones. Flowers meant that Susie herself had been in the office or was about to arrive. She insisted on flowers everywhere, and garden or hedgerow flowers if possible.

Cara walked slowly down the length of the office. It was open-plan and airy, and although the windows were currently black with evening winter rain, in day-time they afforded an astonishing panoramic view of west London: of the river, of trees, which in the summer were as neat and dense looking as green sponges. They had designed the office between them, her mother and her sisters, with natural flooring, display cabinets resembling dressers painted in the trademark duck-egg blue and scarlet and laden with pottery, walls of framed posters and framed tea towels, conference tables like kitchen tables, proliferations of teapots and rows of mugs on hooks, all of it managing to diminish almost to invisibility the necessary computer terminals and whiteboards.

'I want,' Susie had said, standing in the entrance of what had then simply been four thousand square feet of empty office space, 'the buyers from the stores to come in here and *gawp*. I want them to see the brand, and the lifestyle we're selling, like they've never seen anything so clearly before. I want colour, I want warmth and welcome, but I want order. This office must exude efficiency, but it must also exude *home*.'

To Cara's eye, it did. The big white tables on which they all worked were backed by shelves of thoughtfully arranged pottery and walls of romantically shot photographs of pottery: jugs of cow parsley on garden tables, butter-smeared knives on pretty plates, teapots beside tumbles of pastel-iced cupcakes. There were Susie Sullivan lamps next to the computer screens and Susie Sullivan fabrics on the back cushions of some of the desk chairs. The lighting glowed and shone rather than blazed. It looked – well, Cara thought, as she had often thought since they moved from the frankly cramped ad hoc basement offices of the London shop – completely and utterly inviting. However sophisticated you were, however urbane, however much your tastes ran to the impersonally perfected world of hotel living, you could not stand on the threshold of these offices and not feel the impulse to acknowledge the strength and sheer seduction of her mother's domestic vision.

'And there's me,' Susie would say, half laughing. 'There's me who's never thrown a pot in my life. I just – I just see this way of living. The chimney corner. The fireside. The nest.'

Cara walked slowly on down the central aisle towards her own desk at the far end. Her husband, Daniel, was still in front of his screen, and would be, she knew, until she signalled that she was clocking off herself. As commercial director, he made a point of working visibly longer hours than anyone else, and said so. Privately, Cara thought his essential motivation was more that he was not a blood member of the Moran family, but she never said so, and she would never permit anyone else to say so, either. She had met Daniel during her merchandizing training and had recognized in him a commitment to making a business thrive that she was aware of in herself. It hadn't been in any way easy persuading her mother to appoint Daniel as commercial director.

'It's *my* baby,' Susie had said. 'It's mine. And I'm holding on to it.'

'Nobody wants to take it from you, Ma. We just want it to be able to grow up.'

'In the right way only!'

'In *your* way.'

'But Daniel's way isn't my way. Daniel doesn't see what I see.'

'I don't need to,' Daniel had said. 'I just need to do the black magic you can't do.'

She'd eyed him, taut with suspicion. 'What d'you mean?'

'I mean,' he said carefully, not looking at Cara, 'predicting what you don't know on models from the past, which you do.' He'd paused. Then he'd said lightly,

'Maths is so useful. For analysis. And you don't have maths.'

Later, acquiescing with every sign of reluctance, Susie had said to Cara, 'I hate needing something I can't do.'

That was ten years ago now. In ten years, with the help of Daniel and – she had to admit – herself, the company's turnover had gone from two million to almost thirteen. It had been a battle. It was still a battle. At every turn, at every suggestion, Susie cried that they were losing the essence of her vision, that this precious baby of hers was becoming less personal and, in consequence, more inauthentic. At the moment – and it had been rumbling on for months – there was the ongoing problem of getting Susie to see that in franchising out her designs to tinware companies or bedlinen manufacturers, she only had to give them her vision, not a hundred detailed sketchbooks. Those companies knew how to translate a vision. They were trained for it. But try convincing Ma.

And now there was this house. Cara had not yet had the conversation with Daniel about Susie's house. Daniel had spent the last three years setting up the office team in the face of his mother-in-law's opposition. She wanted what she had always known, she wanted what had always worked for her, and yet she could not resist the idea of growing the company, spreading the word, infiltrating more and more domestic lives with the captivation of her concept. Daniel was, Cara knew, on the very edge of his patience.

'Why can't she see,' he'd demand, 'that if she could only let go of the control of the details, she'd have far more effect and control in the end? Why can't she *see* that?'

Daniel wouldn't like the house project. He'd be utterly exasperated by it. And there was no use asking Pa. Pa was lovely, sweet, but he'd never stood up to Ma over anything. As long as he had his music studio and his guitar and his illusion that his band, the Stone Gods, had once been up there with Pink Floyd, Pa was happy for Ma to do whatever she wanted. If Cara rang him and said, 'What about this house in Barlaston?' he'd say, 'Oh, come on, angel, let her have it. It means a lot to her. And she's earned it, hasn't she?'

Cara stopped by the whiteboard behind her own desk. It was covered in figures she had put up herself that morning in coloured markers. On Monday, her task would be to estimate how much the gifting of products – those personalized teapots that seemed to appeal to so many people for so many occasions – was driving sales, and to come up with a strategy for the next year to present to her mother.

'My job,' she'd said to a business journalist from a national newspaper recently, 'is to nurture our core business while simultaneously introducing quality newness, until that newness becomes core.'

A cottage in Barlaston was not core. And it was not quality newness. It was a distraction. An expensive, unnecessary, wilful distraction.

She crossed to Daniel's desk and stood looking down at him. He was beginning to thin very slightly on the crown of his head, she noticed. She could see his scalp, as pleasingly olive skinned as the rest of him, through his dark hair.

'Dan,' she said.

He didn't look up.

He said, still staring at his screen, 'I'm not really working any more, you know. I'm just stuck.'

'Can I unstick you?'

He leaned back a little. 'What are you offering?'

She perched on the edge of his desk so that she was half obscuring the computer screen. He glanced up at her inquiringly.

'Ma's latest,' Cara said. And sighed, to let him know.

'I needed the A500,' Jeff said.

Grace, who had programmed the satnav and balanced it behind the gearstick because Jeff didn't like the suction marks it left if it was stuck to the windscreen, said nothing.

He went on, 'And then to hit the M6.'

Grace looked out of the window. It was dark and wet, and there was a lot of traffic, and she was tired.

Jeff said, 'Are you listening?'

'Oh yes,' Grace said. 'Did you want a response?'

'Would I have spoken in the first place if I hadn't wanted a response?'

Grace said, still looking out of the window, 'I thought you were just thinking aloud. Seeing as how you have the satnav. And we are *on* the M6.'

There was a brief pause, and then Jeff said with dangerous precision, 'I cannot actually see the satnav. The fucking gears are in the way.'

Grace breathed deeply a couple of times. Then she said, in as conversational a tone as she could manage, 'Where would you like me to put it?'

'Where I can bloody see it.'

Grace reached down and moved the little screen up into the well on top of the dashboard. It immediately fell over.

'Brilliant,' Jeff said witheringly.

'I could stick it on the windscreen . . .'

'I hate it on the windscreen.'

'I've run out of ideas,' said Grace. 'Do you have any?'

Jeff let another silence fall and then announced, 'I am driving.'

'I offered to—'

'You were late, Grace. You kept me waiting. We were

half an hour late leaving. I sat outside that fucking factory for half an hour, waiting.'

Grace turned her head and looked at him. His beautiful profile was outlined intermittently against the lights of passing cars. She said steadily, 'I was working.'

Jeff said nothing. He was of the view that working for a family firm didn't count as proper work in the same way that having a job outside one did. He said that there was always the safety net of capital and job security in a family firm. He often implied that working in a company founded by her own mother was some kind of cop out, which sometimes made Grace feel ashamed and apologetic and sometimes defiant. Jeff himself worked for a friend who ran a garden centre out near Trentham Gardens, something to do with maintaining their database. He didn't like elaborating on it, for some reason, but he got a car out of it, at least, and they weren't exactly onerous hours.

Grace had never, somehow, been able to pin him down about the details of his life or upbringing. He had loomed up out of the mists of the internet, as it were, fully formed but ever elusive, always managing to avoid giving direct answers to any questions, but leaving Grace with the distinct impression that he required recompense for a bad start in life, for an inadequate, now discarded family, for having had to survive on his wits. And his looks. His looks had been her downfall, from the beginning. She had seen his picture on the dating website and gasped out loud, even though she was alone at the time. How could a man who looked like that be unattached for a single second? How could such a god happen to live under ten miles away? And, above all, how could he be remotely interested in her? But then, when they met in Hanley – just for a coffee, as advised by the agency – he had been headily demonstrative of that interest. He had been completely disarming. He still could be – and seemed to know instinctively when there was the need for it.

As if reading her thoughts, Jeff put his left hand out and clasped Grace's nearest one warmly. He said, 'Let's not fight. Let's have a great weekend.'

She squeezed his hand. Even without looking at it, she knew it was an elegant hand, long and strong like the rest of him. His hands were beguiling, just like his teeth were, and his eyelashes, and his thick, extraordinary hair.

'I really want it to be a great weekend,' she said, meaning it.

He released her hand and put his own back on the steering wheel. 'It will be.'

'A nice hotel . . .'

'Oh, we're not staying in a hotel,' Jeff said. 'Not on *my* budget. Matt's giving us his sofa.'

'But I thought—'

'You always think the five-star stuff, Grace. Of course you do. But this is a mate's gig, babe, this is real, this is how ninety per cent of the population in this be-nighted country *live*.'

Grace tried to feel as if her hand was still in his. She said, 'I am fine with Matt's sofa. Really. It's nice of him to have us.'

'You'll like him.'

'I'm sure I will.'

'Amazing on drums. Awesome.'

Grace swallowed. 'That's tomorrow night, isn't it?'

'Plus some jamming tonight. It'll be like it used to be – impro and ideas till dawn.'

Grace opened her mouth, and shut it again. Did he mean jamming and improvisation on drums in the same room as the sofa? She felt for her phone in her pocket.

'Jeff?'

'Uh-huh?'

'I've just got to make a quick call.'

'This is Friday fucking night, babe! Can't you even switch off work mode on a Friday night?'

'It's not work.'

He said roughly, 'What is it then?'

28

'I have to ring my mother.'

'Why?'

'It's . . . it's a bit of a crisis. A sort of family crisis. I promised my sister.'

There was another silence. Taking it as assent, Grace began to dial Susie's number. As she did so, Jeff indicated to the left and swerved the car to a sudden and dramatic halt on the hard shoulder.

Grace stopped dialling. 'What are you doing?'

'Stopping the car.'

'But why?'

Jeff stared straight ahead. 'I'm not having this.'

'Not having what?'

'I'm not having your bloody family all over our time together. Your bloody family, your fucking family firm. Honestly, Grace, when are you going to grow up and not be at their beck and call every minute of every bloody day?'

Grace waited a moment and then she said inadequately, 'I'm not.'

'Well, what are you doing right now? *Right now?* When we are on our way to what should be *our* weekend away, in Edinburgh?'

'But,' Grace said levelly, 'it's something that can't wait, which I promised my sister I'd talk to my mother about. It's about a property. It's about preventing a big unnecessary expenditure.'

'It's always about money, with your family.'

'That is so not fair—'

'It's true!' Jeff shouted.

'I only want to make one phone call—'

'To your fucking mother! Again!'

Grace said, 'Can we drive on?'

Jeff folded his arms. 'No, we cannot. Not till this is sorted.'

'Until my phone call is sorted?'

'Until,' Jeff said, hunching down in his seat with folded arms, 'your priorities are sorted.'

Grace said nothing. She was shaking slightly, and the traffic thundering past only feet from them was making the car shake too.

Jeff said, staring straight ahead, 'It's been like this all along. You fit me into bits and pieces of your life when your fucking family doesn't need you to do something for them. All I ever get is what's left over. They come first, last and in between, you're just their plaything, they can do whatever they like with you, because little baby Grace can't do without her toys and her family have the power to take all those toys away in a nano-second if she's naughty. I am absolutely fucking *sick* of coming way, way after all your family!'

Grace slipped her phone back into her pocket and gripped it like a talisman. She said, 'How far to Manchester, do you think?'

Jeff grunted. 'I have no idea. Forty minutes, maybe.'

'Then would you drop me off there?' Grace said. 'Drop me off in Manchester, and I'll get a train back to Stoke.'

CHAPTER TWO

The Parlour House stood end on to the lane. It was built of softly coloured old brick, with a central door under a small pedimented porch, a white-painted window either side and three on the floor above. It had a reproduction coachman's lantern beside the front door – *That's going*, Susie thought – and an oval black iron plaque screwed to the end wall which faced the lane, with THE PARLOUR HOUSE embossed on it in white. There was a wicket gate, a brick garden wall, a square of rough grass and a yew tree. It was, to Susie's eyes, deeply and uncomplicatedly satisfactory.

It was also empty. The owner, tiring of waiting for a buyer at the house's initial and unrealistic price, had given up trying to sell it occupied, and had gone to live in a bungalow near her daughter in the New Forest. She had left behind pink carpets, a fretworked fitted kitchen and the coachman's lantern. She had not, the agent said, been a Staffordshire woman, but had come up to the Potteries when her late husband had got a job with one of the local companies making hotel ware, and had subsequently been marooned in Barlaston by his death only two years into retirement.

'I was born in Barlaston,' Susie said to the agent.

The agent smiled at her. 'Moran isn't a very local name.'

'It's my married name,' Susie said. 'I was born a Snape.'

'Ah,' said the agent, who had been born in a suburb of Birmingham.

'Barlaston was full of Snapes. And then I married a Moran.'

The agent glazed over slightly. He had thought, judging by Susie's jeans and boots and hair, that she was going to be one of his classier and more entertaining clients. But she was behaving more like the kind of people who researched their genealogy on the internet. He didn't actually care where she came from or what she was called. He just wanted her to accept the reduced asking price, pay her deposit and get the sodding house off his books. The owner was a pain, ringing up from Lyndhurst umpteen times a week and demanding to know why he wasn't presenting her with a fat cheque. He made an effort. 'Barlaston must have been lovely back then.'

'It's lovely now,' Susie said indignantly.

He thought of the shop front in Barlaston's tired little

shopping parade which read RETIREMENT PLANNING LIMITED and said gallantly, 'Well, if you were born here . . .'

'It's a gorgeous village,' Susie said. 'It was a very *deliberate* choice of Wedgwood to move their factory out here. For the workers.'

The agent said nothing. He had stupidly handed the Parlour House keys to Susie, so he couldn't even jingle them in a jolly way and suggest that they get a move on.

As if she'd read his mind, Susie shifted the keys in her hand so that she was holding the main one ready. 'Tell you what,' she said. 'You have my name and number, and I can hardly nick a whole house, can I? Leave me to look round it again on my own and I'll drop the keys back at your office.'

He hesitated. 'If you're sure . . .'

'More than sure. In fact, I can't decide with you hovering. If you want to have any chance of a sale, your only hope is to leave me to think on my own.' She eyed him shrewdly. 'You want a sale?'

'Mrs Moran, I . . . Yes.'

'Then scoot,' she said. She glanced at him. Bad skin. Worse suit. She put her hand on the wicket gate and said dismissively, 'The keys will be through your door by lunchtime.'

*

Susie supposed, as she stood in the small, damp-smelling front room, that when her great-grandfather worked in this building, the whole ground floor would have been the dairy – stone-floored, slate-shelved, with a pump somewhere central and a long gutter for the water and waste to run away, and a milky, cleanish, sourish smell in the air that you could never get rid of. It would have been cold and draughty, clanking with churns, and the dairymaids would have worked bare-armed with chapped hands and their hair tied up in nets. She'd be respectful of that legacy, she thought. She'd empty out this warren of gimcrack little rooms and turn the ground floor back into a single space, with the steep stairs rising unrailed out of the centre, and a solid fuel cooker and a wood-burning stove, and families of jugs on the windowsills. Maybe rag rugs on the floors – modern rag rugs in bright colours. Waxed stone floors, with modern heating pipes underneath so that when you came down to make tea in the morning and let the dog out and the cat in, and you noticed that the yew tree in the garden was spangled with new spiders' webs—

Stop, Susie thought. Stop there. The girls do not want me to buy this house. Daniel does not want me to buy this house. Leo has not expressed an opinion, and Jasper, as usual, has said if you really want it, doll, you go right ahead and buy it. Neither of which is a satisfactory response in any way, because all Leo and Jasper mean is that they'd like to side with the girls and Daniel, but they don't quite dare. Even so, I hear them. I hear what they don't say as loudly as what the others do say. Even Grace, who I think had been crying when she rang, although she insisted she was fine. I thought she was going to Edinburgh, but she seems to have changed her mind. And she wouldn't come this morning. I wanted her to come with me to the Parlour House, but she wouldn't. She said I had to make up my own mind on my own. She said that's what I've always done. I suppose I have. Only child, absent parents. No, correction: only child, hopeless parents, as well as absent. It teaches you to know what you need. What you want. And I, standing here on a Saturday morning with the winter sun shining on the dirty windows of the building where my great-grandfather worked most of his life, want this.

Susie went slowly up the stairs, a narrow cottage staircase, the walls marked with faint rectangles where pictures once hung. The upstairs rooms were what her grandmother would have called poky – a favourite criticism from a woman whose husband installed her in a large and solid Edwardian house in Barlaston, which he had designed in imitation of one of the Wedgwood family houses, right down to the flying stone staircase in the portentous central hall and the proliferation of red and blue Turkey carpets.

Susie had loved that house. It was her childhood home, after all, as her grandparents had brought her up. Her grandmother had been born in a back-to-back in Burslem, and had found herself transported to become the mistress of Oak View, in Barlaston, well south of the six towns and the pits and the pots of her growing up. She'd met Susie's grandfather when he'd interviewed her to be an apprentice fettler for his newly opened pot bank in Hanley. She'd left school on the Friday, and her mother had found her a job at Snape's pottery on the following Monday. Young Mr Snape chose all his own staff in those days, liking as he did to know everything about everyone who worked for him. And he'd looked at Jean McGrath, and imagined the silica dust that was so difficult to extract from the fettling shop in the factory getting into her unquestionably precious lungs and causing the horrors of emphysema, that infamous potters' rot, and had decided then and there that he had other ideas for her.

Susie had adored her grandfather. He had known even as a boy that his spirit could not bear to follow his father into agriculture. He apprenticed himself to Royal Doulton, working his way swiftly up the ranks, trading on the side as he went – local coal, local barge transport along the canals, imported china clay, imported pit props, machinery imported from Germany to make porcelain, from Birmingham to make flatware. By the time he was thirty, he was able to open his own pot bank in Hanley, making pottery spongeware. By the time he was forty, he was married to Jean McGrath, and had installed his wife and infant son in a house built in careful imitation of a previous age. And by the time he was seventy, the market for spongeware had dwindled to almost nothing, and the no longer infant son had abandoned his parents, his native country and his only child to take off with that child's eternally adolescent mother to live a carefree, barefoot and unabashedly addled life on the island of Lamu.

Susie never went to Lamu. She was asked to go, in the vague, indifferent way her parents always suggested anything, but she refused. She liked the anachronistic routines of Oak View, which went on steadily, even after her grandfather had failed to revive his business with tissue printing on eighteenth-century shapes and had sold Snape's factory to a firm that made cheap commercial ware for modest family-hotel chains and the new motorway cafés. Her grandfather was, she saw, a trader at heart, more than an entrepreneur. He continued to deal in the commodities he knew, eternally on the telephone, with rolls of used notes in his pockets, secured with elastic bands.

He was a Methodist, her grandfather, as her grandmother had become, but that didn't stop him from sending Susie to school at St Dominic's in Stone, where she was one of only a handful of girls who weren't Catholic. His values remained the sturdy, aspirational, paternalistic values of his own young manhood, and his only grandchild was going to profit from his success, if he had anything to do with it. He never mentioned his only son, and if the subject ever came up between Susie and her grandmother, Jean would say, 'Well, there must have been bad genes among the good genes in the McGraths, and your poor father inherited all of them.'

Susie had once asked if her grandparents ever shared what must have been a fierce and abiding disappointment in their only child, and her grandmother, sealing jars of hot marmalade with discs of waxed paper, had simply said, 'That's not for you to ask, pet, ever.'

After St Dominic's, Susie had gone to art school in Liverpool, to study photography. She had rapturously embraced the flower power of the seventies, returning to Oak View with friends in tow who wore half-cured embroidered Afghan sheepskin coats and Schubert spectacles. Her grandparents had regarded these students in their loon pants and vast-sleeved shirts, the boys with hair as long and riotously curly as the girls, as if they were creatures from another planet, but their otherness had been no reason not to feed them with pies and porridge, and put them to sleep under

39

Yorkshire wool blankets and Paisley quilts. Marijuana smoking was banished to the garden and there was little alcohol in the house beyond her grandfather's whisky decanter and the treacly sherry used to soak sponges in trifles, but Susie couldn't help noticing that her friends angled for invitations to Oak View, and her grandparents, in their turn, regarded their visitors with the benevolence usually reserved for abandoned dogs.

So there was a lot of explaining to do to a lot of people when Susie decided, halfway through her second year, that she disliked photography, was tired of education and educational establishments, and wanted to roll up her sleeves, and *start*.

'Start what, exactly?' her grandfather said.

'A business. Like you.'

He regarded her matter-of-factly, and said, 'I failed at business.'

'Well, you had to give up the pottery.'

'I'm a dealer. I'm a trader. I'm lucky that I'm not on a market stall, hustling. I couldn't run a business. I couldn't get the spirit of it right. I couldn't believe in what I was making.'

Susie waited a moment. She wound a long lock of her hair round her finger, and inspected the ends. Then she said, 'I could, though.'

'Could you, now?'

'I could. I could revive your old business.'

'Too late.'

'No, it isn't.'

'Nobody wants spongeware.'

Susie said, 'People want home life, though.'

'What's that got to do with it?'

'They would like to have the kinds of kitchens and home lives where spongeware is just right. Handmade, but not as ritzy or formal as bone china. Accessible. Approachable. Pretty. Kitchen-table china you could eat your crumpets off.'

Her grandfather watched her for a while. Then he said, 'I'm not buying that factory back for you.'

Susie put her chin up. 'I'm not asking.'

He grunted. 'What's your plan then?'

'I'm going to London.'

He grinned. 'Of course you are. What else would you do at twenty?'

'But I'll be back. I'll be back before I'm thirty.'

He put a hand out and brushed her cheek. 'I'll be dead by then.'

'Oh, I'll be back long before you're dead.'

'I'll be worth something to you, dead.'

She said soberly, 'I don't want to think about that.'

'No good not being realistic.'

She dropped her hair and looked directly at him.

'And there's something else to tell you and Grandma. I've met someone. He's studying industrial design, but that's not where his heart is. His heart's in music. He plays the guitar in a group. He's called Jasper Moran.'

Susie and Jasper set up their joss-stick-scented first home in a London basement, in Fulham. It was damp and chilly, and they adored it, festooning the ceilings and walls with Indian scarves and saris and cooking ferocious chilli con carne on a Baby Belling cooker which emitted blue sparks if you touched it with damp hands. Jasper's group, the Stone Gods, had been signed up by EMI – their recording label, Parlophone, was to their profound gratification the same as the Beatles' – and they were plainly bound for great things. While Jasper was out playing or recording, Susie had no intention of staying at home to water their infinite cascades of spider plants. She got a job in the half-hearted shop of a run-down pottery in Fulham, which made – to her mind – cod artisan pottery decorated with clumsy faux-naïf transfers. Within three months, she had improved the look of the shop, and within six, the sales figures. At the end of a year, she bearded the owner in the nicotine-thick fug of his disordered office and offered to buy him out.

He winked at her. He had long grey hair tied back in a ponytail with a length of red woollen tape.

'What with, ducky?'

'A loan from the bank,' Susie said.

'And what bank is going to give a twenty-one-year-old a big enough loan to buy out a hundred-year-old pottery and retail premises?'

Susie stared at him. She had no intention of telling him that the loan would come from her grandfather's bank, in Stoke-on-Trent, and that her grandfather was tacitly underwriting the loan.

She said, 'I have the loan already.'

'Really?'

'Really,' she said. She indicated the heavy black handset phone that sat in the muddle of his desk. 'Ring them and ask.'

Nineteen seventy-eight, the year Susie turned twenty-two and Jasper twenty-four, was momentous for both of them. The Stone Gods got to number four in the charts and played live on *Top of the Pops*; Susie bought the pottery and named it Susie Sullivan after her grandmother's Irish mother, an immigrant to Liverpool whose family, along with hundreds of others, had been recruited to Stoke to work in the Potteries; and they got married in a registry office, Susie in a cream lace mini dress with trumpet sleeves and a floppy-brimmed straw hat wreathed in daisies. Jasper wore a purple velvet suit with flared trousers and took his bride off to Morocco for their honeymoon, whence she returned with ankle bracelets and the backs of her hands stippled with

43

indigo. The basement flat was exchanged for a narrow, dilapidated house with mushrooms along the skirting boards and panels of Formica across the fireplaces, and when the cheerful chaos of their London life became briefly too much for them, Susie would drive her yellow Citroën 2CV, with its frog-like headlamps, up to Oak View, and climb under the Paisley quilts, secure in the knowledge that life in that solid household ticked on as comfortably and reliably as an old clock.

And then, suddenly, her grandfather died of a stroke. One moment, it seemed, he was on the telephone in the room that had always been designated his office, rather than his study, and the next he was lying on his side of the marital bed upstairs, under a sheet, waiting for the undertaker. When he had fallen in his office, crashing against a bookcase, he had managed to cry out, incoherently but loud enough for his wife, watching racing from Doncaster on the television across the hall, to get to her feet and make her purposeful but unsteady eighty-four-year-old way to his side. He was conscious, but he could not speak. By the time Jean had manoeuvred herself on to the floor beside him and heaved his head into her lap, he had had a second stroke, and was dead. In the time it had taken for the final furlongs to be run at Doncaster, he had gone from being upright and articulate to dead. It took rather longer for Jean to reach a point where she could move his head to the floor, and get herself to her feet and a telephone.

Susie wondered if her father would come from Lamu, for the funeral. Her grandmother said that she was perfectly indifferent.

'If he comes, he comes. I wouldn't turn him away, but I wouldn't welcome him, either.' She had not glanced Susie's way. 'And we'd neither of us thank you for trying to persuade him. He's got the information and that's all I want done.'

He didn't come. But it seemed half of Stoke-on-Trent did. St Peter's Church was packed, and the service was relayed on loudspeakers into the churchyard, where the original Josiah Wedgwood lay under his table tomb, fenced in with iron railings.

After the funeral, Susie and Jasper returned to Oak View with Jean, who informed them that she was selling the house and moving to a bungalow on Barlaston Green, near the library. She said, looking straight at Susie, that she wanted no arguing. Then she left them at the kitchen table with the familiar blue-and-white Burleigh teapot and a ginger cake of her own making, and went slowly and alone up to bed.

Susie had looked at Jasper across the table and said, sadly, 'I never managed to tell her that I was pregnant.'

*

45

Cara Moran was born in London in 1980. Her sister Ashley followed two years later, and then, after a further gap of six years, there was Grace. In the course of those eight years, it became plain to Susie, if not to Jasper, that the Stone Gods' early promise was unlikely to come to anything much, and it became simultaneously evident to both of them that there was in Susie both an unstoppable force and a remarkable capacity to achieve. The old pottery building in Fulham was sold to a developer, and a purpose-built unit was rented instead on a small industrial estate in Lavender Hill. A new corner site was acquired for the shop, with a warren of haphazard offices in the basement underneath, and the pottery gradually transformed itself into a powerful, unmistakeable, fresh modern take on traditional spongeware.

And then when Grace was eight, and the lower ground floor of their second Fulham house had been newly converted into a music studio for Jasper – 'Don't ask me about it,' Susie said to her oldest daughter. 'Just don't ask me' – Susie's grandmother developed bronchitis and then pneumonia and died in the University Hospital of North Staffordshire. She left her pearls to Cara, her amethysts to Ashley, her cameos to Grace and her two platinum Swiss watches to Jasper. Everything else – which was nothing like it had been in her husband's heyday – she left to Susie, including all the documentation relating to the purchase and subsequent sale of the factory where Jean McGrath had gone to apply for a job as an apprentice fettler all those decades before.

For Susie, there was no decision to be made. She was in her mid thirties, with a growing family, a growing business, and a raft of powerful impulses driving her on, chief of which was a determination to commemorate her grandfather in the most appropriate place and manner conceivable. His old factory in Hanley, flanked by wasteland on one side and a scarcely used canal on the other, was now only occupied by its owner in a single wing. The central block, where her grandparents had met, was boarded up, and the secondary wing, where the stores had been kept and machinery repaired, had broken windows and planks nailed across the main doors. In the yards between the wings, where cobblestones had once kept the horses' hooves from slipping, and buffer stones had protected the corners of the buildings from heavily laden carts, weeds were growing dankly and half-heartedly, and there were drifts of litter and cigarette butts in the gullies. It was not, Susie thought, standing looking at it all on a leaden March morning, a factory in good health. Everything was dispirited; everything spoke of decay. It was a business limping along making cheap goods for an unenthusiastic market. Seventy

47

people laboured in that rundown building, making nothing that they, or anyone else, could take pride in. She turned up her coat collar. Well, it was time to change all that. It was time to energize, to put the heart and the craft back into the old Snape pottery, time to give the people of Hanley a proper reason to live and work where they did.

Looking at the factory now, she thought, as she stood gazing out of the upstairs window at the Parlour House's unkempt but promising garden, you could still see the original pot bank. The canal was still there, of course, with an old bottle kiln on the far bank, one of the few survivors of its time. The stretch of wasteland on the other side had been reclaimed from rubble and weeds and planted optimistically as a meadow. But the factory itself looked cherished now, its brickwork repointed, its slate roof solid, its whole appearance softened and mellowed with duck-egg-blue paint on all the woodwork and climbing plants trained up the walls. Susie had left the Snape Pottery lettering on one wall, but had added SUSIE SULLIVAN above it in bold white letters surrounded by the daisy and diamond motifs that had been her first bestsellers. It had never failed to thrill her, arriving by taxi from Stoke station and seeing the factory standing there looking so coherent, so collected, with lights in all its windows, cars in its yard, and stack after tidy stack of her diamond-patterned boxes visible in the warehouse wing, packed full of pottery destined for stores in London, stores in Edinburgh, and kitchens the length and breadth of the country.

She gripped the sill of the window she was standing by. It meant so much to her, that factory, that business. It didn't just represent what she had built, or where she had arrived at; it represented her past, her grandfather's past, the past of those six towns and the riches of the land they were built on, as well as all the unimaginable human effort that had gone into digging coal out of its depths, and fashioning its clay into every kind of object required by domestic life. And it was this, this belief that she grasped the essence of this part of England, as well as the essence of what people wanted in terms of home and hearth, in taming some tiny patch of the wide, wild world to be a reliable sanctuary, that made her resist relinquishing any control of the business to outsiders.

Her brand was essentially her invention. Without her, it was traduced somehow, diluted, distorted. She understood the figures – good God, hadn't she looked after all the books herself for twelve years? – and she understood the ambition. But none of *them* – Cara and Daniel and Ashley and Grace – seemed to grasp how intrinsic her eye, her sense was to the success of the whole business.

Which was, really, what this cottage was about. With the Parlour House, she could go back to where she had begun, she could make it into something that demonstrated incontrovertibly to them that her concept, her comprehension of a particular longing and dream and aspiration in the public, was not just at the heart of Susie Sullivan pottery, but what made it *work*.

'You,' she said out loud to the empty house, 'are going to show them. You are going to show what I don't seem able to explain.' She patted the wall next to the window. 'You, Parlour House, are my trump card.'

CHAPTER THREE

Daniel expected to find his father-in-law in his studio. It was a Saturday morning, after all, and his mother-in-law was away in Staffordshire, so Jasper would have made one of his habitual pint mugs of strong tea and be where he was always happiest, down in the lower-ground-floor studio, fiddling about on the keyboard with a new idea for a song, or trying it out on his guitar.

Daniel had a front-door key to his parents-in-law's house. Neither Susie nor Jasper had – to Daniel's initial surprise, and abiding delight – any conventional sense of privacy, or indeed of any formalized generational divide. Their daughters had been brought up very much as their equals and companions, and neither of the parents had the faintest concept of requiring a respectful distance to be kept around their private lives. In consequence, the Victorian family house in which the three girls had done most of their growing up was open to all of them. Cara had simply never surrendered her own keys, and nobody had ever expected her to.

So, this Saturday morning, armed with two Americano coffees and a bag of croissants, Daniel let himself into Radipole Road, allowing the front door to bang shut behind him to announce his arrival. Then he called out his father-in-law's name, expecting to receive no response before opening the sound-proofed door under the stairs and descending to the music studio.

Instead, from the far end of the hall, Jasper shouted, 'Kitchen!'

He was sitting at the kitchen table, in the blue-painted carver chair that had somehow become his, with a newspaper spread out in front of him. He was in his habitual black jeans and black T-shirt, and his longish pepper-and-salt hair was tousled in a way Daniel had at first thought was casually contrived, but had come to realize was just the way it was. He had a mug in front of him, large tortoiseshell-framed spectacles on his nose, and his usual amicable air of being unsurprised to see anyone.

He took his glasses off and beamed at Daniel. 'Morning, mate.'

Daniel put down the cardboard cup-holder and the bag of croissants. There was, as usual, music playing on the stereo system. Jazz this morning, somebody brilliant on a saxophone. 'Some breakfast, Jas? Are you ready to follow one variety of caffeine with another?'

'Always ready,' Jasper said. He pushed the newspaper to one side. 'And I shouldn't be reading those reviews. All these new kids on the block, with their synthetic music, in their pathetic suits, God help us, all computerized and packaged. Does nothing but get me down, insofar as I let anything get me down.'

Daniel extracted one coffee cup from its cardboard grip and set it in front of Jasper. 'That'll get you up again.'

'But vinyl's back,' Jasper said. 'Kids are collecting vinyl. It's the same with these ebook things. After a while, people want solid stuff again. They get sick of grasping at air.'

Daniel sat down at an angle to his father-in-law, ripped open the croissant bag and pushed it across. He said nonchalantly, 'Susie back today?'

Jasper took the lid off his coffee. 'Who knows?'

'Has she rung?'

'Yup.'

'And?'

Jasper took a gulp of coffee. He said, 'You're not getting a reaction out of me that easily, mate.'

Daniel tore off a piece of croissant. He said, 'It's a family matter, Jas. It's a family decision.'

Jasper leant back in his chair and said mildly, 'I don't see that, Dan.'

Daniel leant forward. He had not only rehearsed what he would say, but he had assured Cara that his whole approach would be as anodyne as possible. He said carefully, 'She hasn't got the time to give to another house. She can't manage another commitment. I mean, when would she live there?'

Jasper smiled at him. 'When she's in Stoke.'

'But she stays with Grace.'

'Grace has a boyfriend.'

'He doesn't live with her.'

Jasper's smile grew broader. 'You won't provoke me, mate. If Susie wants this cottage, because of her grandfather and her childhood and all that, she should have it. She's got bags of energy. She could run a dozen houses.'

Daniel put the piece of croissant into his mouth and chewed. After a few moments, he said, 'She's amazing.'

Jasper said equably, 'You won't get round me that way, Dan.'

Daniel shifted to hunch over the table and his coffee. He tried to remember what he had rehearsed, on the way to Radipole Road.

'Jas—'

'Yes?'

'It . . . isn't really about this house. Or, at least, the house is only a symptom.'

'Shouldn't you be saying this to Susie, not to me?'

Daniel glanced at him. He said impulsively, 'Actually, I was just looking for a steer.'

'I can't promise anything.'

'I know, I know,' Daniel said, suddenly vehement. 'But as we all live off this company, what happens to it affects all of us, including you, however much you try to avoid responsibility.'

There was a sudden, highly charged silence. Then Jasper said, in the tone of one abruptly faced with unreasonableness, 'Hey, steady on.'

Daniel said nothing. A decade in the Moran family had taught him that Jasper would do anything to avoid a confrontation. So, after a pause and in a much lighter tone, he said, 'Can I explain the situation to you – the situation as I see it?'

Jasper looked relieved. He nodded.

'When I joined this company,' Daniel said, 'it's no exaggeration to say that Susie thought she didn't have the wherewithal to get bigger. She had too many products, she was only making things to order on a three-month lead, the shop was a random mess and the customers didn't know where they were. And also – also, Jasper – she was using any profit she made to offset losses from previous years. Well, look at us now.'

Jasper sighed faintly. He picked up his spectacles and blew on the lenses.

Dan said, 'You know where we are now. You know that when Cara and I joined, you could see visible signs of growth within a year. We go in for classic retail thinking, we're always asking ourselves how we can exploit something that sells. We have grown this company to five times its size in ten years. And we're on a three-year mission to get us to a turnover of £20 million. Are you with me?'

Jasper nodded. He was holding his spectacles out at arm's length and squinting through them.

'Of course,' Daniel continued, 'I don't want it to be twenty. I want it to be thirty. So does Cara. So does Ashley. So would Grace, if she thought about it. We all believe in the product. We are all committed to Susie's vision.'

He stopped. There was another short silence, and then Jasper said quietly, 'But?'

'But, Jas, Susie has to acknowledge what she doesn't know. She has to learn to defer on some things.'

Jasper's gaze swung round to his son-in-law, and rested there. He said levelly, 'Does she now?'

'If she would delegate more, she would achieve more.'

'Ah.'

'She has to lose some control to gain more. She has to allow the next fuse not necessarily to be lit by her.'

Jasper got up and crossed the kitchen to an enormous birdcage by the French windows to the garden. The parrot inside, a yellow-eyed African Grey called Polynesia, sidled along her perch so that she could croon at Jasper through the bars. He put a finger out and scratched the top of her head.

'Suppose,' he said, 'she doesn't want any of this?'

Daniel swivelled to look at him. 'You mean, she doesn't want the company to grow?'

'You'd have to ask her,' Jasper said, his gaze on Polynesia. 'But I'd guess she doesn't want it to get less personal. Because if it isn't personal, then it's had it.'

Daniel said quickly, 'That's my job.'

'What is?'

'To grow the company while retaining its essence. Susie's vision.'

'You,' Jasper said to Polynesia, 'are my ideal woman.'

'Radipole Road, south-west six,' Polynesia said clearly.

'I don't want to even *blur* her vision,' Daniel said, 'let alone lose it. It's a wonderful vision, and it works. But we can't stand still. We have to build on what we have. And Susie has to cooperate with that house she wants to buy.'

'What's that got to do with it?' Jasper said, still scratching the parrot's head.

Daniel let a beat fall, and then he said, 'It's a distraction.'

'She can cope.'

'She will use it as an excuse not to focus,' Daniel said. 'We need her to see what we have to do next to expand

57

the company, not to spend half a million pounds that is of no benefit to the company's future.'

Jasper blew Polynesia a kiss. Then he came back to the table and reached past Daniel for his coffee cup. He said, 'Why didn't Cara come?'

'She's gone to her Pilates class.'

'Not ducking out of things?'

Dan said stoutly, 'She's rung Susie already.'

'To say . . . ?'

'Please don't buy this house. Please listen to us about the best way to franchise the brand out to other manufacturers. Please don't try and dodge the issue of the company's future by getting involved in buying another property you do not need.'

Jasper finished his coffee and put the empty cup down on the table. He said softly, 'Maybe it isn't a distraction.'

'What?'

'Maybe,' Jasper said, staring at the framed Frida Kahlo poster on the wall above the table, 'this house is actually *about* the company. About her fear that you'll grow it into something she can't recognize, something that isn't *her* any more. This cottage is where she can go back to her roots, where it all began. It's a size she can manage.'

Daniel stared at him. 'You think it's deliberate?'

'I think it might be.'

'So . . . ?'

'So she's fighting for some kind of creative survival.'

Daniel got up slowly and walked to the door to the hall. Then he turned, and said to his father-in-law, 'So you won't try and dissuade her from buying this house?'

Jasper didn't look at him. He went on staring at Frida Kahlo's apricot-coloured roses in their fat black vase. He said gently but firmly, 'No, I won't.'

In her flat near the Potteries Museum in Stoke-on-Trent, Grace was ignoring her private telephone. For some instinctive reason, she had never given Jeff her work phone number, so if she switched her private mobile to silent, she would not be agitated every time he either tried to call or sent another aggrieved text.

He had not tried to contact her at all the previous evening. He hadn't spoken another word all the way up the M6, and he didn't speak when he dropped her off at Manchester Piccadilly station. She had got out of the car, clumsily retrieved her bag from the boot, and was stooping to say 'Have a nice weekend' or something equally pitiful, when he slammed the car into gear and roared off. If it had been a more dignified car, and not an ageing Nissan Pixo, his angry departure might have been more effective. As it was, buoyed up by her own indignation and sudden sense of liberty, Grace bought a single ticket to Stoke, a cheese baguette and a quarter-bottle of Beaujolais, and felt that she had not only been justified in refusing to go to Edinburgh, but had somehow triumphed.

This elation lasted until she got home at almost midnight. But then, confronted with a chilly flat, an empty fridge and several messages from her sisters telling her to ring Ma, and from Ma telling her to call, however late, her victory – if that's what it was – suddenly felt hollow and pointless. She dumped her bag in a corner, had a hot shower and got into bed wearing socks and mittens and a T-shirt. Then she rang her mother.

'Gracie! Safe in Edinburgh?'

'I didn't go, after all.'

'Didn't you? Why not? Where are you?'

'I'm home, Ma. I just didn't feel like driving all that way.'

'Oh?'

'And Jeff's mates – it's his weekend, really. He's better alone.'

'Well,' Susie said, 'I'm tucked up at the hotel in Staffs. If you aren't in Edinburgh, sweetie, you can come with me tomorrow, can't you?'

Gracie snatched a tissue from the box beside her bed and blew her nose. 'Don't think so, Ma.'

'Why not? I'd love you to come. I'd really like—'

'I can't decide for you. I can't be anything to do with your decision.'

There was a brief silence at the other end of the line. Then Susie said, 'I imagine you've talked to the others.'

'Of course I have.'

'They don't want me to buy it – Cara and Ashley. Nor does Dan. What about you?'

Grace suddenly felt worn out by the general intractableness of everyone close to her. She said, wearily, 'You have to decide alone, Ma. And you have to have good reasons for your decision.'

'So it's a no from you, too.'

'It's a can't-talk-about-it-any-more-tonight from me.'

She had turned the light off after that and lain awake for hours, not so much going over the evening as circling endlessly round it. In the morning, her phone registered three texts from Jeff – all saying the same thing, as if he had jabbed angrily and repeatedly at the Send button and thus sent the same message three times – and two missed calls. She dressed, tied her wild red curls up into a scarf, and went over to the Potteries Museum café for breakfast: lukewarm tea in a metal pot, yoghurt and a limp Danish pastry, served with a warmth of manner that threw Jeff's behaviour into disagreeably sharp contrast. Then she went back outside and stood on the corner of Bethesda and Albion streets, and looked down the hill at the wide, shallow valley below, full of tumbling roofs, and considered what she should do with the day – or, even, the life – ahead of her.

Behind her was the sturdy Victorian building, striped with lines and arches of sky-blue tiles, that hid her flat from view. Her flat. Her two-bedroom flat with its surprising reception space and magnificent north window which was ideal for drawing next to, and which had sold the flat to her. She had bought it two years ago, before she met Jeff, when she had been promoted to run the design studio at the factory. It had been a real achievement, both actual and symbolic. A flat, a company car, a serious position which gave her valuable independence from the rest of her family in London. So, what did she do? What she did was look at all those achievements, and then compromise them all by taking up with Jeff. Gorgeous Jeff, with his jealousy and insecurity and resentment making him as dangerous and alluring as Heathcliff. She stared at the complicated road junction ahead of her, as if it some-how symbolized her inability to choose a path and set off determinedly down it, without looking back. In her pocket, her phone beeped again, indicating another text. She pulled it out and looked at it.

'Sorry,' Jeff had written. And three kisses.

*

Maisie had drawn, with a green felt-tipped pen, all over her brother's face and then her own arms, and the backs of her hands. Then she had picked up a second pen, a brown one this time, and climbed the stairs with a pen in each hand, the tips tracing wobbly lines up the white walls to the very top. At the top, she sat on the carpet, dismantled the pens and smeared the contents all around her, including on her new grey corduroy pinafore dress with an appliqué elephant on the bib. Finally she went to find her mother, who was having a leisurely Saturday-morning bath, and held out her green and brown hands.

'Messy,' Maisie said.

Ashley, her hair pinned on top of her head with a giant plastic butterfly, was lying in the bath reading an article on Grayson Perry in *The Ceramic Review*. The children had been downstairs, after all – Maisie colouring at the kitchen table, Fred posting plastic shapes into a box – supervised by Leo. She lowered the magazine and regarded Maisie's hands. 'Where is Daddy?'

'They broke,' Maisie said. 'They broke on the carpet.'

'Look at your dress!'

Maisie squinted down at herself. 'What a pity,' she said, philosophically.

Ashley flung the magazine down, out of splashing range. As she began to get to her feet she said again, 'Where is Dadda?'

Maisie shrugged. She leaned over the edge of the bath and dabbled her hands in the water. 'Gone,' she said.

'What do you mean, gone?'

Maisie lifted her hands out of the water and inspected them. She said, with precision, 'He isn't there.'

'Isn't where?'

Maisie sighed. She said slowly, 'He isn't in the kitchen.'

Ashley seized a towel and wound it tightly around herself, under her armpits. She took Maisie's hand. 'Come with me.'

Maisie hung back, dragging on her mother's arm. She said, 'Oh, I need to wash my messy hands.'

Ashley stooped and whirled Maisie up into her arms. The towel untucked itself and fell to the floor.

'Fuck,' Ashley said. She set Maisie on her feet again and seized the towel.

Maisie said, 'He went to the loo.'

'Who did?'

'Dadda. He said, "I'm just going to the loo. You go on with your drawing." But I needed to come upstairs.'

'What does that mean?'

'I needed to do big drawing, you see. Very big drawing.'

Ashley leant over the bath and flipped out the plug. Then she took Maisie's hand again and ran her down the landing. She stopped at the top of the stairs and surveyed the scribbles.

'Oh, *Maisie*!'

Maisie looked nonchalant. She said carelessly, 'I expect it will wash.'

'Maisie, you *know* not to draw on walls. You *know* not to draw on the carpet or the floor. You *know* all that.'

Maisie burst into sudden tears. She screamed, 'I'm not naughty! I'm not! I'm not!'

Leo appeared at the bottom of the stairs and looked up.

'Oh my God.'

'So much for my peaceful Saturday-morning bath,' said Ashley.

Leo began to climb the stairs. He said sorrowfully, 'Oh, Maisie—'

'Don't say that!' Maisie shrieked. 'Don't say that!'

Leo reached the landing. He sat on the top step so his face was on a level with Maisie's.

She cried, 'I'm not naughty! I'm not—'

'But you are, Maisie. Look at the poor walls, look at the poor carpet. Never mind your new dress.'

'And your poor Mumma,' Ashley said.

Leo didn't look at her. He said, still regarding his daughter, 'Mummy can now go back to her bath.'

'But,' Ashley said, adjusting her towel, 'Mumma has let it out now.'

65

Leo didn't flinch. He said, 'Then Mumma can run another one. And Dadda is not going to apologize to Mumma for going to the loo for three minutes, in case she was planning to suggest it.'

Maisie said, between sobs, 'I didn't mean to.'

'Yes, you did,' Leo said. 'You let yourself do it. You allowed your hands to uncap those pens and then draw with them, all the way up. It wasn't a mistake.'

Ashley knelt on the stained carpet. She took Maisie's hand. 'Look at me.'

'No!' Maisie roared.

'No!' Fred shouted, from the bottom of the stairs.

He had crawled out of the kitchen and was now on his knees, clutching the bottom step.

Ashley leapt to her feet and raced down to him. 'Freddy!' She bent over him, clutching the slipping towel.

'No,' he said again, waving her outstretched hand away. He glanced up the stairs, longingly.

'Not Fred,' Maisie said indistinctly.

Ashley bent down and scooped Fred up with her free arm. He protested at once. Ashley said to Leo, 'I'll take him to the bathroom with me.'

'I thought you wanted to be peaceful.'

Ashley climbed back up the stairs, Fred kicking under one arm. As she stepped round Maisie and Leo she said, crossly, 'Fat chance of that.'

Leo didn't look at her. He put a hand out and took Maisie's nearest one. He said, 'Maisie is going to help me clean the walls and the carpet. And she is going to think how to say sorry.'

Maisie glared at him. She said again, but without conviction, 'I didn't mean to.'

From the bathroom came the ringtone of Ashley's mobile.

Leo said, unnecessarily, 'Your phone.'

Ashley swung Fred into a different position. 'It'll only be Ma again.'

'This cottage—'

'I don't want to talk to her about it. If she's going to buy it, whatever we all think, why doesn't she just get on and do it?'

'She'll have her reasons.'

'She can always justify anything she wants to do.'

Leo got to his feet and bent to pick Maisie up. He said, 'I think that's my line.'

Ashley regarded him, the towel and Fred clasped awkwardly in her arms. She said dangerously, 'Are you criticizing my mother?'

'I wouldn't dare. I know how much we owe her.'

There was a brief silence.

Then Ashley said, without looking his way, 'But you resent it.'

Leo adjusted his hold on Maisie. He said carefully,

'No, I don't resent it. I just think that sometimes all the good stuff comes at quite a price.'

'For you.'

'For us.'

Ashley stood looking at him. Both children were still and silent. She said again, 'For you.'

Maisie put her face into her father's neck. He took a deep breath. 'Yes,' he said, almost defiantly, 'for me. But not exclusively for me. For *us*. It doesn't help the dynamic between *us*.'

Ashley hitched Fred a little higher in her arms. 'So what are you going to do about it?'

'I – haven't decided,' Leo said. He gave Maisie a brief kiss and then he added, with marked emphasis, 'Yet.'

Cara was making a salsa. She had assembled all the ingredients – an avocado, plum tomatoes, a small scarlet chilli – like a cookbook photograph on the breakfast bar in the flat, and had put beside them the huge stone pestle and mortar that they had bought during a holiday in Lombardy. The pestle and mortar didn't come out of the cupboard very often: Cara had read an article on the arthritis that afflicted huge numbers of women in the Third World who spent hours each day grinding the ingredients for their basic food. Grinding was clearly only to be undertaken for reasons of occasional and specific authenticity.

She had bought a rye sourdough loaf from an artisan baker to accompany the salsa. It sat at the end of the breakfast bar in a stout, gusseted brown-paper bag, and beside it lay a slab of Italian butter, on a small slate. There would also be olives and fennel-infused salami. It was the kind of deliberate and delicious Saturday lunch that she set herself to prepare almost as a therapy, as a way of winding her mind down from the intensity of the week, after Pilates had done the same for her body.

It was hard, switching off. You could tell yourself that you were infinitely more effective at work if you had thoroughly re-booted at the weekend, but this was one of life's many occasions when the theory was impossible to put into practice. After all, she and Dan were now, really, the engine of the company. Between them, they had rescued it from its hand-to-mouth state, and given it a promising future as well as a healthy present. There were now twenty-four people in the office and more than two hundred in the factory, including an excellent new website guy in the former, and a factory manager, Neil Dundas, who didn't, like his predecessor, want to pick a fight with Dan, in the latter. She picked up the avocado and flicked out its little nub of stalk. It was all looking gratifyingly *good*.

Cara ran a knife smoothly round the avocado.

The figures last week were admittedly down on the same week the year before, but overall, sales were up thirty per cent. It was the result of an accumulation of small things: the chocolate-drop-filled daisy mini-mugs were doing well, royalties were coming in from the tinware company and the paper-napkin company for using Susie Sullivan designs. And, of course, the marked-down stuff was just flying out. She pulled the avocado gently in half and inserted her knife tip under the stone. Discounting was never a problem for a company with its own factory, and one of the golden rules of merchandising was that you must mark a product down the moment that you notice its sales declining.

Daniel's key scraped in the front-door lock across their open-plan sitting room. Cara picked up a spoon and began to scoop the avocado flesh out of the shell of its skin into the pestle. She said as he came in, 'Good news.'

'Oh?'

'Ash got that contract. I checked her emails this morning. They want a special line, just for them, but they also want twenty grand's worth of core stuff.'

Dan slung his black-leather satchel on to the chair by the front door and pushed the door shut. 'Excellent. Does she know?'

'She'll see for herself later. Saturdays, she's knee-deep

in toddlers. She'll be thrilled. She thought she'd blown it. So funny. The wet wipes . . .'

'Don't you want to know how I got on?' said Dan.

Cara shook a few drops of Tabasco on top of the avocado. 'I'm putting off asking you. You don't look a happy bunny to me.'

Daniel came across and peered into the pestle. 'Yum. I'm not.'

'He wouldn't help?'

'He won't try to dissuade her,' Daniel said. 'He wouldn't even countenance it. He sees no reason why she shouldn't have it, if she wants it. He thinks that if her reasons are nostalgic, or creative or whatever, that's fine.'

Cara turned towards the kettle. Those tomatoes would need skinning. She said, 'Why did I ever think he'd take our side? Or that he'd at least agree to talk to her?'

'We had to try.'

Cara ran water into the kettle. She said, 'I can't actually remember him standing up to her about anything. Even with us girls, he didn't. But then, he didn't really have to, because he was doing most of the mothering anyway, and we cut him a lot of slack for just quietly getting on with it.'

Daniel dipped a finger into the avocado pulp and then licked it. He said neutrally, 'D'you resent that?'

71

'What?'

'That your mother wasn't there for you when you were small, because of the business?'

Cara watched the kettle boil. 'No.'

'Really?'

'He was so good at it,' Cara said. 'All our friends loved him. Making music and making cakes. What more could you wish for?'

Daniel watched her. He said, 'But you don't want children . . .'

'Nor do you!'

'Agreed. But I just wondered . . .'

The kettle pinged itself off. Cara picked it up and came back to the breakfast bar.

'Dan, I'm not in the mood for an analysis of my childhood. Dad was great. Ma was fantastic. The company is pretty well all in all to you and me. Enough, don't you think?'

'There was just something about your father this morning. Something a bit . . . oh, I don't know . . . lonely, or – or abandoned.'

At the far end of the breakfast bar, beside the loaf in its brown bag, Cara's telephone emitted a brief yelp, signifying that a text had arrived. She indicated with a jerk of her head that Daniel should pick it up.

'Do see—'

He glanced at the screen and held the phone out towards Cara.

'What?' she said.

'Look,' he said. 'She's done it. She's made an offer.'

CHAPTER FOUR

'All I'm asking,' Jeff said, 'is that you give me a bit of a break.'

It was seven thirty in the morning and the design studio was empty, save for the two of them. Ben and Michelle, Grace's assistants, would not be in until eight. Jeff, who normally avoided coming to the factory, as if merely being on premises owned by Grace's family would somehow contaminate him, had known that he would catch Grace there alone, on a Monday morning, if he was early enough.

He was not only early, but also shaved, and bearing flowers and a round golden box of chocolate truffles. Grace was in her weekday uniform of jeans, battered knee boots and a fisherman's sweater, with no make-up and her hair held back by an old bandana of her father's. She had never felt less like smiling.

She stood by the window, with its checked curtains, where she had been when Jeff walked in, and looked past him. He was still holding the flowers. Pink oriental lilies. Where had the poor things been flown from? He held them up.

'If you aren't even going to speak to me, babe, then I might as well put these in the bin.'

He made a move towards a galvanized dustbin that stood at the end of the display table. It had 'Paper Only' painted neatly on the lid in black.

'Not in there,' Grace said automatically.

He dropped them on the floor. 'You don't want them, do you?'

Grace said nothing.

He held his empty hands out in supplication. 'Please, babe.'

She slowly turned her gaze to look at him and said, 'Please, what?'

'Please gimme a break.'

'Why?'

'Because—' He stopped, and then he said, dropping his hands, 'Because you mean the world to me.'

Grace waited a moment, and then she said levelly, 'No, I don't.'

He took a step towards her, over the flowers.

'Please don't come any nearer,' she said.

He stopped a yard from her. 'I mean it, babe. I'm sorry. I'm sorry about the weekend. I don't know what got into me. I missed you. I missed you all the time. It . . . it just felt kind of . . . pointless, being there without you.'

Grace moved backwards, away from him, and put the central unit between the two of them.

'I'm not interested, Jeff.'

'Let me explain a bit more—'

'No.'

He waited a moment. Then he bent, picked up the lilies and put them on the nearest surface, in front of Michelle's computer. He said, his voice catching, 'Don't say this is the end, babe.'

Grace sighed. She folded her arms. 'I'm the one who needs a break.'

He said, suddenly eager, 'I'll give you anything you want.'

'I don't trust you. I need time away from you. I need not to see you.'

His smile was hopeful, boyish. 'Anything you say. I'll do anything you say.'

The door to the studio opened. Michelle, wearing her quilted parka and an enormous knitted bobble hat, like something from a Scandinavian fairytale, came in on a gust of cold air and chatter.

'Oh my God, it's Arctic out there, and *icy*. I was sliding all the way from the bus. I mean—'

She stopped. She looked at Grace. Then she looked with visible interest at Jeff. 'Whoops. What have I walked into?'

'He's just leaving,' Grace said.

Michelle's eyes slid from Jeff's face to the lilies lying across her keyboard.

Jeff said to Grace, 'OK, he's leaving. If you promise he can come back again.'

'I'll have you back,' Michelle said. 'Any time.'

Grace stepped sideways and picked up the lilies. She held them out to Jeff. 'Take them.'

'Only if—'

'I need space,' Grace said. 'I need time to think. I don't know.'

Jeff took the lilies. He said with fervour, 'I'll take that as a yes.'

'Just go.'

He walked to the door and paused, his free hand on the handle, turning to look back at Grace with meaningful ardour. Then he let himself out and they heard his booted footsteps resounding down the outside staircase.

Michelle dropped her bag. 'Wow,' she said. 'And all that before breakfast.'

'Sorry that you—'

'Don't mention it. I like to start the week with a bit of drama. So that's the famous Jeff?'

Grace nodded.

Michelle said, 'Handsome is as handsome doesn't?'

Grace said, 'It wasn't a very good weekend.'

'He works for that garden centre, doesn't he? Out Trentham way?'

'Yes,' Grace said shortly.

'What does he do there?'

Grace didn't look at her. She said, 'It's a bit vague . . .'

'Depressing, you mean,' Michelle said. 'It must be one of the most depressing garden centres in England. And plants are supposed to cheer you up, aren't they? Living things, and all that.'

Grace looked away in silence.

'OK,' Michelle said, 'I get the message. I can take a hint. I just like to know what's going on, same as you do, if only you'd admit it.'

She took off her bobble hat and hung it on the bent-wood coat rack in the corner. She said, 'And a little bird told me that your mum's buying a house in Barlaston.'

Grace stared. 'What?'

Michelle unzipped her parka.

'You can't keep anything to yourself round here. You know that. Especially if it concerns your mum. So it's true, isn't it? I can tell from your face, just as I can tell that if your Jeff wasn't so hot you'd have given him the Monday-morning push.' She paused by the central unit and looked down at the golden box. 'Wow,' she said. 'Chocolates! And I'll have to eat them all, won't I? Because you simply couldn't face them, could you?'

*

There was nobody at home, in Radipole Road, except the parrot. Jasper had left one of his comical doodle notes on the kitchen table, saying that the cleaner couldn't come because she had a child off school, and that he would be back about six, possibly with Brady and Frank, and if so, he'd get a takeaway for all of them.

Apart from the note, the kitchen table was empty, save for a Susie Sullivan jug of small, forced irises. The irises had no doubt come from Holland. The jug was from the Rise and Shine range, twenty years old and still selling.

Susie crossed over to the birdcage. Polynesia, busy investigating something under one wing, affected to take no notice. She was at the far end of her perch and, apart from the small clucking sounds integral to her search, offered no greeting.

'Polynesia,' Susie said, 'just because I'm not Jasper—'

At the sound of his name, Polynesia extracted her head and eyed Susie sideways.

'I'm sorry it's only me,' Susie said. 'But it's better than being alone, isn't it?'

Polynesia clucked briefly. Then she sidled along her perch so that she was nearer Susie, but not near enough to be touched.

Susie said, 'You've had him to yourself all weekend, after all.'

Polynesia considered this. Then she edged back the way she had come and put her head back under her wing.

'It's a bit much,' Susie said, 'to have a parrot that won't even *speak* to me. I think I'll get one of my own for the Parlour House, just to put your beak out of joint.'

'You bugger off,' Polynesia said, indistinctly but unmistakeably from among her feathers.

Susie laughed. 'You're a baggage, Polynesia Moran. You really are. Isn't it lucky for you and me that Jasper seems to like baggages?'

Polynesia's head shot up again. 'Polynesia Moran,' she said. 'Jasper Moran. South-west six.'

Susie went across the room, by force of habit, to the kettle. Beside it, Jasper had left a pile of mail, the more interesting envelopes slit open with their contents re-inserted sideways, to indicate that he had read them. The girls – well, not Grace so much, but Cara and Ashley – had been saying for years that Susie should have an assistant, someone dedicated to running her life, from organizing her correspondence and the diary to collecting her dry-cleaning. But she had always refused. She had office staff both in London and Stoke, she said, and she had Jasper, who had been in at the very beginning of the company, which was more than any of the girls had been. In any case, she didn't want more people in her life, more people to accommodate and consider.

'What she means,' Ashley said to Cara, 'is that she doesn't want anyone to know exactly where she is or what she is up to. And, situated as I am right now, I can't blame her.'

Jasper never questioned anything. He knew she didn't mind if his studio was full of sundry musicians, and by the same token, he didn't mind if she was, unpredictably, somewhere other than Radipole Road. They had, she thought, and not without a touch of self-congratulation, reached a point of immense mutual respect and comfortableness, and the liberty they both cherished would only be diminished by the introduction of an assistant – however delightful – who would, of necessity, know every detail of their lives.

They had, after all, managed an overall harmony for the past thirty years that was nothing if not impressive. They were still in only the second house they had ever bought, and if it now boasted a hi-tech music studio and sound system and a lavishly enormous hot-water tank, it was still basically no more than a Victorian terraced house with a fifty-foot garden – now cunningly landscaped – and a paved patch in front where passers-by threw crisp packets and stringy wads of chewing gum. As they both had a horror of pretension in any form, this house and a mildly amateur way of approaching the nuts and bolts of Susie's business life suited them admirably. Cara and Ashley and Daniel could chastise Susie for a lack of professionalism as much as they liked, but they knew that it was all about control. If you stayed in the house you knew, with domestic arrangements that weren't just familiar but entirely manageable, with as few intimate human commitments outside the immediate family as possible, then not only were you free to concentrate all your energies on creativity, but you remained undeniably in charge.

And that, Susie thought, flicking through the envelopes, is what suits me. I've been in command of my own life since I got my first bank loan, and nothing – *nothing* – is going to take that away from me. She put the last envelope down on the stack – nothing there that needed any immediate action on her part – and carried the kettle over to the sink to fill it. Coffee first, and then a brisk walk to the office with the details of the Parlour House on her laptop. She wouldn't explain or justify her decision; she would simply announce it. And add that she had had an offer accepted of forty-five thousand below the asking price.

Polynesia had shunted herself along her perch once more until she was as close to the bars of her cage as she could get.

'You bugger off,' she said again.

Susie was talking in the steady, unhurried way she had that was so difficult to argue with. Her laptop was open on the boardroom table, showing a shot of the Parlour House taken from the lane, with an improbable hydrangea-blue sky behind it.

'It really was that colour on Saturday,' Susie said. 'And the house is so sweet – just a cottage really. I made the offer at lunchtime and Mrs Whatsit from Lyndhurst had said yes by mid-afternoon. Exchange of contracts by the end of the month and completion to suit me. Perfect.'

Ashley did not look across the table at her sister. She knew, from a sidelong glance, that Cara was looking down at the figures in front of her, and not at either the screen or her mother. Cara wanted a normal Monday meeting, as scheduled. She was trying to move on, round an immovable, immutable obstacle. Susie, on the other hand, only wanted to talk about the house.

'I'll use it when I'm in Stoke. I'm there a day or two a week, as it is, and maybe Jasper will come and join me sometimes.' She paused, and then she said, 'I'm longing to show it to you. And the PR people. It will be great for publicity.'

Neither Ashley nor Cara said anything. Cara was scribbling in the margins of her notes, her head bent. Her hair was pulled back in a ponytail, so that Ashley had a clear sight of the tautness of her jaw. It looked as if her teeth were clenched again. Ashley's dentist had told her that she must make a conscious effort not to grind her teeth, and to relax her jaw and her shoulders. 'Drop both,' he'd said. 'Your shoulders are not attached to your ears.'

Susie looked across the table at Cara. 'Where's Dan?'

Cara didn't look up. She said, 'He's got a meeting, Ma.'

There was a brief pause. Then Susie said, 'We always have a Monday meeting, the four of us.'

'I know,' Cara said. She put her pen down. 'But it was the only time this particular management consultancy could see him.'

Susie sighed. 'Not that again.'

'Ma, it's a recognized process of development. We've been through all that – you know we have.'

'And I've accepted it. From fifteen to twenty is a logical progression—'

'But not,' Ashley said, 'what we could do.'

Susie drew the laptop towards her and leant forward to study the picture on the screen.

Cara said, 'Could we talk about gifting, instead?'

'Of course,' Susie said, not looking up.

'It's growing,' Cara said. 'The personalized stuff is just flying out, particularly on the internet. Can we—'

'No,' Susie said suddenly, shutting the laptop smartly.

'No, we can't. This will lead on to you telling me that I must delegate more, that it's no longer all about me and I must recognize that. And I don't want to hear it again.'

'But you just said—'

'Cara,' Susie said, 'I will talk about anything, but I am not going to be lectured. And it has nothing to do with family, before you accuse me of that, either. I am buying this house because I must have somewhere of my own – somewhere I can think, and draw, and plan, somewhere I am not badgered to let go of this, or change that, or delegate the other, until I sometimes feel that nobody remembers where this company, and all the people who depend upon it, came from in the first place.'

Ashley put the heels of both hands into her eye sockets and pressed until there were preoccupying explosions of colour behind her closed lids. This moment was not unlike today's breakfast, in essence, when Fred, holding his plastic bowl of cereal out sideways, his round brown eyes fixed on her face, had slowly and purposefully tipped it upside-down. Watching the cereal fall to the floor was very like watching her mother breathe now, with deliberate regularity.

She said from behind her hands, 'Ma, we never quarrel.'

Susie said, staring straight ahead, 'I'm not quarrelling.'

'But we must,' Cara said tightly, 'be able to discuss everything. Freely. We *must*.'

'I know,' Susie said. She was gripping her laptop now. 'I know we must. But I just can't – *can't* give up what I know is the heart of the thing.'

There was a silence. Then Ashley took her hands away from her eyes and said, 'I wanted to talk about the late-spring catalogue.'

'Of course.'

'And some proposed partnerships for special editions.'

'As long as they are a good fit for us.'

'She knows that, Ma,' Cara said wearily.

'And I imagine,' Susie said to Cara, 'that you are waiting to tell me that mug sales are down sixty per cent—'

'Forty-four, actually,' Cara said.

'But you won't even acknowledge that I am buying this house. And that this house, in the heartland of what this company is all about, is also going to feed the creativity that lies at the very centre of everything we do.'

Cara and Ashley looked at each other. Cara shrugged slightly. Then they looked at Susie.

'If you want it,' Ashley said, 'you have it.'

Susie picked up her laptop. 'You'll see,' she said.

*

It was an hour before the factory workers clocked off for the day. Five days a week, they were in before six in the morning and gone by three in the afternoon, leaving behind them the ghostly racks of cast but undecorated ware to be fired in the kilns overnight.

Grace was always soothed by the factory. It was partly those long, dusty, brilliantly lit rooms dedicated to the steady application to making something; partly the people – the casters and the fettlers, the jiggers and jolliers, the girls cutting the sponge shapes with soldering irons, the women decorating and banding on their paint-splashed revolving tables, the glaziers dipping each piece into the lavender-hued tanks of glaze, all by hand, every piece touched by hand – and it was also partly being out of the studio, away from the telephone, away from problems. There was no point taking her phone into the factory. She couldn't have heard herself think, let alone speak. And there was such a luxury in switching the thing to mute and leaving it behind on her desk, as if it were no more important than an empty notepad.

The casting shop was always impressive. Fourteen casters working between pairs of immense slatted benches, with the liquid clay slip in which they worked piped along the ceiling in great yellow hoses. Seven tons of it each day, seven tons of china clay and chemicals and water mixed each night in the blunger until it was the right consistency to run down the hoses and into those plaster-of-Paris moulds which produced the mugs and the jugs, the teapots and the vases, the bowls and the cups – over four hundred pieces from each man every day, lined up on the wooden trucks to be wheeled away for fettling.

Grace paused beside Barney Jilkes. He had a visible gold tooth, a snake tattooed around his neck and had left school at fifteen, following his father down the mines for a year – 'Only a thousand feet down. I were too young to work the coalface' – before taking a trade test to work at Wedgwood. His mother had been on the switchboard there; she was known as the Voice of Wedgwood. He'd applied for a job at Snape Pottery the moment Susie had taken it over, almost as a prank. 'I'd never worked for a woman before. Thought it'd be a laugh. Best thing I've ever done.'

'Bloody awful day,' he said to Grace now, not pausing in what he was doing for a second.

'Oh?'

'Three losses! Three! I never have losses. I haven't lost anything in months!'

'There you go, then. Think of those months, not today.'

'I've let myself down,' Barney said. He reached forward to fill a mould and the snake on his neck rippled faintly.

Grace said, 'Nobody'll say anything.'

'They don't say. But they think it. They know. Me dogs'll know, the minute they see me.'

'Forget it, Barney. The rest of us will. You're a brilliant caster.'

'Five hundred and fifty-two pieces, me best day.'

'How are the whippets, talking of dogs?'

Barney's expression softened. He rubbed a plaster-flecked fist against his temple. 'Champion, Grace. Especially the little blue.'

'If it's any comfort,' Grace said, 'I'm having a mildly shit day, too.'

Barney wagged a finger at her. 'Now, now, language.'

'You're a fine one to talk.'

'I'm a fella, Grace. And you're a—'

'Please don't say lady.'

He grinned, and stepped sideways to set a small tureen on the truck beside him.

'Dogs,' Barney said, 'is easier than this lady-and-gentleman malarkey. They don't bother messing about. They're just dogs and bitches.'

Grace moved on, smiling, down the casting shed, through the area where the dense great discs of china clay awaited the blunger and on into the fettling shop, where rough edges and seams were smoothed off with knives and sponges. She always paused here, among the regimented shelves of unfired ware and the blue-overalled women – always women, in a fettling shop – and thought of her great-grandmother, coming here in search of a job and finding herself in front of the great man himself, except that he was a youngish great man, and the assessing way he looked at her had little to do with judging the kind of fettler she might make. It was the stuff of fairytales, really it was. Jean McGrath, from an Irish Liverpool terraced house in Burslem with no indoor lavatory, being asked out to tea, and then a country walk, and then the cinema, by Mr Snape of the pottery. Who then produced a ruby and diamond engagement ring from his pocket and went down on one knee in a field out at Barlaston, asking her to marry him and promising her a country house on this very spot if she said yes. Of course, she said yes. And she got a husband and a baby and Oak View. And even if the baby turned out to be a deep disappointment – so weird, Grace thought, to have a grandfather alive who was never spoken of – the baby's baby more than made up for it. When she thought about that – when she thought about what Ma had done, not just for herself but for people like Barney, and Maureen here, in the fettling shop – she felt that . . . well, she felt that if she wanted fifty cottages in Barlaston, she could have them.

'Grace,' someone said.

She turned to see who had spoken. It was Harry, who had spent a lifetime working the kilns, and now, in retirement, took tours of schoolchildren round the factory. He said, 'Michelle's looking for you.'

'Is she?'

'There's someone up there in the studio, looking to see you.'

'Not—' Grace said, and stopped.

Harry patted her arm. He smiled, showing the gleaming new dentures he was so proud of.

'Not him, Gracie. Not lover boy. It's an old geezer, Michelle said. Asking for you.'

'You don't know me,' the old man said.

He was very thin, and tanned, and his white hair fell in a curious kind of bob on either side of his face. Michelle had found him a chair, but he wasn't sitting on it, he was standing behind it, his hands resting on its back. He was dressed in crumpled linen trousers and a long embroidered quilted coat over a tunic of some kind. There were silver and turquoise beads round his neck, and a sort of tooth, curved and whitish, threaded on a long leather thong.

Grace stayed where she was, just inside the doorway. 'No,' she said uncertainly. 'Should I?'

The old man smiled, and raised a braceleted hand as if to wipe the smile off.

'No,' he said. 'Of course not. You've never seen me. I don't expect you've seen a photo of me, even. I'm your black-sheep grandfather.'

Michelle and Ben froze into sudden stillness in front of their computers.

Grace said stupidly, 'What?'

'I'm your granddad,' the old man said mildly. 'Morris. Your old granddad Morris.'

Grace took a huge gulp of air. She said, slightly breathlessly, 'What . . . what are you doing here?'

He laughed, and waved a hand behind him. 'When I walked in,' he said, 'you could see these kids thinking that.'

'Well—'

'I ran out of life, there. It just happened. After your grandmother died.'

Grace said wildly, 'She died?'

'Two years ago,' Morris said. He had a disconcertingly unhurried manner. 'Lung cancer. We flew her down to Mombasa, but it was too late.' He paused and looked down sombrely at his hands. 'Poor chick.'

Grace leant against the door frame. 'I can't think straight.'

He said, 'Well, you could give your old granddad a hug, couldn't you?'

She didn't look at him. She said, 'I don't know you.'

'Well,' he said, unoffended, 'there is that.'

92

'How did you find us? I mean, d'you even know who I am?'

'You're Grace. And—' he turned and gestured behind him again, 'these kids are Michelle and Ben.'

'How do you—'

'The website,' Morris said. He smiled again. 'There's everything on the website, isn't there? Even photographs. You up here, your sisters down in London. I even have great-grandchildren, down in London. It's been amazing, that website. Told me everything.'

Grace took a step or two into the room. 'Does – does Ma know you're here, in England?'

He said calmly, 'I shouldn't think she even knows her own ma is gone.'

'But,' Grace said, suddenly intense, 'what are you *doing* here?'

He looked surprised. 'Doing?'

'Yes,' Grace said. 'What are you *doing* – after decades of no contact, no responsibility, nothing – suddenly turning up here and imagining that any of us would be remotely interested in seeing you?'

There was a silence. Michelle and Ben were still staring stiffly at their screens. Morris took his hands off the chairback and came towards Grace. He had moccasins on his feet, and no socks. He held his hands out towards her, just as Jeff had done earlier, and then dropped them again.

He said, 'I was hoping, I s'pose—' And then he paused.

She didn't smile.

'Well?' she said.

'Grace,' he said. 'I'm eighty-one. I just ran out of road.'

CHAPTER FIVE

Daniel had shut himself in the boardroom. As the office was otherwise open-plan, the boardroom door was the only door in the place, and shutting it made a resounding statement, particularly if you were the only person inside. If closing the door sent a slightly intimidating message to everyone else, then that suited his current purpose just fine.

His purpose was, in essence, to calm down. He could have gone for a walk, of course – into Bishop's Park across the road, or over Putney Bridge with its satisfactorily huge view of the river – but something told him that his agitation might only be increased by leaving the office, and it would be better, really, to take his iPad as an acceptable accessory into the boardroom, where he could pace or gaze out of the window or – the most luxurious option of all – have a private *sotto voce* rant about his mother-in-law and her family and the state of the business.

With, as ever, the exception of Cara. Daniel was truly

sorry for Cara. Cara was not in the office today because she had had to go up to Stoke by train with her mother and Ashley, to meet this outrageous old man who had suddenly turned up in Grace's studio and announced himself to be Susie's father, Morris. At first, when Grace had rung with this implausible story, no one had believed her. It was insane, in these days of worldwide communication, that anyone so closely related could just turn up out of the blue, like a character in a soap opera, all melodrama and improbability. But then the inevitability of the facts began to emerge, never mind the physical presence of the man, and a creeping combination of acceptance and curiosity began to overtake their initial shock and disbelief. The old man in Grace's spare bedroom – his possessions, such as they were, carried in a huge dusty bag fashioned from something indisputably African, patterned in deep red and black – was indeed, it seemed, Susie's father, Morris Snape, returning like an elderly prodigal son to the place he had so emphatically and ungratefully rejected half a century before.

The horror and shock, Daniel had to admit, were – at first, at least – far stronger than the curiosity. Susie was appalled, as were her older daughters. Grace, with this profoundly unwelcome guest in her flat, was said to be despairing. At two in the morning after the revelatory first phone call, Daniel had been aware of Cara lying awake and churned up beside him. He had reached out a hand to take hers, and she'd gripped him as if he were a lifeline and hissed, 'I don't *want* this.'

'I know.'

'He left Ma. As a *baby*. He *abandoned* her.'

'I know.'

'He's a selfish monster. He's never grown up. He's only back because he's run out of options. He just wants to be looked after. And money. Of course, he wants *money*.'

Daniel edged further across their kingsize bed so that he could put an arm across Cara and hold her. 'Your poor mother.'

'She's in shock.'

'Yes.'

'It's awful, Dan, to have to be responsible for someone you really can't bear.'

Daniel had tightened his embrace. He had never had much time for his own parents, but luckily had always been deemed the difficult one, so leaving his filial obligations to his two sisters had merely provoked their resigned acceptance of the inevitable. They had, indeed, formed a small trade union of two responsible, concerned adult children, shouldering the consequences of a third – male, of course – ducking out of his duty. When he had married Cara, his sisters could add 'gold-digger' to his list of failings and cut another notch in their bedpost of virtue. Their general attitude was to be very sorry for him, for his lack of concern and sensitivity, but never to chastise him. As his elder sister, Sally, said to Cara at every opportunity, 'He knows who he's let down, Cara. He knows it perfectly well. As I expect you do. Neither of you need reminding by *me*.'

Daniel let Sally's attitude slide straight off him. As far as he was concerned, she was his sister in name only. She had not cared for his arrival when she was three, and she failed to learn to care for him subsequently. Indeed, she had extended that failure to appropriating their youngest sister, Julie, into her team, excluding Daniel to such an extent that when he met Cara he unleashed upon her all the emotion that had been banked up throughout his childhood with no outlet to offer release. He was like someone, Cara told him, delighted but also slightly dazed, who had a perfectly good home inside their head, but who desperately needed a house to put it into. He'd thought about this, and then he'd said, 'The thing is, Cara, that you are everything to me. Everything.'

He had been terrified that she would want children. He didn't – not because he didn't like them, but because he knew he lacked the capacity for sharing. He might regret that, but he didn't think he could change it. But Cara was a girl, and girls were different. Girls, he thought, wanted babies. They just did. They wanted a man, and then they wanted a baby. But Cara didn't, actually, want a baby. She was very clear about it, and wholly unapologetic.

'I don't want children, Dan. I never have. What's wrong with that?'

He had been flooded with relief.

'Nothing. I just thought—'

'I really like children. I hope Ashley and Grace both have children. I'll be a fabulous aunt. But I don't want my own. I expect a shrink would tell me it had everything to do with Ma being so preoccupied with the business while I was little, so I always felt starved of her full attention or something. I don't know. I'm not sure I really care. I just know myself well enough to know that if I had a baby, I'd be a martyred mother, and I wouldn't dream of asking anyone, let alone my children, to look after me in my old age.'

Dan had gazed at her. He'd said, 'I'll look after you.'

'No, you won't. We're going to work to pay for our own old ages. And before you reproach me for being a selfish cow, I'd like to say that I don't think my choice is better than other women's choices, just different. My grass isn't greener, it's just another kind of green.'

Daniel had reached for her, and held her hard against him. 'I can't believe my luck,' he'd said.

In many ways, and despite the familiarity borne of

a decade of marriage, he still couldn't. When she'd arrived in the sales department of the company where he was already on the buying team, having graduated there from a Saturday job on the tills, he had been immediately attracted both by her looks and her attitude. Her name, Cara Moran, meant nothing to him, but her serious focus did. Like him, she had been good at mathematics and physics at school – she told him quite seriously, early on, that she had considered being an air-traffic controller – and she had, like him, been immediately fascinated by people management and, even more, by customer service and the sales floor. Like him, too, she had seen the fearsome old-school managers in the company as providing an admirable set of ethics rather than merely some kind of outdated authoritarianism, and had been keen to learn from them. After ten days and only one tentative date, he had known that he wanted to marry her when she turned to him at work and said earnestly, 'Dan, what does success look like?'

Well, he thought now, tramping steadily round the boardroom table, his iPad in his hand in case anyone knocked, success does *not* look like haring up to Stoke to fan the flames of a histrionic family farce. The priority this week – long-planned and the culmination of months of preparation – was the final decision about whether to engage a management consultancy to outline the best way to take the Susie Sullivan brand to another level. Would they, as Dan and Cara wanted, consider finally exporting their stoutly defended Made in England product after two decades of rigorously focussed home sales, or would they, as Susie wanted, put their energies into consolidating and extending the home market they already had? (Ashley, he thought, would waver until the last moment and then side with her sister and brother-in-law.)

But Susie had just swept the meeting aside. It had fallen to Dan to ring the management consultancy team and tell them that the meeting – planned for months and with considerable difficulty given the complexity of everyone's commitments – was now cancelled, owing to an unforeseen family crisis.

'But it isn't a crisis, is it?' Daniel had said to his mother-in-law. 'It's a shock and it changes the personal dynamics, but it isn't something that needs instant action. No one's in intensive care, after all.'

Susie had looked at him with an expression he was familiar with, from board meetings.

'He's in Grace's *flat*. In her spare *bedroom*. It's a crisis for Grace, Daniel, at the very least, every day it goes on.'

Daniel had held her gaze. 'Put him in a hotel. I'll organize it, if you like. I'll deal with it.'

Susie had dismissed the suggestion with a single gesture of her arm. 'I can't do that. He's my father.'

'You *can* do that. He's been a disgraceful father.'

'Stop it, Dan. Stop it. You are the last person to have an opinion about family, having virtually no dealings with your own, as far as I can see.'

He'd leant forward very slightly and said, without raising his voice, 'You're going to Stoke, Susie, because you want to, aren't you? Isn't that the truth? You want to dash to Stoke, and you want the girls to go with you, as validation. So that's what's happening. What you *want*.'

He'd waited for her to be angry, but instead her shoulders had slumped and she had said sadly, 'Oh Dan, if only it was that simple.'

But she'd gone anyway. And so had Cara and Ashley, and the atmosphere in the office beyond the closed boardroom door was as unconducive to his usual steady application to the task in hand as it could be. He left his circuiting of the table and went to stand by the window that looked down, past other buildings, old and new, to the river. In the cold light it shone like a sheet of steel, gleaming even under a dull sky. The company was, at this precise moment, flat on budget, two per cent up on last year. But it should be more. It *could* be. He reached out the hand that wasn't holding his iPad and beat it lightly against the glass. If he had anything to do with the future of Susie Sullivan pottery, it *would* be. Whatever the obstacles.

*

'You don't want me here,' Morris said.

His tone was entirely without reproach. He was sitting on Grace's sofa, still wearing his strange assortment of outdated hippy clothing, with the addition of pale-blue woollen socks on his bony feet.

Susie, sitting opposite him on one of Grace's Italian plastic dining chairs, as if sitting upright gave her slightly more authority, said unhelpfully, 'No, I don't.'

Morris sighed. He leant back and looked at the ceiling. 'In your place,' he said, 'I wouldn't want me either.'

'But that doesn't get us anywhere. Talking like that doesn't help.'

Morris waited a moment, then tipped his head forward again and said, 'I suppose you think I want money.'

'Yes, I do.'

He said simply, 'I've never known how you got hold of it.'

'What, me?'

'No,' he said. 'Anyone.'

Susie gave a stifled gasp. Then she said, more shrilly than she'd intended, 'You *work* for it!'

He grinned at her. 'I was never any good at that.'

She looked away from him. 'You're shameless. It's . . . it's despicable.'

'I'm teasing you, duck.'

'Don't call me that!'

'I'll try Susan, then.'

She said, still looking away, 'As you are incapable of working, and always have been, how have you lived all these years?'

Morris leant forward and put his elbows on his knees. He contemplated his powder-blue ankles and said gravely, 'My forgiving old dad.'

Susie's head whipped round. 'I thought he'd cut you off without a shilling!'

'He told my mother he had. Maybe at first he thought he would. But he paid me an allowance every month until he died, and then he left instructions in his will for something similar to go on.'

'There was no mention of you in his will!'

Morris raised his head. 'It was in a separate will. There was a lump sum left with the Kenya Commercial Bank in Lamu, and that was paid out to me in instalments till five years ago, when it ran out.'

'And then?'

'Your Ma was ill. We had a bit of stuff to sell. Paintings and suchlike. I'm a good painter.'

Susie looked round the room. She had sent the girls back to the factory, thinking that they needed to fortify themselves with a dose of normality after the sheer weirdness of their first encounter with their grandfather. Now she rather wished that they were still there, that she had her own touchstones of reality in the room with her. She said, 'I don't even know what to call you.'

He said mildly, 'Morris'll do.'

She sighed. 'So my . . . your wife died and the money ran out and you thought we couldn't refuse to take you in.'

'Oh, you could, you know. But I thought I'd ask.'

Susie was suddenly angry. 'I don't know how you *dared* to think that!'

He gave the smallest of shrugs, moving his hands so that she couldn't help but notice a small gecko tattooed inside one wrist. He said, 'It's changed, Lamu. It isn't the place it used to be. I wasn't at home there any more. I didn't fit in.'

'You don't fit in here.'

He glanced round the room. 'Your Grace has been lovely to me.'

'Grace is lovely to everyone. But you're exploiting her. And I won't have it.'

He said nothing, just fiddled with a frayed sleeve.

Susie said, 'Did you really think we'd take you in?'

'I told you,' he said. 'I thought I'd ask. I had enough for the plane fare and enough to – Oh, what does it matter? I never thought it'd be so cold.'

'You mean that we wouldn't turn a dog away in this weather, so we'd hardly do that to you.'

'No,' he said. 'I meant what I said. I'd forgotten about the weather. I'd forgotten about winter in the Midlands.

You can rant at me all you want. I've been a shocking father, I know that, I deserve everything you want to accuse me of. But the fact remains that I'm eighty-one, I'm on my own and I've hit the buffers. It's my own fault, I know that, but a fact's a fact. I'll go away again, if that's what you want, but I don't think you'd be easy in your mind if I did. I'd like to find some way of fitting in here again, if I can, but I accept I may have burned too many boats for that. I've lived off other people's generosity all my life, and that's how I am. I'm not proud of it, but I'm not going to grovel about it either. The bottom line is, Susan, that I'd appreciate your help now, but I won't think any worse of you if you tell me to get lost. It's up to you.'

Susie stood up. Then she sat down again. She spread her hands out in front of her as if the sight of them, of her wedding ring, would somehow provide comfort and guidance. She said slowly, 'Your turning up like this is a nightmare. A complete nightmare. And your exasperating passivity only makes it worse. You've never lifted a finger to earn anyone's respect all your life, and it looks to me as if you have no intention of changing your ways. And I haven't the first idea what to do about it. That's the truth.'

'What's the proverb?' Jasper said. 'About a bad penny?'

Daniel put his beer bottle down on the pub table

between them. 'It's something to do with a counterfeit coin always finding its way back into circulation.'

'And that's Morris. Odd, to have a father-in-law after pretty well forty years of marriage without one.'

Dan said, 'Don't you want to go up to Stoke to meet him?'

Jasper laughed. He tipped his beer up and took a gulp. 'Susie didn't want me to.'

'Did you offer?'

'Sure. Just her and the girls, she said.'

Daniel hesitated a moment, and then he said, 'Did you mind?'

'Nah. When have I ever minded a thing like that?'

Daniel picked up a packet of vegetable crisps that lay on the table and pulled it open. Then he held it out to his father-in-law.

Jasper grinned at him. 'D'you think, Dan, that if they're made of parsnip they don't count as crisps?'

Daniel said distantly, 'I prefer them.'

'You're a pompous twit,' Jasper said affectionately. He took a handful. 'Wow,' he said. 'Purple ones too. Beetroot.'

Daniel leant forward. 'Jas,' he said, 'you *must* be concerned about what's going on up there. They've been in Stoke two days. You *must* want to know what's going on—'

'Not really.'

'Jas—'

'Look,' Jasper said, 'it would be hard to be married to Suz if you were quite conventional. But I'm not conventional. Never have been.'

'*I* am,' Daniel said.

Jasper grinned again. He patted Daniel's arm. 'I know, Dan.'

'I have a work ethic, Jas. And that old bastard doesn't sound as if he's ever had one.'

'No.'

'I don't want him sponging off Susie or Cara or any of us. And until there's some kind of plan, I can't be sure he won't manage it, somehow. Just by being eighty-something, for starters.'

Jasper said easily, 'Suz'll think of something.'

'I could shake you.'

'She often says that. But you can't have two driven people in a marriage.'

'Yes, you can.'

Jasper let a beat fall, and then he said, 'What has Cara said to you?'

'That she'll be back tonight and she'll tell me everything then.'

'And the old boy?'

'She says she can't talk about him yet.'

Jasper laughed again. 'Sounds very unsatisfactory for you all round!'

'It is,' Daniel said. 'And on top of all else . . .'

'All else?'

'The company.'

'Ah,' Jasper said. He plunged his hand into the crisp packet again. 'The *company*. That.'

There was a pause. Then Daniel said tentatively, 'Do you hate it?'

'Me? No! I don't hate anything. Why should I hate the company?'

'Because,' Daniel said, not looking at him, 'it means so much to Susie and she's so involved with it.'

Jasper smiled at his beer bottle. 'I was there at the beginning, remember? She tells me everything, anyway. There's nothing about the company I don't know.'

Daniel took a crisp. It was as pointless to contradict such an absurd statement as it was to argue with Susie in certain moods. He said instead, 'Are you curious to meet your long-lost father-in-law?'

'I would quite like to punch his lights out,' Jasper said amiably.

'Me too.'

'Leaving a baby. Leaving your parents literally holding your baby. Not bothering to come back for our wedding. Not bothering to come back for either parent's funeral. Subsidized by your father all your life. What an apology for a human being.'

'But,' Daniel said, 'I have a feeling they'll still come to his rescue. The girls, I mean.'

There was a pause, and then Jasper said slowly, 'I won't like that.'

'Meaning?'

'Just that. I won't like them spending energy on that old waste of space.'

'So,' Daniel said, suddenly intent, 'you *do* mind. You *did* want to go up to Stoke and be a bit of a brake on Susie. You *do* have an opinion about the company.'

Jasper took another gulp of beer, and put the bottle down. He said, 'As far as the company's concerned, I've been glad of it, thankful for it. Over the years I've discovered that if you are furious about your marriage, it's pretty nice to have a super topic diversion, like a business.'

Daniel took a deep breath. '*Furious* . . .' he repeated.

'Not often. Not always.'

'But sometimes. Enough to—'

Jasper stood up. He looked down at his son-in-law. 'I'm off to hear a mate at Ronnie Scott's. A wicked trumpeter. Want to come?'

The design studio was quiet and warm. From the curtained windows, you could see lights were still on in the factory wing across the yard, where the kilns hummed on through the night and the blungers turned

110

the great cakes of china clay into manageable slip, before the morning. But apart from the skeleton night staff and probably Neil, the factory manager, who worked seemingly tireless hours, no one would be there. In the studio, Michelle and Ben's computer screens had been switched off when their owners went home, leaving the room to the three sisters, grouped round the wooden kitchen table which hosted meetings as well as Ben's rigorously vegetarian sandwich lunches, and provided a welcome space for sketching.

There were tea mugs on the table and an open bottle of Prosecco, which Grace had found in the fridge, but which, when it came to it, nobody had felt like drinking. Celebration was clearly out of order, and Prosecco didn't seem appropriate for consolation, either. Grace had opened one of her mother's sketchbooks, which were always lying about on that particular table, and was examining a page of drawings of cutlery, as if some minor design decision would somehow offer a solution to the large and unmanageable personal problem facing all of them. Ashley was leaning back in her chair with her eyes closed and her arms folded, and Cara was sitting bolt upright, her hands around a foxglove-patterned mug, whose contents had long grown cold.

She said suddenly, 'How much longer shall we give her?'

'Who?' Grace said idiotically.

111

'Ma.'

'She'll ring,' Ashley said. 'She'll text. Something.'

'Our train's at six ten,' Cara said.

Ashley opened her eyes. 'We've got an hour and a half. Ages.'

'D'you think she's all right?'

'She'll tell us if she isn't.'

Ashley sat upright slowly. She said, 'She must be knackered by all this. *I* am.'

'Me too,' Cara said. She looked at Grace. 'Gracie?'

Grace traced a forefinger around a sketched spoon and fork. She said, almost inaudibly, 'I'm OK.'

'You can't be, Gracie. He's in your spare room. It's much worse for you than for anyone. Please let Dan find him a hotel, at least.'

Ashley stretched an arm along the table to touch Grace's nearest hand. 'Not just your spare room, Grace, but your *bathroom*.'

Grace gave Ashley's hand a brief squeeze and let it go. She said, 'He's weirdly tidy. And domesticated. I haven't had many men in the flat, but he's by far the most civilized. And clean, actually.'

Cara said, 'Gracie, you don't *have* to put up with it.'

Grace sighed. She pushed the sketchbook away. She said, 'If I don't, then Ma does.'

Ashley looked down at the table top, her expression abruptly chastened. She said, 'But that doesn't seem fair.'

'None of it's fair. That's why Dan wants to put him in a hotel,' said Cara.

Grace said slowly, 'I think Ma is really confused. I don't think she can bear him anywhere near her, but she can't turn her back on him either. She can't behave as badly to him as he has to her.'

Cara took her hands away from the foxglove mug and put them over her eyes. From behind them she said, 'But you can't offer yourself as a sacrifice so that Ma can live with her own conscience comfortably.'

'No,' Grace said, 'I know that. I can't. I won't. It's only temporary. He's only been here three nights.'

Ashley looked at her. She said abruptly, 'What do you truly, honestly feel about him?'

Grace shrugged.

Cara took her hands away from her face. She said, 'I can only just stand to be in the same room—'

'Car, I didn't ask you.'

'Nothing,' Grace said.

'*Nothing?* Just – just, really, nothing?'

'Well,' Grace said, 'indifference, I suppose. My head says he's my grandfather and he's old, and the rest of me says not very much, to be honest. A bit of duty, a lot of indifference. But I do mind about Ma.'

'Yes,' Cara said.

'Me too,' said Ashley.

113

'So,' Grace said, 'there we are. Big old problem nobody wants, Ma least of all, so we have to do something about it, for her.'

Ashley said ruefully, 'And to think we were all so fed up with her, only a week ago, about this house she's buying!'

'That's families,' Cara said. 'Families and businesses. Always a battleground. And it will be again. We're just briefly united, aren't we, by this – this *pantomime* misfortune.'

'He made a curry last night,' Grace said. 'Cinnamon and cloves and ginger and everything. It was amazing.'

'Could you eat it?'

'You mean, could I eat anything he made? Well, yes, I could. I did. And then Jeff finished it.'

'Jeff? What was Jeff—'

'I'm trying to dump him,' Grace said, 'but he won't get the message.'

Cara leant forward. She said urgently, 'Gracie, if he's harassing you—'

'He isn't, yet. And I'm not completely decided.'

'Oh Gracie, please.'

'Car,' Grace said, 'I know he's bad for me. I know he's moody and manipulative and loves himself more than he'll ever love me, but there's something still, just something, and I know it drives you mad watching me not doing what you want, but I don't do things like

114

you, I don't feel things the same way you do, I don't have your certainty about everything . . .'

Cara put her hands out, palms towards Grace, in a halting gesture. 'OK, OK, I get it. I shouldn't have reacted, it's none of my business. I'm just wound up about what's going on, about Ma, about what we do. I'm just—'

'I know what we do,' Ashley said suddenly.

She had pushed herself upright in her chair. The other two turned to look at her.

'What?'

She looked from one to the other. 'Leo would say, work with what you have.'

'So?'

She looked at Cara. 'What do we have? One unwanted extra house. One unwanted old grandfather.'

She turned to Grace. 'So we put one inside the other.'

CHAPTER SIX

There was, Leo Robbins noticed, a pizza box jammed hastily into the kitchen bin. The jamming had clearly been hasty because the flip-top lid was wedged ajar by a corner of the box. When he opened the lid fully and peered in, he saw the flattened plastic pouches of a sugary children's fruit drink that the nanny had been expressly forbidden to give Maisie and Fred, and a couple of empty yoghurt pots, although the sweetened yoghurt fell into the same banned category. The nanny, a cheerfully unapologetic girl from Margate, had plainly given the children a fast-food supper and then swanned off for her evening's entertainment, leaving the bathroom in disarray and Fred's disposable-nappy receptacle in acute need of being emptied.

Leo was not, personally, sanctimonious or particularly precious about food. But there was a difference, surely, between asking a nanny to avoid specified seductions ingeniously crafted by the food industry, when it came to her very young charges, and coming over all purist. All he and Ashley had ever said to Cheryl was please don't give them sugar-laden, processed junk, and please cook them something fresh for supper every night. And Cheryl had widened her expertly made-up eyes and said, 'Oh, I'd be happy to. I'm a good cook, me. I take after my mum.'

And then, night after night, there'd been children's ready-meal boxes in the bin, and seldom any fruit or vegetable peelings other than banana skins. There was a packet of chocolate-flavoured puffed-rice cereal in the cupboard, and a shrink-wrapped block of child-sized boxes of strawberry-flavoured drink. Cheryl herself, if the contents of the bin were anything to go by, subsisted on crisps and chocolate. Her skin, Leo thought despondently, was immaculate.

After sorting out the bathroom – he must remember to run more sealant along the back of the bath, Fred being such a vigorous splasher – he had gone to check his sleeping children. To be fair to Cheryl, they looked clean and orderly, Fred upside-down in his cot, backed up against one end, and Maisie asleep on her side, her mouth slightly open to accommodate the thumb lying slackly in it, her other hand clutching the rag of cloth that had once been a stuffed mouse made of striped recycled cotton. She was breathing through her nose in little snorts, and Leo had knelt down by her side for a while and put his face close to hers, to inhale that warm and innocent breath. Then he had gently removed her thumb, pulled Fred back into the body of his cot, and gone downstairs to extract all the packaging from the kitchen bin, to confront Cheryl with in the morning.

After that, he decided he would make supper. Ashley had been late last night, too late to eat with him, having travelled down from Stoke with Susie and Cara and then stopped off with them at Radipole Road to be given fish and chips and red wine – his father-in-law's staple comfort menu – before finally arriving home after eleven, slightly wired and dishevelled and in no fit state to give a coherent account of anything. That had occurred at a quarter to six that morning instead, when they had both been woken by Maisie attempting a pee on her own and dropping the toilet roll into the lavatory pan in the process. They had knelt together on the bathroom floor, consoling and mopping and finding dry pyjamas, and Ashley had described her grandfather and the meetings and the talks and had then, leaning against the side of the bath, burst into tears and said, Sorry, so sorry, I don't know why I'm crying but I just *am*.

Maisie had been very distressed to see her mother weeping, and then, of course, Fred had woken and roared for attention, stamping about in his cot and rattling the bars. By the time Cheryl arrived at eight fifteen, her ponytail and make-up both perfectly in place, Leo had been full of gratitude to see her, which had, he supposed, been taken by Cheryl to mean that she could do pretty much what she wanted that day, even so far as giving the children supermarket pizza and sugar water for supper. After all, there were consequences to everything, even if in this instance they were the labyrinthine ones of an unprincipled and amoral old man turning up unannounced and drawing everyone's attention inexorably to him, like iron filings to a magnet.

Leo opened the fridge. There was nothing in it that constituted the solid basis for a meal: no lamb chops or salmon fillets or left-over chicken. There was half a jar of artichokes in oil, the end of a packet of pancetta, a tired bag of salad and various plastic boxes containing forgotten bits and pieces. He would have to do what his famously frugal mother called 'running a teaspoon round the fridge'. Well, he was good at that – an inventive user-up of whatever was on offer. And what seemed to be on offer for Ashley at the moment was not, in his view, acceptable. She was a major contributor to that company, but Leo didn't think she was allowed the voice that such a contribution merited. It was affecting her and, in consequence, was affecting them. And these new developments were going to affect them even more. Which was why, with an appetizing plate of something ingeniously put together out of nothing very much in front of her, Ashley was going to hear how different their life was going to be for the next year at least. Because, he, Leo, was going to tell her.

It was weird, really, how something as trivial as irritation with Cheryl could be so galvanizing. Leo – famous, he knew full well, for being calm and easygoing – was also a master at procrastination and prevarication. Look at the garden. Look at his limping, part-time, half-hearted work. He could work twice as hard as he did; he could accept every teaching job he was offered, not just one in three; he could organize some garden people, at least, even if he didn't want to get out there personally with a rotivator. But he did none of those things. His school reports hadn't exactly said that he was lazy, but they had gone on a bit about his need for confidence and approval, his inability to risk aiming more than just a shade higher than he was already. And he was frustrated with himself. Always had been. 'Come *on*, Leo,' he'd say to himself. 'Just do it.' But there had been too few things that he had felt certain enough about to do. Except marrying Ashley. He had been full of conviction about marrying Ashley, and he had never ceased to marvel that she had married him. And now – at last, and so much more valuable to her than sorting the piffling garden – he had come up with an idea that filled him with energy and rare certainty. An idea that he was going to put to her while she ate the dinner he had made.

'It's the answer, really,' Susie said.

She was in her usual armchair in the sitting room at Radipole Road. One wall of the room was entirely lined with bookcases, painted deep blue, and Polynesia was sidling along the top of these, clucking in appreciation of her freedom. The door to the hall was closed, just in case her notions extended to flying upstairs.

'I hope you're keeping an eye on her,' Susie said, 'in case she makes a mess.'

Jasper had a box of guitar plectrums on his knee and was sorting them. They made small clicking sounds like dice as they slipped through his fingers. He said, 'I'll clear it up. I always do. It's good for her to be out of the cage.' He paused and then he said calmly, 'Do we have to have this conversation every time she's out? When you're away, she's out all the time.'

Polynesia reached the end of the bookcase and was confronted by a large pottery vase. She peered at it.

'Watch,' Jasper said, looking up, grinning. 'She'll tick it off in a minute.'

'Why don't you bugger off?' Polynesia said to the vase.

Susie didn't look up. She said, 'That's what she says to me.'

121

Jasper was delighted. 'Does she?'

'She only loves you. You know that.'

'I didn't know she told you to bugger off.'

'Since you presumably taught her to say it, I think you probably *did* know. Actually.'

Jasper smiled at her. 'Want a fight?' he said kindly.

She shook her head.

'Bugger off,' Polynesia said again to the vase. 'Off. *Off*. South-west six.'

Susie said, 'I'd rather talk to you about . . . about Morris.'

Jasper stopped sifting. He said, 'Well, you've seen him and sorted him.'

'He isn't sorted. He's in Grace's spare bedroom.'

'Dan offered to book a hotel room.'

Susie sighed. 'Jas, don't be obtuse. Whatever I feel or don't feel, he's old and he's my father.'

Jasper said reasonably, 'Old people manage perfectly well in hotels.'

'Why are you being like this?'

Jasper lifted the box of plectrums off his lap and set it on the floor.

'Suz, I'm not being like anything. But I can't work out what you want from me. You don't want me to come to Stoke, you don't want me to meet Morris, but you do want me to agree with you and support you while you keep changing your mind. If I were you, I'd put

Morris in a hotel for now, and then send him back to Lamu with a remittance to keep him there till he pops his useless clogs. But you won't do that, so I can't help you.'

Susie stirred in her chair as if she was trying to get comfortable. She said, almost as if Jasper hadn't spoken, 'Maybe Ashley's right. Maybe it *is* the answer.'

Jasper got up, crossed to the bookcase and stood directly below Polynesia. She bent down immediately, crooning and clawing at the painted wood with her gnarled grey talons.

'Jasper.'

'Yes.'

'What do you think of Ashley's idea?'

He put a hand up so that Polynesia, bending dangerously low, could have her neck feathers ruffled. He said, 'Suz, I don't have an opinion.'

'You must do!'

He turned round, retrieving his hand. He said soberly, 'You know my opinion. I couldn't quite get why you needed to buy the Parlour House, but you assured me it was creatively essential and I believed you – I believe you so I went along with it. Now you tell me that it's the place to park Morris while you think what to do with him next, and as you don't want to take my advice about him, I'll go along with your wishes again. I don't want to argue with you, I don't agree, but you'll have to put up with that. I'll go along with what you want, but you can't have agreement as well. You'll have to reconcile yourself to that.'

Susie looked at the fireplace. Jasper had lit a fire, hours before, and it had now burned down to a soft red glow in a heap of feathery ashes.

She said, 'I can't behave other than very well, in the circumstances.'

Jasper came back to his chair and lowered himself into it. He looked across at her. Forty years together and he could still sometimes glimpse the girl in the straw hat wreathed in daisies, even if that girl had never been as blonde as the woman before him now.

He said, 'Accepted standards say you should do your duty. That means seeing that he is warm and fed and looked after. Well, you'll do that. You and Grace are doing that already. But circumstances do *not* say that you should behave towards him as if he'd been, to the smallest degree, the kind of father he bloody well should have been.'

'But I have to live with myself afterwards,' Susie said unhappily. 'I have to make a decision that I feel comfortable with.'

Jasper shrugged. 'I'm not interested in martyrdom.'

'Nor me.'

'Nor do I think I can go on with this conversation much longer. I'm revolted by the mere thought of the

124

man, but he's not my dad, thank the Lord.' He stood up, slightly stiffly. 'You decide what to do and I'll try and live with it.'

Susie looked up at him. 'Only try?'

'Yup.'

Jasper went back to the bookcase and looked up at Polynesia. She had now decided that the vase was a friend and was leaning against it, murmuring. He said, 'I'll do my best. Like I've always done. I'll do my best to support you in this ridiculous daddy palaver, as I've done in everything else. Put him in the Parlour House if you must, but I'd send him packing back to Lamu with enough money to keep him there. Money he'll forfeit if he tries to get on another plane. That's what I think, and I'm not changing my mind and I'm not saying it again. And now,' he said, reaching up to grasp Polynesia's feet, 'I'm going to put madam here back in her cage, and then I'm going to bed.'

'He's very . . . peculiar,' Cara said. She was pushing linguine round her plate, whose rim was decorated with a precise ring of clam shells. 'Tall, and very thin and very brown, with straggly white hair tied back and lots of threads and thongs and beads tied round his wrists. Grace says he's very clean.' She gave a brief shudder. 'I don't care if you could eat off him. He gives me the creeps. Especially as he and Ma have the same eyes. I kept looking at his eyes and thinking "How *dare* you have her eyes?" even though I knew it was insane.'

Daniel reached across the restaurant table and poured more sparkling water into Cara's glass.

She said, 'I'm not very good at forgiving people. I mean, it wouldn't matter to me how beautiful some-one was, if their behaviour was shite. And his has been shite personified. Being anywhere near him made me feel kind of . . . *contaminated*.'

'I know,' Daniel said. He let a little silence fall, and then he said, 'Could we talk a bit of business?'

Cara put her fork down. 'I would *love* to talk a bit of business.'

'We have to reschedule that meeting.'

'Of course.'

'And I think, Car, that we have to talk to Ashley.'

Cara had picked up her wine glass. She put it down again abruptly. 'Ashley? Why Ashley?'

'Because I've been doing a bit of thinking while you were away, and I think we need Ashley to understand something.'

Cara leant forward. 'Have you been talking to Leo?'

Daniel smiled at her. 'You know I hardly ever talk to Leo. Lovely chap and all that, but not an inhabitant of my planet. No. I think we have got to talk to Ashley, on her own, about where we go from here, and what needs to be different.'

126

'Now? Right now? After what's happened?'

Daniel said seriously, 'Especially after what's happened.'

Cara pushed her plate aside and folded her arms on her table mat. She said, 'D'you know, Dan, that what I hated while I was in Stoke – I mean, I hated seeing Ma so upset and Grace being so shoved about, as usual, but what I hated was that *he* – that all this stuff about *him* – was getting in the way of the company, kind of distancing it, as if he had the power to somehow blot it out for us, this thing that Ma started, that we've all made, that's our lives, really, and he could just wander in, all old and forlorn and greedy, and just kind of get in the way, obliterate it, make us all forget to put it first, where it should be . . .' She began to hunt about in her pockets for a tissue. 'Sorry, Dan, sorry. And all the people in the factory were so sweet. I mean, they were fascinated, of course, but so concerned and puzzled. Oh damn. Have you got a tissue?'

Dan passed his napkin across to her. Then he reached to touch her elbow. He said, 'I know, sweetheart.'

She blew her nose on the napkin and said gratefully, 'I know you do.'

'That's why I want to talk to Ashley. I want to try and depersonalize the whole thing. I want the brand to be as cosy and domestic as ever, but I want the company to grow up and be altogether more professional.'

127

Cara blotted her eyes and put the napkin down. She said, 'But what about Ma?'

'That's it, really.'

'What, Dan? You're not plotting . . .'

'I'm evolving,' Daniel said. 'I want to evolve the company. Susie could be the best ambassador the company could ever have.'

Cara looked at him for a moment, then she sat back and put her hands in her lap. 'Wow,' she said admiringly.

He glanced up. 'D'you get it?'

'Our spokeswoman,' Cara said. 'Our living advertisement. On panels, talking about entrepreneurs . . .'

'Woman entrepreneurs.'

'School boards, mentoring groups, non-executive positions in other companies . . .'

'All that.'

'Well done, Daniel!'

'And,' he said, 'if she can't bring herself to send Morris away, it'll shield her from him. She'll be too busy. We'll keep her too busy.'

Cara beamed at him. 'What if she won't agree?'

'That's why we need to talk to Ashley.'

'And Grace?'

'I don't want to sound heartless,' Dan said, 'but I can't save Grace without her consent.'

'Morris, Jeff . . .'

'Did you and Ashley bully her when you were kids?'

Cara looked indignant. 'Never! Anyway, she was too dreamy to bully. You could never get a grip on Grace. Still can't.'

He leant across the table again, holding out his hand. 'So. My plan?'

She put her hand in his. 'Go for it.'

'You look worn out,' Leo said.

Ashley made a face. 'It's the default look for all working mothers of small children. Panda eyes, washed-out clothes garnished with sick . . .'

'I didn't mean that.'

'Oh good,' Ashley said. She was lying on the sofa with her shoes off.

'I meant,' Leo said patiently, 'that you look as if you've had a really harrowing few days, which you have.'

'And tomorrow it's the shop visit to Bicester Village, plus a meeting.'

'Ash,' Leo said, 'don't do that. Don't destroy relaxing time by winding yourself up about tomorrow. Anyway, you like shop visits. You like going to Bicester.'

Ashley gave a small groan. She closed her eyes.

Leo crossed the room to sit beside her. Behind him, in the kitchen part of the half-done family room, candles flickered on the table he had set for supper.

'Ash,' he said again.

She opened her eyes and regarded him balefully.

He said, 'What would you say if I told you that you never had to work again?'

Ashley stared at him for a moment. Then she said, 'I'd be thrilled for half a day and then I'd go mad.'

'Quite.'

She struggled to sit up. 'What are you talking about?'

'Well,' Leo said, 'we can't go on like this.'

'Like what?'

'Muddle and chaos and Cheryl, and you shattered and the kids fed crap and nobody really *settled*.'

Ashley was now upright and looking at him with suspicion. 'Leo, what are you saying?'

'Well, I'll tell you what I've been thinking after you've assured me again that you really do want to work.'

'Of course I do! If there was anyone else doing my job in the company, I'd want to kill them!'

'Fine. Good. Just checking. And what about home life?'

Ashley gave the room a cursory glance. 'Hardly magazine standard, but roughly on a par with everyone else of our age and stage.'

'But could do better?'

'Of course it could be better. Nicky was better. Cheryl's only average on good days. I asked Maisie what she liked about her and she said her eyeliner.'

'I have a plan,' Leo said.

'We can't have a plan right now. Not with all the Morris stuff going on—'

'The Morris stuff makes it perfect timing for a plan. That Barlaston house of your mother's, and now Morris – it's ideal. It throws everything up in the air. You're brilliant at what you do in the company, but you need more clout. Maybe a pay rise. Maybe a payment structure like your parents have. I don't know. I don't care much, except that I want to see you listened to more. And you won't be listened to more if you can't give more mental energy to work, and you can't give more mental energy to work if you're worrying about Cheryl feeding the kids badly and spending time in cafés with other nannies instead of teaching Maisie how to ride her bike. So . . .' He paused and looked at her. He was smiling.

'So?' she said.

'I'm going to do it.'

'*What?*'

'For a year, anyway. We're sacking Cheryl, saving the money and I'm going to look after the kids and run the house.'

Ashley gulped. 'But what about your teaching?'

He waved a hand. 'That can wait.'

'But Leo . . .'

'I want you to have this chance,' he said. 'I want to

131

be at home with the children. I want to do this family thing properly. I *want* to.'

Ashley nodded slightly. She said, 'Are you sure? All that repetition? Making lunch every day for Fred that he won't eat? Hanging out with other mothers at play-group? Hearing about other fathers on business trips to Singapore?'

'All that. Quite sure.'

Ashley got slowly to her feet. 'Gosh.' She looked down at him. 'I was quoting you in Stoke. I was telling them that you always say, work with what you have.'

'Well, then.'

'Everything seems in a bit of a state of flux, at the company.'

'Perfect.'

'The big meeting cancelled because of Morris, Dan and Ma being at loggerheads; Grace not knowing what she wants so everyone thinking they know for her; do we export, don't we . . .'

'Exactly.'

Ashley put a hand out and ruffled Leo's hair. 'You can't just do the house and the kids. You'll go mental.'

'I won't. I'll be good at it. I'll like being good at it.'

'Just a year.'

'Or more, if I like it.' He smiled up at her. 'I might even get round to the garden.'

'I'll believe *that* when I see it.'

He stood up too, and said happily, 'So you'll be the breadwinner, won't you?'

She nodded again, without complete conviction. 'Maybe.'

'No. Certainly. That'll be our deal. You bring home the bacon. I'll cook it and feed it to the children.' He put his arms round her. He said into her neck, 'It'll be brilliant.'

'Sacrifices worry me.'

'It's not a sacrifice,' he said. 'It's what I want!' He pulled back and looked at her. 'My wife, the bread-winner.' He smiled and kissed her nose. 'Just like your mother.'

Jasper was asleep. He was lying on his side with his back to Susie, in his usual sleeping position, and his breathing was quiet and even in a way that was almost impossible to achieve if you were only pretending. But then, if he was pretending, Susie thought, it was because he didn't want to talk any more: he was tired of what she wanted to talk about, so, asleep or really awake, it was clear that he was of no use to her.

Nor was it any use lying awake in the dark going round in mental circles. It would, surely, be more profitable to get up and go downstairs and attempt to comfort herself with the soothing ritual of tea-making – proper tea leaves in a proper pot – rather than lie in a tangle of thoughts and creases under a duvet which was alternately too hot or not warm enough. Jasper's imperturbable capacity to sleep through life's turbulences had been infinitely comforting and instructive at the beginning of their relationship; now it was beyond mere irritation, and was a symbol of his increasing detachment from everything that concerned her. His languid humour had been irresistible to her once, so sophisticated, so darkly witty. Now it just seemed, too often, to be merely childish, tiresome evidence of his inability to take life seriously, to see what had to be done, day after day, just to make things work.

Well, she thought, turning away from him on to her left side for the umpteenth time, it was no good finding fault with every useless man in her life right now, no use deploring them for their shortcomings. In fact, uncomfortable though it might be to think about, was there something similar in Jasper and Morris? Was there something in her father's deeply flexible – to put it politely – approach to life that she had unconsciously chosen to replicate in her marriage? And what about her role in whatever had gone wrong in either the past or the present? Her father had never come to find her, but then she had never been out to find him either, or her poor little mother, because it was always easier to stay where she was, safe and admired and encouraged, and where, above all, the action was. What she could not explain to Jasper was that the sight of Morris in his beads and crumpled linens was filling her with terrible guilt, guilt at having made so little effort as a daughter to either parent while her mother was alive, and then being filled with nothing but revulsion when her father stumbled into their carefully constructed lives, bringing with him no reproaches of his own beyond the fact of his continuing and now almost helpless existence.

I can't tell even Jasper that, Susie thought, staring at the faint lines of city night light at the edges of the bedroom blinds. I can't admit all that. Any more than I can face what I might have done to him – to Jasper – all through these years, and to the girls in various ways. The sort of thing Ashley might be inadvertently doing to those littlies of hers, my grandchildren. Grandchildren? What am I doing with grandchildren, when I can't even sort out my feelings about my own father? What am I doing fussing over jug spouts and pansy prints when I don't have the answers to such huge human questions? Except that without the jugs and the pansies, I probably couldn't face anything, manage anything, achieve anything. I love them. I love thinking about them. I love the fact that because of them over two hundred people earn enough money to feed and clothe their families. I *love* that. I do.

She turned on to her back once more. Jasper hadn't

stirred. He breathed on, steadily, peacefully, regularly. She put a hand out to touch him, and then hesitated and pulled it back again. Be fair, she said to herself, be fair. You told him that whatever you decided had to be something you could live with, so apply that smug statement to him, as well as to Morris. Don't ask him to do what he can't do, feel what he can't feel. Morris isn't his problem, and you've made it plain he's not a problem for sharing. Why did you do that? God knows, but you did, and it's done now. You've slammed the door in Jasper's face, haven't you?

She stared hard at his back in the gloom. He was sleeping, as he'd slept for as long as she could remember, in boxer shorts and a huge, thin, Sea Island cotton T-shirt, navy blue or black, and laundered now to a uniform dark grey. She watched the slight rise and fall of the fabric as he breathed, and felt her thoughts ebbing and flowing with his breaths – thoughts of remorse and anger and guilt and resentment and disappointment and determination and fear and sadness and satisfaction. And worry. There was always worry. It lay in wait at every turn, unhurried in its persistence, but always ready to seize an opportunity. And what, it said to Susie, at twenty to four in the morning as she lay wakefully beside her slumbering husband, are you going to do about Grace?

CHAPTER SEVEN

'My granddad worked here,' Morris said.

Grace stood just inside the doorway of the Parlour House's small sitting room, and watched him. He was wearing a long, sleeveless knitted waistcoat over his linen tunic, its edges blanket-stitched in brown wool. He pointed at the floor.

'There'd have been a central drain here in the old dairy, running all along. A channel – a stone channel. My granddad didn't learn to read till he got married. My granny taught him.'

'Oh,' Grace said. She glanced out of the windows. They were very dirty, and the sky beyond them was no brighter.

'I expect she was ashamed that he couldn't read,' said Morris. 'It's quite a common thing in families, shame.'

Grace went on looking out of the window. She said, without emphasis, 'Yes.'

'I went off before my old dad really woke up to being ashamed of me. And then I come back all these years later, and it's waiting for me, as if it had never been any different.'

Grace said uneasily, 'I don't actually think it's that.'

Morris turned to survey the fireplace. It was made of reconstructed stone, and had a phoney, quilted look. 'Oh?'

'I don't think that anyone's actually ashamed of you. But it's a bit disconcerting that you don't seem to feel any shame yourself. That's what I mean, I think.'

'How do you know what I feel?'

Grace said with more spirit, 'By how you act. You act as if you weren't responsible for yourself and nobody should have ever asked you to be.'

Morris said, slightly defensively, 'I took myself off, you know. Out of everyone's hair.'

'Leaving a baby.'

He looked at her. 'Is that what everyone's so worked up about? Our leaving your mother behind? Where she'd have ten times the life we could ever have given her?'

'That's not the point. That's easy to say, looking back.'

'Even you,' Morris said. He pushed his hands up into the opposite sleeves of his tunic. 'Even you end up holding that against me.'

'Of course I do.'

'And would your mother have had a fraction of the success she's had if she'd grown up on a beach in

138

Lamu speaking Swahili and running wild? You have no idea how basic life was there, how many handouts we were grateful for. Our house wasn't much more than a shack. We shouldn't have stayed. But it's the first place we landed when the balloon went up with your great-granddad, and we got stuck. We meant to move on – at least, I did – but somehow we stayed. I'm telling you, if it was no life for us two, what kind of life would it have been for a clever child?'

Grace sighed. 'It's no use making excuses with hindsight. You left her. You didn't keep in touch.'

'Nor did she.'

Grace took a step back towards the door to the little hall. 'I'm going to pretend I didn't hear that. Or, even better, that you never said it.'

He said, as if grumbling to himself, 'You don't know what it's like, never to get used to being who you are.'

Grace took a deep breath, as if to steady herself. She said, in as level a tone as she could manage, 'Well. Do you think you could live here?'

Morris looked up at the small chandelier on the ceiling. It was made of wrought iron and pink glass. 'I should think so.'

'Ma's going to rip it apart. She's going to kind of empty out the ground floor, and start again. It would mean camping here, really.'

139

He gave a small shrug and took his hands out of his sleeves. 'I've never lived any other way, duck.'

'But in a tropical climate. This would be cold and uncomfortable.'

'Not in summer.'

'We don't have summers any more. Not real ones.'

He eyed her. 'Trying to put me off living here, are you?'

'No,' she said. 'But trying to get you to be realistic. Ma says you can live here, but I'm just telling you that it won't be comfortable.'

He went slowly across to the window. He said, looking out, 'You want your flat back.'

Grace sighed. 'I want my privacy back. I'm used to privacy.'

He turned round, grinning. 'You want to move that boy in. That Jeff boy.'

'No.'

'Good-looking boy.'

'I don't want Jeff—'

'You do,' Morris interrupted. 'That's the trouble. You want him, and you know he's no good for you. But you're giving in to the wanting, aren't you?'

Grace said nothing. She stared fixedly at the fireplace.

'Know something?' Morris said. 'I was wrong just now. I was wrong to say you didn't know what it was like, never getting used to being who you are. You *do* know, don't you?' He let a beat fall, and then he said softly, 'You're just like me. Aren't you?'

Cheryl said that being sacked was fine by her. She hadn't liked the job much anyway – though don't get her wrong, the kids were quite cute – because the early starts really messed up her life and the commute was terrible. And frankly, the money wasn't all that wonderful, and she'd got a friend who worked shifts in a call centre who made the same money without the hassle, and some weeks she had three days off in a row, which Cheryl thought was really how the work–life balance should be.

'Why don't you apply for a job there, then?' Leo asked her pleasantly.

She had rolled her eyes slightly. 'Oh, I will. When I've had a holiday. My boyfriend's getting a summer job in Ibiza, in one of the clubs.'

'Cleaning, is he?' Leo said, suddenly exasperated.

She stared at him, the penny dropping abruptly. Then she hoisted her fringed handbag on to her shoulder. 'I don't have to take this,' she said, 'Not from someone who hasn't even *got* a job. And a *man*, at that!'

When the front door had slammed behind her, the house had shuddered and then seemed to settle, quietly and steadily, as if reminding itself that dramas were an aberration and not part of a regular pattern. Leo climbed to the top of the house, to tidy the children's bedrooms, and then descended all the way down to the basement kitchen, collecting laundry and used mugs as he went, until he reached the washing and drying machines, those symbols of cleanliness and order. In seventeenth-century Holland, he remembered from A-level History of Art, cleanliness had been seen not just as a virtue, but as a symbol of social harmony and prosperity. There was no reason why a load of his own family's laundry, washed, ironed and restored to its relevant shelves and drawers by him, shouldn't have an equally congenial effect on all of them. When Ashley had been pregnant, or having her two brief, impatient spells of maternity leave – 'I can't pretend that I'm not itching to get back to work, however much I'm thrilled to be a mum,' she'd said frequently – he had been an excellent house husband, after all. Susie had wanted to pay for a nanny, but Leo had put his foot down, insisting on their need and ability to manage alone, just the three or subsequently four of them, and had been rewarded by the grateful gleam in Ashley's eyes. He could resume the role that had, temporarily anyway, suited them very well. He could at least try. Whatever he managed would be a first step, at least, towards reclaiming control of their lives and ultimately – grandly – their destiny.

It was a comfort to think that he and Ashley were both simultaneously reclaiming authority over their working and domestic schedules. Here he was, stuffing socks and T-shirts into the washing machine, with Fred having his morning sleep upstairs and the prospect of a buggy walk to collect Maisie from nursery school, followed by a commendable lunch of leftover chicken casserole. And there was Ashley, at work after a fine morning walk to get there, with a healthy packed lunch in her work bag and a firm intention to speak to Cara and Dan at the end of the day, in order to explain their changed domestic circumstances and her intentions for her professional future. By the time she got home, the children would be bathed, fed (tomato soup and cheese toasts, possibly), and even if supper wasn't started, the kitchen would be tidy and welcoming. He felt a small surge of elation. If this was contributing, then maybe it was going to be more fulfilling than he had dared to hope.

He straightened up. Above his head, Fred was abruptly awake and bellowing, rocking his cot so that the headboard banged against the wall. There was a distinct mark on the wall already, which threatened to develop, any minute, into a crack in the plaster. It was obviously necessary to move the cot away from any wall, at once. It was also necessary to put washing powder into the machine, select the right programme for reasons of economy and ecology, and switch it on. Leo hesitated for a moment, his hands full of a tangle of Maisie's tights. The banging upstairs intensified, culminating in a crash. And then there was silence. Leo dropped the tights and ran.

'Pa!' Grace said, holding her telephone to her ear.

'Don't sound so surprised.'

'Well, I am. I haven't spoken to you for ages.'

'Days.'

'And it's the afternoon.'

'Where are you?' Jasper said.

'In the studio.'

'So you're back.'

'Back?'

'From Barlaston,' Jasper said. 'From – the new house.'

Grace cast a glance at Michelle and Ben's studiously turned backs. Then she crossed to the studio door and let herself out on to the iron landing at the top of the outside staircase.

'I'm outside now,' she said, 'and it's freezing.'

'Gracie,' Jasper said, 'I'm ringing to see if you're OK.'

Grace screwed up her eyes. In the yard below her, a gaggle of schoolchildren were being herded from the factory towards the pottery café. In the school holidays, you couldn't move for children painting pottery in the café, pottery that then had to be labelled and fired and

144

labelled again. It had been Susie's idea, fifteen years ago – long before everyone else had thought of it – children putting their names, their handprints, their mother's names on—

'Grace?'

'Pa,' Grace said, 'I'm fine. I really am.'

'But Barlaston . . .'

'I think it'll work. I think he'll agree to live there, even with builders in. He's not really bothered about comfort.'

Jasper made an exasperated sound. 'I don't care what bothers him or doesn't. You know what I want.'

'Yes. Ma told me.'

'I don't want you exploited, either. Making you show him round the house is exploitation.'

'I offered to,' Grace said.

'She shouldn't have let you.'

'It's easier for me, I'm a bit distanced. I'm not his daughter.'

'You're mine,' Jasper said, 'and I'm worried about you. You don't sound right to me.'

Grace turned to face the wall of the studio. It was a little less windy with her back to the yard. 'I'm tired, that's all,' she said. 'I'm not used to having anyone else in the flat.'

'He shouldn't still be there.'

'Pa, please.'

'I'm coming up to Stoke. I'm going to sort it.'

'No!' Grace shouted.

'Why not?'

'I don't want it sorted. I mean, I don't want you to sort anything. I'll sort it my own way.'

'Don't you want help?' Jasper said.

Grace leaned her forehead against the brick wall of the studio. It was cold and rough and impersonal. 'I don't want any more dramas,' she said.

'I won't make a drama. You know me, I don't do drama. But I draw the line at having you exploited in all this nonsense.'

Grace closed her eyes. She said, without thinking, 'I'm not being exploited. I'm just – trying to work out who I am.'

'*What?*'

'I don't mean that. I didn't mean that, Pa. I just mean, please can I do things my own way?'

'Even if it means other people bullying you?'

'They're not.'

'Oh God, Grace,' Jasper said, suddenly weary, 'have it your own way. Reject help. Tell me I shouldn't have rung.'

'I like you ringing,' Grace said lamely.

'I haven't seen you for weeks.'

'Only about three.'

'Grace, what is going on?'

Grace took her forehead away from the wall and rubbed it. She said, 'We're really busy. I mean, exceptionally, for this time of year. Usually it goes completely dead after Christmas.'

'I didn't mean that. As well you know.'

'I'm OK,' Grace said. 'And I'll be down to London soon.'

Jasper said sharply, 'When you've finished doing your mother's bidding.'

There was a sudden surprised silence.

'Gosh,' Grace said. 'That wasn't like you.'

Jasper took a breath. He said, 'Perhaps you should pay more attention.'

'To you?'

'Yes, actually.'

'If you and Ma are fighting,' Grace said, 'it's none of my business.'

'I see.'

'Pa, I have to go. I've got work to do.'

Jasper sighed. 'Sorry, Gracie.'

'Me too. Sorry, Pa.'

'Will you ring me? If I can do anything?'

'Yes. Yes, of course.'

'Bye, darling.'

'Bye, Pa.'

Grace clicked her phone off and dropped it into her pocket. Then she opened the door to the studio.

Michelle was standing by the kettle, her weight on one hip, holding the Valentine's mug that she had appropriated for her own use – 'Be prepared,' she said, 'that's my motto' – a single teabag held between finger and thumb.

She looked at Grace. 'Lover boy?'

'What?'

'On the phone. Was that hot Jeff?'

Grace took a chair at the central table with its back to the rest of the room. 'It was my dad,' she said. '*If* it's any of your business.'

Ashley decided that she would not talk to Cara and Dan in the boardroom. That would look altogether too elaborate. It would be better to sit at the meeting table, where buyers and other visitors were welcomed, in the alcove flanked by shelves of pottery grouped by design, and with a view out to the south and to the river. There were high stools around this table, which lent the area informality, and a whiteboard on the wall which gave the sales figures in the shops for the week, divided by coloured marker into three columns – the actual sales, the target sales, and the sales compared with the same week in the previous year. Ashley knew those figures by heart, as she did every week. Dan had already said that he was not interested in seeing any more minus signs.

Ashley had made coffee in the Italian screwtop device which Cara and Dan said made the best coffee. Ashley suspected they said that because the process was more laborious and therefore, in their opinion, more authentic. Dan had refused an office request for an espresso machine, pointing out that the building had an excellent café on the ground floor, but he had imported an electric ring to sit beside the office kettle all the same, to enable the coffee pot to be used. Ashley told herself that she would not even comment on that, let alone allow herself to get steamed up about it. Dan and Cara were a pain about coffee, as they were about anything to do with food and drink, and Ashley just had to accept that, in the same way she had had to accept having a mother who was late for every school sports day – if indeed she made it at all – and having a lovely-natured, supportive husband who, it seemed, was without significant personal ambition. They all were as they were. And just at this moment, she was determined to focus on raising her personal profile in the company.

Cara and Dan arrived simultaneously from their separate desks, and put their BlackBerries down next to the coffee pot.

Dan said, nodding at it, 'Thank you for that, Ash.'

Cara looked at Ashley's mug. 'What are you drinking?'

'Green tea.'

'Are you detoxing or something?'

'No. Just trying not to overload the system. Now that life is going to be rather different.'

Cara made a face, misunderstanding her. 'Oh, I do hope not.'

'I didn't mean him. I meant at home.'

'Wow,' Cara said. 'What's happened?'

Dan poured coffee into two small mugs from the A for Apple range. He pushed one towards Cara and glanced at Ashley. 'A good thing, from the look of you.'

Ashley said proudly, 'We've sacked Cheryl.'

'Great,' Dan said.

Cara paused with her coffee mug halfway to her mouth. 'You always said she was lazy about everything except dolling herself up.'

'It was the children, really. She was feeding them such rubbish, all packet stuff and sugar. One of the reasons we took her on was that she said she could cook. Well, she didn't, and so Leo fired her, and we're going for a totally new regime.'

Cara took a sip of her coffee and put the mug down. 'Like what?'

'Leo,' Ashley said carefully, 'is going to be a full-time house husband. He's going to look after the children, and cook, and do the laundry. He suggested it. He said it was what he wanted to do.'

'Good for Leo,' Dan said. His tone was faintly hearty, as if he knew he should applaud Leo's choice, but couldn't quite believe in it.

'That's wonderful,' Cara said, 'if that's what he wants. Wonderful for the children—'

'And me.'

'Yes, of course. And you.'

'Because,' Ashley said, looking down at her tea, 'it sort of . . . frees me, doesn't it?'

'Frees you?'

'Yes,' Ashley said. She looked straight at her sister. 'It frees me up to have a much greater commitment to the company. And if I have a greater commitment, then it follows that I should have a greater say.'

There was a small silence. Dan made as if to say something, and Cara reached across to squeeze his forearm to restrain him.

She said to her sister, 'What do you mean?'

'I mean,' Ashley said, 'that I'll have more headspace. For marketing. More time to analyse the website. More time to spend on the data from the Collectors' Club. More attention to give to advertising and partnerships with other companies. Increasing the number of catalogues from four to eight, say, with two or three around Christmas.'

'All good,' Daniel said, too quickly.

'But?' Cara said.

151

'But?'

'You implied that all this increased application on your part should somehow be recognized . . .'

'Yes,' Ashley said.

'We do recognize—' Dan began. Cara tightened her grip on his arm. She said, 'What are you saying?'

'I'm saying that you and Ma don't regard me as equal. And I think you should. Merchandizing and marketing should be equal.'

'In – in standing?'

'And remuneration,' Ashley said.

'Ash, we get paid the same—'

'But there's two of you. And no children.'

'We can't compensate you for having chosen to have children.'

'No,' Ashley said. 'But you can recognize that I am as professional as you two and Ma. I am as crucial to this company. And what I do for the company – and even more, what I *will* do, now that Leo has made this amazing offer – should be acknowledged, both in how I'm treated in the company and what I'm paid.'

'But Ash—'

'This is a *family* company,' Ashley said. 'The money it gives Ma and Pa is pretty ad hoc. I don't mind that, but I do mind being treated as a lesser contributor than you two. Especially now.'

Daniel looked at Cara. He said, slightly impatiently, 'May I speak, please?'

She took her hand away. 'Of course.'

'Ashley,' he said, 'we can't magic marketing into more than it is.'

She held his gaze. She said, 'I'm not asking that. I'm just telling you that I'll be adding value.'

'Could you—'

'Listen,' Ashley said. 'The brand used to depend on Ma and Pa's home life, didn't it? When we were little. All those photoshoots of us eating toast and catching tadpoles and doing the Christmas tree. Well, Ma doesn't really have a home life now, does she, whatever she says? So it could be *my* home life instead – mine and Leo's and the children's. Our lives are very much like an updated version of how we used to live, and that's crucial to customers, you know it is.'

Cara said carefully, 'Are you insisting, Ash? On something that should be a joint decision?'

'No,' Ashley said. 'I'm just emphasizing how valuable I am. Forty thousand online mailshots increase sales about three per cent. Double the mailshots, using Maisie and Fred, thus keeping it in the family as we've always done, and we'll double the increase. The Collectors' Club will go wild – so many of them are grandparents. I'm just pointing out to you that you need me, and I want that recognized.'

'By paying you more?'

'By at least having a discussion about payment. For all of us.'

'Including Grace?'

'Of course.'

'*Now?* While business is so—'

'Now,' Ashley said.

Cara sat back on her stool. She didn't look at Daniel. 'Wow. There's so much to think about.'

'No, there isn't,' Ashley said. 'I've made it perfectly plain. It isn't at all complicated, and it completely chimes with the brand ethic.'

Cara glanced at Daniel. She said, 'I didn't mean that.'

'Oh?'

'I meant—' she said, and stopped. Then she said, 'Ash, we were discussing something else, Dan and me. We were talking about another shift of emphasis – something that would actually sit very well with what you were saying.' She pushed her coffee mug away. 'What Dan and I were discussing was, in fact, a bit of a change in direction for . . . for Ma.'

There was a note on the kitchen counter in Grace's flat, in Morris's curiously feminine hand. It merely said that he was out and would not be back till late. He would not be there for supper. He had signed the note with a flourishing M and a kiss, and left it under a jar of fig

154

mustard that it would never have occurred to Grace to buy.

She sighed, and dropped her bag on the floor. Of course, she had given keys to Morris, and then Susie had given him some cash, and it was not up to Grace to monitor how he spent that cash. It was irritating not to know where he was, in the same way that it would have been irritating to have a wayward teenager in the flat who one was fundamentally responsible for, while acknowledging the need for them to have a degree of independence. It was a relief not to have Morris there all evening, shuffling about the sitting room in his blue socks, but at the same time it was mildly agitating not knowing where he was, what he was doing, or when he would be back.

She ran water into a glass and drank it, then filled the glass a second time and carried it into the sitting room. The room was tidy, but to judge by the dented cushions had recently been occupied. Grace told herself not to be neurotic about how many people had been in her flat, or to speculate as to what they might have been doing there, and sat down on her sofa with the remote control in one hand and her glass of water in the other. She would watch whatever came up on the screen, until her brain was sufficiently relaxed to be of use to her.

She was no sooner seated than the buzzer to the

street door of the flats sounded. Heaving herself to her feet, Grace put her water and the remote control on the coffee table and padded over to her front door, and the small security screen set into the wall beside it. The screen showed Jeff, in jeans and a leather jacket, holding a bunch of flowers.

Grace leant on the wall beside the screen.

'Go away,' she said into the speaker.

'Why?'

'I don't want to see you.'

'Babe, you always say that.'

'This time, I mean it.'

'I've got something to say to you.'

Grace said, 'You've always got something to say to me. I don't want to hear it. Where's Morris?'

'How would I know?'

'Because he's not here, and you are, and I suspect there's a connection.'

Jeff leant towards the screen, his face distorting as he did so. 'He's in the pub. Drinking lager and lime, like a good boy, and playing darts.'

'And you cooked this up between you?'

'Babe,' Jeff said, 'we get on, your granddad and me. I need to talk to you. I need to see you alone.'

'Go away,' Grace said.

'Let me in. Please, Grace, let me in.'

'No,' Grace said.

Jeff took something out of his pocket with his free hand, and dangled it close to the screen. 'Look,' he said.

She peered, then said faintly, 'Keys.'

'Your keys,' Jeff said. 'Your granddad's keys. He lent them to me.' He blew a kiss at the screen. 'I'm coming up.'

CHAPTER EIGHT

'Am I hearing what I think I'm hearing?' Susie said. She was in the kitchen at Radipole Road, sitting at the table with Frida Kahlo's roses on the wall above her.

Cara, sitting opposite with her back to the room, was folding the arms of her sunglasses around the stem of the wine glass in front of her. She said steadily, 'I don't know why you sound so outraged.'

'Because I *am* outraged,' Susie said. 'This is *my* company, conceived of, started and grown by me. I found the factory. I have been at the forefront of reviving English spongeware. I have grown the workforce from seventy to over two hundred and twenty. I *am* Susie Sullivan pottery. And now you tell me that I should step aside to be a sort of superannuated *president*, or something equally remote, and leave the running of the company to you and Dan?'

Cara unfolded her sunglasses and laid them beside her wine glass with precision. She said, 'And Ashley.

And Grace. And I didn't put it at all like that.'

'But that is what you *meant*.'

'Ma,' Cara said, 'nobody is disputing what you've done, what you've achieved. In fact, nobody wants to do anything but applaud and admire you for the amazing success you've had and the huge numbers of people whose lives have been transformed by you. But nothing stands still. What we're trying to do is take the company forward. We're trying to adapt it to be what our customers want it to be. *Now*. They've changed, as times have changed. As doing business has changed. There are things about Susie Sullivan's way of doing business that have to change, too.'

Susie hadn't touched her wine. She turned the glass now, restlessly. 'You're saying I'm holding it back, though, aren't you?'

'I'm saying that if we want it to grow – and I think we all do, including you – then we have to embrace, not fear, other people's expertise.'

Susie took her hands away from her wine glass. 'Which means you think I'm holding it back. Say it, Cara. *Say* it. I don't trust other people to see what I see. This company is my baby.'

'No, Ma. That's just it. It isn't a baby. It's grown up, and it's got all kinds of other relationships in its life, just like grown-ups do. It's not – I hate saying this, but it's not just your baby any more. And hasn't been for ages.'

Susie pushed her glass away. She said, 'Who cooked this up? Dan?'

Cara didn't look at her. She said, 'It was evident to all of us. It's evident to everyone. It has been for ages. It – it just fell to me to talk to you. We thought that if Ashley came too, it would look like we were ganging up.'

'Well, aren't you?'

'Having the same opinion isn't the same as ganging up.'

Susie leant forward, put her elbows on the table and covered her face with her hands. From behind them, she said, 'And all our old core customers?'

'We're not forgetting them,' Cara said. 'We'll never forget them. They're crucial. But we need new customers all the time, and we need to show the old ones fresh ideas. That's where you would be so brilliant.'

'Please don't stoop to flattery.'

Cara stood up and carried her wine glass over to the sink, to tip the contents down the drain. She said crossly, 'It doesn't help to make a business discussion personal.'

Susie took her hands away from her face. 'How can it not be personal when the very essence of the business is personal? It's the intimacy of my vision that makes the whole thing *work*.'

'I know that. But it's still a business.'

'The minute you introduced Dan—'

'Don't start, Ma. I'm warning you.'

Susie said, more reasonably, 'He can't help it. Nor can you. Both graduates of the chainstore university break-out department as you are. So is Ashley, really.'

Cara said patiently, 'It's modern business practice, Ma.'

Susie looked across the room at her. 'But we're a family.'

'Yes.'

'A family currently rather besieged by its own problems.'

'I know,' Cara said.

'It isn't just Morris . . .'

'I know.'

'It's Grace,' Susie said. 'She keeps stepping in to protect me, and I let her, and then it goes wrong, and I blame myself, and I'm right to. What am I doing? What am I going to do about Grace?'

'Include her.'

'In what? In marginalizing me to the edges of the very company I'm the centre of?'

Cara said nothing. She came back slowly to the table and picked up her sunglasses.

Susie brushed a hand across her face. 'Of course we must include Grace,' she said. 'It's no excuse that we live here and she lives there and we're bad at making sure she comes to London.'

'No,' Cara said.

'But I'll tell you something. If you propose to Grace what you've just proposed to me, she'll side with me.' Susie glanced up, without smiling. 'I can guarantee that.'

Morris said that he'd heard of a hotel on Winton Square where there were rooms to be had for forty pounds a night. The reviews online described the standard as being poor to fair, but he didn't mind about that. He just thought it was time he got out of Grace's hair.

Grace said she couldn't think of him staying in a poor-to-fair hotel for forty pounds a night. 'But nor,' she said, 'can you go on staying here. Not after giving my keys to Jeff.'

Morris said, wheedling slightly, 'I thought I was doing you a favour. You and Jeff. I thought I was helping.'

Grace looked at the ceiling. 'No, you didn't. You were making mischief. You *liked* making mischief.'

Morris waited a moment and then he said, 'Well, you got your keys back, didn't you?'

Grace lowered her head again and regarded him. She decided neither to reply nor to smile. The scene with Jeff the night before had been, well, horrible. There had even been a brief appalling moment when she thought it might become physical, frighteningly physical, after she had stupidly made an attempt to snatch the keys from his hand, and had caught a flash in his eyes – only a flash – that had been distinctly chilling. In the process of trying to retrieve the keys, which he was holding out, teasing and grinning, she had tripped and fallen against the edge of the coffee table and banged her shin, hard. It had hurt at once, the sharp, deep pain of bruised bone. And it had made her cry out and double up, and when she did that, Jeff had dropped to his knees beside her, dropping the keys in the same instant, and said, 'God, sorry, babe. Sorry, it was only a game, honest. Only a bit of fun—'

But none of it had been fun. None of it. Not for weeks, with Jeff, and certainly not since Morris had arrived. It had, instead, been an increasing and debilitating strain, filling the days with a kind of tension that entirely obscured not just any pleasure in work, but work itself. Add to that the uneasy feeling that she had brought the current chaos on herself because she was too appeasing, too needy and – if Morris was right – too afraid to be left alone with the unwelcome reality of her own personality, and the mess she was in was unbearable.

It was equally unbearable to think of sharing it. The brief pride she had felt in assuming responsibility for Morris now seemed pathetic and impractical. The choice of Jeff as a boyfriend seemed to be nothing but the calamity Cara had always said it would be. The fact was that in the case of both men, she, Grace, couldn't continue, let alone finish what she had chosen to start. She was stuck with a couple of wrecks, and the last thing she could face, in her predicament, was asking for help and admitting that she couldn't cope with what she had elected to take on.

'So you're going deaf and dumb on me, now, are you?' Morris said. 'Can't hear, won't speak.'

Grace said, 'You can't stay in Winton Square.'

'And you say I can't stay here.'

'I said I can't have anyone staying here that I can't trust.'

'It was just the once,' Morris said. 'Just a joke.'

'I'm not discussing it.'

He looked suddenly sober. 'Have you told your mother?'

'No.'

'Are you going to?'

'No.'

Morris sighed. He said, 'You're a funny one.'

Grace reached for her bag. 'I'm going to work.'

'And me?'

'You can stay here. For now. Or you can go out. But if you go out, you can't come back till I'm back. I'm not letting any keys out of my sight.'

Morris leant against the wall and folded his arms. He

said, 'I didn't mean this to happen. I didn't mean to be like this.'

Grace glanced at him. 'Nor did I.'

'Duck, what are we going to do?'

Grace moved towards the front door. As she reached it, she turned briefly and said, 'I have no idea.'

Jasper spent the afternoon with Brady and Frank in his studio. He and Brady had known each other since the early days of the Stone Gods – those heady, promising days of the Parlophone signing, which had not so much come to an end as petered out almost invisibly, so that when it transpired that Brady had been playing his bass in another group for at least two years, there had seemed to Jasper absolutely no point in taking it personally. So he hadn't. He had simply gone along to the gigs where Brady was now playing, and integrated himself comfortably with the other musicians, one of whom was Frank, who could really play any wood-wind or even brass instrument you asked him to, and the three of them had settled into an easy routine of jamming together occasionally, mostly in Jasper's studio, because why wouldn't you use a great facility like that if it was available to you?

In any case, even if it was never mentioned, there was the kind of money in Jasper's life that there never had been and never would be in either Brady's or Frank's.

They had been jobbing musicians all their lives and even if they didn't actually envy Jasper his studio and the advantages of the life provided by his missus, they weren't going to turn their noses up at what he had to offer, either. On those jamming afternoons, they brought a token handful of beers with them, but then they let Jasper crack open the red wine and go down to the Fulham Road for fish and chips. It was assumed, though never spelled out, that the two of them would take whatever work was offered in pubs and clubs anywhere within reason, and that Jasper wouldn't, because he didn't need to. The discrepancy didn't stop them thinking he was a good guitarist; they just knew he was a guitarist who could play for pleasure and not for necessity, and that he would never know what it was like on the last tube home at night on the Northern line. Neither of them, out of tact, ever mentioned the fact that Jasper hadn't actually been offered a gig in a decade, and that the continued existence of an agent was quite unnecessary.

That afternoon, they'd all been in a nostalgic mood about the death, a few months earlier, of Dave Brubeck, and had spent hours leisurely riffing on 'Take Five' and 'Blue Rondo', until Frank said he had to get back – his daughter was singing in a gig at a pub in Hoxton and he'd promised he'd go – and he'd taken himself off towards the Underground, carrying the clarinet and the piccolo he'd brought in an old nylon gym bag.

'Don't budge, Brade,' Jasper said to Brady. 'No need to go too.'

Brady put a final chip in his mouth and pushed the paper they had been wrapped in away. He said, 'I'm in no hurry.'

Jasper leant across the kitchen table and poured more wine into Brady's glass. It was an unspoken rule that even if drink was taken into the studio, food should never be. When it came to eating, they always trooped obediently up to the kitchen, even if they never bothered with plates. It would have been disrespectful, somehow, to have contaminated the music and instruments with the odours of frying.

Brady said, 'Of course, I was at the Monterey Jazz Festival in 2007. I saw him live.'

Jasper took a sip of wine. 'You said.'

'Did I?'

'You probably told us a dozen times this afternoon.'

'Jeez,' Brady said, 'Mo's always telling me I drive her nuts, repeating myself. She says it's quite boring enough the first time, let alone the tenth. D'you get that?'

'Not really.'

'Well,' Brady said, 'it's different for you, isn't it? I mean, Susie and Mo might both be women, but they're from different planets. I can't get Mo to budge from the house and Susie's never in hers.'

'No.'

''Course, we only had the one lad, Mo and me, and what does he do but up and off to Vancouver. I often wonder if it'd have been different with girls. Girls stick around more, don't they? As far as family goes, seems to me girls are a better investment.'

Jasper licked a forefinger and pressed it into the salty crumbs that remained in his fish-and-chip wrapper. He said mildly, 'Not really. In my experience.'

Brady glanced at him. He said, 'You must be so proud of your girls.'

'I am.'

'All chips off the Susie block. Success stories, every one.'

Jasper gave a small sigh. 'Looked at like that, yes. Every one.'

'Looked at like what?'

'Career,' Jasper said. 'Ambition. Getting somewhere in business. Yes, all three of them.'

Brady waited a moment. He watched Jasper lick more batter crumbs off his finger. Then he said, 'You OK, Jas?'

Jasper thought a moment, then he pushed his reading glasses up on top of his head. He said, 'I dunno, really.'

168

'Something happened?'

Jasper squinted at his wine. He said, 'Well, yes. Susie's useless old dad turns up, doesn't he, out of the blue. But it's not that. Well, it's not just that. It's what you said. She's never here. There's no life *here*. There's me and the parrot' – he turned and threw an affectionate glance over his shoulder towards the bird, who was apparently dozing on her perch, – 'and we kind of wait. Except we don't really know what we're waiting for.'

'Her old dad, eh?'

'He showed up in Stoke. Grace took him in. I've never met him. I don't want to meet him, to be honest. If I met him, I'd want to flatten him. And the girls all getting into a flap about him doesn't help. It doesn't help at all. It just makes me—' He stopped. 'D'you know, Brade, it wasn't wonderful before. And now it's a whole lot worse.'

Brady leant back. He said slowly, 'And there's me thinking the sun never went in for you.'

'Don't get me wrong,' Jasper said, 'I never wanted Suz to be different. I'd never have stopped her, because I never wanted to stop her. She's amazing. She's a force of nature. I'm proud of her. I admire her. But it's me, Brade. I don't know where I fit in now, with the girls in the business too. I thought of offering granddad services to Ashley, but then I thought, you sad old git, what are you, begging for favours because you haven't pulled your bleeding finger out all these years? You haven't made the effort, you've just lain dozing under the mango tree watching for lunch to fall off on to your stomach.'

'Hey,' Brady said, 'steady on.'

'Sorry,' Jasper said. 'Sorry.' He tapped his glass. 'It's probably making me maudlin.'

Brady looked round the kitchen. He said, 'You were a hell of a father. You brought up three kids here.'

'Yup.'

'Homework . . .'

'The kids' friends, toast, spaghetti . . .'

'And now it's you and the bird.'

'Mostly.'

'And this old boy . . .'

'He hasn't changed things, really. He's just woken me up to it all, I suppose.'

Brady leant forward. He said, 'You're saying you're lonely, Jas?'

Jasper took his reading glasses off his head and put them on the table. Then he rubbed his eyes. 'I'm not lonely,' he said. 'I don't seem to do lonely, really. It's something else. It's . . . it's more that I don't know what I'm for, any more.' He looked across the table at Brady. He said, 'Can you tell me, Brade, what the *point* of me is?'

*

170

For Christmas, Cara had bought Daniel a Boardman Performance Hybrid Pro bike. It had a super light-weight frame, and had been designed to use all the features of track cycling that would benefit the leisure or commuting rider. Daniel was just such a rider. Cara might prefer to commute by bus or on her feet, but Daniel had always, except in the foulest weather, cycled to work.

Since the arrival of the Boardman – carefully re-searched and selected by both of them – Daniel had wanted to do more than commute by bike. Most week-ends he took himself off on a serious cycle circuit, one involving both distance and hills, and returned home on the kind of endorphin high that he knew benefited every other aspect of his life.

But today was rather different. Today, the prospect of a challenging bike ride was more welcome than usual, the psychological benefits being even more attractive than the physical ones. Cara was in the Fulham Road shop with Ashley and the marketing team, Susie was on her way up to Stoke to try and sort out the situation with Morris and Grace, and he, Daniel, was in the office in a deeply unsettled frame of mind.

The trouble was Cara. Daniel had never had any quarrel – well, not any quarrel of consequence – with Cara. He and Cara saw eye to eye on everything, really, and certainly everything of importance. It was a source of both pride and pleasure to him that they shared so much, morally and philosophically. They might fine-tune details rather differently, but they came at life and other people from a satisfactorily similar standpoint. In business and social life, Cara was Daniel's best ally, as he was hers. They had got through many a tricky meeting by exchanging fleeting glances which confirmed to one another that they were neither mistaken nor alone.

But last night, Cara had returned from Radipole Road after an extremely important meeting with her mother, which they had carefully discussed in advance, and said that she wasn't going to talk about it.

'But you *must*,' Daniel said unwisely. 'You have to. It was a crucial conversation. We *planned* it. You must tell me what she said.'

Cara was in the middle of opening a packet of bresaola. She put it down on the kitchen counter. 'I *mustn't* do any such thing.'

Daniel came and leant on the other side of the counter. 'Cara,' he said, 'this is a *joint* approach. You and me. For the future of the company. *Our* future. I thought you were for it.'

She looked at him. 'I am.'

'Well, then.'

Cara pushed the bresaola aside. 'Ma was upset,' she said.

'Well, of course. Of course she was. We knew she would be.'

'No,' Cara said.

'What do you mean, no?'

'I mean that she was upset in a way I hadn't reckoned on. Distressed. Angry, but *personally* angry.'

Daniel waved a hand. 'Well, what did you expect? I mean, obviously she was going to react like that.'

Cara went on looking at him. 'But I didn't think it would make me feel like it did. It didn't occur to me that I'd—'

She stopped. She looked down at the counter. 'I don't want to talk about it. I don't want to talk about Ma.' She stopped again, and then she said, as if to herself, 'Poor Ma.'

'What?' Daniel said.

Cara moved away from the counter. She said again, but louder, 'Poor Ma.'

'Poor? Your mother *poor*? When the only obstacle to our—'

'Stop it!' Cara shouted.

Daniel was startled. He stood still and watched her. She had her back to him now, and he wasn't sure if she was crying. He said softly, tentatively, 'Cara?'

She flung her head up, not looking at him. She said, 'I'm going to have a shower,' and then she walked past him, into their bedroom, without another glance.

He knew she hadn't slept. He hadn't, either. He had no idea how to resolve the situation, being a complete novice at not having Cara's compliance, Cara's support, Cara's unasked-for solidarity. When the faint, late dawn began, he finally fell asleep, and woke to find Cara's side of the bed empty, and a note by the coffee pot to say she had gone into work early. She had put an 'x' at the bottom of the note, but it looked perfunctory. It wasn't a real kiss; it was just a punctuation mark. He had showered and dressed, made a double espresso – never a sensible start to any day – and cycled to work with a heart as heavy as lead.

And now, three hours into the working day, his heart was no lighter. Cara had scarcely acknowledged him – or, rather, had displayed none of the marked affection he was frankly longing for – and had then taken off for the London shop without saying, as she usually did, when she would be back. Daniel could settle to nothing. Disciplined, focused, energetic Daniel could think of nothing at all except that, for some reason he could not fathom, Cara had elected to side with her mother for the first time in their lives together, and the result was that he felt utterly and painfully excluded.

Sitting here at his desk was plainly completely pointless. All he was doing was fretting, nagging and needling away at himself in a way which, on top of a bad night, was exacerbating rather than resolving the problem. He stood up. At the next desk down the room, beside Cara's empty space, sat Kitty, their assistant, her smooth fair head bent conscientiously towards her screen.

'Kitty,' he called.

She gave a little jump. 'Yes?'

'I'm just going out.'

'Oh.'

He knew she wouldn't ask where. Or why, for that matter. He made himself smile at her. 'I'll be a couple of hours, OK? Can you field my calls? I'll leave my phone here.' He made a show of putting the phone down beside his keyboard, and smiled again. 'In case Cara calls.'

The country-house hotel, just south of the six towns, where Susie often stayed on her visits to Stoke gave her her usual bedroom, and Morris a much smaller one at the back with a narrow, very basic bathroom and a bed covered in mustard-yellow candlewick. Morris said it was fine. There was a bed, hot water and a telly: what more could he need? He'd smiled at the receptionist and told her he'd grown up in a house just like this one, only a few miles away. She didn't smile back, and informed him she came from Riga.

In the enormous lounge of the hotel – once a stately drawing room and now oppressively crowded with sofas – Susie had ordered tea for herself, and a brandy and soda for Morris. The receptionist from Riga had brought both in silence and Susie's thank-yous had sounded unnaturally loud and forced to her, in consequence. There had been no other guests in the lounge but them, and the fire that had been lit in the grate much earlier had now burned down almost to silence too. Susie handed Morris his glass of brandy and the accompanying can of soda, poured a cup of tea, added milk, and then sat back and waited.

Morris decanted soda water into his glass very, very slowly. Then he set the can down carefully, took a considered sip, and put the glass down too. Finally he said, 'I was trying to do something for myself, Susan. I was trying to spare Grace. After she told me she had no idea what to do with me.'

Susie said nothing. She drank her tea and looked at the dying fire.

Morris went on, 'She likes that Jeff, you know.'

Susie took another sip of tea. She set the cup down on the nearest side table with a small bang. She said, 'Well, *we* don't like him for *her*.'

Morris crossed his legs. He was now wearing plum-coloured socks and his knitted waistcoat was garnished with an abstract ceramic brooch. 'We can't choose people for other people,' he said. 'We can't dictate that. We like who we like and we don't like who we don't like. That's human nature.'

'It's still not helpful,' Susie said, 'to encourage destructive relationships.'

Morris took another sip of brandy. He said, 'I didn't, Susan. I just accepted his offer of somewhere to stay, to get me out of Grace's hair. I thought she'd be pleased. I thought you'd like me to solve the problem for you.'

'It doesn't solve any problem to have Grace or me in any way obliged to Jeff.'

Morris looked at her. He said, slightly piteously, 'What was I to do, Susan, till I can move into your house?'

She gave an irritated little shrug. 'I'd have done what everyone said I should have done in the beginning, and put you in a hotel.'

'This'll be cheaper.'

'And more complicated. I bet Jeff leapt at the chance.'

Morris linked his hands around his knees. 'I can help his boss, see. I'm good with my hands. He says there'll be plenty to do out at Trentham Gardens, fixing things. I'd like to have something to do.' He glanced at Susie. 'You're not listening to me.'

She withdrew her gaze from the fire. 'No, I'm not.'

'Thinking about Grace? Lovely girl.'

'No, actually,' Susie said.

'What then?'

'Nothing to do with you.'

Morris looked unoffended. He released his hands

and picked up his brandy glass. He said, 'It's not like I thought it'd be, you know. I thought you'd have a big house up here, full of rooms, and everyone would be busy and sorted. I thought I'd find myself a corner somewhere and help out a bit somehow, and we'd all bed down together after we'd got over seeing each other again. But it's not like that, is it? It's not settled and sorted in the least, it's all up in the air and you're never in the same place for two minutes and I'm beginning to wonder if this husband of yours exists, or whether you've just invented him. And the girls don't seem right to me, none of them – none of them quite, well, stable. Everything in motion all the time, everybody rushing everywhere—'

'Please stop,' Susie said.

He leant forward and said kindly, 'You upset?'

'No.'

'Susan—'

'Just don't say any more. You're in no position to say *anything*.'

Morris took another sip of his brandy. He said, 'I know you think I'm the last straw, turning up like this. But maybe I'm not.' He leant back again. 'Maybe,' he said, 'I'm just what you need.'

CHAPTER NINE

To Ashley's surprise, Daniel was leaning against her car in the car park under the office, tapping away at his BlackBerry. Ashley was carrying her workbag, her handbag, and a supermarket bag containing the two-litre cartons of full-fat milk that Leo had asked her to pick up. 'Dan?' she said simply.

He looked up, dropped his BlackBerry into his jacket pocket and came forward to relieve her of her burdens.

'Were you waiting for me?' Ashley said.

'Yes,' he said shortly.

'Are you OK? Why didn't you find me in the office?'

Dan stood by the boot of the car, holding the milk and Ashley's workbag. He indicated with a nod that she should unlock it.

Ashley scrabbled in her bag for the keys. 'What's the matter?'

The boot lid swung slowly into the air. Loading the bags inside, Daniel said tersely, 'You could *see* what was the matter.'

Ashley said, 'Well, the atmosphere in the office wasn't wonderful today, but it often isn't very—'

'You could see that Cara wasn't speaking to me,' Daniel said, slamming the boot shut.

Ashley opened her mouth, and shut it again wordlessly. Then she gestured towards the car. 'Shall we talk sitting down?'

Side by side inside, facing the grey concrete wall of the garage, Ashley waited for Dan to speak. He sat beside her, stiff and silent. After a minute or two, impatient with whatever internal struggles he was having, she said, '*Why* isn't Cara speaking to you?'

He said, 'I don't know.'

'You *must* know. People always know why they're in the doghouse.'

'I'm not in the doghouse. Or if I am, I don't know why.'

Ashley sighed. She wasn't in the mood for this kind of conversation. She was fond of Dan in that tolerant, faintly resigned way that family choices of partner often require, but she frequently thought he could be a bit more relaxed about some things, not insist on so much, obsess less about details. In any case, she wanted to get home and see how Leo's day had gone, how the children were, whether Fred had slept for only an hour or the usually fatal two, whether Maisie had wept at nursery school. She said, not altogether encouragingly,

180

'You'd better tell me about it,' and failed to stop herself from adding, 'I suppose.'

Daniel looked away from her at the car parked alongside. He said, 'Cara went to see your mother on her own, as agreed, to propose the new plan about Susie's involvement in the company, and when she came back she was clearly upset, and refused to tell me what had happened. I mean, *refused*. Wouldn't talk about it, wouldn't tell me anything. And then twice – *twice* – said "Poor Ma," but not to me. To herself.' He turned and looked at Ashley. 'So, as you spent the morning together, I thought you could give me a bit of a steer. Tell me what I've done that's so awful. In her eyes, anyway. All I've actually done is what we all three agreed in the first place. For which I now seem to be being punished.'

Ashley folded her arms and said non-committally, 'All she said this morning was that Ma was very upset, and we'd have to go easy.'

'Go easy?'

'On pushing the idea of changing her role in the company.'

'Well,' Daniel said exasperatedly, 'why didn't she say that to *me*?'

Ashley looked down at her lap. 'Maybe she didn't think you'd listen. Maybe she thought you'd argue.' She glanced at her brother-in-law. 'Maybe she's cross with you, now that Ma's taken it badly, for having had the idea in the first place.'

Dan stared at her. '*What*? How unjust is *that*?'

Ashley shrugged. 'She had to carry the can, didn't she? I mean, she was the one who had to actually *say* it to Ma. I know she offered, but it must have been a horrible thing to have to do, to have to say to your own mother, look, you've got to give up complete control, you've got to get used to the idea of stepping aside—'

'Jesus,' Daniel said furiously. 'What *is* all this? What are you *talking* about?'

Ashley looked at him, and then she unfolded her arms and put the car key into the ignition. She said, not especially warmly, 'So you don't see—'

'No, I do not,' Dan said with emphasis.

'Perhaps we shouldn't expect you to.'

'*What*?'

She turned to look at him. 'Well,' she said, 'you can't be expected to feel what we feel, can you? I mean, you can't help it, Dan, of course you can't, but – you're not family, really. Are you?'

Neil Dundas had been manager of the Susie Sullivan factory for three years. He had been working as assistant manager at an artisan pottery in Ross-shire, some way north of Inverness, when he had seen Daniel's advertisement for a new manager, all the way south in Stoke-on-Trent, and had applied eagerly at once, although without much hope that he would get the job. But Daniel had responded within twenty-four hours and invited him down to Stoke. He had been interviewed by Daniel, by Susie herself, and by Cara, both separately and all together. Susie interviewed him in the factory café, over his first Staffordshire oatcake – it bore no resemblance whatsoever, he thought, to a Scottish one – and asked him, almost as her first question, 'Could you stand up to Daniel?'

He had his mouth full. He'd nodded.

'Could you *argue* with him?' she said.

He swallowed the oatcake. 'Yes,' he said.

'Are you sure?'

'I have a reputation for arguing,' Neil said. 'Ask my boss. Ask my mother. If I think something's right, I'll argue it for ever.'

She'd smiled at him and said, 'I don't exactly want to *encourage* any arguing, ever. But if you are the interface between the workforce and the office staff, then you have to be braced for a few fisticuffs.'

Neil had smiled back. It had occurred to him to blurt out that no son of his mother's knew the meaning of appeasement, but in the same instant he'd realized that it wasn't necessary. This woman pouring tea for him out of a teapot of her own design, in a factory she had rescued almost from dereliction, was actually offering him a job that was in her gift to give him. He was, in fact, having tea with the boss. And the boss liked him.

'Once I've understood your message,' he'd said, looking straight at her, 'that'll be the message from the factory. Loud and clear.'

He'd loved the job from the outset. The pottery he had worked in before was small and craft-driven, specializing in wood-ash glazes and unthreatening natural designs, so to be involved with a product that was still handmade, but commercially visible and successful, was immediately energizing. It was, he discovered, an advantage to be Scottish – foreign enough to be exotic, but egalitarian enough to be acceptable and accepted. Neil knew the processes of pottery, he understood manufacturing life and he was completely comfortable with the workforce. The fact that he arrived in Stoke in a state of disarray was only to his advantage, especially as far as the women in the fettling and decorating shops were concerned. The disarray was caused by his wife of two years declaring that she couldn't possibly leave her family and friends in Dornoch, never mind the coast, the sands and the sea, to move not just to *England* but to a decayed industrial city of slag heaps and general depression. So Shona had stayed in the Highlands, and after a swift divorce had married a man who worked for the

Forestry Commission in Morangie Forest, and cut Neil out of her life as completely as if he'd never been in it.

Neil had, at first, been utterly dismayed by a marriage – even a brief one – being treated as if it had never happened. But Susie had rescued him. She didn't use tea and sympathy as a remedy, she used work. He joined the company one September, just before the Christmas production push, and it was February before he came up for air again to discover that, despite the economic gloom that was settling like coal dust across the country, the company had had one of its most profitable Christmases ever. Even Daniel, with whom there was an almost perpetual locking of horns, was congratulatory. But when he went to find Susie, scribbling away at something in the design studio, and tried to thank her, she hadn't even looked up at him.

'All your own work,' she said. 'Don't thank me.'

As far as Neil Dundas was concerned, the factory was Susie's, and Susie's alone. The heartbeat of it, the actual product, the workforce, the human energy, were all because of her. He appreciated that the London office was necessary, as well as the policies and programmes for expansion and progress that emanated from it, but as far as he was concerned, the actual manufacturing was what counted. And pottery was, in his mind, true manufacture, sinewy and practical. Checking the trolleys ready to be loaded into the kilns, inspecting the benches and work stations in the long, brightly lit rooms of the factory, dealing with the vagaries of life presented by the workforce, these were all in his blood. He bought a flat in Burslem, a car that had been assembled in the UK and a season ticket for Stoke City football club, and joined a local ramblers group. When asked if he missed the beauty of the Highlands, he grinned and said he'd rather have life than beauty.

Life, if he'd been asked to define it, consisted largely of the factory, partly of his own active existence, and in small but significant part of Susie and her daughters. He was fascinated by all of them, coming as he did from a severely traditional background which held inflexible views about the obligations and suitable occupations of men and women. His mother had been a nurse before she married, but gave it up when his elder brother was born and never thought of returning. She made herself useful in the community, but never for money, because to do so, it was implied, would have somehow been an affront to his father's manliness. Coming from such a background caused Neil to wonder very much, when he first met Susie. The wonderment only increased when he then encountered her daughters. There were, by his calculation, five people who ran the Susie Sullivan pottery, and four of those people were women. After three years of working for them, the wonderment might have worn off a little, but the respect had grown. Especially for Susie. Susie ran that factory – or, at least, influenced that factory – with an instinctive mixture of the personal and the impersonal that he doubted any man could manage. They all knew her as a person, but they knew she was the boss as well.

Her daughter Grace, however – the daughter whom Neil had much the most to do with – was more of an enigma. She was talented, no doubt of that, and popular round the factory, and she had no airs and graces about the practicalities of what they did. In fact, out of Susie's three daughters, Grace was the only one who could actually *do* all the processes on the factory floor. Neil knew she could; he'd watched her. Her eye for what would or wouldn't work in a functional sense was second to none. And she had a good manner with the workforce, always herself, but comradely somehow, kind without patronage. But for all her warmth and approachability, he couldn't quite get a handle on her. She was just a little cool, just a little distant, just a fraction out of reach. It wasn't grandeur, but she was elusive, all the same. She looked vulnerable, but also unavailable to be helped. It made her very interesting and disconcertingly attractive. Whenever Neil saw her unmistakeable red head across the yard, or through the design-studio window, he experienced a little jolt of electricity that could easily throw him off balance.

Not for long – but long enough to make him aware of it, and to make him anticipate, more keenly than was comfortable, the next time it might happen.

The existence of Jeff in Grace's life was painful to Neil. He told himself that Jeff was just an irritation, but he knew he was kidding himself. At first, Jeff's height and looks were almost beyond bearing, but as his personality became evident, indulgent exasperation at Grace's choice gradually softened the blow of his appearance. Neil could shake his head at her folly, while making an automatic note of all Jeff's failings and inadequacies, which were now mounting up to a shocking tally. He had had to watch them, as he had had to watch that strange old boy who said he was Grace's grandfather arrive with his carpet bag of trouble, and move in on her as inexorably as Jeff had done. It was frustrating to watch, agonizingly frustrating. But watch he had to. It wasn't so much that she was the boss's daughter – this wasn't the nineteenth century, after all – but more that riding to her rescue would make her angry, and make him look a complete idiot. They had a working relationship, and that was that. If his heart smote him on seeing her looking so strained and tired, it couldn't be helped. Grace Moran had never given him the slightest hint that she saw him as anything other than a work colleague, and that was a fact that he would simply have to bite down on.

So when she came into his office unannounced and said she'd like to tell him something, he was completely unprepared. His office was small and chaotic, the door permanently wedged open with lever arch files of press cuttings, and lit by a single fierce fluorescent strip light which threw violent and unbecoming shadows on everything underneath it. It gave Grace's face a truly terrible pallor, as well as darkening the evident smudges of weariness under her eyes.

Neil half rose from behind his computer. 'Excuse the mess—'

'I can't see it,' Grace said. She waved a hand, as if the clutter of papers was indeed invisible.

He stood more upright and edged round his desk towards her. 'Are you all right?'

'Tired,' Grace said.

Neil moved a pile of stuff off a plastic chair to the floor, and indicated that she should sit down. He said, 'None of my business, but it's been a rough old week.'

Grace sat. She pushed her hair back and said, 'What goes on here is everyone's business. And yes, it's been rough.'

He picked up one of the many used mugs on his desk. 'Tea?'

'Don't bother.'

'It's no bother. Nor's coffee. I can nip to the café—'

'Neil,' Grace said, 'I don't need tea or coffee. I just want to tell you something.'

He said, 'Anything,' too quickly and instantly regretted it.

Grace looked at the door. 'Does it shut?'

Neil manoeuvred his way further round the desk and nudged at the lever arch files with his foot. 'Let's try.'

'I don't want to be furtive . . .'

'But?'

'But I really just want *you* to know. In case . . .'

He shut the door with difficulty, and stood leaning against it. 'In case?'

'Well,' Grace said, 'I think someone should know where I am. If you don't mind being that someone.'

A spasm of fear clutched him. She was about to tell him that she was going away for the weekend with Jeff, and Susie had made it very plain that she disliked and disapproved of Jeff. So Grace was about to ask him not to tell Susie—

'I've got to get away,' Grace said. 'Not for long. Just a few days. I've—' She stopped.

He waited.

'I've just got to be by myself. No family, nobody. I feel completely . . . *pummelled* by them all.'

Neil was almost giddy with relief. He said cautiously, 'Why are you telling me? Don't get me wrong, I'm very flattered you are – but why me?'

Grace gave a little sigh. She glanced up at him with a small smile. 'Well, you see me coming and going more than anyone. You're in daily touch with Ma. You can fend any of them off, if there's a fuss.'

'A fuss?'

'If anyone wants to know where I am.'

He relaxed against the door. 'And where will you be?'

She said slowly, 'The Lake District. A hotel. I'll give you the number.'

'And for how long?'

'Just the weekend. Maybe a bit longer. I'll see. It depends on whether I can sleep.'

'Grace,' he said, 'are you not telling your mother?'

She glanced at him again. 'No, I'm not telling anyone but you. I want to slip out, and then slip back again. I am absolutely exhausted with everything being such a big deal.'

'Are you asking me to cover for you?'

Grace looked slightly startled. 'I don't think anyone will even notice I've gone.'

Neil took the plunge. 'Not even Jeff?'

She put her hands in her hair again, and pushed it back. She said, 'It won't hurt him to wonder.'

'So this is really—'

'No,' she said quickly. 'No, it's not a game. I wouldn't ask you to be part of a game. I shouldn't have said that

– I don't mean it. I just mean I need to get away from all of them.'

Neil stood more upright, an inch or two away from the door. He said, 'So, if anyone asks me, what do you want me to say?'

'That I'll be back by Wednesday. Latest.'

'Is that all?'

She got slowly to her feet. 'Yes, please. That's all you know. That's all I've told you. Just delete everything else.'

He said, 'They'll ring your mobile.'

She looked at him. 'And I won't answer it. I'll only answer it if you ring me, because then I'll know it's an emergency. OK?'

He smiled at her. Her sudden confidence was like an unexpected present.

'OK,' he said.

'If you eat that,' Jasper said to Maisie, indicating the cubes of cheese and discs of cucumber on the plate in front of her, 'then I might find you something special.'

Maisie regarded him. She had already inspected the contents of his pockets and found a bus pass, a crumple of old receipts and a button. She said sternly, 'You haven't got anything special.'

He picked up a cheese cube and held it out. 'Not in my coat, I haven't.'

Maisie leaned forward and took the smallest possible corner off the cheese cube. She said, 'Where's Grandma?'

'Working.'

'Like Mumma.'

'Yes,' Jasper said. 'Very like Mumma. Eat your cheese.'

Maisie folded her arms on the table. She said, 'Cheryl gave us Jammie Dodgers.'

'And your dad and I are giving you cheese.'

Maisie made a face. 'I want Cheryl back. I want Cheryl to be here *now*.'

Jasper smiled at her. He said, 'Fred's eaten *his* cheese.'

'Where's Dadda?'

'Gone to check something.' He turned and looked at Fred, in his high chair. He said, 'Hi there, big boy.'

Fred, his cheeks packed with cheese cubes, beat his hands on the tray in front of him, setting cucumber discs jumping.

'I want a Jammie Dodger,' Maisie said.

Jasper bent to pick up a fallen slice of cucumber. He said indistinctly, 'One, that's no way to ask. And two, not a hope. This house is a Jammie-Dodger-free zone.'

Maisie gave an experimental roar. Fred imitated her, his mouth full of cheese. Jasper straightened up and put the food in both his hands down on the table. He said, 'If you're hungry, you eat what's in front of you. If you're not hungry, you don't need to eat.'

Maisie stopped roaring. She said, in a perfectly normal voice, 'What about the special thing?'

'If you're not hungry,' Jasper said, 'there's no need for specials.'

Fred leant forward, grunting urgently, his mouth still open.

'Eat up,' Jasper said to him. 'Swallow.'

Fred gulped.

Maisie said, 'If I eat my cheese?'

'Then we'll see.'

'Why aren't *you* working?'

'I am,' Jasper said. 'I'm helping Daddy look after you. That is most surely work.'

'When I'm a princess,' Maisie said, 'I can have wings. And eyeliner.'

'Only if you eat your cheese.'

Fred gave a final gulp and roared again.

'What does he want?' Jasper said to Maisie.

She picked up a slice of cucumber and took a tiny nibble.

'Probably a Jammie Dodger,' she said.

There were feet running down the stairs to the basement kitchen, and Leo appeared. He looked to Jasper's eye both collected and cheerful. He'd looked like that when he'd opened the door to Jasper, two hours ago. He'd looked, it occurred to Jasper, as he had probably looked himself, twenty-five years ago, with the kitchen full of little girls, and Grace on his hip, eating a breadstick. He'd been a rarity then, an oddity, a commented-upon phenomenon, a man at home competently coping with two little girls and a baby, and seemingly never happier than when the kitchen was full of children finger-painting and plaiting each other's hair, children whose attention he could command in an instant, just by picking up his guitar. Leo didn't have a guitar. But he had, it seemed, a presence. The kitchen was not the kitchen of a man out of control or even a man who wanted to be somewhere else. It was the kitchen of a man with a plan.

Jasper said to him, 'We haven't given up on the cheese. But it's taking a while.'

Leo looked at Maisie's plate. He said, 'I'm not impressed, chicken.'

Maisie flopped back in her chair. 'I'm too tired to eat.'

'Fine.'

Fred was packing cucumber into his mouth with the flat of his hand.

'Steady on, Freddy,' said Jasper.

'Thank you for holding the fort,' Leo said.

'I like it, you know.'

Maisie said, 'I need Mumma!'

'You're an old hand, Jas.'

'A bit out of practice.'

'I need a biscuit!'

Fred choked, and a mass of cucumber flew out of his mouth and landed wetly on the tray of his high chair.

'You're such a twit,' Leo said to him, thumping him gently on the back.

'I said,' Maisie shouted, 'that I need Mumma!'

'We heard you.'

'Now!'

Leo lifted Fred out of his high chair and sat down opposite his father-in-law with Fred on his knee. He said to Maisie, 'Where do you think Mumma is?'

Maisie glowered at him. 'Working,' she said witheringly.

'Where?'

'At the office!' Maisie shouted.

'Why?'

Maisie jerked herself upright. 'To buy me a *present*!'

Leo wiped Fred's face. He said cheerfully, 'Now you're being silly. You know why she's working.'

Jasper looked at his son-in-law. He said, 'Do *you* know why?'

Leo unhooked Fred's plastic bib. 'She's good at it,' he said. 'We all like doing what we're good at.'

'Don't feed me a line,' Jasper said. 'Don't fob me off.'

'I'm not.'

'Leo,' Jasper said, 'I'm not asking for no reason. I'm interested. I'm interested to know what you really think.'

Leo lowered Fred to the floor. Then he leant across the table, put a cube of cheese on top of a slice of cucumber and pushed it towards Maisie. 'Eat up.'

She bent forward, and without using her hands began to nibble clumsily at the cheese.

Leo said, 'What I really think is that you do as much of what you like doing as you can, and as much of what has to be done as you can stand. In my view, it's better to get *something* done than try and do everything perfectly. So if Ashley likes what she does at work and can make enough money to support us, then I'm happy to make that possible. Or at least try to. It's early days. I like this home stuff. *You* should get it, Jas. You liked it, too. God, man, you were a pioneer!'

Maisie quietly picked up her cheese and cucumber and put it in her mouth. Neither her father nor her grandfather took any notice.

Jasper said, 'Early days.'

'I know.'

'What about your own disappointment?'

Leo looked at Maisie. 'Don't feel any,' he said.

'I didn't. Not for ages. I was glad not to be the breadwinner. Still am, probably. But not being the breadwinner and not fulfilling one's personal ambition either – well, that's something else.'

Leo looked embarrassed. He went on regarding Maisie, who was chewing ostentatiously.

Jasper said, 'Wanting to do something and being driven to do something aren't quite the same.'

'Two more bites,' Leo said to Maisie, 'and then you can have the strawberries Grandpa brought.'

'He shouldn't have,' Jasper said. 'Flown in from Israel or somewhere. All those wicked air miles.'

'And then a Jammie Dodger?' Maisie said.

'There aren't any.'

'There are! There are! Cheryl put them in the tiger tin!'

'They've all gone,' Leo said.

Maisie opened her mouth to roar again.

'Stop,' Leo said.

She glared at him, her mouth still open. But she didn't scream.

'Good,' Jasper said admiringly.

Leo reached across the table and held out another cube of cheese.

'As I said, Jas,' he said, 'we all like what we're good at.' He inserted the cheese into Maisie's open mouth. 'And anyway, what's happening here is just as important as what's happening in the office. In fact, if I wasn't doing this, Ashley couldn't manage to do what she does.' He smiled at Maisie, who was chewing, her eyes on her father's face, then glanced across at Jasper. 'Any more than Susie could have done without you.'

Jasper ducked his head. He stooped sideways to hand Fred a plastic train that was just out of his reach. Then he said, 'I know, I know. But that – well, that was then.' He glanced at Leo. 'Early days, you know.'

CHAPTER TEN

Jeff's flat was very small. It was on the first floor of a modest purpose-built block at the back of the garden centre where he worked, and the view was either of rows of container-grown shrubs, or of a car park beside a disused cinema now given over to bingo.

Jeff himself slept on the couch so that he was near the immense television whose screen dominated his sitting room. He was a tidy man, and during the day his bedding was rolled up and stored in the room that was to be Morris's. It contained a headless bed, a built-in cupboard, a stepladder, a travel bag and no curtains. On the bed were two pillows and the fat roll of Jeff's duvet. The walls were blank and the view was of the car park. It was as far from the ramshackle house at the back of a palm-fringed beach that had been Morris's home for half a century as it could be.

Susie had driven Morris out to Trentham Gardens. Jeff had offered to collect him but Susie had been very firm in declining. She had borrowed Grace's car and put Morris, his carpet bag and a box of groceries inside and driven out of the city. She told Morris, as if he was a newcomer to the area, that Trentham Gardens was lovely, really quite posh for Stoke, having been the Duke of Sutherland's estate, with the park laid out by Capability Brown. The park itself was now just a gorgeous playground, she said, attracting over three million visitors annually, and all free. But Jeff's flat was not, as it turned out, in the salubrious part of Trentham Gardens. In fact it was only nominally anywhere near it. Susie's positive talk, Morris noted, died away as they drove further and further from the park and the lake and the carefully designed chalet-style retail centre. They ended up beside a building which made Morris remember, weirdly, a fact he'd known when he was a boy, growing up in Barlaston, which was that all the hills in the Stoke area had once been coal-waste slag heaps. Industry had such a terrible gift for uglification then, and obviously still did. No wonder it was hard to be back.

Susie unpacked her box of groceries, made him tea and a ham sandwich, and found sheets for the bed in the curtainless room. Jeff had left a note to say he'd be back at six and they'd go out for a curry. She didn't seem to want to talk much any more, and Morris didn't quite have the nerve to encourage her. They inspected the bathroom – clean, but very small – and back in the kitchen Morris took an obedient but unenthusiastic bite of his sandwich. Then Susie said, with difficulty, 'It's only for a few weeks.'

Morris put his sandwich down. 'And I'll be helping out in the garden centre.'

Susie glanced out of the window. 'Looks like all they sell is Leylandii.'

'I'll be fine, Susan.'

She didn't look at him. She said, 'I'd really rather you were in a hotel.'

'I wouldn't.' He leant towards her, grinning, 'Did you see that carwash place we passed?'

'Where?'

'On our way here. It said "Best Hand Job In Town". Jeff told me they're all run by Afghans.'

'Oh,' Susie said. She wasn't smiling.

He shrugged slightly. 'Only trying to cheer you up.'

'I don't want to leave you here.'

'I'll be fine.'

'But it's . . . it's not . . .'

'Well, it's not Grace's flat, I'll give you that. But it'll do fine for now.'

He wondered, for a split second, if she'd kiss him when she left. But she didn't. She didn't even look as if the thought had occurred to her. She handed him a new mobile phone and an envelope of cash, but she didn't come any closer than that. And then she said that Grace needed her car back, for some reason, and she must go. So she went, rather suddenly and quickly, and left him standing there in Jeff's bleak little kitchen, with his mug of tea and a half-eaten sandwich.

He carried them both into the sitting room and sat on Jeff's couch. Things change, he thought, all the time – a great moving carpet of change that you can't stop and you can't get off. When I was growing up, the Wedgwood factory was in Etruria, right bang in the middle. Now the factory's out in Barlaston and there's a ski slope where it used to be. I left a baby and now she's a complicated woman with a business and grand-children. I don't know the grandchildren. I don't know her. I don't know how to handle her, what line to take. But then, I haven't known what's what for as long as I can remember. I seem to have lost my bearings. I didn't know Lamu any more, not once they started building the new port and all those roads and planning an oil refinery, and I could see all the beauty and remoteness just vanishing under concrete. But then, I'm just an old relic, an old has-been, aren't I? I don't really know what I know. I don't know what I think I'm doing, here or anywhere. Morris picked up the sandwich, looked at it and put it down again.

He lay back against the cushions and looked round the room. It was tidy, but in an unlived-in way. No pictures, no colour, nothing that didn't serve the purposes of watching television. Jeff's running shoes were together in a corner, and above them, on a hook, the hooded top of a tracksuit. Otherwise, apart from remote controls and a neat stack of magazines, there seemed to be no indication of personality. The man who appeared to be in focused pursuit of Grace, and who seemed to possess some force of will, lived in this anonymous place in an equally anonymous way. It was dreary, Morris thought, dreary. Deeply dreary.

He tilted his head back and looked at the ceiling. It had been painted white once, but the corners and edges had now darkened to grey. He took a breath. He'd told Susan that he'd be fine in Jeff's flat for a few weeks, and he would be. He'd make an effort to be. It struck him that he could actually put some energy into not being a problem, a nuisance. He felt suddenly rather surprised. He'd caught himself making a mental effort. That was novel. Very novel indeed. He raised his head and regarded the blank black glass of the television screen. He worked slowly backwards through his thoughts. Why had he determined to live with Jeff in this dismal flat until he could move into the Parlour House? Because, he realized, he was glad to do something for his daughter and granddaughter; he was actually pleased to be able to relieve their burdens, even a little.

Good God, Morris thought to himself. Holy Mother

of Whatsit. He was smiling. He was sitting on a faux-leather couch in a disheartening room belonging to a man he had no feelings for really, one way or another, and he was *smiling*. I'll be blowed, he said to himself; don't know what's come over me. He leant forward and picked up his sandwich. It had been nice of Susan to make it, after all. Even if she couldn't manage a kiss.

Michelle Knight had put quite a lot of energy over the last few years into making it possible for Neil Dundas to ask her out on a date. She'd had the same boyfriend since she was at school, and despite hoping that someone a bit more exciting than Mark would change things during her college years, it hadn't happened, and Mark was still around, working now for a huge earth-moving-machinery company out towards Uttoxeter, and apparently content with the same friends and the same personal life he'd had since he was eleven.

Michelle was fond of him and exasperated by him in exactly the way she was with her two younger brothers. They, like Mark, still lived at home, and got their washing done and their lunchboxes filled, whereas Michelle shared a flat with a girlfriend, and preferred to meet her mother in town for a coffee, rather than get sucked back into all the old routines of her growing up. She thought her brothers were infantile, and said so, and tried quite hard not to think the same of Mark, who joined the men in her family for all the Stoke City home games at Britannia Stadium, and had found a framed photograph of Stanley Matthews on eBay, dated 1963, for her father's last birthday. He was lovely, Mark: pleasant-looking, kind, polite and familiar – oh, so familiar – but something nagged at Michelle that a more adventurous and interesting alternative might be out there.

Neil Dundas had struck her as more interesting the moment he arrived. He was so very dark-haired and his accent was so very Scottish and he was so evidently approved of by Susie that he'd had a kind of distinction for Michelle all along. Also, at the beginning he had the faint melancholy glamour of being abandoned by his wife and of then seeming wonderfully unconcerned about replacing her. He'd presumably *had* other girl-friends, but nobody had seemed to stick. And he hadn't looked bothered. He hadn't looked lonely. He looked like a man for whom a relationship was not crucial, which might mean he was still, uselessly, missing his wife, or it might mean something much more attractively complicated.

Michelle was not a girl to give up. Whenever there was a pretext to seek Neil out and ask him something, she took it. She was not prone to self-doubt, in any case, and because of Mark she had never known the peculiar humiliation of rejection. So when Grace was not in the studio on Monday morning, and Ben rang in to say that he thought he'd got the flu, Michelle decided that work could wait for the ten minutes it would take her to go and find Neil Dundas and ask him – all innocence – where Grace was.

She found him by the kilns. He was examining the computer panels that regulated timings and temperatures. He said, 'Morning, Michelle,' without looking at her.

'How d'you know it's me?'

'I always know it's you,' Neil said, still looking at the keypad, and then added, before she could assume anything, 'I can recognize the footsteps of all of you.'

'All of us?'

'All you girls,' Neil said. He pressed a couple of keys. Then he stepped back and looked at her, and smiled.

She pushed up the sleeves of her sweater. 'Where's Grace?'

'I have no idea.'

'She's not in the studio. And Ben's got flu or something.'

'Is that a problem?'

'Well,' Michelle said, 'it's not, as it happens, today. But why isn't she here? Susie'll be in later.'

Neil hesitated. He was wearing a deep-blue denim shirt under a V-necked sweater, and the blue looked really good with his hair.

Michelle said, 'I'm not up for any more dramas.'

'Meaning?'

'Her granddad. The boyfriend.'

'You love them,' Neil said. 'The dramas.'

She grinned at him.

He added, 'And you're hoping I'll give you another one.'

She ran a hand through her hair, carelessly. 'Anything to liven up a Monday . . .'

'Well,' Neil said, 'she'll be back by Wednesday. She's fine.'

'So you know!'

'Only that.'

'What about Susie? When Susie comes in, what'll you say?'

'Just that,' Neil said.

'Is she with Jeff?'

'No,' Neil said, too quickly.

Michelle paused. She folded her arms and regarded him, her head slightly on one side. 'Neil,' she said, 'why do you know any of this? Why did she tell *you*?'

Leo, Ashley noticed, was asleep. He had been watching *Newsnight* beside her, talking desultorily, and then she was suddenly aware that his silence was more than just not speaking, and when she turned her head she saw that he was asleep, his head against the sofa back with his mouth slightly open. Her first thought was how like Maisie he was, and her second was that he never went to sleep in the evenings, that it was she who often nodded off, and had to be roused by him and pushed yawning towards the stairs.

She took a long look at him. He really was very like Maisie. The same tawny, curly hair, the same clear complexion, the same square chin. But Fred was more like him in temperament than Maisie was. Maisie was, in truth, very like how Ashley remembered Cara being as a child. Indeed, there were moments now, even, in the office, when something Cara did or said reminded Ashley forcibly of Maisie.

She put a hand affectionately on Leo's nearest thigh. He didn't stir. No wonder he was tired. He had gone at this whole new lifestyle with such gusto, eliminating rubbish from the fridge and the food cupboards, sorting out the clothes that even Fred had grown out of, running a crisp new line of sealant along the back of the bath and the basin, and around the rim of the shower tray. All that on top of the chore – yes, it *was* a chore – of taking Maisie to nursery school, and collecting her, never mind sitting through those interminable children's meals with their endless requirements of diversion and negotiation. But he said he liked it. He said he knew he'd only been at it a week, but he liked it.

'And,' he'd said, draining pasta over the sink in clouds of steam, 'think of the money!'

She did think of the money. She'd thought of money all her life. Friends had assumed that because her mother had her own business, the Moran family had always had the luxury of not having to think about money, that money had just been there, comfortably, easily, perpetually, and that if it wasn't, for some reason, Ashley's mother only had to order five hundred more mugs to be made and it would magically appear again. But, as Ashley grew tired of saying, if you have a working *mother*, if it's your *mother* who is providing for the family, and not traditional old dad waltzing out of the house for twelve hours a day to do something nobody's very interested in, then you are very conscious of money, because it's the need for money that dictates your mother's absence.

And her absence had been, if not exactly painful, in Ashley's experience noticeable. Jasper had been a fantastic father – always there, invariably tolerant, constantly accommodating. But despite all the warmth he generated, Susie needed to be back for the family circle to be complete. Ashley had often wondered if Cara's resolve not to have children stemmed from those years of Susie's absence, although she had to admit that Susie's presence, when it intermittently arrived, had not always been an altogether harmonious or completing element. She brought energy back into the house, certainly, but she also often brought a kind of jangle too, a crackle of unfinished and unresolved things. Evenings huddled up on the sofa with Pa, watching a movie on television with bowls of popcorn he'd popped himself in a saucepan the size of a bucket, were in truth a better recollection of childhood security.

Anyway, Ashley thought, moving her hand softly against the denim of Leo's jeans, look at me. I'm doing exactly what Ma did and Leo is doing exactly what Pa did. In fact, I've battled to do my version of what Ma did. I've tussled with guilt and pressure and exhaustion and anger, but somehow I've always known that I'd rather battle than give up either side of my life. I couldn't bear not to be a mother. I couldn't bear not to work. I couldn't bear, most of all, to be beholden to some man to pay the bills, not to be independent, not to call my own shots. So we'll see if it works out, this new regime, this new deal between us. The children have eaten more vegetables this last week than in the rest of the year put together. And by the time I'd paid Cheryl, and her tax and all the National Insurance, there wasn't much change out of seven hundred pounds, which is what Leo brought in, just about, when he was working.

So even if we won't be better off, we won't be much worse off either, and psychologically we'll be in far better shape. I won't be running to stand still any more, to pay for childcare we both knew was inadequate. Ashley looked at Leo's sleeping face again, and felt so very grateful to him for making it possible.

She reached up to kiss him in gratitude, gently, but meaningfully. On the sofa cushion beside her, her phone began to vibrate, its screen flashing. 'Grace,' it read.

She scrambled off the sofa and carried the phone to the far end of the room, pressing it to her ear. 'Gracie?'

'Sorry it's so late—'

'That's OK. Are you OK? Where are you?'

'In my flat,' Grace said. 'I'm at home, with all the doors locked.'

'Did you go away with Jeff, this weekend?'

'No.'

'No? But nobody could find you—'

'I was here.'

'You sound odd. Are you—'

'I'm fine,' Grace said. 'I was going to run away, and then I didn't. I stayed here. I just – well, I just shut down, here. I'll go into work on Wednesday.'

Ashley leant against the long cupboard where the mops and the vacuum cleaner lived. She said, 'We haven't talked properly in ages.'

'I know.'

'Not since we came up to meet Morris.'

'He's gone,' Grace said.

'I heard.'

'He's at Jeff's place.'

'Yes.'

'Where's Ma?'

'I thought that she was up in Stoke with you,' Ashley said.

'I don't know. I didn't go in today.'

Ashley shifted a little. She said, 'You don't sound quite right to me.'

'I don't know whether I am—'

'There's been a lot going on down here. Cara and Dan and me. Leo . . .'

'What about Leo?'

'He's taken the children over.'

'Wow,' Grace said. 'Is that OK?'

'I don't know yet. But he seems determined to make a go of it.'

Grace said suddenly, 'I'm in a bit of a mess.'

'Gracie. Are you pregnant?'

'No!' Grace said. 'God, no. But – look, I can't say what I want to say over the telephone. I'm just a bit done in by everything up here—'

'Come to London.'

'Well,' Grace said doubtfully, 'I might.'

'Come this weekend. Come on, Grace. Just come. I can tell you everything. It's been such a mental time,

213

Ma's house and Morris and trying to restructure stuff and everything. You can see the children.'

'I'd like that.'

Leo appeared suddenly at the other end of the room, rising from the sofa in a haze of sleep and standing, swaying slightly, outlined against the muted television screen.

'Get a train on Friday,' Ashley said. 'The children'll be thrilled to see you.'

'Yes,' Grace said. 'OK.'

Ashley felt a little surge of vitality, an electric charge of being in control, and strong enough to prop up those who were faltering. 'Fab,' she said, 'see you Friday,' and flipped her phone shut. Then she walked across the room and put her arms round Leo. 'I was going to kiss you just now,' she said, 'but my phone rang. So I'll do it now, instead.'

'Michelle says that you know where Grace was this weekend,' Susie said to Neil Dundas.

It was late afternoon and the factory was quiet. It was the time of day Neil usually liked best, walking through those long rooms filled with the day's productivity, the air settling after the disturbance caused by a couple of hundred occupied people, the kilns humming their way through their night-long programmes.

He said, not pausing in his rapid checking of a

truckload of ghostly fired jugs, 'I don't. I didn't.'

Susie was holding a clipboard against her. She always had a clipboard when she went round the factory, for scribbles and sketches. She said, 'I rather think you did. I think she told you.'

Neil picked up a jug, inspected its base and put it back. 'She told me she was going away for a few nights and that she'd be back on Wednesday at the latest, and that nobody was to worry.'

'Why do you think that she told you?' Susie said.

Neil turned to look at her. He said firmly, 'Because I wouldn't make anything of it, and I'd leave her alone.'

Susie crossed both arms across her clipboard. 'I'll ignore that.'

Neil turned back. He said, 'Did you need her, anyway?'

'What?'

'Well, did you need to speak to her this weekend?'

'I needed,' Susie said reprovingly, 'to check that she was all right.'

'Can't help you there.'

Susie waited a moment, and then she said, 'It seems she didn't go anywhere. She's just staying in her flat.'

Neil began to push the truck aside, to make way for another. 'I wouldn't know.'

'Neil,' Susie said, 'what's eating you?'

He pulled the second truck loaded with small tureens

into place. He said, 'Forgive plain speaking, but you can't have it both ways.'

'I like plain speaking,' Susie said. 'What do you mean?'

He turned to face her. 'This might be a family business. But it's a business. There are orders to fill, and it's my job to fill them. It isn't my job to keep an eye on your family. You shouldn't be asking me where Grace was this weekend.'

'But she told you—'

'She told me,' Neil said, 'because I wouldn't make anything of it. It was a *fact*. She said she wouldn't be in on Monday or today. One of the casters is off too, because he's taking his mum to hospital, and we can't use the flatware machine tomorrow because it's being serviced. Those are the staffing *facts* I am working around. Grace was merely one of them.'

There was another pause. Then Susie said, 'Point taken.'

Neil turned back to the tureens. He said teasingly, 'Thank you, Boss.'

'But I would have liked to see Grace this weekend,' Susie said. 'I was out at Barlaston with the architect, and I'd have liked her opinion. She didn't answer her phone.'

Neil said nothing.

She watched him for a while, and then she said,

'Have you made the samples for the coffee-shop special edition yet?'

He let a beat fall and then he said, 'Yes, I have,' in the tone of one who really wanted to say, 'Of course.'

Cara had bought an organic, free-range chicken. It had been an eye-watering price – even if not as eye-watering as a poulet de Bresse, which she had not permitted herself even to consider – but it came covered with assurances of quality and compassionate rearing, and in any case, Dan loved chicken. Which was the whole point. When Dan got back from a punishing cycle ride, Cara would have stuffed the chicken with breadcrumbs, olives, lemons and basil, and roasted it to perfection. She would even use some of the aged balsamic vinegar they had bought in Modena together in the stuffing. Dan would notice and approve of these details, and he would realize what she was saying, in roasted chicken rather than in words.

The thing was, Cara discovered, that she didn't want to say sorry. She didn't think that there was any need to apologize for feeling so acutely and suddenly protective of her mother, nor for simultaneously resenting Dan's attitude. That attitude – that demand to know exactly how Susie had been browbeaten into submission – had really offended her. It had stuck in her gullet, both because it assumed that the two of them were detached from, and somehow superior to, the rest of the family, and also because it assumed that Susie was some kind of obstructive, obstinate idiot. Which was, Cara felt, most unfair.

These feelings were extremely disconcerting. They had never happened before. Before, she and Dan had taken for granted that their united front was naturally progressive in the best possible, incontrovertible way. But something had shifted, and that certainty no longer appeared so unassailable. Cara had a hot flush of shame at the memory of some of the conversations about Susie that she had had in the past with Daniel. Now, for some reason, her exasperation with Susie felt like something she was naturally allowed to have, just as Ashley and Grace and Pa were, but that Daniel and Leo – if he ever joined in – were not. Absolutely not. If Daniel spoke disrespectfully of Susie again, Cara was determined to put him forcibly right. Conversations about Susie's limitations would be severely policed in future. She felt very strongly about that.

On the other hand, she knew that Daniel was often right. There was no question about that. He was a brilliant commercial director, and he was also very patient, really, in his dealings with the whole Moran family. Pa loved him, after all, and so did she. He was her chosen companion, her best friend, her ally and her supporter. He had backed her up in so many business disputes where she had actually turned out to be right. They agreed about friends and holidays and leisure pursuits and money and, crucially, about not having a baby. She really wanted to make peace with him and to demonstrate her very real love for him, but she couldn't say sorry. So the perfect chicken, filling the flat with its irresistible aromas when he returned and found candles lit and music playing, would wordlessly say it all for her.

As was her habit, Cara laid out all her ingredients on the kitchen counter. It would be soothing to chop and slice and stir, and she was keenly aware of needing to be soothed. This sudden urge to defend Susie, almost to *protect* her, had apparently come out of nowhere, striking her not while she was still arguing crossly in Susie's kitchen, but on the way home, when she had been flooded with sudden anguish about leaving Susie alone in Radipole Road with the aftermath of their exchange to deal with. But what was that about? There'd been plenty of occasions in the past when she'd felt nothing but fury at Susie's abiding unreasonableness or obduracy, and hadn't felt a shred of remorse. In fact, over time, she'd got quite used to switching into exasperated-daughter mode in almost every conversation with her mother, and who could blame Dan for picking up on that and following her lead? She had grown to regard her frustrated attitude towards her mother in their business dealings just as the way things would always be. She had fallen into a habit, taking Dan with her. And now that habit had been roughly, unavoidably shaken.

But by what? Cara began to fish the olives out of their jar of oil. Could it possibly be the arrival of Morris? Could it be that his appearance on the scene had made starkly vivid the idea of Susie being casually abandoned as a baby by her parents, however loving and capable her grandparents had been? Was the presence of this strangely elusive but burdensome old man a catalyst for the kind of empathy that Cara had never felt before? Had never, if she was frank with herself, *bothered* to feel before? She lined the olives up on her chopping board and began to slit them open to extract the stones. Had she and her sisters just never looked beyond their own emotionally secure childhoods, to picture what Susie had never had? Had they just focused on the advantages she had undoubtedly received, or the comforts and security that her achievements had given them all?

She lifted the board and scraped the olives into her bowl of breadcrumbs. Whatever had happened in her mind, it was deep and disconcerting. It was also pre-occupying her in a way that preparing the stuffing for the chicken didn't seem to be helping with at all. And in addition, she realized with dismay, it was making her lonely. Because of the complexity of her feelings, and their contradictions, she couldn't discuss them with the one person she had grown to rely upon turning to. She could give Dan a perfect chicken by way of not saying sorry, but she couldn't ask for his help in disentangling her feelings. It was a most unwelcome first in their marriage.

She picked up the lemon and the grater, held them over the bowl of breadcrumbs, and suddenly couldn't see. Oh God, she thought. Oh *God*. I'm crying.

CHAPTER ELEVEN

'For a slip-cover tin,' the production director said to Susie, 'you're looking at about a pound a tin, for orders over three thousand. And for hinged-lid tins, about half that.'

They were sitting in his office, which had been converted from a Victorian barn within sight of the M6. The barn, and the farmhouse it had once served, had long since lost all agricultural connections, and were now reincarnated as a small light-industrial estate with a tidy road system edged with orderly municipal planting. Susie, who liked randomness in natural things, found these trips to Tinware for Today aesthetically offensive, but it was a small British company, founded by an enterprising man who had grown up in Newcastle-under-Lyme, and therefore it ticked all her required boxes for local manufacture. She had discovered the company almost fifteen years ago, when it was just a fledgling start-up, and had been the first manufacturer to give it a substantial order. Since then, she had gone there twice a year, to present her new designs in person and to talk them through, in every detail, with the team who would produce Susie Sullivan tin trays, lunchboxes and biscuit tins.

Susie looked at the prototype tins on the production director's desk. They were unadorned in any way, just cylinders and cubes of silvery tinware, with the odd heart shape or oval among them. There was a small, round tray to one side, gleaming like a moon.

She had not made a specific point of flagging up this visit. If Daniel or her daughters wished to look at her open diary, they would notice that the biannual visit to Tinware for Today was scheduled, but she had not drawn their attention to it. It wasn't deviousness, she told herself, it was more a need to reassure herself that she was still in charge, that the company functioned on fuel provided by her input and her hands-on approach. In any case, Nick Jarvis, the production director of Tinware for Today, was new to the job, and therefore needed to be made aware of the significance of Susie Sullivan pottery to his company. He also needed to know who was ultimately in charge. He was looking at her now, slightly questioningly, and then said with a hint of defiance, 'That's a very good price.'

Susie reached out and touched a lunchbox, with its pleasingly retro handle. 'It is,' she said. She didn't look at him. 'Too good, in fact.'

He gave a small bark of laughter. 'I don't have many customers who complain about *that*!'

Susie went on looking at the lunchbox. She said lightly, 'Well, I'm not your average customer.'

Nick pulled himself together. He said hastily, 'I never intended to imply that.'

She picked up a cylindrical tin and inspected it. 'This is seamless.'

'Of course.'

'And what we pack our cookies in.'

He said politely, 'I'm aware of that.'

'And you are offering it to me at much less than I've paid for it before?'

He smiled, and said with a small air of triumph, 'That's the current price, Mrs Moran.'

Susie put the tin down carefully. She said casually, 'And where are you sourcing the sheet metal from?'

Nick said cheerfully, 'China, of course.'

She looked directly at him. 'Exactly.'

'But—'

'I don't want to use sheet metal from China,' Susie said, 'however cheap it is. I want to use the sheet-metal manufacturers I've always used, in Sheffield.'

'But that might be twice the price—'

'My pottery,' Susie said, still regarding him, 'my brand says Made in Britain underneath every item. Made in Britain. Every mug, every paper napkin, every biscuit tin. To me, Made in Britain means that everything – the china clay, the paper, the tin, the glass, *everything* about the product is made and sourced here. There are manufacturers in my industry, Nick, who have their products made in China and only decorated here, which still have Made in Britain stamped underneath. That, to me, is a lie. I won't have it. I want Made in Britain to mean what it says. And that goes for the tinware we buy from you.'

Nick shifted in his chair and pushed his designer spectacles up his nose. He said, 'I haven't had many dealings with Sheffield—'

'Well, you'd better start.'

'If you're prepared—'

'I'm prepared,' Susie said. 'I'll argue the price with you, but I'm prepared.'

He said unwisely, 'I'll get back to you with a quote—'

'No, you won't,' Susie said. 'You'll ring them now. While I'm here. We'll get a price sorted before I leave. And the design. I need to talk to your team about the design, as I always do.'

Nick leant forward, smiling, but his smile was far from certain. 'Perhaps,' he said, 'you could leave your ideas, your sketches . . .' He stopped. Then he said, 'My second bad idea, obviously.'

Susie smiled at him kindly. 'You have a lot to learn.'

He attempted a shrug and thought better of it

halfway through. He said lamely, 'I'm three weeks in.'

'And I,' Susie said, 'am well over thirty years in. Probably since before *you* were born.'

'Not quite.'

'Long enough to know both my product and my customers, wouldn't you say?'

Nick nodded.

Susie stood up. 'You ring Sheffield,' she said, looking down at him, 'while I go and find the design team. No—' she added, holding out a hand to stop him rising, 'don't move. I know where I'm going. And when I'm back, we can haggle over what I am prepared to pay for sheet metal made in Britain.' She paused and gave him a brief smile. 'OK?'

Jeff said he owed Morris a drink. Even a double. He said that his boss was so thrilled with the prototype bird house that Morris had made that he, Jeff, was benefiting from the reflected glory.

Morris, sitting on the couch in Jeff's sitting room, looked at his hands and said that it was nothing. 'I made spirit houses in Lamu. They were an idea that came from Bali or someplace, originally. You had this little house on a pole outside your own house, for the spirits to live in, and you left them offerings – flowers and things. I made them in exchange for – well, it was a barter thing. Kept us going sometimes.'

Jeff was sitting on the floor, propped against the wall by the television. His long legs were stretched out in front of him, elegantly crossed at the ankle. He said, '*Us*. You don't talk about her much.'

'Who?'

'Grace's granny,' Jeff said.

Morris sighed. He said, 'Paula.'

'That her name? Grace's grandma was called Paula?'

Morris smiled to himself. He said, 'I called her Stella. Stella the star. She never grew up.'

Jeff was watching him. He said, 'In what way didn't she grow up?'

Morris pulled a face. 'She never thought about the next day. Or the next week, or year. She was all impulse and reaction. Rain or shine, she just lived it, like a cat or something.' He glanced at Jeff. 'She'd never have managed life here.'

Jeff took a swig from the can of Coke Zero he was holding. He said nonchalantly, 'D'you think Grace is like her?'

'Why d'you ask?'

'Just wondered.'

'Did you now?' Morris said.

Jeff set the can down on the carpet tiles beside him. He said, 'Grace is very special.'

'Yes,' Morris said shortly.

'And it sounds as if Stella was.'

'She was an eternal child,' Morris said, 'if that counts as special.'

'Maybe that's why I want to look after Grace.'

'Really?'

Jeff nodded solemnly.

'Well,' Morris said, still looking at him, 'she's got Stella's hair.'

'I love her hair.'

'She was one big freckle after a year in Lamu. Reminded me of a flame or something, red hair and all those freckles.'

Jeff smiled to himself. He said confidingly, 'Grace has freckles—'

'I don't want to know,' Morris said.

Jeff looked tolerant. ''Course you don't. You're her granddad.'

Morris nodded.

Jeff picked up his drink again and squinted at the can. 'You got plans for this weekend?'

'Not unless my daughter calls me.'

Jeff said, 'Think I'll try and see Grace.'

'Oh?'

'Well, we haven't been in touch this week somehow. Not since you moved in, in fact. I'd – I'd like to know her reaction to that.'

Morris adjusted some of the woven bracelets around his left wrist. He said, 'You want her to say thank you?'

'Oh no,' Jeff said.

'Really?'

Jeff looked sideways, towards the window. 'I'd – like to know if she's noticed.'

'Well,' Morris said, 'I would think she's noticed that I'm not in her flat, wouldn't you?'

Jeff said, suddenly piteous, 'I miss her.'

'Me too,' Morris said.

Jeff swung his head back to look at Morris and said decisively, 'I'm going to call her this weekend.'

Morris smiled at him. 'No point.'

'What d'you mean, no point? What would you know—'

'She isn't there,' Morris said.

'Isn't where?'

'She isn't at home.' Morris went back to rearranging his bracelets. He said with just a hint of satisfaction, 'She's gone to London for the weekend.'

'I love you,' Maisie said to Grace.

She had climbed into Grace's bed some time before dawn and was now lying on her side, her head on Grace's pillow and her nose only inches from Grace's own.

Grace was struggling to open her eyes. She said indistinctly, 'I love you, too.'

Maisie pushed her face even closer to Grace's, so that

her breath was warm on Grace's skin. 'But I *really* love you,' she said.

Grace didn't try to open her eyes. 'You mean,' she said, 'that you want me to wake up.'

'Yes,' Maisie said.

'I can't.'

'Oh,' Maisie said, in imitation of her mother's inflection, 'I think you can.'

'Not yet.'

'It's the morning,' Maisie said.

'No—'

'Oh yes,' Maisie said. 'Mumma went downstairs to make tea.'

'Did she?'

'So it's time to get *up*.'

Grace put a hand on Maisie's solid little side. 'Don't bully me, Mais. Please.'

'I want you to *play* with me.'

'Not yet.'

'Now!'

'In a minute,' Grace said.

'You don't say that,' Maisie said sternly. 'You *never* say that. Not to a *child*.'

Grace laughed and opened her eyes.

'That's better,' Maisie said approvingly.

'You're awful.'

Maisie moved so close that her eyes crossed, trying

to see Grace properly. 'I need to play Lego Friends.'

'Not *need*,' Grace said. '*Want*.'

Maisie took no notice. She said, breathing into Grace's mouth, 'You have to help me.'

'She doesn't *have* to do anything for you whatsoever,' Ashley said from the doorway.

Maisie shot up in bed. 'Mumma! It's the morning!'

Ashley was carrying a tray of mugs. She wore a cardigan of Leo's over polka-dotted pyjamas and her feet were thrust into immense sheepskin slippers that made her look like Donald Duck.

Grace raised herself on one elbow. 'Oh, Ash—'

Ashley put the tray down on the bedside table. 'Hot chocolate for Maisie. Tea for us. Budge up, I'm getting in.'

'But I need to *play*,' Maisie said.

Ashley kicked off her slippers and began to climb into bed beside her sister. She said to Maisie, 'Have you done a pee?'

'Yes,' Maisie said.

'Fibber,' Ashley said. 'Go now.'

'No.'

'Go *now*. Or I will pour your hot chocolate down the loo.'

Maisie began to slither slowly out of the bed. She said, 'I don't want to go by myself.'

Grace reared up a little further. 'I'll come with you.'

231

'No,' Ashley said. She put a hand on her sister's arm. 'She can manage perfectly well on her own. Anyway, Leo's in there. Shaving.'

'I don't want Dadda to help me.'

'Then do it yourself.'

Maisie had reached the floor. She glowered at her mother. She said, 'Don't talk to Grace.'

'What?'

'Don't talk to Grace when I'm not here.'

Ashley said, laughing, 'But she's my sister!'

Maisie walked very slowly to the door. She looked back at them, side by side in bed. She said, 'I got there first. I was there in the night time.' Then she slid from view.

Grace struggled to sit up. She said, 'She's wonderful.'

'Did she wake you?'

Grace pushed her hair back. 'Not when she got in, whenever that was.'

'I think she's going to be a bit like Ma when she grows up,' said Ashley. She handed a mug of tea to Grace. 'Where *is* Ma, by the way?'

Grace took the tea and held it with both hands. 'Not at home, I don't think. Maybe in Barlaston.'

'We should know.'

'We often don't.'

'No,' Ashley said, 'we often don't. And she doesn't want us to. Is it a kind of control?'

Grace took a gulp of tea. 'God, that's good. That first mouthful of tea in the morning – nothing like it. It might be control, but I think it's more to do with liberty. I think she kind of craves freedom – can't bear to be told, or confined or anything.'

'Which is where Cara and Dan have got it so wrong,' Ashley said, settling back into the pillows. 'They tried to assign her a *role*. And even if she didn't hate the role itself, she wouldn't have been able to stand the mere idea of having one in the first place. Certainly not one that someone else has devised for her.'

Grace said, 'Did Cara think of the idea? It doesn't sound like Cara.'

'It was Dan.'

'Oh,' Grace said. She held her mug against her chin. She said, 'He so wants the company to prosper and *grow*.'

'Grace,' Ashley said, interrupting, 'we can talk about them later. We've got all weekend to talk about the company. But what about *you*?'

Grace closed her eyes briefly. She said, 'Nothing much.'

'*Gracie*. Don't be irritating. Tell me.'

Grace reached to put her mug down beside the bed. She said slowly, 'I – just started some things that I can't finish.'

'Morris? Jeff?'

'Both.'

'We all do that,' Ashley said. Her tone was encouraging. 'We all hope we can sort things, and then we find we can't, and it's often not our fault that we can't.'

Grace slid back down in bed and closed her eyes again. She said, 'I shouldn't have started it.'

'Jeff?' Ashley said again.

'Cara said don't. Cara said it was almost always dangerous online. But when I saw this photo and realized he lived so close—'

Ashley said, in an extremely reasonable voice, 'It isn't a crime to fancy someone, you know.'

'But now he's kind of hooked on hating my family, but wanting to be part of it,' Grace said. 'The thought of Morris in his flat is so complicated it makes me want to run away. Or go to bed for a week.'

Ashley looked down at her sister. She said gently, 'Morris is actually Ma's problem, Gracie. If she doesn't want him in Jeff's flat, then she has to put him somewhere else. It isn't up to you.'

Grace opened her eyes. 'I was trying to help.'

'I know.'

'I mean,' Grace said, rolling on her side towards her sister, 'I know you and Cara think Ma is holding the company back in lots of ways, and I expect you're right – at least, partly right – but I can't help seeing her point of view, too. I can't help wondering what it must feel like to start something as important as the company,

234

and nurture it all these years, and watch it grow, and employ people and become a household name, and then be told by your children that you've got to change and play a different role and let them take over all the modern aspects of business that they now understand better than you do.'

There was a pause. Ashley put her mug down, too, and folded her hands in front of her. She said after a while, 'I don't think Cara and Dan are doing very well together.'

Grace raised her head. 'Really?'

'I had a weird encounter with Dan. He was waiting for me in the office car park. He asked me if I knew why Cara wasn't speaking to him.'

Grace pulled herself into a sitting position again. 'Isn't she?'

Ashley was looking straight ahead. She said, 'They came up with this scheme that Ma would step down from being the MD, really, and Cara went round to Radders to tell her this and had some kind of epiphany on the way home about Ma's position and what they were asking of her, and she seems to have been angry with Dan about it ever since.'

'It fell in,' Maisie said from the doorway. She was wearing only the top half of her pyjamas.

Ashley began to scramble out of bed. 'Not *another* one, Mais. Not *another* loo roll.'

'Well,' Maisie said cheerfully, 'there you go.'

Grace said, 'Ash, can we—'

'In a sec,' Ashley said. 'I'll just have to rescue the bog roll. And see where Leo was, why he didn't—'

'He went downstairs,' Maisie said. 'With Freddy. Freddy did a huge—'

'I don't want to know. Grace doesn't want to know either. Where are your pyjama trousers?'

'Wet,' Maisie said. She looked up at her mother. 'Oh *dear*,' she said, with emphasis.

From the bed, Grace began to laugh.

Ashley turned and looked at her. She made a gesture of mock despair. 'What to do?'

'It's good for us,' Grace said, still laughing. 'It's so good for us. Maisie, you are just what we need.'

Maisie put her hands on her hips and struck a pose. 'Oh, I *know*,' she said, with satisfaction.

Jasper was watching snooker on television, world championship snooker, live from Sheffield. He would have preferred to watch football, but the only football on television that night was Spanish, and he wasn't enough of a fanatic to prefer Spanish football to snooker. In any case, there was something quite soothing about snooker, the darkened indoor quality of it, the formality of the players' clothes, the solid click of the balls. It was also something to be doing, an anodyne occupation for the moment – twenty-four hours after he had expected it – when he would finally hear Susie's key in the lock.

She had rung and texted him as usual, every day. She had, also as usual, recited a list of commitments which meant that she couldn't quite plan, as she didn't know exactly where she'd be, when. He had given up saying, 'But you always keep your appointments at the factory, and at everything to do with the factory, to the minute,' because it was pointless and undignified. Her reply had invariably been, 'But Jas, I'm always back. I always come back in the end,' and, of course, she always had. Punctually, regularly when the girls were small, and then gradually less consistently as they grew up, until the unannounced randomness of her returns was pretty well complete. Now, this evening, he heard her open the front door, shout 'It's me!' as if it could ever conceivably be anyone else, let the door slam behind her and add with relief, 'Hello, home.' He waited. There was a soft thud as she dropped the bag she was carrying on the hall floor, and then the scuffle of her kicking her shoes off.

'Jas,' she said from the sitting-room doorway, her tone plainly anticipating a warm welcome. 'What a few days!'

He smiled at her from his armchair, but he didn't get up. 'I bet.'

She padded across and bent to kiss him. She said, 'Why are you watching snooker?'

'I felt like sport,' he said, 'but not Spanish football.'

She gave his arm a kindly pat. 'I didn't know if you'd be here. Thought you might be round at Ashley's again.'

'Nope,' he said, 'not again. Hungry?'

She considered this. 'Not really.'

'Glass of wine?'

She began to move back towards the door. 'Just tea, I think. I'll get it. Lots to tell you.'

Jasper grunted. He turned back to the snooker.

Susie paused in the doorway. 'Jas? Are you sulking?'

He went on looking at the television. He said, 'Why would I be sulking?'

'Because I wasn't back yesterday. Because of the new cottage. Because of Morris.'

Jasper waited a moment, and then he said, 'Even *you* must think it's a bit odd that I haven't met him.'

'What d'you mean, even me?'

'Well,' Jasper said evenly, 'you lead very much the life you choose to lead. Your rules are not really designed to take account of anyone else's wishes. You are a law unto yourself, Suz. So your attitude to a long-lost parent isn't going to be exactly conventional, is it?'

Susie came back into the room and stopped a few

feet from Jasper's chair. She said, 'I'm not pleased to see him, Jas.'

He went on steadily looking at the snooker. He said, 'I know. We all know. But it isn't unreasonable, is it, to think that when you have a big personal problem in your life all of a sudden, you might think of sharing it with your husband?'

Susie said, with difficulty, 'I'm . . . not very proud of him.'

'Which only underlines what I've just said.'

Susie sat down on the arm of the sofa and looked at her stockinged feet. She said, almost under her breath, 'Sorry, Jas. I'm sorry.'

He picked up the remote control and aimed it at the television. In the silence that followed, he said, 'Sorry about what?'

'If – if I've looked as if I'm shutting you out.'

'I'm used to that, Suz. I'm used to you and the business. But this is a bit different, don't you think? Your own father?'

She said, still staring at her feet, 'There's been such a lot going on. Cara and Dan wanting changes, Ashley wanting more of a say, poor Grace in such a mess—'

'And none of it,' Jasper said, 'for sharing?'

She said again, 'I'm so sorry.'

'I never know what you're really sorry *about*. Sometimes I think you're just sorry you've dropped a ball in the juggling act. Sometimes I wonder how sorry you're really capable of being about other people's feelings, especially if you've had a hand in hurting them.'

Susie raised her eyes. She said, 'Have I hurt you?'

He didn't look at her. 'Yes.'

'Jas, I never meant—'

'Please don't start on that. Please don't tell me about your intentions and how they got corrupted by subsequent events. Please don't make excuses.'

Susie was silent for several long seconds, then she said, 'Can I at least try to do better?'

'Like how?'

'Like us going for a long walk together tomorrow, down by the river or something, and having a meal out at the pub.'

'Sorry,' Jasper said, 'I can't. Not tomorrow.'

She was startled. 'You *can't*? What are you doing?'

'You mean,' he said, 'what can I be doing – me, Jasper, who never has any commitments beyond lounging through life on his wife's money?'

'No,' she said. '*No*. I didn't mean that. I never meant—'

'I'm working,' Jasper said flatly.

Susie stared at him.

He picked up the remote control and switched the snooker back on. 'I'm playing in a gig tomorrow, Suz. With Brady. We're rehearsing in the afternoon and playing in the evening.' He dropped the remote on to the arm of his chair. 'In Shoreditch,' he said.

'You must come more often,' Leo said to Grace. They were washing up together. Ashley and Fred had gone upstairs for a nap, and Maisie was on a beanbag in front of a Peppa Pig DVD, with her thumb in.

Grace said, 'I'd like that.'

Leo was washing up with conspicuous competence, rinsing the soapsuds off saucepans and peering at them to see if there were any smears that he had missed.

'It can't be good for you, work and play being so local all the time.'

'I like it,' Grace said. She was polishing wine glasses slowly, with a cloth. 'I like Stoke.'

'I didn't mean that,' Leo said. 'I just mean that it's small.'

Grace set a wine glass down. She said, 'There's nothing the matter with Stoke, you know. It's me. I got in a bit of a tangle.'

Leo untied the butcher's apron he was wearing and pulled it over his head. He said, 'You and Ash need to see more of each other.'

'Yes,' Grace said. 'I'd forgotten how well we get on.'

'Especially now.'

Grace picked up another wet glass. 'What's special about now?'

Leo hitched himself on to a corner of the kitchen table. 'Well,' he said, 'you can see that things round here aren't quite what they used to be.'

Grace pushed her cloth inside the wine glass. She said warmly, 'I think it's great of you to take on the children and the house and everything. Ash says it's going to change so much for her.'

'I mean it to. And for the children.'

'Of course,' Grace said politely.

'But it isn't just to avoid the childcare problems we've had in the past, you know. It's more than that.' He looked at the second glass Grace had set down beside the first. 'The thing is, you and Ash should have as much clout in the company as Cara and Dan do.'

Grace said quickly, 'They're very fair.'

'Fair,' Leo said, 'is all very well, from a position of power. But you and Ash don't have the power that they do. And you should.'

Grace hung her tea towel over the back of the nearest chair. She said, 'Maybe I prefer influence to power. Perhaps it suits me better.'

'That's just semantics,' Leo said. 'This is a family business and there must be equality. Ash and I have made a kind of deal in our marriage and home life. You and she need to make one in your working lives, too.'

Grace looked at him for a long moment. Then she

said, 'Leo, is this why you've decided to take on the childcare? To free Ashley up to . . . to go for something?'

He stood up and crossed the kitchen briskly towards the kettle. 'Yes,' he said, with his back to her. 'Coffee?'

CHAPTER TWELVE

'I've come,' Cara said, 'to say sorry.'

She stood just inside the boardroom door, holding the handle. Susie was sitting at the table, her sketchbooks spread around and her laptop open. She glanced up at Cara as if she couldn't quite remember who she was, and said absently, 'You what, darling?'

Cara shut the door behind her. She said, 'I shouldn't have spoken to you like that. I shouldn't have stormed off.'

Susie was wearing her reading glasses. She took them off and laid them on the nearest sketchbook. She said, 'I have to hear these things, I know I do.'

Cara took a chair opposite her mother. She said, 'It wasn't meant to sound so antagonistic.'

'No.'

'Ma, it wasn't a *criticism*. It was meant to be a suggestion. That's all.'

Susie said sadly, 'I think it's my week for criticism.'

'What d'you mean?'

Susie sighed. She picked up her glasses, fiddled with them a bit, then put them down again. She said reluctantly, 'It was a rather . . . *painful* weekend.'

'Ma!' Cara said. 'In what way?'

Susie pushed herself back in her chair. She said, 'Is Dan out there?'

'He's on the phone. He's busy.'

'Are you both—?' She stopped.

'Sort of,' Cara said. She leant forward. 'But what about you? Was it Morris?'

'Only indirectly.'

'Then?'

Susie looked away. She said unhappily, 'Your pa.'

'Pa?'

'He's very angry with me.'

'Oh,' Cara said with a shrug. 'Take no notice. Pa's never cross for more than five minutes, he can't keep it up.'

'He's really angry,' Susie said. 'Coldly angry. He was out all yesterday, playing some gig with Brady. I wanted to go and hear him, but he said no.'

'He said *no*?'

'He said he didn't want me to.'

'Childish,' Cara said.

'Not really. More . . . more like someone having to

245

resort to doing something very obvious to get a point home to someone else who won't listen.' She looked at Cara. 'Have you spoken to him?'

'Not since last week.'

'And?'

'He was perfectly normal. We fixed a night for supper this week, talked about Leo and Ash a bit, he said he thought Grace was better. Nothing out of the ordinary.'

Susie said, 'He thinks he should have met Morris.'

'Well, shouldn't he?'

Susie picked up her glasses again. She said slowly, 'I don't really want Morris mixed up with my real life.'

'Ma, you mixed *us* up pretty quickly!'

'I know. It isn't rational. It isn't even excusable. But if I keep Morris up there, then . . . then I can somehow pretend that he – oh, I don't mean that, I don't mean that he doesn't exist, but I can stop him sort of *leaking* into my life.'

Cara watched her mother's fingers playing with the tortoiseshell earpieces of her glasses. Then she said, in a much less conciliatory tone than she had used before, 'Ma, that is utter bollocks.'

'But—'

'Stoke means the world to you, because of the factory. The cottage at Barlaston is important, you said, because of creativity. Morris is all over all of that, you

246

can't help it, he just turned up there. If anybody's shut out of what really drives you, it's Pa.'

There was silence.

Then Susie said, 'That's what he said.'

'Did he?'

'Not in so many words. But he implied it.'

Cara waited a moment. Then she said, 'Perhaps he's suddenly woken up to the fact that he's kind of – kind of sleepwalking.'

'But he isn't,' Susie said, too quickly. 'We share everything. I tell him everything.'

'No, you don't.'

'I—'

'Not any more,' Cara said. 'You've got out of the habit. Buying the Parlour House wasn't sharing. He didn't think you should buy it, even if he let you persuade him why you had to. And now there's Morris.'

Susie put her spectacles on again. She said more collectedly, 'I thought you came to say sorry.'

'Yes,' Cara said. 'Yes, so did I.' She let a beat fall, and then she added, 'And then look what happened.'

Out of the corner of his eye, Dan watched Cara come out of the boardroom and close the door behind her. He stared hard at his screen, but he was sharply aware of her going across to her own desk, saying something to Kitty, and then, to his surprise, coming in his direction. He gave no sign that he was conscious of her, but merely concentrated on concentrating. She would probably be polite and friendly and removed in her manner to him, as she had been the last few days, so he would take his cue from her and stiffly respond in kind. It was an exhausting and artificial way to behave, but at the moment there seemed to be no alternative. Cara was dictating the mood and it seemed, to his intense frustration, to be out of his hands to change it. At least there was now another date in the diary for a meeting with the management consultancy.

'Dan,' Cara said, in an elaborately relaxed way, 'do you have a moment?'

He decided to play her tiresome game. He said, without raising his eyes from the screen, 'For you, I always have a moment.'

'Hoo – rah,' she said. 'Coffee downstairs?'

He glanced at her involuntarily. 'Downstairs?'

'In the café,' she said, smiling widely. 'Out of the office.'

'Now?'

'Right now.'

'I have a call—'

'Bring your phone. Tell Kitty.'

He pushed his chair back and said suspiciously, 'Do you have an agenda?'

She widened her eyes. 'Certainly not. Why ever would I do that?'

'Oh, Cara, stop it.'

She said, in a much lower voice, 'I want to talk to you.'

'In that case—'

She indicated the boardroom door. 'Just not in the office.'

His phone rang. He picked it up. He said to Cara, 'I'll follow you down.'

She made a drinking gesture. 'Americano?'

He smiled at her. It was such a relief to smile normally at her that he felt almost giddy. He said, meaning far more than just coffee, 'Always,' and put his phone to his ear.

She was waiting for him at a table by the café window, looking out on to the carefully landscaped sweep of turf which hid the car park. There was a glass pot of one of the herbal teas she favoured in front of her, and a white cup and a coffee pot opposite the chair at right angles to hers. He sat down without saying anything and reached across to pour her tea.

'Thank you,' Cara said.

Dan poured his own coffee. He very much wanted to say something, but instinct held him back. So, instead, he took a sip or two of coffee and stared at the green swell of grass outside the long windows, trying to keep his mind as neutral as he possibly could.

Cara didn't touch her tea. She played with the tea-spoon in her saucer, and then she said, 'It's pretty well impossible to get it right.'

Daniel felt his stomach clench in response. He said, 'D'you mean me?'

She flicked a glance at him. She said briefly, 'No. I mean Ma.'

He relaxed as suddenly as he had tensed.

'Ah.'

Cara said, 'I've been feeling awful about her. I thought I'd bullied her, that we hadn't taken into account all that she's achieved, all she's done for the business, for *us*. So I went to say sorry just now. I went to say that I didn't mean to sound so hard and unsympathetic, and that we should probably rethink our proposal about her future role, and there she is, in the boardroom, with sketches of wellington boots, for God's sake, and her laptop open at a picture of that bloody house, and she can't even give me her full attention, can she? She can't even really *look* at me.'

She paused. Daniel decided to go on saying nothing. He noticed that Cara's hands, lying on the table beside her teacup, were shaking very slightly, but he resisted the urge to take the nearest one and hold it, firmly and reassuringly.

'And then it turns out,' Cara went on, 'that Ma

and Pa have had a bad weekend. Ma didn't get back till Saturday night, and Pa was playing on Sunday, *all* Sunday, and he didn't want Ma to go and hear him. And Ma shows no sign of letting him meet Morris, although she's planning to let Morris move into the Parlour House in a week or two, when contracts are exchanged. So Morris gets to live – well, camp, really – in a house Pa hasn't even *seen*. And Pa is fed up about that, of *course* he is. He's known Ma since she was nineteen and he's held her hand through *everything*, and now she won't let him in on the big stuff. She's full of bullshit about it, too, coming up with all kinds of rubbish reasons why she's keeping her life compartmentalized like this. I went in all ready to be sorry and I came out feeling damned if I was any such thing.'

She stopped again and picked up her teacup. Then she put it down again.

'Oh God,' Cara said, 'I'm shaking.'

Daniel said, 'Breathe.'

'I am.'

'No. Breathe properly. Big, deep, slow breaths.'

'I want to cry. Not sad cry – furious cry. I want to help – I want to help *her* – and then she makes it *impossible*. She makes no sense. She is full of reasons, but they make no sense. She just wants her own way, more and more. She only wants our agreement as long as it coincides with her—'

'Stop,' Daniel said. He took a folded handkerchief out of his pocket and held it out to her. 'Here.'

Cara blew her nose.

Daniel said, 'She doesn't really want to alienate Jasper. She relies on him.'

Cara blew again and then used a clean corner of the handkerchief to wipe under her eyes. 'Is my mascara running?'

'No. Well, only a little.'

Cara said, 'She's behaving as if she doesn't need to rely on anybody.'

'It's a reaction to change. Or the idea of change. A sort of defiance.'

'It's doing my head in.'

Daniel put a hand out and tucked a strand of hair behind her ear. He said, 'Don't lose your nerve.'

Cara turned her head to look at him.

He said, 'We're not wrong. We're not wrong about the business, and the way things should be going. We may be frustrated – we *are* frustrated – but we're not wrong.'

Cara made a face. 'Are you sure?'

'Quite sure.'

'What if she just digs her heels in and refuses to compromise about anything?'

'Then,' Daniel said, 'we walk away.'

Cara's mouth fell open. '*What?* From the *pottery*?'

'If we have to.' Daniel held her gaze. 'It's just an idea,'

he said. 'But you can't find the right path unless you consider all the alternatives, even the most extreme ones. That's all I'm saying.'

Cara nodded wordlessly. She gulped. 'Right,' she said faintly.

Grace decided that she would get a lunchtime train back to Stoke, so that she could go round to Radipole Road before she left and see her father. She decided this only at the last moment, over breakfast, when Ashley said to her as she swung out of the house, 'Just remember, Gracie, don't let anyone bully you. Not Ma, not Morris, not Jeff. You don't have to let *any* of them make a victim of you. OK?'

Ashley had bent to kiss Grace, and then Fred, who was sitting stoutly on Grace's knee in his onesie pyjamas, eating blueberries with his fingers, one by one.

Grace had nodded. 'I'll try.'

'Yes, you really must. Generosity is one thing. Allowing exploitation is quite another.'

'I know. At least, I'm practising. In fact, I thought I might start this morning. I thought I might go and see Pa and get a later train after. In my *own* time.'

Ashley picked out a particularly large blueberry and popped it into Fred's mouth. 'You do that. Bye, lovely boy. Bye, Gracie. Come again soon.'

She would, Grace thought. She'd liked it, she'd really liked the distraction of being in Ashley's house, and the gratification of being involved in their domestic lives. It had struck her, more than once, that family life lent a distinct perspective to everything else, a robust sense of proportion. It was demanding and exhausting, but it was also supremely constructive and purposeful. After a few nights in Ashley's spare bedroom, she felt emboldened and heartened. She would take some of these healthy and affirmative feelings round to Radipole Road and bestow them on her father. However experienced he was at running his own life, a Monday morning was always a Monday morning, and he could do with some encouragement.

Jasper had said by text that he'd be at home all morning. When she arrived, and let herself in with her own key, she thought he would probably already be in the studio, but he was in the kitchen instead, making coffee. There was a jar of honey on the table, and a tub of butter and two plates, with a knife beside each.

Grace kissed him. 'Hi there, Pa. Haven't you had breakfast?'

He was pouring boiling water into a cafetière. He said, 'I was waiting to feel like it. And for you.'

'I had blueberries with Fred. And half the banana Maisie didn't want.'

'Maisie,' Jasper said, 'is very decided.'

'Very.'

He glanced at her. He said, 'You look good.'

'I feel it. Nice weekend. I forgot to keep going round in useless circles.'

He laughed. He carried the coffee over to the table. 'Toast?'

'Not really.'

'Oh, go on,' Jasper said. 'Toast and honey. You know you want it.'

'If you eat honey anywhere near Fred, the mess is unbelievable.'

Jasper settled himself in his habitual chair. He said, 'It's incredible how sticky babies are. Have grown-up toast and honey while you can. Put some in for me.'

Grace extracted two slices of bread from the packet. She said, 'Ashley said you had a gig.'

Jasper poured the coffee. He said carelessly, 'I did.'

'And?'

He smiled at the coffee pot. He said, 'I loved it. I did. I *loved* it.'

Grace inserted the bread into the toaster. 'Did they love you?'

Jasper shrugged.

Grace said, laughing, 'Pa? I bet they did.'

'Actually,' Jasper said, 'we wowed them. It was a sell-out and then it just – flew. I couldn't believe it. Three hundred people. Madness.'

'I'm not surprised,' Grace said.

'I even *sang*,' Jasper said. 'I haven't sung since for ever. I didn't mean to – it just happened. We could have encore'd all night.'

Grace came back to the table with the toast and dropped it on to the plates. 'Ouch. Hot. That's wonderful, Pa. So you'll do it again?'

'I think so, yes. Brady says they'll be fighting to have us back.'

'So a happy weekend.'

Jasper pushed the butter towards her. 'No, actually.'

'Uh-oh,' Grace said. 'Don't tell me—'

Jasper spread butter across his toast with elaborate care. He said, 'We don't need to talk about it.'

Grace looked across at him. 'I think we do.'

'It's a bad patch . . .'

'Pa,' Grace said, 'it's a bad *situation*.'

'I'm not going to complain to you.'

'You don't have to.'

'I'm OK, Gracie. I'll just busy myself in the music.'

'No,' Grace said. She dug her knife into the honey jar.

'It used to drive me wild when you kids did that,' Jasper said, watching her. 'There was something about toast crumbs in the honey—'

'Pa,' Grace said, interrupting, 'come to Stoke with me.'

Jasper put his knife down. '*Stoke?*'

'Yes. Now. Come now. Come with me, stay in my flat, go and see this cottage in Barlaston, meet Morris. Just *do* it.'

'I couldn't—'

'Why couldn't you?'

'Behind her back, I couldn't—'

'I don't think that she's been exactly open with you, has she?' Grace said. 'Anyway, it wouldn't be behind her back. It needn't be. You can ring her from the train.'

'Maybe I should ring her now . . .'

'No,' Grace said. 'No.'

'Have you and Ashley been plotting this all weekend?'

'No. Not at all. I've only just thought of it.'

Jasper pushed his plate away. His toast was untouched. He said, 'I'm certainly fed up enough.'

'Then come.'

'But shouldn't I wait till I'm *not* fed up?'

'No,' Grace said vehemently. '*I*'ve suggested this. *I*'ve persuaded you, *I*'m taking you with me on the train.'

He looked at her. He said, 'I've never been disloyal.'

'Ashley would say loyalty was one thing and being a doormat was quite another.'

'Do you both think I'm a doormat? Does Cara?'

Grace bit her lip. 'Kind of,' she said.

Jasper sat back, blinking. 'Wow,' he said.

'Sorry, Pa.'

'That was a bit of a blinder.'

Grace said, astonished at her own persistence, 'You can change.'

'You mean you all think I ought to?'

'We'd like it if you wanted to.'

He sighed. 'Of all of you girls, I never thought *you*'d be the one to tell me to shape up.'

'Nor me.'

'And you promise Ashley didn't put you up to it?'

'All Ashley said was that I was to stop colluding with people who wanted to make me into a victim. I mean, that was her drift.'

Jasper picked up his coffee mug. He said, 'I can't, Gracie.' He glanced over his shoulder towards the bird-cage, where Polynesia was dozing on her perch. 'I can't leave her.'

'Ring Benedita. She'll look after her for a couple of nights.'

'No, I can't.'

'*I*'ll ring Benedita,' Grace said. 'If you feel you can't ask Ma to look after her own parrot for forty-eight hours.'

Jasper took a sip of coffee. He said, 'You're a bully.'

'And you are a coward.'

He shrugged slightly. 'Am I?'

'Pa,' Grace said, 'we none of us want what's happened. And it's none of our faults that it has. But we don't have to lie down under any of it. Come to Stoke with me, and *assert* yourself for once.'

Across the room, Polynesia took her head from under her wing, raised it and surveyed the kitchen. Then she said, in a chatty tone, 'Why don't you bugger off?'

'We love this café,' one of the nursery-school mothers had said to Leo. 'It's completely bomb proof and baby friendly. We usually have coffee together on Wednesdays. Why don't you come? You won't be the only man, promise!'

She had been pretty, lean and energetic looking, with a baby in a sling on her front and her hair sleeked back into a high ponytail. All the time she was talking to him, she was bouncing slightly on the balls of her trainered feet, and her ponytail had bounced in unison. She'd said her name was Amanda.

Amanda's son, Felix, sat at the same table as Maisie at nursery school. When Leo had asked Maisie if she liked Felix, she had rolled her eyes and said, '*Yes*,' with unaffected fervour, so it seemed to Leo that he really should go along to the Wednesday coffee morning and make friends with Felix's mother. In any case, it would be good for Fred to be with other babies, and it would be good for him, Leo, to get a proper insight into the business of making a thorough job of domestic life. So, after he had taken Maisie to school, and peeled her from his leg in the daily sobbing ritual she appeared determined to cling to, he pushed the buggy containing Fred the two streets from the nursery school to the café.

It was, as far as he could see, entirely filled with women. There was an area at the back, up a step, with plastic toys scattered on a smallish square of floor, but all the tables were occupied by young and youngish women, and babies. Leo didn't think he had ever seen so many babies. They ranged from nursing babies through to toddlers, and the noise was indescribable. Dotted about in this sea of babies were the mothers, some holding a child or two – rather absently on the whole – and all of them talking. Some had their laptops open on the tables, most had cups and mugs in front of them, and they looked to Leo as self-sufficient and impenetrable a club as if there was a large notice on the café door saying, 'KEEP OUT'.

Leo scanned the room for another man. There was only one – apparently a grandfather – determinedly reading a newspaper in a corner, with the air of someone who has absolutely no intention of being included. He couldn't at first see Amanda, but then he spotted her, with Felix's baby sister on her knee, in the middle of an animated conversation. He raised his arm to wave to her in a half-hearted way, but let it fall again. Her hair was pinned back in a sleek chignon today, and she appeared utterly engrossed in her companion. It was impossible, Leo thought, to make his way between the tables to reach her, never mind know how he would conduct himself when he got there. 'Hi' and a weak smile just wouldn't cut it – it would simply get washed away in all that liveliness. And anyway, how would Fred cope with a floorful of strange babies, on top of being the only child there not conventionally garnished with a mother?

Leo swallowed. This was ridiculous. He was a qualified, educated, personable man of thirty-four, and Fred was his passport. He just had to lift Fred out of his buggy and stride in, confident and purposeful, trading on his gender instead of feeling incapacitated by it. He looked down at Fred. He was asleep, having nodded off in that sudden and complete way common to babies.

'Freddy,' Leo said to his son, not very loudly.

Fred didn't stir. He had slipped sideways a little, his soft round cheek squashed against the side of the buggy. His fat little hands were completely relaxed on his stomach, which rose and fell evenly under his navy-blue fleece.

Leo looked back at the café. Nobody seemed to have noticed that he was hesitating there. Nobody had looked up from their complete engagement with each other and their children, and observed a lone father hovering – pitiful word, but that's what he was doing –

outside the glazed café door, wearing the expression of, let's face it, a dog hoping for chocolate.

'What shall I do?' Leo said to Fred.

Fred slept on. A small dribble of saliva slid from the corner of his slightly open mouth and ran gently down his chin. Leo bent down, took an elderly tissue from his pocket and wiped Fred's mouth. 'Go or stay,' Leo said to him. 'Up to you.'

Fred's thick eyelashes were completely still on his cheeks. He looked as if waking would be the last thing on his mind for hours to come.

'OK,' Leo said. 'We'll go.'

He turned the buggy. He thought that if Amanda noticed and called out to him, he'd pretend he was only leaving because Fred was asleep. But she didn't. Nobody had seen him there, and nobody noticed him leaving. He was seized by a sudden urge to run, pushing the buggy ahead of him at tremendous speed as if he was being pursued.

Fred slept peacefully on. When they reached home, Leo left him strapped in his buggy in the hall and went down to the basement to make coffee. The need to make coffee suddenly seemed to be tremendously urgent; he needed to make it carefully and deliberately, and to heat milk in the microwave, which he could then painstakingly froth up with the special little gadget Ashley had put in his Christmas stocking. Ashley. He hadn't actually thought of Ashley throughout this – this *episode*. What would Ashley think of him, wimping out on a perfectly friendly invitation just because he was out of his male comfort zone for the first time, in this new chapter that he had been instrumental in starting? Would she be sympathetic? Would she be woman-to-man indulgent? Or would she simply think that his behaviour was, well, lamentable? Leo's father, who was an ardent racing man, would describe him as having fallen at the first fence. And the first fence had been nothing daunting, in itself.

Leo carried his meticulously made coffee to the sofa where they all sat to watch television. The cushions were still dented from the previous evening, and although Leo had determined not to be any more precious about the house than he was about food, the sight of the crushed and flattened cushions, scattered with crumpled sheets of the *Evening Standard* brought home by Ashley the night before, was disheartening. They looked as he felt – distinctly ashamed of them-selves.

He sat down, his elbows on his knees, holding his mug of coffee. He looked at the foam on the top – the foam he had made. It lay in an even, light blanket, the edges just touched with coffee colour. He thought of how he had felt at the weekend, how confident he had been, especially with Grace, telling her in a forthright manner how she must conduct herself in future, stand up for her talents, stand up to her mother and her older sister, support Ashley in getting due recognition. He shut his eyes. What a load of cobblers, he told himself, what bullshit; who did I think I was kidding? Do this, do that to Grace, and three days later you're too chicken to walk into a café full of mothers, even though Fred gives you the perfect excuse.

He bent his head, sucked at the foam blanket. He would not, he thought, tell Ashley about this morning. He would, in fact, tell nobody. His only witness, luckily, had been asleep, and, in any case, couldn't talk. He would be cheery with Amanda when he saw her at nursery-school pick-up that day, and pretend he'd had an appointment that prevented him from coming, and then he'd make a firm date to join them all next Wednesday. By next Wednesday, he would have obliterated the memory of today and tidied it away to the back of his mind as one of those beginner's mistakes that could happen to anyone.

He looked round the room. Breakfast still lay sprawled messily across the table, and he knew a tangle of bedlinen had been dumped on the floor in front of the washing machine, but not yet put in. That meant the beds upstairs were awaiting clean sheets, and, while he was up there, he should really sort out the bathroom. He took another noisy slurp of coffee. Trouble was, he thought, he didn't feel like doing any of it. In fact, he felt an enormous resistance to doing any of the domestic chores that needed to be done before it was time to collect Maisie, a resistance that surprised him by its strength. He hadn't made any allowance for the loneliness of his determinedly chosen new domestic role. Or the repetitiveness or the banality. He had longed to be welcomed in among those young women, and had been ashamed of the longing, ashamed to demonstrate it. Had he, he wondered, elected to do something he was actually going to fail at, as he had failed at so many things before?

There was a wail from the hallway upstairs. Fred was awake. Domestic life, said the wail, did not allow for options. And it was entirely oblivious to gender.

CHAPTER THIRTEEN

'No,' Grace said, 'I'm not coming with you.'

Jasper tried again. 'Just to introduce us. Just that first moment—'

Grace was checking that she'd got her keys and her phone and other essentials, her head bent over her bag. 'No,' she repeated. 'No, Pa. I've held your hand all the way up here and got you this far. Now you have to do the next bit. He won't bite you.'

Jasper looked at Grace's car keys, which she had pushed towards him on her kitchen counter. He said, 'But I can't promise not to bite *him*.'

'Go right ahead, then.'

'You're no help.'

'But I *am*,' Grace said. 'I'm whatever that thing is, in physics. A catalyst?'

'I'm no good at confrontation,' Jasper said. 'You know that.'

Grace slung her bag on her shoulder. She said remorselessly, 'You managed yesterday. Talking to Ma, telling her what you were doing.'

Jasper sighed. 'I was still quite cross, yesterday.'

'Stay cross for today, then.'

He glanced at her. 'No relenting then?'

'No,' she said for the third time. '*No*. None.'

And then she gave the car keys another nudge. 'Come on, Pa. Drive me to work and then go on to Trentham Gardens. He's expecting you.'

And that, Jasper thought, driving west out of Stoke, was an added burden. To have surprised an unwanted and historically despised father-in-law would have given Jasper the upper hand. To have him waiting instead, with time to prepare his reactions, was quite another matter. But Grace had insisted. Grace had rung her grandfather and informed him that her father was coming out to Trentham Gardens, and Morris had said he'd be in the workshop at the garden centre that Jeff's boss had found for him. She'd said he'd sounded unperturbed, but that he was like that anyway, rolling with the punches, going with the flow. Jasper had said distastefully, 'You almost sound as if you approve of him,' and Grace had replied, 'I don't. But there are bits of him I seem to be able to tolerate,' which Jasper had found peculiarly irritating. He realized he wanted to be backed up in his lifelong conviction that Morris had defaulted on every area of any self-respecting man's life.

Susie had been baffling on the phone, as well. She had sounded as if she was relieved that Jasper was taking the initiative over meeting Morris, but simultaneously both anxious and angry that he was doing any such thing.

Jasper had said at one point, 'Are you actually asking me not to?'

And she had said hastily, 'No. No, not at all. I just wish . . .'

'What do you wish?'

'I just wish,' she'd said maddeningly, 'that all this didn't have to happen.'

'For God's sake!' he'd shouted, and then there'd been silence, and he'd thought she might be crying and was just about to say something else, something gentler, when she'd said unexpectedly and in a much calmer voice, 'Thank you for doing this, Jas,' and he was left to grapple with yet another switch of mood.

'You drive me crazy,' he said to her. 'Do you know that?'

'Yes,' she said, sounding not in the least contrite.

'*Crazy.*'

'Thank you, Jas,' Susie said, her voice suddenly full of warmth. '*Thank* you.'

They were thanks he could not quite believe in, even

now, five minutes away from his destination. They were more about her own relief than ongoing thankfulness, as Susie's gratitude so often exasperatingly was. But he went on craving her appreciation, all the same, as he went on wanting to relieve her, please her. He got something out of doing things for her – he must do, mustn't he? Why else would he be on this absurd errand to meet someone whose failings had coloured Jasper's life, as well as the lives of all those he held most dear, for as long as he could remember? He swore softly under his breath. His daughters thought, however fondly, that he was a doormat. They thought he let their mother wipe her feet on him. Well, his relationship with Susie was not actually any of their business, however much they considered that it was. But Morris was another matter. When it came to feet-wiping, Jasper was going to make it very plain who would be on the receiving end. And it wouldn't be him.

The garden centre had a patchily gravelled car park, largely made up of shallow puddles. Jasper parked Grace's car close to the entrance and climbed out, avoiding the adjacent puddle with difficulty.

'SPRING BEDDING PLANTS!' an amateurishly written sign said, next to the doorway. 'EASTER HANGING BASKETS!'

Jasper pushed open the door to a sizeable but gloomy shed-like building, full of earthy smells and the piped sound of Dean Martin singing 'That's Amore'. Morris had said to walk right down the centre, past the seed racks and the outdoor furniture, through the double doors, to turn right and then left, and he'd be there at the end, by all the rainwater butts. Jasper looked round. There appeared to be nobody there, not a customer nor a salesperson. In front of him were displays of begonias and African violets in pots, and beyond them, a few dispirited orchids above a neglected plastic pool of water, shaped like a shell.

Jasper set off down the room. Dean Martin sang nonchalantly on and water from an electrically pumped fountain splashed irregularly into the plastic shell. Beyond it, elaborate wrought-iron furniture was grouped under a green canvas parasol, and on one of the tables were several charming wooden bird houses, painted in pale subtle colours that Susie would have approved of, next to a notice which read, *'Unique bird houses from Bali. Commissions taken. Prices on request.'* Beside them was a plastic parrot in a cage, a purple orchid and a pair of heart-shaped sunglasses. Those, then, were Morris's bird houses, marketed as deemed appropriate for the local community. Susie, Jasper thought, would have a fit.

He pushed through the double doors and turned right, then left, as instructed, along a cracked concrete path that ran past rows of shrubs in pots, tied to yellow

270

canes. At the end of the path was a small wooden structure, once perhaps a prototype summerhouse, with a half-glazed door set between two diamond-paned windows. Through the glass, Jasper could see an old man sitting at a workbench, with long white hair tied back at the base of his skull with a length of tinsel. He was dressed in various knitted layers and his feet, clad in powder-blue socks, were thrust into striped canvas espadrilles with the backs trodden down. He was bent over a piece of plywood, a fretsaw in his hand. To his surprise, Jasper could hear jazz playing nearby. He stood there, watching, uncertain what to do, and even more uncertain as to what he was feeling. And then, as if conscious of being watched, the old man raised his head and saw Jasper. For a few long seconds they looked at each other, not smiling. And then the old man put down everything he was holding, rose to his feet, shuffled across the bare floor to the door and opened it. The jazz was suddenly louder. He gave Jasper a tentative smile.

'Hello, son,' Morris said.

The atmosphere in the factory, Neil thought, was always different when Susie was there. It was the same kind of difference that had prevailed in the kitchen of his childhood when his mother was at home, a sense of everything being settled and safe and reliable,

271

underpinned with the best kind of quiet energy. As a boy, he had disliked being at home if his mother wasn't there. These days, thirty years later, he felt much the same, if in a more detached way, about the factory. It was always busy, always absorbing, but if Susie was somewhere in the building, it was better. She gave the place authority. In fact, although a staunch non-believer, he would go so far as to say that Susie conferred on the factory, quite without meaning to, a kind of blessing.

He was aware that everyone who worked in the factory felt it, to some extent. Susie knew everyone by name, after all, and their family situations, and often about their dogs and cats as well as their children. Even the most traditional men, doing the most traditionally male jobs in the factory, like casting, or operating the kilns and the blungers, had succumbed to the particular – and surprising – charm of working for a woman; or, as Neil put it to himself, the charm of working for this particular woman. She might never have thrown a pot in her life, but she was Staffordshire born and Stoke bred, and she had endeared herself to the whole workforce with her egalitarian views on employment and now by buying a cottage out at Barlaston. Some of them had been out to look at the Parlour House, and the general view was that it was pretty but modest. The modesty was much approved of. With her money –

always perceived as some fabulous amount – it was said she could have aspired to the pedimented grandeur of Barlaston Park. But no. She had chosen a cottage, and, what's more, a cottage with family connections. Her great-granddad had delivered the churns of milk to the dairy there, back in the day. She might own a factory now, but she was only three generations away from a farm labourer in Barlaston. You could tell that, some of them said, by looking at her hands. They were the kind of hands familiar to everyone in the factory: hands that were used to doing things, useful hands. When she'd shown some of the decorators how to hand-letter the christening and children's mugs which had been bestsellers now for well over a decade, they'd all marvelled at her deftness. She could draw, she could design, she had bought a factory and built a business. And when she was in the building, there was a definite feeling that those two hundred and twenty souls working there were somehow a family.

Which was why, Neil supposed, he always felt a small lurch of disappointment if she cancelled a visit. She tried not to, he knew that, and there was usually a good reason, to do with the demands of the London office. But not this time. This Tuesday, Neil had expected to see her, and the factory, too, had had an air of anticipation, like children grouped ready for their mother's mildly exciting return, and then Susie had rung to say she couldn't, as it happened, make it till later in the week.

'Sorry,' she said. 'So sorry.'

Neil had waited for her to explain. He said, to give her an opening, 'Everything OK?'

'Oh yes,' she said, as if nothing could ever be anything but OK. 'Everything's fine.'

He waited again.

There was an unnaturally long pause. Then Susie said, 'I'll probably see you Thursday. Friday, for definite.'

'I rather wanted to talk to you about—'

'Not now,' Susie said. 'Sorry, Neil.'

She'd rung off. Not abruptly, but decidedly. She would not be in Stoke until the end of the week, and the design for the coffee-shop chain's special order was proving problematic. He could solve the problem himself, of course, but she didn't like him to do that, she didn't like any changes to be made without her personal sanction. The order had to go out in ten days' time, and if she wasn't going to be in Stoke until Friday, that was three working days lost out of seven. Well, it would be up to him to manage a fast turnaround; but he would, all the same, have given a great deal to know what was keeping Susie in London.

'Neil,' someone said, from his office doorway.

He looked up from his computer screen. Grace was standing there, a huge grey scarf looped round her neck, and her bag on her shoulder. She looked – well, she looked much better. Great, in fact. He stood up, smiling. 'I thought the family'd deserted us—'

'No,' she said, 'you've just got different members of the cast.' She hitched her bag more firmly on to her shoulder. 'My dad's here,' she said. 'He's just seeing my – grandpa.'

'Wouldn't it be strange,' Morris said, 'me sleeping where my old granddad used to come to work every day?'

Jasper was standing three feet away from him, in the small sitting room of the Parlour House, his hands shoved into his coat pockets and his collar turned up. He said gruffly, 'I don't know what she sees in this place.'

'It wouldn't be anything you could see,' Morris said mildly.

Jasper grunted. The cottage felt unremarkable to him, chilly and damp and undistinguished. He didn't feel in the mood to be imaginative, let alone appreciative. In fact, he felt thoroughly wrong-footed, and by an old man he had determined to detest, but from the first word, Morris hadn't allowed himself to be comfortably detestable, and that, to Jasper's current frame of mind, was unforgivable. It was unbearable, right now, for the myth not to manifest itself as a monster.

'She probably sees history here,' Morris said, looking

275

at the pink glass chandelier. 'Or she thinks she does. She's made a romance out of history – out of family history. She's made something out of nothing, because she likes it that way. The past is always safer, because it's over.'

Jasper shrugged himself deeper into his coat. He said, trying to antagonize Morris, 'She isn't romancing family history. She adored her grandparents. She owes them everything.'

Morris nodded. He shifted his gaze from the light fitting to his son-in-law. 'Yes,' he said. 'She does.'

'Without them—'

'Yes,' Morris said again. 'I know. She was the child they always wanted. She fitted them. Hand in glove.'

Jasper walked across to the window and looked out at the rough little garden. There were a few celandines in the grass by now, and a blue spear or two of grape hyacinth. He debated what to say next, what other long-overdue accusations he could justifiably throw at Morris.

Then Morris said, without rancour, 'My old dad loved Susan as much as he couldn't stand me.'

Jasper waited a moment, then said, his back to Morris, 'So that's your excuse, then?'

'No,' Morris said equably. 'But you could say it was my reason.'

'For abandoning your child?'

'We didn't see it that way. And even if you'd like to pick a fight with me, I still don't.'

Jasper turned round. He said, 'I don't want a fight. But I want you to know what a shit I think you are.'

Morris looked completely unruffled. 'I'm a nuisance,' he said amicably, 'but I'm not worse than that. I was a young man. I was – well, stuck with a girl, a sweet girl, but only a girl, who I'd married because she was pregnant. I couldn't be a fraction of what my dad wanted me to be, and my mother always took his side. So it seemed to me to be best if I just cleared off. Just got out of everyone's hair and took poor Stella with me, because she could hardly manage herself, let alone a baby. So we left the baby to be managed properly, as you would see it. To be fed and cared for and disciplined and educated like you're supposed to do with a child. Stella couldn't manage it, and neither could I, with Stella, and with things with my dad like they were.' He paused and then he said, 'And I didn't have the nerve to come back. Or to ask Susan to come to us. Living hand-to-mouth in not much more than a shack on a beach. A remittance man. A good-for-nothing remittance man, my old dad said.'

Jasper said steadily, 'Is any of that supposed to make what you did any better?'

Morris looked entirely undisconcerted. 'Of course not. I didn't tell you because I wanted to be whitewashed.

277

I just told you how it was. How it came about. I can't change the past. I can't change who I was. Any more, son, than you can.'

'Don't call me son.'

'Suit yourself,' Morris said. 'I could call you lad, like my old dad called me when I was still too small to have disappointed him yet.'

'My name is Jasper.'

Morris grinned. 'What a label to hang round any kid's neck.'

Jasper said furiously, 'You are so bloody infuriating—'

Morris held up a hand, its palm towards Jasper. 'Peace, lad. Peace. I told you I was a nuisance.'

'Too fucking right.'

Morris lowered his hand and put it in the pocket of his strange outer garment. He said, 'We shouldn't fight. We're on the same side as far as Susan and the girls are concerned.'

'*My* girls.'

'I know that.'

'My girls,' Jasper said, 'who are all stressed out about what to do with *you*.'

Morris looked round the room. He said, 'If it'd help Susan to have me live here, I'll do it. I'll do whatever helps her. But if I was left to myself, I wouldn't choose here.'

Jasper eyed him. 'What d'you mean?'

'I mean,' Morris said, 'that I only came back here because I knew it's where I'd find Susan. But I don't want to be here. I don't want to be in Stoke, or even in Staffordshire. This place has bad memories for me, bad vibes. I'd be happy to be anywhere but here.'

Jasper crossed the room and leant against a wall. He said, 'I thought you liked your billet with Grace's boy-friend. I thought as long as you had bed, board and no responsibilities, that was fine by you.'

Morris sighed. He took his hand out of his pocket and looked at it, turning it over and inspecting the back, where bluish veins stood out like miniature tree roots. 'I was getting out of Grace's hair. I read all the runes wrong, so I did what I always do. Made myself scarce.'

'I thought Jeff offered.'

'He did,' Morris said. 'He wants to get back into Grace's good books. But she shouldn't let him.'

'It's none of your business.'

Morris said quietly, still looking at his hands, 'She's my granddaughter.'

Jasper took his shoulder away from the wall. He said, 'Only in name.'

Slowly Morris raised his head and regarded his son-in-law. He put both his hands back in his pockets. He said, 'If you could get over your temper with me, we might get somewhere.'

Jasper wandered back to the window and stared out. He said mulishly, 'There's nowhere to get.'

Morris waited. Then he shuffled across the room and stood beside Jasper, looking out at the garden. He said, 'As long as I'm still breathing, lad, I'm afraid that there is. I'm here. I exist, and no amount of wishing I didn't on your part or mine is going to make any difference. I had a bad childhood here, but I know that's no excuse in your eyes for what I did later. But I did, it's done, and Susan's a marvel in spite of it – or *because* of it, neither of us will ever know. But if you could stop using all your energy telling me how atrocious a father you think I've been, we might have a chance of making my existence easier for Susan. And that's what we both want, don't we?'

'If I fancy someone,' Michelle said over her shoulder to Grace, 'I'll forgive them pretty well anything.'

Grace was at her computer. The drawings of wellington boots her mother had sent up were not, of course, compatible with the standard leg lengths or widths of the manufacturer who was interested in using their designs. The company was English, but the boots themselves were made in China, inevitably. What Susie wanted could be made closer to home – in France, as it happened, by a superior company who offered eight calf widths for every shoe size, but the figures made no sense, even if they agreed to take Susie's designs. The English company was cheaper, less specialized, and resistant to some of Susie's design requests. There were battles ahead. She said distantly in reply, 'I don't fancy Jeff.'

'Yes, you do,' Michelle said. 'You'd have to be off another planet not to. *I* do. Ben does. Don't you, Ben?'

Ben gave no indication he had even heard her. Michelle went on, 'Ben's pretending not to hear me.'

'Get back to work,' Grace said.

'I am working. I'm just talking while I work. I have the spec of the new cat design just about there. Ben wouldn't eat any of Jeff's chocolate truffles because Ben wants to stay slim and lovely for someone just like Jeff, don't you, Ben?'

'Don't answer her,' Grace said. 'Ignore her. Shut your offensive mouth.'

Ben said, 'The cat design doesn't look right on the dinner plates. It's too big. Maybe just the rim—'

'I ate the whole box,' Michelle said. 'They were amazing. I allowed myself two a day. I'd rather have had Jeff, though.'

'Have him,' Grace said.

Michelle turned round from her screen. She said, 'You're joking.'

'No, she's not,' Ben said.

'I'm not.'

'But he's part of the family! Your granddad's living there—'

'That's neither here nor there.'

Michelle got up from her chair. 'I bet Jeff thinks it is.'

'Well, he's wrong.'

Michelle came across to Grace's computer. She said, 'What's got into you?'

'Resolve,' Ben said. 'Unlike you. Anybody's for a box of chocolates.'

'Jeff isn't anybody.'

'He's nobody,' Ben said. 'Being hot isn't enough, in the long run.'

'What would you know?'

Ben turned round. He said, 'Look at Grace.'

'I am.'

'How does she look?'

Michelle considered. Then she said, 'OK, actually.'

'Not like she did a month ago?'

'Can I join in?' Grace said.

'Not yet,' Ben said. He looked at Michelle. 'Grace looks better?'

'Sort of – yeah, she does.'

'No Jeff for most of the time,' Ben said. 'All kinds of upsets, like her granddad, but not much date time with Jeff.'

Michelle said to Grace, 'Are you just going to let him nick your boyfriend?'

Grace stared at her screen in silence.

Ben said slightly scornfully, 'Jeff's straight.'

Michelle bent closer to Grace. She said, 'You're never going to dump him. Lose the fittest man in Stoke and put your own grandfather out on the street?'

Grace didn't turn. She moved her computer mouse to adjust something. Then she said, 'If you don't get back to work, you'll find there isn't any work to get back to.'

Michelle gave a yelp of laughter. 'Who says?'

Grace glanced up at her. She wasn't smiling. 'I do,' she said.

There was a sudden and faintly alarming silence.

'Wow,' Michelle said.

'Goodness,' Susie said. 'Are you still here?'

Ashley was at her computer in an otherwise empty office. Cara and Dan had left half an hour ago, saying that they were going to the gym.

Ashley didn't look up. 'It was a Bicester day,' she said. 'I only got back at four.'

'And?'

'Good,' Ashley said. 'We did a spring-sale mailshot for Bicester, and their sales were up eight per cent last week. Six mugs for the price of five shifted over three hundred.'

'Excellent,' Susie said. 'Well done. That was a good sale catalogue.'

Ashley focussed on her screen to turn it off. 'Ma?'

'Yes?'

'I want to talk to you about catalogues, actually.'

'I rather wanted,' Susie said, 'to talk to *you* about your father.'

Ashley looked up at her. 'Why? What's he done?'

Susie perched on the edge of Ashley's desk. 'I think it's what *I*'ve done. Or haven't done.'

'In what way?'

'Grace has taken him up to Stoke with her. To meet Morris and see the cottage. They only rang to tell me once they were on the train. And they don't seem to think they're the ones in the wrong. I feel hurt, and I'm puzzled.'

Ashley leant back and folded her arms. She said sympathetically, 'Oh, Ma.'

Susie said, 'It's so weird, being in Radders with no one there except a sulking parrot who won't even look at me.'

'Why didn't you say? Why didn't you come round to ours?'

Susie fiddled with a pencil lying on Ashley's desk. 'I don't seem to feel very fit for company. I didn't want to talk about it, somehow. It made me feel a bit – wobbly. But I'm certain, at the same time. I mean certain about the business.'

'Pa did need to meet Morris.'

'I know.'

'And see the cottage.'

'He'll hate it,' Susie said. 'And he'll hate Morris. It's an awful idea, it's a disaster. I don't know what got into Grace. I can't think why she didn't tell me.'

Ashley looked straight ahead at her blank screen. She said, 'I wouldn't have told you, either. And I think she's right. You can't control everything. You can't just connect with Pa when it suits you.'

There was a pause. Then Susie said, 'He likes his own life. He likes his freedom as much as I do.'

Ashley looked at her watch. 'Ma, I should go. Do you want to continue this in the car?'

Susie got off the desk. 'Not the way it seems to be going, no.'

'You mean my not instantly agreeing with you?'

Susie said sadly, 'It's more complicated than that. I wanted your father uncontaminated by Morris, for one thing.'

Ashley began to drop things into her handbag. 'He's not *that* awful!'

'That's not what you thought when we were up in Stoke.'

'I'm getting used to the idea of him. We all are. Anyway, he's . . . having an effect on everyone.'

'That is partly what I'm afraid of,' Susie said.

Ashley stood up. 'I didn't mean that. I meant he's

285

having an effect on our dynamic. We all seem to have moved round in the dance a bit.'

'I know,' Susie said. 'And it isn't good.'

'But it is,' Ashley said. She hoisted her bag on to her shoulder and flipped her laptop shut before sliding it into her workbag.

'Ash?'

'We're – all a bit different,' Ashley said. 'All of us. It's good. Grace. Leo and me.'

'Leo?'

'Looking after the children. Sacking the nanny. Like I told you.'

Susie said faintly, 'Like Pa—'

'No,' Ashley said, 'not like Pa. Things are different now. It's different for men at home these days.'

'Oh.'

'And Ma—'

'What?'

'Another thing,' Ashley said, moving away from her desk. 'While we're talking about change, there's something else Leo and I were discussing. We talked it over with Grace at the weekend. And Cara and Dan think it's a good idea. It's about the children's catalogue.'

'Oh?'

'I think that it should be shot at our house this time. With Maisie and Fred. We need a new setting for the family shots – we've done Radders to death, don't you think?' She reached the door and smiled back at her mother. 'I just thought I'd mention it, so you can think it over. OK?'

Polynesia had not touched the sunflower seeds or the out-of-season blackberries that Susie had left for her that morning. She was at the far end of her perch, against the bars of her cage, staring out of the French windows at the wet garden. She looked smaller somehow, and faintly bedraggled, as if her feathers were damp.

'He'll be home tomorrow,' Susie said. 'He'll be back. Perhaps we'll both have a lot to say to him.'

Polynesia shrank her head down into her neck and closed her eyes.

'Please eat something, at least,' Susie said, indicating the blackberries. 'Don't give him something else to be fed up with me about.'

Polynesia swivelled her head and opened one eye. Then she yawned, showing her little black darting tongue, and closed her eye again.

Susie returned to the kitchen table, where she had left a mug of tea. A feeling, not of liberation, to which she was accustomed, but of isolation was threatening to overwhelm her. It had been coming on stealthily, ever since Jasper had telephoned from the train to Stoke the day before, and the conversation with Ashley had unleashed the final wave of it. Under normal circumstances, her reaction would have been to go up to Stoke immediately, to head straight for the factory and reassure herself of her significance there, her effectiveness, her centrality to the whole purpose and success of the enterprise. But she couldn't do that, not tonight. Jasper was up there, with Grace. Jasper had seen the Parlour House and met Morris, and had neither rung nor texted afterwards. When she had rung him, his phone went straight to voicemail. Grace had answered her phone, but had said that she hadn't seen her father and that she was going out for a drink with Neil before she went home. She'd been as sweet as ever, but had declined to, well, *engage* with her mother, not by being obstructive but merely by being elusive. Ashley was at home with her family. Cara and Dan were at the gym and were then going out for a Chinese. They had suggested Susie join them, but she had felt reluctant to agree. So here she was, in Radipole Road, alone and . . . and lonely. There was no getting away from it. That's what she was. Lonely. She glanced across at the parrot cage.

'Please?' she said again.

CHAPTER FOURTEEN

'Hey!' Leo said in surprise. 'Come on in!'

'I should have rung,' Jasper said.

Leo stood aside, holding the front door open. On the floor behind him, Fred was sitting up on his padded bottom, jiggling excitedly at the sight of his grandfather.

Jasper stooped to pick him up. 'Hi there, Freddy.'

Fred hit him lightly with the plastic brick he was holding.

Leo said, 'What brings you here?'

Jasper took the brick out of Freddy's hand. 'Just passing.'

'Really? Coffee?'

'Please,' Jasper said, and then to Fred, 'You're all dribble.'

'He's teething,' Leo said. 'Poor Fred.'

Jasper kissed his grandson's forehead. 'Poor little sod. Hard to find a dry bit to kiss.'

Leo went ahead of Jasper down the basement stairs at speed, calling over his shoulder, ''Scuse the mess!'

'Can't see it.'

'I decided I'd get resentful if I tidied up all the time.'

Jasper came carefully down the stairs behind him, carrying Fred. He said, 'Resentful of Ashley?'

'Well, it might have manifested itself like that. And I didn't want it to,' said Leo.

Jasper reached the bottom of the stairs and stooped to set Fred down. 'Have your brick back now, Freddy.'

Fred turned away, ignoring the proffered brick, and began to crawl rapidly towards the television.

'He wants the remote,' Leo said. 'What is it about buttons and sockets and switches and kids?'

'I think,' Jasper said, 'it's just a reaction to always being given what society thinks is age appropriate. At any age.'

'Kettle or machine?'

'Kettle. I like a big cafetière of the old-fashioned stuff.'

Leo carried the kettle to the sink, stepping over the toys and clothes on the floor. He said, 'I drink so much coffee-shop coffee these days.'

Jasper was watching Fred pull himself up on the low table by the television. He said affectionately, 'You boys together. Always out.'

'Actually,' Leo said, 'it's our new social circle.' He put the kettle back on its power pad and switched it on. 'Maisie's school mothers.'

'Yummy mummies?'

'Only some of them,' Leo said.

They both laughed.

'Good for you.'

'Actually,' Leo said again, 'I made a bad start. I just kind of funked even talking to them. But I did a coffee-shop thing the other day, and it was weird but it was OK in the end. In fact, I quite liked it.'

Jasper moved to retrieve the remote control from Fred. He said casually, 'Is that dangerous?'

Fred roared.

Jasper put the DVD control into his hand instead. 'I imagine the DVD isn't switched on?'

'No,' Leo said. 'And no to the other, as well. I'm not in the market for straying.'

Fred thumped down into a sitting position, clutching the second remote.

'Sorry,' Jasper said.

'It's OK.'

'I'm just always a bit sensitive about – well, you know, I'm Ashley's father.'

'And I'm her husband. I suggested this arrangement.'

Jasper looked up. He said, 'I shouldn't have said what I did . . .'

'No. I'm not a cliché, Jas. Any more than you are. I'm not out to punish Ashley for earning more than I ever will. I'm just trying to get the hang of keeping the domestic show on the road.'

There was a small silence, broken only by the bubbling of the kettle. Then Leo said, 'You OK?'

Jasper made a face. 'Yes and no.'

The kettle switched itself off. Leo rummaged in a cupboard for mugs, his back to his father-in-law. He said, 'Want to talk about it?'

'Not really.'

'Suit yourself. How was Stoke?'

There was a further silence. Jasper sat down on the low table next to Fred, who was frowning at the remote and determinedly pressing its buttons. Then he said, with deliberate energy, 'It was good. I went round the factory. I haven't been round the factory in five years. It was amazing how many of the same people are still there – same old faces. Lovely, really. I found myself promising to go and do a gig up there some time. Of course, there's a worry about the future, about the skills gap. The girl apprentices will stay on the whole, but they have awful trouble keeping the boys. They'll do three or four mornings and then they won't get up. They can't take the discipline of an early start – it's easier to stay on benefits than get up at five in the morning and learn a skill.'

Leo carried the cafetière and a couple of mugs over to the table where Jasper was sitting. Fred looked up at his approach and grunted urgently.

'What's up with you, Freddy?' said Jasper.

'He wants a biscuit,' Leo said. 'Coffee for us means a biscuit for him. He thinks.'

'Can he have one?'

'No. He can have a carrot or an apple.'

Jasper looked down at his grandson. 'Poor old Freddy.'

Leo said, 'What about the cottage?'

Freddy gave an experimental roar. Leo went across to the fridge, opened it and took out a packet of carrot sticks. He extracted one and held it out to Fred. Fred looked outraged and glared at his grandfather. Leo said, 'It's all you're getting.'

'Wow,' Jasper said to Fred. 'Tough old daddy love.'

Fred began to wail.

'Ignore him,' Leo said. He put the carrots back in the fridge. 'Bring your coffee over to the big table.' He picked up the coffee pot and his own mug. 'What did you think of Susie's cottage?'

Jasper followed him, leaving Fred indignantly on the floor by the television. He said carefully, 'Her vision. Her need. Her thing, you know.'

'So you didn't like it?'

'I'm no good outside a city. I can't see rural potential.'

'So you didn't like it,' Leo repeated.

Jasper shifted his mug, not looking at his son-in-law. 'Not my thing. No, I suppose I didn't.'

'Nor did Ashley,' Leo said, 'if that's any comfort.'

Jasper was still staring at his coffee mug. He said, 'I don't want to fan flames.'

'So you'll say nothing? To Susie?'

'Not sure yet.'

Leo got up from his chair and went to stoop over his son and fish something from his mouth. He held it up. 'A hazelnut. Where did he find a hazelnut, for God's sake? We haven't had hazelnuts in the house since Christmas. Jas, what have you come to say?'

Jasper gave his coffee a nudge. He said, 'I was getting to that.'

'It's taking you a bloody long time.'

'I've got a suggestion . . .'

'Have you? For me?'

'Well, yes.'

Leo came back to the table and sat down, dropping the hazelnut into a nearby bowl left over from breakfast. He said, 'Come on!'

Jasper turned his head slowly and looked at him. 'You might think I'm off my trolley.'

'Try me.'

'Brace yourself,' Jasper said. 'It's about Morris.'

Cara lay on the sofa in the sitting-room part of their large open-plan flat. It was an Italian sofa, which she and Dan had spent as much time researching and sourcing as they had his bike. It was angular and sleek,

294

upholstered in soft dark-blue fabric, with brushed-steel legs, and it was long enough for Dan to lie on although he was more than six feet tall. So Cara could stretch out quite flat, as she was now, her head on a cushion, staring out at the twilight sky visible behind the roofs and chimney pots of the houses behind their block of flats. It was a greyish-mauve sky, without stars, and every few minutes an aeroplane crossed it, surprisingly slowly, with winking red and white lights and a roar of engine noise subdued by double glazing.

Dan was out. He was having yet another meeting with the management consultancy – oiled this time by alcohol. The man who had started the consultancy had been a colleague of Dan's in their early years at a major chainstore, so there was the advantage of mutual liking and respect, and the disadvantage of embarrassment over the number of delays and cancellations there'd been in arranging meetings with Susie Sullivan pottery. Dan had first approached Rick about how to expand the company, as well as rebranding it – this being Rick's new area of expertise – without losing core customers or the integrity of the initial vision. The company, Dan felt, was stuck. Not irrevocably, but halted at a crossroads. He had wanted Cara to go with him for a drink with Rick that evening, but she had said that he should go alone.

'Because you think it would be better if it was just

me and him?' Dan had said. 'Or because you don't want to?'

Cara had hesitated. Then she'd said, 'Both, actually.'

Dan had opened his mouth to protest.

'Please,' Cara had said, holding her hands up, as if at gunpoint. 'Don't push me, don't ask me. Just go. Give him my love.'

Dan had leant forward and kissed her cheek. 'OK.'

'Thank you.'

He'd regarded her. 'You all right?'

She'd nodded. 'I'm fine. I'll be fine.'

'I'll pick up something on my way back. Chinese?'

Cara had smiled at him. 'Japanese,' she said, and then again, 'Thank you.'

So, here she was, on the sofa, Laura Marling on the iPod, green tea cooling in a mug beside her. Her mother was in town, as was Ashley. Grace was back in Stoke, with their father. She had no impulse to ring any of them; no desire to. She didn't even, she realized, have any curiosity about them, about what the current difficulty was between her parents, or what her father had made of Morris or the Parlour House, or what Leo felt about being a house husband, or the state of Grace's love life. It wasn't that she didn't care. It was more, right then and there, lying on the sofa with Laura Marling singing softly in her ear, that she couldn't reach caring. It was as if, just for the moment, she was detached from all of them, like a helium balloon that's escaped its tether and gone bobbing up into the clouds, above all the busyness. I can see them all, Cara thought, but I can't hear them. And it isn't bothering me.

Very occasionally, in childhood and adolescence, she had felt like that. In the middle of the hubbub of family life – in the middle, even, of organizing her sisters' lives, which she had always been renowned for – she had suddenly felt detachment drop on her like a magic invisible cloak, distancing her from everything that was going on. When she was very young it had slightly frightened her, but she grew to tolerate and then to welcome it, this feeling of stepping out of the heat and din and action into a cool, calm place where one could just unaffectedly *be*. Her mother, for all her remarkable energy, could always create that effect, it seemed, just with her presence. The house would be in uproar, all those years ago – full of all of them, full of schoolfriends, full of music – and Susie would return, slam the door behind her, shout 'Home!' and the whirling kaleidoscope would still, and order would return.

Cara turned her head and looked at her mug. If she were to drink some tea, it would mean rearing up from the cushion to a sitting position, taking out her earphones, and reaching for the mug. From where she lay, that whole procedure just seemed to be too much trouble. She was quite content without tea, anyway; quite content just to lie there and think about drinking it sometime soon, when the prospect of sitting up seemed less of an effort.

She had loved it when her mother was at home, loved it to the point of craving it. When she was a child, she had always longed for Susie's return, and felt an immediate settling of internal anxieties once she was back. But as adolescence dawned, so did a whole range of new feelings – feelings that were very much less docile and manageable. She had felt fury and resentment towards this other, clearly imperative element in Susie's life, which presented such an irresistible alternative to the family. Her early teens were spent in a turmoil of hotly defending Susie in public, while raging at her in private: raging at her mother finding anything more compelling than her children; raging at what she saw as the bitter, unfair consequence of Susie's choice – namely that she, Cara, as the eldest, had to do so much to compensate for Susie's absences.

Jasper had been wonderful. He really had. He had been the most assiduous of fathers, the most loyal of husbands. Even at her most furious, Cara had known that she would only redouble the injustice of the situation if she took out her rage on him. And to take it out on Susie was simply pointless. Susie was impervious. Smiling, steady, consistently affectionate when around, and unreachable when not, Susie had been impregnable. So Cara, incapable of shaking Susie's implacability about her work–life balance, had retreated to her own occasional detachment. Better in the end, surely, to distance yourself than to bloody your knuckles hammering on a door that would never open.

She remembered thinking, when she was about sixteen, that she hated the very idea of high-achieving women, that she wasn't remotely interested in equal opportunities, and that, given her looks and her determination, she would marry a very rich man and spend her life without needing to prove herself to anyone. But her brain wouldn't, in the end, allow her to surrender to this vision. Her own mental energy and appetite, her own urge for achievement wouldn't let her rest for long in dreamy contemplation of a gilded cage. She found herself with excellent A-level results, and a propelling force in her personality which could only be called ambition.

So here she was, qualified, capable and effective, beached on the expensive Italian sofa that she had paid for out of money she had earned. The same could be said of the shoes kicked off on the floor beside the sofa and all the technology that lay within her reach – all those screens and gadgets of communication – as well as the copper pans hanging over in the kitchen, and indeed the very flat itself. She had taken advantage of everything that her mother had offered, and had harnessed her own talents to those considerable opportunities, to great effect. She had brought Dan into the company – possibly the best thing that had ever happened to the business, after Susie herself – and between them, they were responsible for most of the innovation and growth that had got the company to where it was today.

She shifted a little. The sky through the big window was now dark and reddish, the planes distinguishable only by their wing- and tail-lights and the peculiar high roar of their engines. Dan would be back soon, bringing those crackling translucent bags that the local Japanese takeaway packed their fragrant food into, and with him would come news of his meeting and the accompanying resultant energy, as well as affirmation of their chosen view of the future. Dan's return would be both reassuring and confirming. And it might signal a new start for Cara, something of a breakthrough. It came to her, with a little thrill of excitement, that she might be able to let go of being constantly angry with Susie, if she didn't work alongside her any more.

Jeff had persuaded Grace to go for a meal with him in a local pub. She had demurred at the prospect of dinner, but had agreed to lunch, and maybe also a walk, since the pub he had chosen was in a country park, on a canal, and was quite difficult to find. He said it was a great pub, serving real ale. Grace said she wasn't interested in beer, he knew that, and he said he'd only mentioned it to give her a flavour of the place, to emphasize its individuality.

The pub was brick-built and in a complicated location, with a tree-covered hill behind, a canal and a railway line in front, and a crowded car park. Jeff said they could go for a walk, and then come back for a drink and a bite of lunch when there weren't so many people.

Grace said, 'It's going to rain.'

Jeff was wearing walking boots and a tan suede bomber jacket that Grace didn't recognize. It was the wrong colour for him. Too gingery. And his hair needed cutting. He pulled a huge commercial umbrella out of the Nissan Pixo and flourished it at her. 'All prepared!'

Grace sat in the open doorway of the passenger seat, with her feet on the tarmac. She said, 'Jeff, I don't really want to go for a walk.'

He lowered the umbrella to the ground and leant on it, as if it were a walking stick. He said, 'Do you mean with me?'

Grace gestured at the parked cars all round her. She said, 'I don't want all this. I don't want today to be a – a *date*.'

'Then why,' Jeff said slowly, 'did you agree to come?'

She looked up at him. She was wearing a cotton scarf like a headband, subduing her hair. She said, 'You badgered me. You went on and on at me till I said yes. I shouldn't have.'

'*I see,*' Jeff said.

'Do you?'

'You give in, you agree, because you haven't got the guts to tell the truth. Ever. Have you?'

Grace pushed her scarf back an inch. 'I was planning to tell you in the pub. In a public place. I don't want to be in a country park with you – I want to be where there are other people.'

Jeff gave a snort. 'Am I that scary?'

'No,' Grace said. 'It's just easier for you not to lose your temper when there are other people about.'

Jeff leant on the umbrella and squinted up at the sky. He said, 'Here's me, doing your family quite a favour, because one member of it – *not* your granddad – means a good deal to me, and all the time, this particular person is planning to dump me in the public bar of a busy pub on a Saturday lunchtime.'

'It's no surprise to you,' Grace said. 'Don't pretend it is. And I never asked you to take Morris in.'

'Extraordinary how nothing is ever your fault.'

'Yes, it is,' Grace said. 'Doing nothing is. Appeasing

and placating and giving in is. I didn't want to come out with you today, but I thought I ought to. I thought I ought to say we're finished to your face.'

'Are we?' Jeff said, still staring at the sky. '*Finished?*'

'Yes, we are.'

'Suppose I don't see it that way?'

'You can't have a relationship with someone if they don't want one back.'

'But you play games with me, Grace. You give me little hints, little chances, and then you turn your back. There's a nasty word for girls like you.'

Grace stood up. She said, 'I'm trying to do the right thing. But you can only ever see things from your own point of view, so doing the right thing is wasted on you. I'm going into the pub to ask them to call me a taxi.'

Jeff held up his hand. 'Wait.'

Grace suppressed a sigh. She was waiting to feel the familiar clutch of fear. It was certainly incipient, somewhere in the pit of her stomach, but it wasn't leaping up her throat yet. She looked at Jeff and said flatly, 'What?'

'I'm not a bully, Grace. I'm not unreasonable. But I have had a lot to put up with. You've messed me about something chronic. On top of all I've had thrown at me ever since I was a kid, I meet someone like you, who only wants to add to everything I'm dealing with already. You're a massive stress, Grace. Massive.'

She waited.

He jabbed at the ground with his umbrella. 'But I happen to think you're worth it. I really do. I think you're a girl in a million.' He smiled at her. 'That's why I took your granddad in.'

Grace opened her mouth to say an instinctive thank-you, and shut it again. Instead she said, 'Morris can come back to my flat tonight.'

Jeff stared at her. He shook his head disbelievingly. 'You are a piece of bloody work. Didn't you hear a word I said?'

Grace went on looking at him in silence.

He said in a different tone, 'Is there someone else?'

She shook her head. 'No.'

'Who were you having a drink with then, the other night?'

'A colleague,' Grace said. 'He manages the factory.'

'It's pretty sad, your life, isn't it?' Jeff said. 'If it isn't work, it's family. And as family *is* work, that's all it ever is.'

Grace moved a step or two away. 'I'm going into the pub.'

He shrugged. 'I won't stop you.'

'And you can tell Morris to pack. It's been good of you having him. We all think that.'

'*We,*' he said contemptuously. 'The fucking family again, the royal fucking we.'

'Stop it,' Grace said.

'Make me.'

'I don't want to. I don't want to have anything more to do with you. I just want to say goodbye and I'm sorry that it didn't work out.'

He moved towards the boot of the car, opened it, and threw the umbrella inside. He said wearily, 'Get in.'

'No, I—'

'I'll drive you back, Grace.'

'No.'

'Your granddad can stay till he moves to your mum's cottage.'

'No.'

Jeff slammed the boot shut. He didn't look at Grace. He said, more distastefully than angrily, 'Have it your own fucking way.'

She took a huge breath. 'Thank you—'

'I won't stop you,' he said. 'Why would I try to stop you? In fact, what have I ever—' He paused and then he said, 'Just go.'

'I'm going.'

'I just wish—'

'Don't,' Grace said. 'Please.'

He turned his back. Grace began to walk rapidly between the cars towards the pub, feeling in her pocket for her phone. She wouldn't ring a taxi, she thought. She would ring Neil. Neil had said she should get in touch if she was ever stuck, or needed help, or there was anything he could do. He wasn't on a hike that weekend, she knew, so he'd probably be in the factory, doing those strangely attractive weekend rounds in the empty rooms, among the empty work stations, while the kilns hummed on like the factory's heartbeat. And if he was in the factory, perhaps he wouldn't mind coming out to Consall, or wherever she was, and driving her back to Stoke.

As she reached the pub entrance, a car roared out of the car park behind her; Jeff's Nissan Pixo, being driven as if it were a Ferrari. She watched it for a few seconds, careering down the lane and over the canal, and felt a pang of distaste at how messy their final exchange had been and how badly she had handled it, despite all her new intentions. And, however much she tried to pretend otherwise, there was a small and deeply unpleasant sliver of regret. Was it for Jeff, or just her old friend, habit? She dialled Neil's number and put her phone to her ear. How long did it take to stop missing what was familiar, even if that very familiarity had only been bad for you?

'Grace!' Neil said, his voice warm with surprised pleasure.

She looked down towards the canal. There was a

306

longboat coming slowly towards her with a man and a dog by the tiller and two children waving enthusiastically at the stern.

'Neil,' she said, 'I'm really sorry to interrupt your Saturday, but I've done a bit of a stupid thing.'

CHAPTER FIFTEEN

It was, Ashley noticed with an undeniable sense of achievement, after midnight. Leo had gone upstairs an hour earlier and Maisie, who had found pretexts for three appeals to her parents during the evening, had finally gone to sleep with an abandonment that suggested she had never thought of doing anything else. After Leo had gone to bed, Ashley had spent at least twenty minutes tidying up – picking up toys from the floor, smoothing out the clothes in the ironing basket which had been corrugated by the tumble-dryer, polishing the sink and the taps with wads of kitchen paper.

'Don't do it,' Leo had said earlier. 'Don't waste your energy doing domestic stuff that doesn't matter. Save your energies for work. That's the *deal*, Ash. It's what we agreed.'

Leo had said a very great many things that evening in addition to that remark. In fact, he had startled Ashley with his sheer assertiveness, the force of his opinion. She wasn't used to that. She wasn't used to a Leo who didn't quietly oblige or elude or compromise; she was familiar with a Leo who had always appeared to accommodate other people at almost any cost to himself. In fact, there had been times since Maisie was born when Ashley had wondered if, being so used to her father's capacity for tolerance, she had instinctively chosen a mate who resembled him, at least in this respect. Leo didn't sulk or shout or insist, just as Jasper never had. It might be difficult to motivate him to finish projects – or, as in the case of the so-called garden, even to start them – but there were no flashes of temper or any evidence of a desire to dominate. Which made his pronouncements over supper – a very passable kedgeree that he had even managed to get the children to eat earlier by putting it down in front of them unannounced and subsequently refusing to bargain – all the more extraordinary. He had swallowed a mouthful then said, not looking directly at Ashley, 'I saw your dad yesterday. He came round. And I've agreed that we'll take Morris in – for the moment anyway.'

Ashley had dropped her fork, like someone reacting melodramatically in a movie, scattering grains of rice across the table.

'What?'

Leo had loaded up another forkful, spearing a piece

of fish. He said casually, 'I think Jasper rather took to him. I mean, he didn't *want* to, having built up such a head of steam about the past, but then he was a bit disarmed when they met, and he discovered that Morris had his reasons for behaving as he did, even if they aren't ones you'd necessarily accept.'

Ashley picked up her fork again and jabbed at the air, in Leo's direction. She said, '*What* did you say just now, about us taking him in?'

Leo took a gulp of water with his free hand, then looked at Ashley. 'Morris told Jasper he doesn't want to be in Stoke. He doesn't want to be anywhere near Staffordshire. He only went there to find Susie, because he knew she'd be there. But it's got bad memories for him and he'd love to leave. So Jasper thought that he could come to London and that we could have him here.'

Ashley shouted, 'We could *not*!'

Leo waited a moment. He put his fork down. 'Why not?'

'He's a detestable old man! I don't want him here. I don't want him anywhere near my children.'

'Your dad didn't find him detestable.'

'No!' Ashley shouted again.

Leo said, 'We've got a spare room. He likes kids. He could babysit.'

'I don't *want* him here! I don't want him in our lives!' She was breathing hard. 'I *forbid* it!'

Leo said calmly, 'You can't.'

She glared at him. 'What d'you mean, I can't?'

'You can't forbid something out of hand like that, not any more.'

'What are you *saying*?'

'I'm saying,' Leo said steadily, 'that I'm running our home life now. I may not be doing it exactly as you'd like it done, but you can't insist on domestic control if you're no longer responsible for it. Ash, be reasonable. We've only been at this new regime a few weeks, but it's working. The kids are happier and better fed, you're less stressed and I'm getting there. It's going to *work*. But if I decide that I wouldn't mind another adult in the house – just for a trial period, mind, I'm not suggesting any more than that – then my decision will carry. I run this side of things; you run the earning side. You can't do both, and you can't cherry-pick the bits of my part of the deal that you'd still like to have charge of.'

Ashley sat back in her chair, her hands on the table. She said wonderingly, 'How long have you been thinking like this?'

He shrugged. 'It's come on me gradually. A week or two, maybe.' He turned to look round the room behind him. 'It's a bit of a mess, but that doesn't matter.' He turned back to look at her again. 'My aim is to get stuff *done*, not to do it perfectly. Food, clean clothes, conversation. That's it. Fred doesn't give a monkey's whether I've ironed his T-shirt or not. And don't say you do, because that's only because you're afraid you'll be seen as a bad mother if he isn't pristine. Nobody judges me like that.'

Slowly, Ashley leant towards him again. She said, 'You've winded me. I don't know what to say.'

He gestured at her plate. 'Eat up.'

'I'm not sure I can.'

'Eat it, Ash. You know what a sweat it is to make food that people won't eat.'

Ashley said, as if still trying to grasp the idea, 'You told my dad that we'd take Morris in, to live here?'

'Trial period only. I said three months.'

'Three *months*?'

'He may drive *me* crackers. The kids may not like him. But I said we'd give it a go.'

'*We*—'

'Yes, Ash. *We*. It'll take the heat and melodrama out of this whole situation. It'll calm things down. It'll calm your mother down.'

'So I don't have *any* say?'

He smiled at her. 'If you have a really good reason, of course you do. But you don't. Anyway, I'm running the family now, and I say we give old Morris a whirl. It's an experiment. And I'll be the first to admit it if it doesn't work.'

'Why won't you even *discuss* it?'

He smiled at her. 'Because I know what you think. Flat denial born of prejudice.'

'But—'

'Look at me, Ash,' Leo said, leaning forward.

Reluctantly, she raised her head.

'And give me your hand.'

'No.'

'Ash, *give* it to me.'

She put one hand out across the table towards him. He grasped it firmly. He said, 'My dad was a tyrant at home. A petty tyrant. He was overbearing and I hated it. I hated it for my brother and me and especially for Mum. Well, that was a generation ago, and he was old-fashioned then. Now, there's a woman like you in about a quarter of all UK households – a woman who out-earns her partner, partly because of the long over-due emphasis on girls' education and partly because the modern workplace needs brains rather than brawn. I'm fine with that, Ash. In fact, I'm more than fine – I think you are amazing, doing what you do, and doing it so well. I'll make sure our kids know I think that, too. But the balance has got to level out a bit to make it work at home. I've got to be able to call the shots round here – not moral or ethical ones about the kids, they're for both of us – but I've got to be able to run this house my way, not your way, with me doing the donkey work and you not here.'

Ashley nodded slowly.

Leo said, 'Your dad was a bit of a pioneer, if you think about it. Didn't you ever resent Susie being so wrapped up in the business?'

Ashley whispered, 'That's why I wanted to be around, for Maisie and Fred.'

'But it drove you mad. It drove you nuts not being able to concentrate on your job.'

There was a long pause. Then Ashley said, still in a whisper, 'I know. Guilt—'

'I don't have guilt,' Leo said. 'But I don't have your drive, either.'

Ashley closed her eyes. She said quietly, 'I love my job.'

'You're allowed to. You are absolutely *allowed* to love doing what you are good at.' He squeezed her hand, 'You're *allowed* not to take a back seat. Ash—'

'Yes.'

'Look at me,' he said again.

She opened her eyes.

He said, 'I'm not diminished by you being the bread-winner. I'm just going to do the other stuff rather differently from the way you did it.'

'Which includes having Morris living here.'

'As an experiment.'

She sighed. 'OK. As an experiment. I suppose. Leo, I don't *know* him.'

'None of us do. I don't.'

'Does Ma know?'

He gave her hand a little shake. 'Maybe by now. Maybe your dad has told her now. But she kind of forfeited the right to have a say in where he goes.'

'She thinks he's going to the cottage.'

'He doesn't want to.'

Ashley slowly withdrew her hand. She said, 'Does it matter if he doesn't want to?'

Leo grinned. 'Things don't tend to work if the participants don't want them to. Look at you and—'

'Please don't.'

He was gazing at her. After a pause he said, 'Ash, I'd love us to go upstairs now. But I know it's no good asking. I can see from your face that you aren't in the mood.'

She stared at him. 'Are you telling me that after a day of Maisie and Fred and the house and kedgeree, you still feel like *sex*?'

He went on grinning. 'Yup,' he said.

Well, she thought, you had to marvel at that. You had to admire and rejoice in a man whose self-esteem seemed so undiminished by the domestic round. She'd got up from the table then, and kissed him with gratitude and wonder, while at the same time making sure that it was a kiss that could not be construed as a prelude to anything further. He'd laughed when she

315

took her mouth away, and said that if there was nothing worth staying awake for, he'd take himself off to bed, and she'd heard him going up the stairs humming, like a man who had a lot to look forward to. She had been amazed to find herself half hoping he'd come down again and just – just take over.

When a few minutes had passed and it had become clear he was not planning on returning to carry her dramatically upstairs, she had tidied the kitchen, checked her emails and turned on the television for a final discouraging world news bulletin. When midnight came, it brought with it a peculiar sense of elation she couldn't identify, because, technically, everything she had heard that evening should have caused her heart to sink, rather than to lift. She aimed the remote at the screen and looked for a few seconds at the blank rectangle of black glass in its glossy black frame. 'Telebusy,' Maisie called it. 'Can I watch the telebusy?' Ashley dropped the remote on to the low table beside a Barbie wearing, obscenely, nothing but an open mauve plastic mackintosh, and Fred's blue sippy cup with its half-worn-off transfer of Elmer the Elephant in his patchwork skin.

Home life, she thought. Work life. Family life. And now Morris! Maisie will hate his hair.

*

316

'I don't want you to think of this as a date,' Grace said to Neil.

He smiled at her. 'I wouldn't dare. Anyway' – he looked round the museum café – 'breakfast, or brunch or whatever this meal is, is as vanilla as it gets here.'

Grace looked past him, through the floor-length windows towards the huge blond block of the Central Library.

She said, 'I love it here. I often come.'

'It reminds me of an Edinburgh tea-room.'

'That's why I like it. Welcoming. Unthreatening.'

He laughed. He said, 'Scones. Milk in a metal jug. Have you heard from Jeff?'

Her head snapped round. 'No,' she said abruptly.

'Are you expecting to?'

'I'm not thinking about it.'

He nodded. 'Good girl.'

She leant forward and said earnestly, 'I'm not the good one, Neil. You're the good one, taking Morris in for us all.'

'For *you*, to be precise. And for your mum. He's no bother.'

'Another person in your private space is always a bother.'

'It's not that private,' he said. 'It's where I lay my head, that's all. And he's off at the garden centre all day. They've sold fifteen of his bird houses, he told me.

He bought me a bottle of whisky as a thank-you, and I haven't the heart to tell him that I must be the only Scotsman living who doesn't drink the stuff.'

'Don't you like it?'

'I'm a beer man,' Neil said. He reached for the teapot. 'Beer and tea.'

Grace pushed her cup towards him. She said, 'And now he's going to London.'

Neil poured. The tea was clearly too dark, and cooling. Without speaking, he got up and took the teapot back to the service counter for a refill. Grace watched him, his sturdy figure in unfashionable jeans and a slightly shabby corduroy jacket. The sight was undeniably comforting. The woman behind the counter, smiling and obliging, plainly thought so too. Grace saw her put teabags into a clean pot and fill it from the urn, and then wave away Neil's obvious efforts to pay her for a second pot. He came back to the table and set the tea down.

Grace said, 'That's one reason I come here. They're so lovely, the people.'

Neil resumed his pouring. He pushed her cup back towards her. He said, as if there'd been no interruption, 'So Morris is off to London.'

'Yes. Ashley rang me. They're going to have a trial of three months, having him living there with them.'

'Is that OK?'

Grace added milk to her tea. 'She sounded a bit stunned. She said—' She stopped.

He looked up at her. 'What?'

She said awkwardly, 'It's sort of . . . family stuff.'

'Not to be shared with the factory manager, you mean?'

Her face flamed. She said hastily, 'It's got nothing to do with – with that. It's just that I don't know you very well.'

He said comfortably, 'Only well enough to ask me to rescue you, last Saturday.'

'Neil, I'm so sorry.'

'You, young lady,' he said, his tone still entirely un-offended, 'have got your wires a bit crossed, haven't you? Especially with your granddad in my bed and me on the sofa?'

Grace bent over her tea, so that her hair would at least partly screen her face. She said again, 'I'm so sorry.'

'Och,' he said, 'I believe you.'

She said, still staring at her tea, 'Ashley said she had never known Leo so masterful. Leo is her husband.'

'I know.'

Grace said, 'Shall I just go out and come in again? I'm making everything worse.'

'I'm helping you dig the pit. I'll stop now.' He put a hand on her wrist for a fleeting moment. Then he said, 'Does your mum know?'

319

Grace slowly raised her head. 'About Morris?'

'Going to London.'

She said, 'I haven't rung her since I heard. And she hasn't rung me.'

'She hasn't rung me either. Normally, she's on the phone two or three times a day, but I've heard nothing since Thursday. She's in London?'

'I think so.'

'And that cottage?'

Grace managed to look at him. She said, 'It's just sitting there.'

He moved a few things round unnecessarily on the table top. Then he said, with sudden force, 'You mustn't do that.'

'What?'

'Just sit there.'

She looked at him intently. 'What do you mean?'

He said, 'You know what's the matter with girls like you nowadays? Clever, talented girls like you? You get discouraged. That's the problem. You get disheartened, dispirited. You won't go for gold because you grew up believing you'd never get it. Shall I tell you something?'

Her mouth was slightly open. She shook her head faintly.

He said, leaning forward, 'You're a better designer than your mother.'

She made a rapid, dismissive gesture. 'Oh, I'm not.'

'You *are*,' he said. 'You may not have her get up and go, or her drive and tenacity in business, but you're a better designer, you understand how things work as well as how they look. If you put yourself out in the marketplace, you'd be snapped up.'

Grace said, almost in a whisper, 'That sounds almost like *sacrilege*.'

'No, it's not,' he said. 'Nobody's a bigger fan of your mum than I am. But she's got to see what she has in you, the potential the business has in you. And the beginning of that is *you* seeing it, overcoming all those years of being obliging and not speaking up and sorting out other people's mistakes. You should *assert* yourself.'

Grace put out a hand and moved a couple of teaspoons to lie parallel to one another. She said uncertainly, 'Ashley said something of the sort.'

'Good for her.'

'So if two of you . . . ?'

He picked up the teapot again and held it over her cup questioningly. He said, with emphasis, 'Then it must be true.'

Cara stood in the boardroom doorway with an expression of astonishment.

'Ma!'

Susie was sitting at the table, her laptop in front of

her and several sketchbooks scattered about. She said levelly, not really looking at Cara, 'Don't sound so amazed.'

'But it's *Saturday*!'

Susie put her glasses on. She said, 'I know it is. And I could be as surprised as you. What are *you* doing here on a Saturday?'

Cara took her bag off her shoulder and dropped it on the floor. 'Where's Pa?

'Rehearsing,' Susie said briefly.

'With Brady?'

'I presume so.'

'Don't you *know*?' Cara said, pulling a chair out.

Susie made a show of peering at something on a page in the nearest sketchbook. 'He doesn't want me to know.'

'Ma,' Cara said, 'don't be an idiot.'

'He doesn't want me at the gig. He isn't rehearsing at home. It's just more of the same.'

Cara sat down. She had planned to start mapping out a new gifting strategy to drive the company's growth in a way that would both satisfy Daniel and Rick and also be acceptable to Susie. She wanted to come up with something original. But as she had tried to explain to Dan, not all newness worked merely because it was new. And when you were faced with someone like Susie, who preferred depth to novelty, the problem was, in marketing speak, challenging. Which meant very difficult. And to find Susie sitting here, in the very place where Cara had sought space and quiet to think, translated very difficult into impossible.

'Shall I make some coffee?'

Susie waved a hand towards a cafetière on the table. 'Made some.'

'It'll probably be cold. I'll make some fresh.'

'I think that we should start discounting the mono-chrome diamond mugs,' Susie said, as if Cara hadn't spoken. 'Don't you always say discount the very minute sales start to decline?'

'Ma—'

'And the under-ten-pound price point. Don't you think there should be a far bigger range there, for the summer, in London?'

Cara said gently, 'Ma, I said that to you weeks ago.'

'Well, now I'm agreeing.'

'Good.'

'Gifting for tourists and visitors.'

'Ma—'

'What?'

'What are you working on there?'

Susie held up her sketchbook. Cara leant forward. 'Shells?'

'Summer range,' Susie said. 'Blue on cream. And star-fish. I might call it Seaside. Or Bucket and Spade.'

'Right,' Cara said, almost inaudibly.

Susie picked up her sketching pencil. She said, not looking at Cara, 'Why are you here?'

'I was going to work.'

'Were you? On what?'

'Ma,' Cara said, 'what's eating you? Why are you in such a temper?'

Susie added a detail to a shell. She said, still looking at the page, 'I'm not in a temper. But I'm – hurt. Upset. Yes, that's what I feel. Completely and utterly upset.'

Cara adjusted herself to sit very upright, her hands folded in her lap. She said steadily, 'Do you want to tell me why?'

'Do I have to?'

'Yes, Ma, you do.'

Susie stopped drawing and threw her pencil down. She took her glasses off and looked across the table and out of the window. 'Suddenly,' she said, 'nobody is talking to me. This is my company, and all our livelihoods, and lives, are bound up in it, and nobody is telling me what is going on.'

Cara waited. She thought of Dan, on one of his vigorous Saturday-morning cycle rides, and tried to imagine how he might urge her to – to *manage* herself, in this situation. He would be on her side, at least, and that, with a small but steady flame of fury beginning to burn in the pit of her stomach, was both a spur and a reassurance.

Susie went on, still looking away from Cara, 'I find all kinds of plans and arrangements are being made, both private and professional, without even mentioning them to me, let alone *consulting* me.'

Cara said steadily, 'You didn't tell anyone about your visit to Tinware for Today. The first we knew about it was when Dan got a quote from the sheet-metal people in Sheffield.'

Susie ignored her. She said, 'Arrangements about Morris. Taking no notice of the Parlour House and the plans I've made for it. Going to see Rick Machin without even mentioning it to me.'

Cara crossed her arms. She waited a moment, and then she said, 'Everyone else knew. Everyone else was in agreement about Morris coming to London. Ashley told me that yesterday.'

'Nobody told me. Nobody told me *anything*.'

'I'm sure Pa did.'

Susie looked down at the table. She said, in a tone of bruised surprise, 'He told me as a fait accompli. He never asked me. He just said he had stayed with Grace and met Morris and been to see Leo and it was sorted. Just like that!'

Cara said steadily, 'It *is* just like that.'

'I – I can't quite believe it.'

325

'Believe what?'

'That you've all taken all these decisions without even asking me what I thought!'

'Ma,' Cara said, 'we knew what you'd think.'

'Which was what?'

Cara took a deep breath. Then she said, 'Control, control, control.'

There was a highly charged silence. Then Susie said, 'Is that what you really think?'

'It's part of what I think.'

'You make it sound as if I want my own way at all costs.'

'It sometimes feels like that.'

'Cara,' Susie said, raising her head, 'don't you see?'

'See what?'

'That I want to make things *right*? For as many people as I can? Is that – is that just control?'

'I think,' Cara said, 'it's how it ends up seeming, yes.'

'But I believe—'

'I know what you believe,' Cara said, interrupting. 'I know what you've achieved, for hundreds of people, because of what you believe. It's wonderful. *You*'re wonderful. But you think that there is only one way of doing everything. And that *isn't* right. It isn't working. You have to be able to see that there are different ways of realizing your vision, and they aren't automatically wrong if they don't coincide with your way.'

Susie got up and went round the table to the window. Cara didn't look at her. She sat where she was, her arms folded, and waited.

After a long and uncomfortable pause, Susie said without turning round, 'Is this a plot?'

'No.'

'Did you all get together and decide to defy me?'

'*No*. It's just happened. We couldn't get past you, so we've had to go round you. Separately. Dealing with what had to be dealt with, as it came up.'

'Even Morris.'

'You didn't know what to do about Morris.'

Susie turned round very slowly. She said unexpectedly, 'No, I didn't.' And then she added under her breath, 'I hated that. Not knowing what to do.'

'You're allowed,' Cara said, surprising herself, 'not to know what to do when you're the child.'

Susie's gaze sharpened suddenly. She looked directly at Cara. 'D'you mean – you?'

Cara nodded. The energizing flame of anger inside her had turned into something much less easy to harness, threatening tears. She swallowed hard.

'Would you like just to say whatever it is you want to say?' Susie said.

Cara shook her head to dispel any incipient weeping. She said loudly, 'I hated you putting work before me when I was growing up. I hated not being able to *do*

327

anything about it. I just had to take what was handed out to me.'

Susie came slowly back to the table and sat down. She said softly, 'Of course.'

'We just had to take what *you* decided. Ash, Grace, Pa. Everyone. It's always been about what you wanted.'

'Or what I was compensating for.'

Cara scrabbled in her bag for tissues. 'We all do that. You're not unique.'

'I know.'

Cara found a pack of tissues and extracted one. She said, blowing her nose, 'There's *always* choices, Ma. Always. You can't blame other people for what you choose, whatever the circumstances.'

'I wasn't trying to. I was just explaining—'

'Why,' Cara said, suddenly raising her voice, 'don't you stop explaining and justifying and try just saying bloody *sorry* instead?'

Susie gave a little gasp. Then she said, 'I *am* sorry. I'm sorry about more than you can imagine.'

'And Pa?' Cara demanded. She thumped her bag down on the floor again.

'What about him?'

Cara blew her nose again. Then she said, in the same tone but without the volume, 'Why don't you try saying sorry to Pa, for starters?'

CHAPTER SIXTEEN

Brady and Frank had a conversation about whether they should ask Jasper outright if they weren't welcome at Radipole Road any more. Neither of them wished to have to spell out what a good gaff it was to visit, how much they appreciated a well-equipped studio, never mind the fish and chips and red wine, as well as the fact that as Jasper's missus had her own busy life, they were never interrupted or made to feel that they had outstayed their welcome. Without wishing to come right out and say so, they both admitted that they missed the advantages and comforts of Radipole Road, and were disquieted by the possibility that their visits had been stopped because they had been seen to be taking advantage or being exploitative. It occurred to them that Susie might have counted the number of empty wine bottles in the recycling bin. Or thrown a strop about people having the run of the house behind her back. Or something.

'Maybe,' said Frank, 'you upset her by teaching that parrot to swear.'

Brady was nursing a pint of Guinness. Its health properties were such, he was wont to say, that it didn't really count as alcohol. Even pregnant women drank it. He said gloomily, 'She was swearing long before I got to her. It wouldn't be that.'

'I reckon that Jas and his missus have had a falling-out,' Frank said. 'It'll be money. It never works, in the end, a woman out-earning a man.'

'Jas is OK with that.'

Frank turned his glass round thoughtfully. He said, '*I* wouldn't be.'

'Jas has never known anything different. Thirty-five years I've known him, and she's always made the money.'

'Worms turn,' Frank said.

Brady lifted his glass and carefully drank a mouthful of thick foam from the top of it. He said, 'I'll bet you it's not us, it's to do with them.'

'That's what I just said.'

'Did you?'

'Yes,' Frank said. 'They've had a falling-out and we've copped it.'

'Ah,' Brady said. 'But we've had more work – and with Jas – since we haven't been to his.'

'Nothing to do with it.'

'I'll bet you it's not just coincidence.'

'Whatever it is,' Frank said, 'it's got him off the pot.'

Brady picked up his glass again, and halted with it in mid air. He said, staring at the door, 'Talk of the bleeding devil—'

Jasper came sauntering into the pub, paused, looked round, clocked them with a gesture and went over to the bar to order a drink.

'Do we say anything?' Frank said.

Brady set his glass down again. 'One more mouthful of this and I'll be game.'

'Don't ask about his marriage.'

'Don't be a dickhead,' Brady said. 'Would I?'

'I'd like to know . . .'

'He doesn't look to me like a man out on his ear.'

'I meant about his studio,' Frank said.

Jasper came slowly towards them, concentrating on not spilling his drink. He said cheerfully, 'Lowlife in a low pub. I knew I'd find you here.'

'I've been drinking in here for a good fifteen years,' Brady said. 'Maybe twenty.'

Jasper looked at their glasses. 'I'll get a second round in.'

Brady put his hand flat on the top of his glass. 'Not for me, mate, ta all the same.'

'Frank?'

'Save it for Friday,' Frank said.

'What's the matter with you both? I want to celebrate.'

Frank looked at Brady. Brady said, 'It's been so long, mate, I've forgotten how.'

Jasper set his glass down carefully in front of him. He said, 'I've found a studio.'

There was a pause. Then Frank said, 'You've already got a studio.'

Jasper slid a handful of change into his jeans pocket. He said, 'In Hackney. It's in a converted factory. Amazing. All studios with kids making a million things in them. Knitwear, shoes, light fittings. And then there's this studio, completely soundproofed, just sitting waiting for us, like it was meant.'

They sat in silence, regarding their drinks.

Then Jasper said, 'Aren't you pleased?'

Brady gave Frank a quick glance. He said, 'Jas, mate, we thought we had a studio. At yours. No studio's going to be as good as that one.'

There was another pause, and then Jasper said firmly, 'No.'

'No what?'

'I don't want to use that studio. Not any longer.'

'Ah,' Frank said, too quickly. 'We wondered if we weren't welcome any more, if Susie—'

'It's nothing to do with Susie,' Jasper said. 'It's my decision. I don't want to play in that studio. Not any more.'

They regarded him, and then looked at each other.

'Jas? You OK?'

'Yes,' he said.

'It's gold dust, that studio.'

'I know.'

'Hackney's not exactly Fulham—'

'That's what I like.'

'You having a bit of a crisis, mate?'

Jasper picked up his glass and took a gulp. He said, 'I'm bringing the parrot.'

'What?'

'I've bought a travelling cage. When we use the studio, I'm bringing the parrot.'

'You off your trolley?'

'No,' Jasper said. 'I'm back on it, as it happens.'

Frank said, 'So it isn't us? It isn't something we've done?'

'What isn't?'

'Us not coming round to yours any more.'

Jasper looked at him. He was laughing. 'God, no,' he said. '*God*, no. You two are the reason we're moving to Hackney.'

'But—'

'Can't you see?' Jasper said. 'Can't you see that I'll be free?'

*

Morris sat opposite the children at the kitchen table. Maisie was eating toast soldiers and Fred was packing discs of banana into his mouth as if it was essential to accommodate all of them. While she ate, Maisie was watching Morris with a steady and appraising eye.

She had declined her father's suggestion that she might help Morris to unpack. Morris had arrived with his strange luggage on a National Express coach from Stoke-on-Trent, having refused a train ticket and paid for the bus himself. In addition to the carpet bag, he had brought a bird house for the children, painted celadon green with their names on the sides, garlanded with flowers and butterflies.

'Say thank-you,' Leo had said to Maisie.

She'd shrugged. 'I can't.'

'Yes, you can. You can say thank-you for the lovely bird house.'

Maisie had tugged on Leo's arm to get him to bend over her. She'd said in a hoarse whisper into his ear, 'There are no *birds* in it.'

'There will be,' Morris had said. 'When we put it outside. In the garden. With nuts and seeds in for them to eat. They'll come when there's something for them to eat.'

Maisie had looked as if she'd believe that when she saw it. She'd accompanied her father firmly downstairs, leaving Fred investigating the carpet bag.

'I'm your great-granddad,' Morris had said to Fred. 'I never thought I'd be anything, and here I am with you.'

Now he was opposite both of them at the table. Leo had gone to the corner shop for something or other, leaving Morris in charge, and indicating as he did so that it wouldn't be the last time; that he had started as he meant to go on. Maisie ate and stared, never taking her eyes off Morris. He made himself look back at her, consoling himself that she had jam smeared across one cheek and, comically, on the end of her nose. When she had eaten all the strips of toast, she drank noisily from a plastic mug of milk, holding it in both hands and still staring at him relentlessly over the top. Then she put the mug down with a bang, gave a little gasp and said, 'Your hair is like a *witch*.'

Morris smiled at her. 'Witches are women.'

'They're spooky,' Maisie said reprovingly. 'Witches are bad guys.'

'Ah,' Morris said.

Fred made a choking sound and a plug of banana shot out of his mouth and landed sloppily on the tray of his high chair.

'He always does that,' Maisie said.

Morris got up and went round the table to pat Fred on the back.

'Harder,' Maisie said.

335

Morris didn't look at her. 'I'll do it my own way, missy. You OK, lad?'

Fred stretched his arms up to be lifted out of his chair.

'Not till he's finished,' Maisie said. 'It's the *rule*.'

'Granddads,' Morris said, 'have their own rules.'

He heaved Fred out of his chair and carried him back round the table to sit him on his knee. Maisie began to scramble off her chair. She said, 'I need to sit on your knee too.'

'I thought that I wasn't in your good books,' Morris said. 'Wrong bird house, wrong hair . . .'

'Lift me *up*.'

'Can't.'

'Yes, you can.'

'Not with one arm. One old arm. Got Fred in the other one, see?'

Maisie began to push an empty chair next to Morris's. She said severely, 'You need sorting.'

'You can say that again,' Morris said. 'D'you think you'll be the one to do it?'

Maisie adjusted the chair so that it was as close to Morris's as she could get it. Then she clambered up inelegantly, and stood on the seat so that she could inspect Morris's hair with full and close disapproval. She said, 'This won't do.'

Morris was feeding Fred morsels of digestive biscuit.

He said, 'It's been like this since I was sixteen. You sound just like my old dad. He couldn't stand long hair on a man either.'

'Are you going to live here?' Maisie inquired.

Fred leaned forward to lick crumbs off Morris's fingers. Then he settled himself back into the crook of his arm, as if against pillows.

'You're a nice lad,' Morris said, and then to Maisie, 'And yes, for the moment. If you'll have me.'

Maisie considered. She put a hand out to touch the black ribbon tied round Morris's ponytail, and shrank it back again. 'I think so,' she said.

'You sound a bit doubtful.'

'Well,' Maisie said, 'we're pretty full up with people.'

'You don't take up much space. Nor does the little fella.'

'I'll grow you, you know. Till I'm *huge*.'

'You might be,' Morris said. 'I was six foot two once upon a time. Tall genes in the family.'

Maisie leant against him. She said breathily in his ear, 'Witch hair, witch hair, witch hair.'

'You tickle—'

'Witch hair, witch hair—'

'Maisie, would you like me to do something for you?'

'Yes.'

'Something you'd like and I wouldn't?'

'Yes,' Maisie said.

'I'm not promising,' Morris said, full of sudden joy at the two solid small bodies pressed against him, 'but I might consider – just consider, mind – cutting it off.'

From the kitchen table at Radipole Road, Susie rang Grace. She had started to ring from an armchair in the sitting room, but restlessness had propelled her out of it and back down the hall to the big kitchen, with its French windows to the garden. The great parrot cage was in its usual place next to the glass doors, and beside it, on the floor, sat a much smaller and less decorative cage, with a sturdy handle on the top.

'Are you going travelling?' Susie said to Polynesia.

Polynesia pretended not to hear her, as usual. She had taken up her stock position, if Jasper was out, at the furthest end of her perch, and was staring distantly at nothing.

'Where are you, Ma?' Grace said.

'In the kitchen at home, being ignored by the parrot. She is brilliant at ignoring, especially me. It looks as if she's planning to get away, though. There's a much smaller cage on the floor here, a new one. Do you know anything about a new parrot cage?'

'No,' Grace said. 'Should I?'

'I thought your father might have said something to you.'

'Ma,' Grace said, 'you're the one who lives with him. Why don't you ask him yourself?'

Susie paced back down the kitchen. It was on the tip of her tongue to say that she might technically be sharing a house with Jasper, but that she didn't appear, at the moment, to be sharing anything else of any significance. She swallowed. Grace would not want to hear that. Nor would Cara or Ashley. There were some elements in a marriage that it would be entirely inappropriate – awful if invaluable word – to burden the consequences of that marriage with. She said instead, 'Have you talked to Ashley?'

'Haven't you?'

'Gracie—'

'Morris is your father, Ma. It's up to you to ring Ashley. Or even go round there and see for yourself.'

There was a charged silence. Then Susie said carefully, 'Are you cross about something?'

'Me? No. Why would I be?'

'It's just that it isn't like you to talk like this. You sound like Cara.'

'Perhaps it's time I sounded more like her. If I do.'

Susie stood at the far end of the kitchen, between the table and the painted dresser which housed all the early prototypes of her pottery, those mugs and jugs and bowls decorated with strawberries and daisies and dots and diamonds that she had stood in the factory holding, all those years ago, in a kind of wondering ecstasy. She put out a finger and stroked the shiny curve of a small blue-spotted Dutch jug. She said, as neutrally as she could, 'Cara and I had a sort of row—'

'Cara didn't describe it like that.'

'So you've talked to Cara?'

'Of course.'

'Gracie, why is no one talking to *me*?'

Grace said maddeningly, 'I'm talking to you now.'

Susie closed her eyes briefly. She had the phone in one hand, and the little Dutch jug in the other as a kind of instinctive talisman. She said, 'I wish I understood what's gone wrong. What I've done wrong.'

There was another silence. Susie pictured Grace pulling out one of her long, springy curls, as she was in the habit of doing whilst telephoning. The silence went on long enough for Susie to wonder if Grace had just quietly ended the call, when she said in a much more familiar tone, 'I don't think it's as straightforward as that, Ma. I don't think it's a question of having made a sudden mistake, or anything. I think it's been brewing for ages and none of us realized what was going wrong until it was suddenly impossible to ignore. And Morris – you can't ignore Morris.'

'He's changed everything—'

'No, he hasn't. It's too easy to blame everything on

340

him. He's just brought everything out into the open. Not by doing anything – just by arriving and creating a problem.'

'What do you mean by everything?' Susie said, putting the jug gently back on the dresser.

'Changes,' Grace said.

'Changes? What changes?'

'The need for them.'

'But we *are* changing. We're changing all the time. We're evolving—'

'I'm not talking about the product, Ma. I'm talking about management. The way we're structured. The way we're paid. The way we interact with each other.'

Susie leant on the kitchen wall next to the dresser. She felt that she ought to flare up at this moment, hold her ground, fight her corner as she always had, as she had believed that she should. But for some reason, she couldn't find either the conviction or the energy to resist.

Grace said, 'Ma?'

'Yes?'

'Are you OK?'

'Perhaps,' Susie said uncertainly. 'Probably. Gracie, I don't really know.'

'What are you doing at home, on a work day?'

'I'm leaning on the kitchen wall.'

'Why?'

'I don't know. I just feel – exhausted.'

'You're never exhausted.'

'Darling,' Susie said, pressing her forehead to the wall. 'What do you think I should do?'

'I think,' Grace said, 'that you should pull yourself together.'

Susie gave a rueful laugh. 'You don't sound very worried about me.'

'I'm not.'

'Thank you, darling—'

'I'm not, because you can sort this. You can sort all of it. If you want to.'

'*Want* to!'

'Yes,' Grace said. 'And now, Ma, I've got to go. I've got work to do.'

'Could you possibly give a message to Neil?'

'No,' Grace said, 'I couldn't. You'll have to ring him yourself.' And she put the phone down.

Susie stayed where she was for a few moments, her phone in her hand. Then she said to Polynesia, 'She put the phone down on me. Grace actually put the phone down on me. *Grace!*'

Polynesia stirred not a feather. She went on looking out at the garden, her back to Susie. A car went past, down Radipole Road, too fast, music blaring, leaving the atmosphere quivering faintly in its wake. Susie took her forehead away from the wall and dropped the phone on the table. Even Grace had said that the major log in the current jam had her name on it. Grace! She walked back down the kitchen to stand by the new portable cage.

'Are you all just leaving me?' Susie said to Polynesia.

Ashley said firmly that she didn't want to talk in the office. Daniel had suggested the boardroom, but Ashley said that she would prefer to be out of the office altogether, so the three of them were in a wine bar on the Fulham Road, sitting on velvet-covered chairs round a plate of Spanish ham that Daniel had ordered with their drinks. Ashley was drinking fizzy water, and had had a haircut, Cara noticed. It suited her. As did her navy-blue sweater dress, which Cara didn't recollect seeing before – any more, as a matter of fact, than she remembered those particular ankle boots. Cara tried very hard never to assess, let alone judge other women by what they wore. But you couldn't help *noticing*, could you?

Ashley rolled a piece of ham into a cigarette shape and ate it, ignoring the bread basket. She added a wedge of lime to her water. She looked remarkably together, Cara thought, especially for someone with two small children at home, let alone an unwanted grandfather in her spare bedroom. Cara shuddered inwardly at the thought of Morris anywhere near her and Dan's flat, their private space. But Ashley looked strangely unruffled. In fact, since these recent upheavals in her private life, Ashley had looked a great deal less harassed and flung-together than she had done in the days of Leo being out at work and a full-time nanny at home.

Cara glanced at Daniel. He seemed in no more of a hurry than Ashley to get down to business. He was sipping thoughtfully from a glass of Riesling – Riesling was his latest wine thing – and asking Ashley peacefully about how things were at home, and she was replying, equally comfortably it seemed to Cara, that it was all remarkably OK, thank you, and the children had rather taken to him, and he was weirdly quite easy to have around, and had even made a start on the garden, having an aptitude for plants and outdoor spaces. Even Maisie, Ashley said, whose wellington boots were as pristine as when they left the shop on account of her fierce insistence on only ever wearing her buckled shoes, had consented to put them on to join Morris in the garden. It was a first. She had thought Maisie was going to be like one of those cats that single girls have as baby substitutes, who are terrified of any surface that isn't carpeted because they are never allowed out.

'Doesn't he creep you out a bit, Ash?' Cara said.

Ashley picked up a second slice of ham. 'Less than I

thought he would. He's very clean. And now the hair's gone—'

'Gone!'

'He had it all cut off. For Maisie. They went to the barber together. It's so short now, it's practically shaved. A definite improvement. And Maisie has stopped bossing Fred around, now she's got Morris to boss instead. So that's a relief.'

'I'm glad something is,' Cara said. She took a sip of her wine. 'Ma's in a very odd mood, she hasn't mentioned the Parlour House for ages, Grace is being very elusive, and Pa is having some kind of mid-life crisis and hiring a studio in *Hackney*. What's all that about?'

'Perhaps it's nearer these gigs he's doing,' Daniel said. He glanced at Cara. 'Should we be going to hear him?'

She gave a small snort. 'No. Absolutely not. He's got this state-of-the-art studio at home—'

'But perhaps it feels a bit disconnected,' Ashley said.

Cara shrugged. 'Maybe. I don't think that we can worry too much at the moment about Pa's *Great Gatsby* desire to relive the past.'

'That's a bit harsh.'

'I'm feeling harsh,' Cara said. 'I'm angry with both of them. Pa has just stepped away from us, and Ma is expecting us to fall in with what she wants, because in the end we have to. They're both being a kind of exaggeration of what they used to be, and totally ignoring each other, as if they have no responsibility for one another. It's driving me nuts. So I'm trying not to think about it. I'm practising detachment. It's wonderful when it works.'

Ashley looked across at her brother-in-law. She said, 'What do you think, Dan?'

He gave a small shrug. 'Not a lot, actually.'

Cara looked aggrieved. 'Dan!'

He smiled at her. 'Other things on my mind, sweetheart.'

'You're so lucky, not being family,' said Ashley.

'I know.'

Ashley took a sip of her water. She said, laughing a little, 'Maybe that's the only thing you have in common with Leo!'

'I like Leo.'

'I'd be very fed up with you if you didn't like Leo.'

'Ashley,' Cara said suddenly, turning towards her, 'why are we here?'

Ashley sat back. She crossed her legs and flicked something invisible off her sweater dress. Then she said, 'Me, actually.'

'Go on,' Cara said. She looked at Dan for his customary support. He didn't look back. He was smiling in a mild kind of way at Ashley.

'Two things,' Ashley said.

'Well?'

'The first is the catalogues. I want the photoshoots to happen at my home now, as I said before. My home which might soon have a garden. It's too late for an Easter catalogue now as well as the spring one, but I want one for next year. As well as early and late summer, with special gifting pages. And I want to change the design and the typography – matt finish and italic handwriting. And before you object, I have worked out the costs, and increased sales will more than compensate for the price of producing and mailing more catalogues as well as updating the website.'

She stopped and picked up her glass. Cara glanced at Daniel again. His expression hadn't altered. She said aggrievedly, 'You never consulted *me*.'

Ashley took a gulp of water. She said, 'I am now.'

'That speech didn't sound like a consultation. It sounded like a fait accompli. Dan?'

Daniel shifted a little in his chair. He said imperturbably, 'I can't see any real problem with any of that.'

'Dan!'

Ashley nodded at him. 'Good,' she said. 'Thank you.'

'But *I* don't agree,' Cara said. '*I'm* not just passing this on the nod. I need to see the figures.'

Ashley regarded her. 'I'll email them to you.'

Cara leant towards Dan. She said, 'What's the matter with you? Why aren't you even asking her questions?'

Daniel reached out and patted Cara's wrist. He said, 'Let's see what the second thing is first, shall we?'

'Don't patronize me.'

'Angel, I'm not—'

'Your *tone* is patronizing.'

Ashley cleared her throat. 'Could I just tell you about item two? I have to go in two minutes.'

'Oh, *do* you?' Cara said crossly. 'First, drag us here, all secrecy and self-importance, and then tell us you're in a hurry?'

Ashley sighed. 'I've got children at home.'

'Don't remind me.'

Daniel squeezed Cara's wrist. 'Let her speak, sweetheart.'

Cara glared at Ashley. 'Well?'

Ashley looked straight back at her. She said, 'It's about money.'

'Ah.'

'What I'm paid. How I'm paid.'

Daniel's grip on Cara's wrist tightened. He said, 'Which is . . . ?'

'We know from research, don't we,' Ashley said, as if reciting, 'that men are four times more likely than women to ask for a pay rise. And women are notoriously bad at asking about pay anyway. However, if a woman's pay is set by a committee and based on strict performance criteria, they not only do much better for themselves, but they frequently outperform men. So I want that to happen to us. To all of us. I want the way we're paid to be decided by all of us on the board, and then to be related to performance. Including Ma.' She switched her gaze to Dan. 'Well?'

'Wow,' Cara said. She looked at Dan too. 'Bombshell—'

He said, in the same strangely distanced way, 'Sounds intriguing.'

Ashley said, 'I'm going to push for it. I'm telling Grace next and then Ma. And I'd like your backing.'

Cara was still looking at Dan. She said, 'We'll have to talk about it.'

'I want a decision soon,' Ashley said. 'I don't want to lose momentum.'

Cara leant towards Daniel. She said in a low voice, 'What's the matter?'

He gave her a benign smile. 'Nothing.'

'Yes, there is. There *is*. You're never this disengaged, you're never not involved—'

'Well, maybe I am now,' he said.

'Now?' Cara said. Her voice was alarmed. 'What d'you mean, now?'

He gave Cara's hand a brief final squeeze and let it go. Then he picked up his wine glass. 'I just mean, sweetheart, that I'm possibly not as involved as I was till very recently. And I don't mean just me – I mean you, too.' He took a sip of wine. 'It's just possible, Ashley, that none of this will concern Cara and me for very much longer. But of course we'll help you. For now, that is. For now.'

CHAPTER SEVENTEEN

There were moments most days when Grace reflected how hard she would find it to share her life with anyone on a permanent basis. It was a rare day when she didn't close her front door on the world outside with a feeling of thankfulness and release. She remembered, in childhood, not in the least minding being allotted the smallest bedroom at home, as long as it had a door that closed and no space for a second bed. She had to be coaxed into having friends for tea or birthday parties, or going on school trips, as if the very notion of disliking communal activities was just too peculiar to be permitted. It wasn't, she tried to explain throughout her growing-up years, that she didn't *like* other people; it was just that she really needed lots of time on her own. Her idea of company, she wrote in a school essay when she was twelve, was to be in her room at home with the door shut, and the rest of the family somewhere else in the house, but not beside her. Her English teacher had written at the bottom, 'Well

expressed, even if the sentiments are a little strange!'
But then, as Grace had observed, her English teacher
had been the kind of woman who would have thought
she had fallen off the edge of the planet if she wasn't in
perpetual communication with *someone*.

Since Morris had left, and Jeff had sidled from
centre stage (even if Grace couldn't quite believe that
he had gone for good), her flat had settled back into
itself once more. She had toured it nightly for the first
week, adjusting and tweaking, to remind herself that
it was hers, and hers alone, spreading her sketchbooks
out, hanging favourite garments on cupboard doors,
buying pots of herbs for the kitchen windowsill and
bunches of flowers for everywhere else, even putting a
jug of forced Cornish daffodils on the lavatory cistern.
Late in the evenings, before she went to bed, she would
move things about, changing cushions or lamps,
altering the position of pieces of furniture, in order
to surprise herself in the mornings by seeing the flat
anew. This habit was a private but intense pleasure, like
being alone. It gave her a sensation of quiet control and
also a low but definite hum of excitement. In those
first weeks after Morris went south, Grace revelled in
her own private power.

Which was only increased when Ashley rang to say
she had decided that their pay structure should be
changed, and what they achieved should be reflected

in what they earned. Grace was lying on her sofa, with her stockinged feet propped on one end and her head on the other. She said thoughtfully, 'How would you quantify that?'

'By sales. We look at those and then estimate how we share the profits. Sales are the only yardstick we have for measuring any of our successes, if you think about it, and the only way we can tell if our performance is getting better.'

Grace lifted one foot and balanced it against the opposite knee. She said, 'What did Cara think?'

'She was a bit ratty. But she was in a ratty mood, anyway. I think Dan liked it. Dan's obviously planning some big new move for the company. He wouldn't talk about it, except to say he wanted to discuss it with Cara first, so it's bound to be something that'll upset Ma. All Dan's plans upset Ma. Where is she?'

Grace fitted her left kneecap into the arch of her right foot. She said, 'Up here somewhere, I think. I haven't seen her today. But she was in the factory, I know, because the girls have been painting the ribbons on the Maypole range, and she'll have taught them how.'

'Is she out at Barlaston?' Ashley said. 'What about that house?'

'I haven't asked her.'

'Well, now Morris is here—'

'Is he OK?'

353

'Don't you mean us? Are *we* OK?'

'Are you?' Grace said.

'Most days, yes. None of this *should* work, but it seems to. Morris has been taken up by all Leo's yummies, and Leo has a couple of private pupils he's tutoring.'

Grace took her foot off her knee and wriggled it. She said, 'What about Pa?'

'What about him?'

'I rang him,' Grace said, 'and he said he couldn't talk because he was with somebody.'

'Jesus, d'you think—'

'No, not that kind of somebody. He sounded just the same as normal, only preoccupied. Is he ever at home?'

'I don't think either of them are,' Ashley said. 'I haven't seen Ma in weeks. Maisie and Fred might as well not have a grandmother.'

'Better than smothering.'

'She wouldn't know how to smother if you paid her,' Ashley said. 'It's all she can do to relate vaguely.'

'That's not fair.'

'Isn't it?'

'No, it's not,' Grace said. She swung herself slowly upright. 'Why are we all working with her if she got it so wrong?'

'Gracie—'

'What?'

354

'Do you get the feeling that something's about to happen? That we're all waiting for something to happen?'

'Is that what you're trying to do? Make something happen?'

'If you mean the company—'

'I do,' Grace said.

There was a pause. Then Ashley said, 'I'm alone in the office. Everyone's gone home. It's – great.'

Grace laughed. 'Alone at last. My ideal.'

'It's not being here alone, so much,' Ashley said unexpectedly. 'It's the feeling of being in charge. I like it. I'm sitting at Dan's desk, and I'm looking right down the office, all the way down to the double doors at the end, and I like it, Grace. I really, really do.'

On the train to Stoke-on-Trent Jasper wondered if he was behaving like a character in a third-rate thriller. It was, after all, undeniably furtive to arrange for a neighbour to call in and attend to Polynesia, and then to set off for Euston station without informing either Susie or his daughters. Of course, since he wanted to surprise Susie, there was no point in alerting her, but it was not in character – or at least, not in the character he seemed to have inhabited for almost forty years – to conceal anything quite so deliberately from his children.

He had, over time, developed a method of telling them about his arrangements. He would simply announce in a breezy tone that he was off here or there, but because it never involved any length of time away from Radipole Road, the girls had got into the habit of hardly hearing him, of thinking vaguely, 'Oh, it's Pa. He won't be long,' as if he was a kind of immovable fixture, like a human landmark that had been there for millennia and could thus be taken for granted.

It had come as a surprise to him, a few days ago, to realize that he was going to have to break the easygoing habits of a lifetime and take action because, astonishingly, not only was Susie not going to, but she couldn't. He had avoided her for some time now, because she aroused in him such unmanageable and complicated feelings of anger and distress and bewilderment, but recently something had diminished the anger and increased the distress – maybe it was knowing that she had been at home, alone, without him, in a bizarre reversal of their roles. The anger was an old friend and therefore familiar. The distress was new and violently uncomfortable.

The only course of action, he decided, was to surprise Susie and confront her. And an essential part of the surprise – which would increase the likelihood of getting an authentic response – was for their encounter not to happen in a known context. What was known

– or over-known, for God's sake – was Radipole Road. Radipole Road held not a single element of novelty or surprise for either of them, and in Jasper's view it was no longer the cradle of all that was beloved in that family's history, but rather a hollow reminder of what had once been, and was no more. He had decided firmly that it would be useless to try and talk to Susie in Radipole Road. But it would be wrong to confront her at the office, as well as embarrassing for Cara and Ashley. No, it would be best to appear out of context, to seek her out in the very place where she was least expecting him. And so, after a call to the architect who was refashioning the Parlour House to establish Susie's whereabouts and timetable, Jasper was on his way to Barlaston, via Stoke-on-Trent. His only real responsibility, Polynesia, was at home in her cage with a list of instructions about her welfare on the kitchen table. The neighbour had a key and a list of emergency numbers. If he hadn't been on such a mission, Jasper thought, his gaze fixed unseeingly on the flying countryside outside the train windows, it might have almost felt like an adventure. Stoke-on-Trent twice in a matter of weeks! Unheard of.

'I can't believe how difficult it is to talk to you,' Daniel said to Cara.

Cara was pulling towels off the bathroom rack, prior

357

to washing them. She said huffily, 'That's hardly *my* fault. I'm here, aren't I?'

He stepped into the bathroom and tried to take the armful of towels from her. 'I didn't mean that. I didn't mean you're hard to talk to. I meant that we seem to be so busy that there's never a proper opportunity.'

Cara held the towels defensively. 'Don't. I've got them. I can't talk properly to you, Dan, if I don't feel you're on my side.'

'I am *always* on your side.'

'You weren't the other night. You were siding with Ashley. And you keep going off on your own, and it isn't all cycling, and I'm not going to demean myself by asking—'

'Please put the towels down.'

'No!'

'Cara, sweetheart,' Daniel said, 'that's exactly what I want to talk to you about. But not round the laundry.'

She relaxed her hold on the towels very slightly. She said, her tone still doubtful, 'What are you on about?'

He said with exaggerated patience, 'Where I keep going. What I'm doing. Why I didn't bother arguing with Ashley in the wine bar.'

Cara waited. Daniel reached a second time to take the towels out of her arms. He said, 'Please, Cara.'

She let them go. She said, 'But I want to put a wash on—'

'I'll do it. I'll do it in two minutes.'

Cara said, suddenly flaring up, 'The last few weeks have been such a battle!'

Daniel dropped the towels on the floor. He stepped over them and took Cara by the shoulders. He said, looking seriously at her, 'I know.'

'I wish it wasn't. I wish it was like it used to be.'

'Come and sit down.'

She pointed at the floor. 'I have to—'

'In a minute. We'll do it in a minute.'

'Dan—'

'Cara,' Daniel said, 'I have a plan. I have a plan about our future.'

She shook her head. 'Please don't. It'll be a great plan and she'll just reject it, and then I'll be left with her unacceptable triumph, and your frustration, and as usual I'll—'

'It has nothing to do with your mother. My plan has absolutely *nothing* to do with your mother. Or even the company.'

Cara put her hands to her mouth. 'Daniel, don't—'

He let go of her shoulders and put his arms round her. He said, his cheek against the side of her head, 'I said think outside the box, didn't I?'

'Yes,' she said doubtfully.

'Well, I have. I've thought of our skills and our experience, and then I've thought of where we might employ them. Somewhere where they aren't thwarted all the time.'

Cara said nothing. She was very still, holding herself stiffly in his arms.

Dan said, 'I don't really want to have this conversation in the bathroom.'

She sighed.

He waited a few moments, then he relaxed his hold and slid his hands down her arms to take one of her hands. 'Come and sit down.'

She allowed herself to be led towards the sofa, and then to be seated on it.

'Look at me, sweetheart.'

She raised her chin.

Dan put one hand under it and said sadly, 'You look miserable.'

'I am.'

'It's exhausting you, all this, isn't it?'

Cara looked away from him, dislodging his hand. She said, 'I wish I didn't get so uptight about it all. I wish I could just stand back and get on with my job. But I can't. I can't help being wound up by Ma any more than she can help winding me. I've always reacted to her like this. I can't seem to do normal. It's all huge and fine, or huge and awful. Mostly the latter. I wish she wasn't such a big part of my life, but she is, whatever she does or doesn't do. And I'm worn out by it.'

'I know,' Daniel said.

'And then,' Cara said, swinging her gaze slowly back to take him in, 'I want to protect you and side with you, because I actually think you're right about ninety-nine per cent of the business stuff, and I know that'll be a battle too, and I get in a state about that as well, and I take it out on you even though I know it's not fair.'

Daniel said gently, 'I know all that. I get it. Which is why I think we should put a stop to it, once and for all. You can't go on like this.'

'We can't stop it. I mean, how can we?'

Daniel didn't try to take her hand again. He simply said, looking steadily at her, 'We leave.'

He waited for her to stare at him in amazement. But she didn't. She looked down at the sofa instead, and sighed again. She said quietly, 'Is that where you've been?'

'I've been seeing Rick Machin. Talking about setting up with him. Yes.'

'I thought as much.'

'Did you?'

She raised her eyes. She said, 'You hinted at it before.'

'Well, now I've done more than hint. Are you up for it?'

There was a long pause, and then Cara said, unsmiling but determined, 'I'm up for it. I think.'

*

361

The lounge of the hotel in Barlaston was as uninhabited as it had been the night that Susie and Morris had been there. The fire was burning unenthusiastically, and rain was hammering on the two sets of huge windows, obscuring the view. Jasper and Susie were sitting opposite each other on the sofas flanking the fire, with a pot of tea on a tray between them, and a plate of biscuits which Susie had already dismissed as not worth eating.

'They'll taste of custard powder. We'll get a sandwich if you're hungry.'

'I'm not hungry,' Jasper said. 'I had breakfast on the train. Full English. With baked beans.'

Susie poured the tea. She said, 'Do you not like my house because of how it is, or don't you like it on principle?'

He crossed his legs and leant back. He said, 'I'm no good at country houses or cottages. You know that.'

'You gave me such a fright just turning up like that. I was so surprised to see you that at first I couldn't think who you were.'

He grinned. 'I know. I could see.'

'Well,' she said, 'you said you couldn't talk to me there. You said whatever it was would have to wait till we were somewhere else and concentrating.' She looked round at all the empty sofas and chairs. 'We're here now. So what is it?'

Jasper let a beat fall and then he said, in as relaxed a tone as he could manage, 'Us.'

Susie drank some tea, and then, with a not entirely steady hand, put the cup down in the saucer. She said, clearing her throat and endeavouring to sound as unconcerned as he did, 'Have you followed me all the way to Staffordshire to tell me that you want a divorce?'

Jasper inspected the nails on his right hand. He said, 'Not necessarily.'

'Please don't play games with me.'

He shifted his gaze from his nails to Susie. 'I don't play games, Suz. You know that. I never have. Unless it's the guessing games that I'm forced to play because I never know where you are or when you'll be back, or what you're planning or thinking or wanting or feeling. I haven't come all the way up here to ask you anything. I'm through with asking. I'm done with guessing. I've come to *tell* you something instead. I've come to tell you what I plan to do.'

Susie gave a little shudder. She said, 'You've met someone else.'

'No, I haven't,' he said exasperatedly. 'I'm not interested in romance. I'm not up for another relationship. Suz, it's *me* I'm interested in.'

She put her hands briefly up to her face. 'Sorry. Sorry, Jas. I just thought—'

363

'That I'd have consoled myself in the time-honoured way?'

'Well, you're a very attractive man—'

'And so bloody conventional as to have an affair when I don't like the way my marriage is going?' he demanded.

'No. Of course not. No, sorry. I just meant—'

He leant forward, his elbows on his knees. He said with real energy, 'Suz, it's pretty impossible being married to you. I've been in a smouldering rage about it, a lot of the time for almost forty years. But I've never been remotely interested in anyone else. No one else has ever come close. You may be – you *are* – absolutely bloody *maddening* to be married to, but you are the mother of my children, and you have also taken all the colour out of other women for me. No, I do not want a divorce.'

Susie was sniffing. She took a crumpled tissue out of the sleeve of her jacket and blew her nose hard. She said indistinctly, 'Thank God.'

'He has nothing to do with it.'

She said, laughing uncertainly, 'I'm so relieved.'

'But—'

'But what? Anything . . .'

'There'll have to be some changes.'

Susie blew her nose again. She said shakily, 'Tell me.'

Jasper leant back again and recrossed his legs. He said, 'We are re-forming the Stone Gods. Brady and me. Plus Frank and a guy called Marco who is a jazz pianist. A good one.'

She nodded. 'OK.'

'It's more than OK,' Jasper said. 'It's serious. We have bookings. We're in demand. We are building quite a following on YouTube. We sound a little like Dave Brubeck, only fresher, with a modern twist. I am composing.'

She regarded him. Her nose was pink. She said seriously, 'Jas, that's wonderful. I'm so glad. And . . . and proud.'

He nodded slightly. He went on, 'We have an agent. We won't make Glastonbury, but there's a chance of one of the smaller festivals. I am going to be away a lot, this summer.'

'Of course.'

'I want to buy myself a place near the studio, over in East London. A one-bed flat, say.'

Susie was breathing rapidly and balling the tissue in her hands into a small hard lump. 'Is – is that what you came to say? Are you saying that if I have my – my play place, so can you?'

He shook his head. 'That kind of equation never crossed my mind.'

'Well, does it now?'

'No,' he said, 'it doesn't. I just want somewhere of my own for my new chapter.'

'And where do I come in?'

'Where you always have, Suz. Where and when you choose to. You'll have the cottage, you can come to my flat—'

'But where will *home* be? *Our* home?'

He looked at her. He said, 'We haven't got one of those.'

'We have!'

'Not for years, Suz. A house does not a home make.'

'What do you mean?'

'I mean that Radipole Road no longer has any more heart in it than this hotel does. It hasn't had for years.' Jasper folded his arms as if bracing himself for some kind of onslaught. 'So,' he said, 'I think we should sell it.'

'*Sell* Radipole Road?'

'Yes.'

Susie looked up at the ceiling. She said, fighting tears, 'What about Polynesia?'

'She comes with me. Our mascot. She can learn music instead of swearing.'

'Oh, Jas—'

He leant forward again, uncrossing his arms. He said gently, 'I've made up my mind, Suz. We're selling

366

Radipole Road and moving on. And for once, I'm not asking you. I'm telling you.'

'Who are you?' Jeff said rudely.

He was standing at the foot of the outside staircase, which led up to the design studio. Neil was three steps above him.

'I'm the factory manager,' Neil said. He didn't hold out his hand. 'Neil Dundas. And you are?'

'You know who I am,' Jeff said.

'Touché. Just as you know who *I* am.'

Jeff looked round him as if expecting a sympathetic audience to materialize out of thin air. He said contemptuously, 'This is ridiculous.'

Neil was silent.

Jeff glanced up at him. He said, 'May I pass, please?'

Neil leant languidly against the handrail. 'What is your business up there?'

'I beg your pardon?'

'As factory manager,' Neil said, 'I am entitled to ask what your business is with any of my design team.'

Jeff sneered at him. '*Your* fucking design team—'

'The design team of this factory. This is a workplace. If we have visitors, their purpose has to be known to us.'

Jeff climbed a step or two so that his face was level with Neil's. He said, 'I don't have to have permission from a little jobsworth jerk like you to visit a member of the family who own this place.'

'Ah,' Neil said. 'You mean Grace.'

'I mean,' Jeff said, 'get out of my way.'

'Grace isn't in the design studio. Grace is currently on the factory floor. Of course, if you have professional business with Michelle—'

'Fuck off,' Jeff said. '*Loser.*'

Neil put his hands in his pockets. 'Please leave,' he said.

'Make me.'

'Och,' Neil said, 'I wouldn't dirty my hands doing that. I'd call the rozzers.'

'What is the fucking harm,' Jeff shouted, 'in paying a *courtesy* call on Grace?'

'Not during the working day. I have a factory to run.'

'If you think—' Jeff began, and stopped.

'I don't think anything. I'm not here to think anything about any private life but my own. But I *am* here to run a factory.'

Jeff took a step down again. He said derisively, 'She wouldn't give a short-arse like you a second glance.'

Neil stayed where he was, his hands in his pockets, leaning against the handrail.

'I'm going into the factory,' Jeff said.

'I'm afraid that's not permitted. You are welcome to

join a factory tour if you want to see round. They run at eleven and one.'

'Fuck you.'

Slowly Neil took one hand out of his pocket, withdrawing a phone. 'Perhaps,' he said, not raising his voice, 'you'd like to leave before I need to get you ejected.'

Jeff took another step back. 'You don't scare me.'

'I don't scare anyone. I'm not interested in scaring.'

'What are you interested in, then? Grace? I bet you are, I bet you've got the hots for—'

'I'm dialling,' Neil said. 'And they're quick, if it's the factory.'

Jeff began to retreat, shouting obscenities.

The door at the top of the staircase opened and Michelle came out. She squinted down at them. 'What's going on?'

Neil didn't look up from his phone. He said indifferently, 'D'you know this gentleman?'

Michelle took the two edges of her cardigan and pulled them tightly across her body. Her hair was piled loosely on top of her head and decorated with a large artificial flower. She looked down at Jeff for a long and considering moment. Then she sniffed. 'Never seen him before in my life, have I?'

CHAPTER EIGHTEEN

Fixing her earrings in front of the bathroom mirror was, Ashley told herself, perhaps the only normal thing that would happen in a distinctly weird day. It was even weird to be up here on her own, inserting her lucky pearl and garnet earrings that Leo had given her, while downstairs four generations of her family – *four* – were gathered, waiting for the huge piece of pork that Leo had put in the oven to be roasted. Ashley had said to Leo that she didn't much like pork, and he had replied, very matter-of-factly, that it had been on offer, it was free range, and she was very lucky to have had nothing to do with it until she put it in her mouth. Then he had kissed her firmly and told her that Morris had got Fred almost walking.

'He puts things Freddy wants just out of reach, but not at floor level. He's got amazing patience.'

Which was a quality, she had told herself, that she was going to have to cultivate. After all, it wasn't something that came naturally to her, it wasn't particularly compatible with her energy and drive, but if she wanted to have quite a large portion of her cake and eat it – and she did – then she was going to have to learn patience.

She would start by tolerating Morris. Looked at dispassionately, Morris was a surprising asset in the house: unobtrusive, deft at making and mending, and astonishingly good with the children. But he was there. He was there all the time, even when he was behind a closed bedroom door, and his constant presence was a small inhibition on her liberty, a block on complete privacy. Add to that the way domestic control had gradually slipped from Ashley's grasp to Leo's, so that the contents of the fridge looked like a stranger's to her, and the linen cupboard was now random, and shoes seemed to have spawned across every floor. Ashley felt keenly that there was still a lot to get used to, despite all the advantages, and none of it was either easy or comfortable.

Her feelings were only exacerbated by the undeniable fact that everyone seemed happier. The house felt more open, more relaxed in itself, and so did its inhabitants. Maisie, for example, was distinctly less turbulent, and no longer appeared to need to make every activity, from brushing her teeth to sharing her toys, into a power struggle upon which her very identity depended. She was still unmistakeably Maisie, but less truculently so.

Her nursery school said she hadn't wept there for two weeks.

Ashley put her palms down on the sides of the bathroom basin and leant in until her nose was almost touching the mirror. Did she look good for thirty-one? Or just average? Thirty-one was young nowadays, anyway, even if Ma had been running her own business for a decade by that age. It was never a good idea to make comparisons with Ma, anyway. Ma was an exception to almost every orthodoxy. Always had been. Ma had probably never looked in a mirror and indulged in any doubting or questioning in her entire life. Her certainty was very lucky for her, if not quite so lucky for the people round her.

Those people round her right now, in Ashley's basement kitchen, were people that Susie would probably never have dreamed could congregate in the same room – her son-in-law, her grandchildren and her father. Ashley gripped the basin. She had to go down to them. She had to. But she needed just a few minutes more, to calm herself about the dynamics that awaited her downstairs, the dynamics that Leo had declared needed exposure, and practice, and *normalizing*, which was why he had insisted that Susie came for Sunday lunch.

'Like families *should*,' he'd said, pulling a tangle of socks and tights out of the tumble-dryer. 'Getting it right, like our childhoods never managed to be. Generations round the same table.'

Ashley straightened up and flicked her hair behind her shoulders. Leo was right, even if he did sometimes sound like the soppy Waltons. But, she thought, thank heavens for the children.

Michelle was waiting for Grace in a wine bar on Wedgwood Place. She had a bottle in an ice bucket in front of her, and three glasses, one of which was already generously filled. Grace was used to seeing her in their habitual work uniform of jeans and sweaters – in Michelle's case, vibrantly coloured and patterned sweaters – so to see her gussied up for a night out in platform shoes and nail varnish was startling.

'Goodness,' Grace said, slipping her bag off her shoulder. 'I didn't realize we were dressing up. Sorry, I'm just as usual.'

Michelle waved a purple-nailed hand. 'I didn't say. Doesn't matter. I wanted it to be a surprise, anyway.'

Grace slid on to a stool opposite. She looked at the ice bucket and the glasses. She said, 'Is Neil coming then?'

'Not *Neil*,' Michelle said disparagingly. 'Why should Neil come?'

Grace gave a small shrug. 'I thought you liked him.'

Michelle sat bolt upright and held her left hand up,

its back to Grace. She smiled triumphantly. 'Not any more!'

Grace peered at the outstretched hand. It bore a tiny solitaire diamond, set on a slender gold band, on the engagement finger. Grace's eyes widened. 'Oh my God! Oh Michelle!'

Michelle nodded. She turned her hand over so that she could admire the ring herself. 'I wanted you to be the first to know.'

'Oh, Michelle, *thank* you.'

'I mean,' Michelle said, 'he's been proposing every hour, on the hour, since the dawn of time, till I'd practically stopped hearing him. And then after we'd seen off that useless Jeff of yours, I suddenly thought, Michelle, what *are* you doing, what on *earth* d'you think you're waiting for? So when we came out of that *Star Trek* movie – completely idiotic, I thought – and Mark said he'd heard of some new-builds in Burslem that a housing association was only going to rent to young locals, I thought I'd just say let's go for it, let's apply for a house. And he was so used to me saying no, he didn't react for ages, and then he just stood there on the pavement, with his mouth hanging open, and then he said, "D'you mean you will actually move in with me?" and I said, "No, you numpty, I'll *marry* you." And bless him, Grace, he burst into tears and we had to go into a convenience store and buy Kleenex.'

374

Grace got up and went round the table to give Michelle a hug and a kiss. 'It's wonderful news. *Wonderful*. Congratulations.'

'He'd got the ring in his sodding pocket, and all,' Michelle said happily. 'He's been carrying it round since Christmas. His sister knows a diamond dealer in Birmingham so he'd had the ring for ages. And of course it fits. You could trust Mark to know my ring size.'

Grace straightened up and looked at the third glass. 'Is he coming?'

'Yes. I said I wanted half an hour with you first.'

'It's a real honour, Michelle.'

'As long as you don't think I'm a right whatsit, waving my engagement ring in your face.'

Grace went back to her seat. She said, 'I'm thrilled for you. Seriously. And I don't wish it was me, promise. I don't actually want to be engaged right now. I'm kind of – not thinking about men.'

Michelle lifted the dripping bottle out of the bucket and poured a second glass. 'Only cava, I'm afraid.'

'I like cava.'

'Grace, you're well shot of Jeff. You don't want anyone who wants to hold you back. Mark won't hold me back, I'm telling you, not when I've finished putting a few bombs under him. I've told him quite plainly that I haven't got a job, I've got a career. And if I feel like that, goodness knows how *you* feel.'

Grace raised her glass. 'Huge congratulations. Really. It's wonderful. Here's to a very happy future.'

Michelle picked up her own glass. She said, 'If I have anything to do with it, it will be.' She took a long swallow, then she said, 'What about you, though?'

Grace put her glass down. She said, not looking at Michelle, 'D'you know, I'm OK. I really am.'

'My nan always said it was better to be on your own than with the wrong one. She made no bones about it. Said she'd never have married my granddad if she hadn't been pregnant. And there she was, stuck. Forty-seven years.'

'My parents aren't far off that.'

'I can't imagine it,' Michelle said wonderingly. 'Forty-seven years of Mark.' She laughed and flung her head back. 'I'll be seventy-four. What am I doing?'

'Marrying for the right reasons?' Grace said.

Michelle tipped her head forward again. 'I sodding well hope so.' She held up her glass. 'Drink up. Toast our future. And yours. I know we have our moments, but it's good working for you.'

Grace looked at her. 'Is it?'

'Yes. Why d'you ask like that?'

'No reason.'

'Is there something I should know?' Michelle demanded.

'No. The minute there is, I'll tell you.'

'But you've got wind of something—'

'I'm just looking at my family,' Grace said. 'No more than that. Just looking and considering.'

'Here's Mark,' Michelle said suddenly, getting to her feet. She waved both arms wildly to attract his attention. 'Just look at him, will you? New trainers is my future husband's idea of dressing up.'

It was, Susie reflected, the first time she had sat down to eat with her father in her entire life. He had left England when she was still bottle-fed and she had taken great care, since his return, not to put herself in a position where she would have to eat with him. Cups of tea, yes, a glass of brandy for him, yes, but eating a meal together had seemed altogether too intimate, and too forgiving. And then her son-in-law, unencumbered by all this visceral baggage from the past, had overturned her objections in an instant. One moment Morris was becoming a sizeable problem in Stoke, the next he was in Leo and Ashley's spare bedroom and had peeled the potatoes that accompanied an impressive joint of roast pork. Leo had bought the pork and he and Morris had prepared the lunch. They had made a rhubarb crumble and, rather approximately, laid the table. When everyone was summoned to eat, Susie had suffered a sudden pang of acute isolation: Jasper wasn't there because he was rehearsing yet again, and his absence made her feel exposed, and without a proper role. Seeing all the food on the table and Fred in his high chair also reminded Susie forcibly of long-ago Sunday lunches in Radipole Road, a memory which added to her discomfiture and confusion. She took her allotted place as ill at ease as she ever remembered feeling.

At least Leo hadn't attempted to sit her next to Morris. Morris had, in fact, been placed between the two children at Maisie's insistence, and appeared adept at feeding Fred and persuading Maisie to eat something other than just her roast potatoes. But his evident ease with the children – *her* grandchildren – proved as unacceptable to Susie as having to sit next to him would have been. Just as his calm near-ignoring of her was. He didn't say much, except to the children. But he appeared irritatingly at ease. He ate modestly and quietly, and even if his clothes were as dated and hippyish as before, his hair was now closely cropped and lay on his bony skull in a smooth silver pelt. It was almost unbearable to notice that his hands, skeletal and liver-spotted as they had become, were still more elegant than her own. His demeanour, his mere *presence* in Ashley's house, was deeply upsetting, and created in Susie not just resentment but a feeling that, with all her acumen and achievement and success, she had no idea how to arrange herself in his company at all.

It was Leo who found her later, in the bathroom,

perched on the edge of the bath and blowing her nose ferociously into a length of toilet paper. He closed the door and came to sit beside her. He said at once, 'It's nice having you here, you know. We don't see you enough.'

Susie aimed her wad of paper at the lavatory bowl, and missed. She began to get up to retrieve it. Leo put a hand on her arm, to keep her where she was. 'Leave it.'

'I don't think you should be nice to me.'

'I mean it,' Leo said. 'About being good to see you here.'

Susie looked at the floor. There was a series of small smudged footprints on it, as if Maisie had trodden mud in. She said, 'In my present frame of mind, I can't help feeling that's a reproach.'

Leo waited a moment, and then he said teasingly, 'And so I'm urging Ashley to do what you did because I want her to end up without a family life?'

She turned to look at him. '*Have* I?'

'Don't be daft. This is just a transition. For you, I mean.'

Susie looked wary. She said, 'From what to what?'

'Well,' he said, 'from full-on, full-time entrepreneur and businesswoman to rather more part-time all those things, in order to make way for a bit more family, a bit more home life.'

There was a small silence, and then Susie said, 'I'm

good at business. And I won't have a home much longer. Jasper wants to sell Radipole Road.'

'Yes,' Leo said.

'You *knew*?'

'Yes. I did. I would say that wanting to sell has been coming on for a while, with Jasper.'

'Is it because I bought the Parlour House?'

'No.' He glanced at her. 'Why *did* you buy the Parlour House?'

She said simply, 'I needed to. I really needed somewhere to help me feel what I felt when I first bought the factory. I needed to get back to the roots of it all. And I thought that buying somewhere up there which had family connections would join the dots and I'd feel as I felt twenty years ago.'

'Not possible.'

She sighed. 'Sometimes you have to try something to discover that it won't work. But that doesn't invalidate the impulse.' She glanced up at him. 'Is that what was going on with Jasper?'

'You'd have to ask him.'

'Sometimes,' Susie said, 'I think I am deliberately kept out of the loop. And then I wonder if it's just me. Maybe I haven't listened to anyone for ages, either.'

Leo glanced at her. He said, 'You can't do everything. That's why we all need to stand up and shout at you sometimes. Just to kind of say, hey, we're here too.'

She nodded, not speaking.

He said in a softer voice, 'You're a cool mother-in-law, you know.'

She was truly startled. '*Am* I?'

'Yup,' he said. 'Not emotionally possessive of your daughters. Treating us sons-in-law like humans. Never expecting any of us to be grateful for anything you give us or enable us to have. In my book, that's pretty good.'

She put her hands to her face. 'Goodness—'

'But maybe you *could* be a bit more hands-off now? Maybe you could step back a bit and, well, get to know Maisie and Fred a bit better?'

She dropped her hands and smiled a little ruefully. 'Do you mean I should step aside for Ashley?'

Leo stood up slowly. 'I might do,' he said.

She looked up at him. She said, 'Is this a plot? Were you sent to talk to me?'

He shook his head. 'Pure impulse,' he said. 'I saw you leave the table.'

'Promise?'

'Promise.'

She stood up too. 'I don't want to be pensioned off—'

'No one's suggesting that.'

'I can't *not* work.'

'That isn't on anyone's agenda. It's just – working differently. Working from another angle.'

She smiled at him again. She said, 'You're a clever boy.'

'Not really.'

'I don't know many men who are so good at people.'

He ducked his head. 'Thank you.'

'I'll think about what you said. I can't promise anything, mind, but I'll think. But while we're on touchy subjects, perhaps you can help me with something else. Perhaps you can do your different-angle thing for me in another area. Can I ask you something else? Something I need advice on. Leo, what am I to do about Morris?'

Morris had taken to being the last person downstairs in the evenings. He said that at his age he didn't need the sleep, and in any case, in all his life with Stella, he'd been the first one up and the last one to bed, because that had just been how things fell out between them, naturally. It had also been a source of important solitude for him, the quiet time of midnight, especially when there was a moon, and the raucous time of dawn, with all the tropical birds. For years, he had started every day sitting on the worn, paint-blistered steps of the beach house in Lamu, the first joint of the day between his fingers, the jungle chorus getting into its rowdy stride all around him and the sun rising ahead of him out of the quiet waters, bringing with it its daily blast of light and heat. To balance that with the silky quiet of darkness at the end of the day, a quiet only broken by the rustlings and faint chirrupings from the vegetation around, was a luxury. It was, probably, his only luxury. There were days when he had considered starvation a more attractive proposition than the prospect of yet another bowl of rice, maybe decorated with the bones and fins of some flavourless and dark-fleshed little fish. The idea of roast pork would have been as fantastical in Lamu as the idea of a well-appointed bathroom with constant hot water, and no opportunity for snakes to slither in through gaps in flimsy walls and coil themselves round the bucket that served as a toilet. Moving slowly around Leo and Ashley's incredibly solid-feeling kitchen last thing at night, washing up stray mugs, picking up stray toys, was a nightly miracle for him of permanence in living. It might have its claustrophobic side, but that was far outweighed by its sheer concrete evidence of a settled existence.

He was standing by the sofa in front of the television, a sock of Fred's in one hand and a double-handled pink plastic cup in the other, when Ashley came down. She was in pyjama bottoms and a camisole under a long grey cardigan, and her hair was pinned up roughly with a couple of clips. Free of make-up, she looked to Morris about fourteen – an age he had, over the years, become used to Stella being somehow arrested at. But Ashley, his and Stella's granddaughter, seemed to Morris to be arrested by nothing. He held up Fred's sock. 'Just clearing up a bit.'

Ashley didn't smile. She said, 'I came down for some tea.'

'Would you like me to make it?

She went across to the kettle. 'Heavens, no.'

'Only asking.'

She had her back to him, filling the kettle. She said, not turning, 'Sorry.'

He shuffled across the room and put the pink mug on the counter above the dishwasher. He said amiably, 'It's been a bit of a day.'

Ashley began opening cupboards in search of mugs and tea.

'It has. Where's the valerian?'

Morris leant against the counter, smoothing Fred's sock between his fingers. He said, 'Long ago, when I didn't fit somewhere I just pushed off. If things didn't work out, I made myself scarce. Can't do that now. I would if I could, you know.'

Ashley put a box of teabags next to the kettle and extracted one. She said, still not looking at him, 'It's not you, actually. It's me. And possibly Ma.'

Morris went on smoothing the sock. He said indistinctly, 'Can't blame her.'

Ashley turned round. 'I don't. I understand her. I understand me, too, being on her side. But understanding her doesn't mean she's right. Or that I am.'

Morris didn't look at her. He said, 'What's done is done. You can't change things by wishing.'

Ashley switched on the kettle. She said, watching it gather itself up to boil, 'Nor can you change other people.'

'That's why I used to run.'

Ashley flicked a glance at him. 'No running now.'

'No. And . . . and you get stuck with the consequences.' He grimaced at the sock and then he said, 'I've never been much of a one for saying sorry, but I'm sorry for that. Just as I'm sorry about Susan.'

Ashley went back to watching the kettle. 'Have you said that to her?'

'No.'

'Why not?'

He paused, and then he said, 'Haven't dared.'

'You should dare,' Ashley said. 'You ought to.'

Morris laid the sock beside the mug. He said, 'D'you think it would help?'

'Yes, I do. She's having an awful time. And you're not. Are you?'

He said quietly, 'I'm glad to be here, Ashley.'

The kettle gave a short scream and subsided. Ashley picked it up and began to pour water into her mug. She said, 'And I'm trying to get used to it. The children like it, Leo likes it, and I am going to try to like it. I have to somehow get over your – unforgivableness. As well as just having you here. That's *my* problem. But Ma is different. Ma is your problem, at least in part. You have to help her. Try and make it up to her by helping her now, helping her to forgive you and to move on from where she's been all her life, because of what you did.'

Morris was silent. He stood leaning against the kitchen counter, his head bent and his hands, as was his wont, in his opposite sleeves.

Ashley left her teabag to steep and leant back too. She put her hands into the pockets of her cardigan and wrapped it across her. She said, 'You defied convention by running away. Well, now you've come back, and you've got to face the fact that people like Leo and me are dealing with it in a very different way. Just as Ma did, except that you were too far away to see it. Leo gets it. Leo understands that, just like Ma, I really wanted children, but I really want life too. Wanting fulfilment doesn't stop just because you've become a mother, and I'll always be torn because mother love is such a fierce feeling. Leo understands that I'm torn like this, he gets that I've got a kind of hunger in me, the kind of hunger Ma had, and he also realizes that Ma has let the balance of her life slip recently, and that you are actually one of the people who can help her get it right again, help her see that however brilliant the company is – and it is – it can't give her everything she needs. It satisfies one hunger, but not the other. She's so much more than a mother and grandmother, but she's both those vital things, too. And at the moment, you're not helping her be either, because you're not showing her that you're on her side.'

Morris didn't look up. He said gruffly, 'I'm the last person she wants.'

'No,' Ashley said. 'Nobody feels that about their fathers. Not deep down. Anger's only a way of showing how miserable you are.'

'She's got everything she needs. She doesn't need me.'

'She does,' Ashley said. 'She *does*. Don't you even want to *try*?'

He glanced at her. Then he looked back at the floor beyond his feet. 'Yes,' he said.

Cara let herself into Radipole Road, and allowed the front door to slam shut behind her, deliberately.

'Hi there!' she shouted.

There was no reply.

'Pa!' Cara shouted. 'Ma?'

Silence. The hall lights were on, but ahead of her the stairs were in darkness, and so were the kitchen and sitting room. She went down the hall rapidly and fumbled for the light switches, a whole bank of them sleekly set into a brushed-aluminium plate which had been put up when the house was rewired for Jasper's studio. The kitchen sprang into abrupt and brilliant light. It was empty. Tidy and empty. Even the big parrot cage was empty, the door open and a scattering of striped seeds lying on the floor. A Susie Sullivan jug of improbably orange gerberas on the table was the only sign of life.

Cara went back down the hall to the sitting room. It had the air it always had after one of Benedita's visits, the cushions unnaturally plumped, as if the whole room was standing to attention. The TV guide was folded back to show a date two days previously. It was weird, Cara thought, ghostly. Deckchairs on the *Marie Celeste* and all that. No sign even of Polynesia.

Switching on lights as she went, Cara climbed the stairs. Her parents' bed was made, but there was a towel hanging over a corner of the bathroom door and one of their toothbrushes was still faintly damp. To her relief, her mother's familiar make-up bag was open by one of the two washbasins, with its usual comforting jumble inside, and there was laundry in the dirty-clothes basket and her father's slippers – ancient, dark red leather with no backs and worn soles – lying by the shower.

Cara shivered. It was not just strange, but wrong, somehow, to be investigating her parents' bedroom for signs of life. When she was little, she remembered feeling an absolute right to possession, a natural justification at barging into her parents' room or conversations whenever she felt inclined to, as if they could never have a greater concern than with her. In fact, she had felt the need to test that concern almost constantly, to challenge them to have any commitment more pressing than their children, as if she knew that one day she would inevitably find them wanting. Well, she supposed, in purely orthodox terms, her mother would have been found wanting. Her mother was often away, and was constantly preoccupied. But she had, at the same time, created for the household a stability that the mothers of most of Cara's friends took for granted, the only difference being that it was their fathers who provided it.

Cara picked a lipstick out of her mother's make-up bag. It was the same brand, same colour she had used for ever. Like her scent, it was instantly recognizable as Susie's. The lipstick itself was also worn down in the idiosyncratic shape of all Susie's lipsticks, with a curious little peak at one side. The sight of it made Cara suddenly ashamed of herself. It was like looking in the drawers of her parents' bedside tables on the sly, and being rewarded – or punished – for such snooping by finding evidence of the sort of bedroom games that it was absolutely unthinkable for her own mother and father to indulge in. She clicked the lipstick shut hastily and dropped it back into the make-up bag. She was aware of her reflection in the well-lit mirror above the basin, but she couldn't actually look at it. Feeling abashed was one thing. Seeing it written plainly on your thirty-three-year-old face was quite another.

She went quickly out of the bathroom and bedroom, turning off the lights as she went. She would go down to the kitchen and leave her mother a note, saying that she had come round to see her on the off-chance, but no more. She would leave the note where they had always left everything of significance for Susie: on the counter not far from the kettle, weighted with a chipped plaster-of-Paris parrot that Grace had made at school when she was eleven.

As Cara reached the bottom of the stairs, a key sounded in the front door. Cara froze. The door opened and Susie stepped in, uncharacteristically clad in a shapeless old padded jacket of Jasper's, with a striped muffler tied over her ears. She paused, took in Cara and gave a gasp of surprise.

'Darling!'

Cara hurried forward. 'Sorry, Ma. I should have texted. I didn't mean to give you a fright.'

Susie's cheek was cold against Cara's lips. She said, 'I wouldn't have picked up a text anyway. I've got my phone in my pocket, but it's turned off.'

'Where have you *been*?'

Susie pulled off the muffler and shook her hair. 'Walking.'

'*Walking?*' Cara said. 'But you never walk.'

Susie smiled at her. 'I did just now.'

'I couldn't think where you were. I thought you'd be back from Ashley's by now.'

'I was,' Susie said. 'I am. But I wanted some exercise. I wanted to do a bit of thinking, and it's easier walking while you think, isn't it?'

She pulled off Jasper's jacket and looked at it. 'We bought that in Berlin. We hadn't reckoned on it being so cold. It must be more than twenty years old.' She looked at Cara. 'Lovely to see you, darling.'

Cara began to move down the hall towards the kitchen. She said, 'I'll put the kettle on.'

Susie stood where she was, holding Jasper's jacket. She said, 'Cara?'

'Yes.'

'It's Sunday night. Are you – are you here for a reason?'

Cara stopped walking. She turned in the kitchen doorway and put her hands on the frame. 'Yes,' she said again.

Susie folded the jacket and laid it on the hall chair.

Then she moved across to a mirror on the wall and ran her fingers through her hair. She said, 'Nothing awful happened?'

'No,' Cara said. 'It's just that I – well, I've got something to tell you.'

CHAPTER NINETEEN

Maisie had a haircut for the photoshoot. Usually she wriggled and raged on a bathroom stool, swaddled in a towel, while Ashley darted at her curls with a pair of scissors. But today, in honour of the first fully fledged professional photoshoot to happen in her very own kitchen, she was taken to a real hairdresser, propped on a pile of magazines to raise her high enough for the stylist to cut her hair properly, and swathed in a black nylon cape that fell in bat-like folds almost to the floor.

As long as she was in the hairdresser's, and absorbed by her own reflection in the mirror in front of her, she was, Ashley reported, angelic. But once back at home and presented with the new dark-blue, white-collared corduroy dress, with matching blue and white striped tights, that had been chosen for her to wear for the catalogue photographs, she disintegrated into sudden and complete fury. She was *not* wearing that dress. She was wearing her favourite princess dress from her dressing-up box, the one made of scratchy panels of iridescent gauze, with artificial jewels glued gaudily to the bodice. She did not shout, she screamed. Then she cast herself down on her bedroom floor, like someone helpfully demonstrating a textbook tantrum, and, while still yelling, kicked her feet so hard against her chest of drawers that her shoes fell off.

'I'm afraid that it's a complete meltdown,' Ashley said, coming down to her unrecognizably styled kitchen. 'She's *purple*.'

Leo was sent up to try and calm her. When that failed, Morris, who had worked a small miracle by creating a sufficient semblance of a garden outside the French doors to satisfy photographic requirements, went upstairs to try his luck at pacifying her. He returned to report that he had managed to get her to stop screaming, but that nothing he said would induce her to put on the blue dress instead of the princess one. He said she had got into bed fully dressed, clutching the princess dress, and was lying under her Hello Kitty duvet, smouldering with determination.

Susie, who had been rearranging the mugs and jugs and bowls on Ashley's dresser in a way that aroused familiar admiration in everyone there, turned round and announced unexpectedly that she would go up.

Ashley was astonished. 'Oh, Ma!'

Susie gave a daisy-patterned jug a little nudge to the

left. She said, surveying it, 'When are the other children coming?'

'In ten minutes,' Leo said. 'Amanda's bringing Felix and the baby, and there's a couple more from school.'

'Right,' Susie said. She crossed the room to a box packed with various items from the new range to be photographed, and picked out a couple of mugs. 'Wish me luck,' she said, and went out of the kitchen. Everybody present – Ashley, Leo, Morris, and the photography crew, headed by the company stylist, who had chosen Maisie's catalogue clothes – watched her go in respectful silence.

Maisie's room was dim. She or Morris had pulled the curtains across when she retired to bed, leaving the eerie gloom of partly obscured daylight. Maisie lay on her side in bed, her thumb in her mouth, and stiff folds of glistening gauze clamped in her arms.

Susie put the two mugs she was holding down among the litter of small plastic objects on top of Maisie's chest of drawers. Then she said, 'I think I'll draw the curtains.'

'No,' Maisie said, round her thumb.

Susie went across to the window. 'The thing is,' she said, pulling them apart, 'that I can't see in the dark. I'm not a cat, I'm a grandmother, and I need light to see by.'

Maisie took her thumb out. 'My eyes hurt!' she shouted.

Susie went back to pick up the mugs, and then sat down on the edge of Maisie's bed and held them out. 'See those?'

Maisie squinted. 'Yes,' she said reluctantly.

'What's on them?'

Inch by inch, Maisie half sat up. Her newly cut hair clustered round her head in soft curls.

'You look lovely,' Susie said.

Maisie peered at the mugs, ignoring the compliment. 'Balloons,' she said.

'And this one?'

'Flags.'

'Bunting, actually. And there's some with kites. We're going to take pictures of them, you see – pictures of you, and Freddy and Felix and all the others, with this lovely new china, for a special children's catalogue. We've never had a catalogue just for children before, so you will be the first children ever to be in a catalogue on your own. This is special china for that catalogue, special china for children. It's called Balloons and Bunting. That's the name of the range. It was designed by your Aunt Grace.'

Maisie crawled slowly out of her nest of gauze and bedclothes and reached out to touch the mug.

Susie said, 'What colours can you see?'

Maisie sighed. It was astonishing, Susie thought, to bellow your eyes out for over half an hour and be without a blotch or a tearstain ten minutes later.

'Red,' Maisie said. 'Blue. Green.'

'But not pink.'

'I *like* pink.'

'So do I,' Susie said. 'But deep pink. Or soft pink. Not bubblegum pink.'

'Pink is my *favourite*.'

'This china, Maisie, is for *all* children. Not just you. This is for boys as well as girls, and big children as well as little children. And for these very special photographs, we need all the children – and you are the chief child – to wear colours that match the balloons or the kites or the bunting. So if you wear bubblegum pink, you won't match. So you can't be in the photos, I'm afraid. Fred will be, and so will Felix and his sister, but we'll have to do without you, because you won't match. It's very sad, because we wanted you to be the chief child in the photos. But there we are.'

Maisie sat for a moment, looking at the mugs. Then she looked back at the garish shimmer in her bed.

'If you scream again,' Susie said pleasantly, 'I will just go downstairs and leave you here, and tell the cameraman to photograph the other children because you won't be coming. What a pity. What a shame.'

Maisie gave a shuddering sigh. She glanced with

distaste at the dark-blue dress hanging trimly on her wardrobe door. Then she climbed slowly off her bed and stood in front of Susie, her chin raised in defiance. 'I've got my Sleeping Beauty pants on,' she said, *anyway.*'

'I saw the studio lights were still on,' Neil said, 'so I guessed you'd still be working.'

Grace was sitting at the big table, staring at the screen of her laptop. She had hardly glanced up when he came in.

'I'm not working,' she said. 'I'm looking at the photos from the shoot today. Ashley's just sent them. They're amazing. Absolutely amazing. We've always had good photos, but we've never had ones as good as these.'

Neil went round to stand behind her, instructing himself, as he did so, not to lean too close, not to allow his mind or his senses to register anything beyond what was on her screen. It showed a picture of Maisie and Fred, apparently lit only by the candles in the background. Maisie, in dark blue, her stout striped legs ending in red suede boots with thick soles, was standing on a chair concentrating on pouring milk from a Balloon jug into a Kite mug in front of Freddy. He was in his high chair, in a checked blue shirt with buttoned cuffs, and he had flung his short arms into the air in a gesture to match the look of rapture on his face. Both children appeared entirely oblivious of any camera, their faces caught in the glow of what they were doing.

'It's a winner, isn't it?' Grace said.

Neil cleared his throat. He moved sideways to avoid the distraction of Grace's vulnerable back view. 'It certainly is.'

'There's loads of them. That one is obviously the cover shot, as Ash says, but there's lots of others nearly as good. A fantastic one of a wonderful baby with her face almost obscured by the mug she's drinking from. And a sweet little boy counting M & Ms on a Bunting plate.'

'You must be thrilled.'

'I am,' Grace said. 'They plainly had such a good day.'

Neil propped himself against the table and crossed his arms and ankles. He said, 'I didn't mean that. I meant you must be thrilled with the range. All your own work.'

Grace gave the laptop a shy smile. 'Well, that too.'

'The idea of a children's catalogue—'

'I think that was Ashley.'

'No,' Neil said, 'it was you. It was Ashley's idea to increase the number of catalogues, but the idea of having one to launch a specific children's range was you.'

'Oh,' Grace said. She didn't look at him.

'And the designs for that range were yours, too.'

Grace leant forward to look at a picture of Maisie sitting on a stool, with a bowl in both hands, staring straight and solemnly to camera. She said, almost under her breath, 'It's just as well that today was good, actually.'

Neil waited. He watched her flick through a few more slides. He noticed, slightly to his despair, that as well as the scattering of freckles across her nose and cheekbones, she had a single darker one, almost like a beauty spot, just above the left-hand corner of her mouth. He said, too loudly, 'Say again?'

Grace didn't look at him. She said, 'Ma rang. Just before Ashley sent these through.'

Neil looked down at his feet. He said as brusquely as he could, 'Remembering episodes in the past, Grace, are you sure you want to share this kind of thing with me?'

Her face flamed. 'Oh God.'

'Well,' he said, 'I'd just like to be sure. Where I stand.'

'I should never—'

'No,' he said. 'You shouldn't.'

She gave him a quick glance. Her face was still pink. She said, 'I don't know what came over me.'

'Nor do I. I just don't want it to, again. I'd prefer not to know than be sent back below stairs.'

Grace cleared her throat. She shook her head, then said, 'I want to tell you. Please don't hold an insane and clumsy stupidity against me.'

'Look at me,' he said.

She turned her head, very slowly. She said, 'I'm so sorry. I really am so sorry.'

'I know. And I'm a chippy Scot. But I won't mention it again.' He held her gaze. 'What is it? What did Susie want me to know?'

Grace swallowed. She pushed her hair off her face in a characteristic gesture. 'Cara went round to see her, on her own, on Sunday night. In order to say – to tell her – that she and Dan have decided to leave the company.'

Neil gave a long, low whistle.

'Yes,' Grace said.

'*Leave?*'

'Yes.'

'Leave completely? Quit being commercial and merchandizing directors?'

'Yes.'

Neil uncrossed his ankles and moved to bring a second chair close to Grace's. He sat down and leant towards her. 'Why?'

Grace turned to look at him. She said, 'Why do you think?'

'Isn't it a bit drastic?'

'Not for them,' Grace said. 'No, I don't think so. You can't go on wanting and needing change, and not getting it, for ever. And anyway—' She stopped.

'Anyway what?'

'Anyway,' Grace said carefully, 'they weren't ever as committed to the *product* as some of us. It was the systems they liked. They are brilliant at running and promoting a company, and that's what they're going to do.'

'Which is?'

'They're joining this friend of theirs, Rick Machin. They're going to start up something new with him, re-branding companies which have got tired or are losing momentum. Any kind of company, Ma said, starting with a hotel chain and a firm that makes warehouse systems. She said Cara was very fired up about it, about the idea, the independence—'

'Independence?'

'From a family company, I suppose.'

Neil straightened up. He looked round him. 'D'you keep wine in that fridge?'

'No,' Grace said. 'Only milk.'

'You need more than milk. So do I. This may even be a more-than-beer moment.'

'Neil,' Grace said, 'we shouldn't be *celebrating*.'

'I wasn't thinking of that. I was thinking of shock. Medicinal drinking.'

'Oh,' she said. 'Shock.'

He stood up and held out a hand to her. 'Come to the pub with me. Bring those pictures.'

'Neil—'

'Don't turn me down.'

'I wasn't going to. I was just going to say how weird I felt, how I thought I shouldn't feel what I'm feeling.' She reached forward and closed her laptop. Then she stood, too, and stayed there, looking down.

'Which is?' he said.

She didn't move, but he could see that she was trying, without much success, to suppress a smile.

'Excited,' she said.

'I can't stop crying,' Cara said. 'I don't know why I keep crying. I don't want to cry like this.'

Jasper pushed a box of tissues towards her. He said, 'I had a Latin teacher once whose favourite saying was "There is no change without sacrifice".'

Cara snatched a handful of tissues and blew her nose. Her appearance, Jasper noted fondly, was as together as it ever was, but her nose was touchingly pink.

'Coffee?' he said. 'Tea? Something stronger?'

She made a little waving-away gesture, then she blew her nose again. She said, 'I want this new future to happen. I really do. It's exactly what we like doing and we can do it together. But it's just awful, leaving. I feel like I'm leaving far more than I ever felt it on my wedding day. That felt like adding Dan. This feels like – like *emigrating*.'

Jasper ran water into the kettle. 'When you girls were

growing up, I learned not to come running if one of you screamed blue murder. It usually meant you'd only broken a fingernail.'

'This isn't melodrama, Pa,' Cara said. 'It's real drama. Dan and I are changing every single relationship in our lives except the one we have with each other.'

Jasper put a Susie Sullivan teapot – Poppy Fields range – on the counter and dropped in a couple of tea-bags. He said, 'Sweetheart, we're all doing that, even your mother. We've all been flung up in the air and we're all coming down again in different places. It won't mean the end of things. It'll just mean seeing it all from another angle.'

Cara opened the fridge and took out a plastic container of milk. She said, looking into the fridge, 'Heavens, there's nothing *in* here. Just milk and a lemon and some contact lens saline.'

'There hasn't been much more than that for ages.'

Cara shut the fridge and put the milk down by the kettle. She said, 'Is that why you're moving out?'

Jasper put both palms down flat on the counter and stared at the kettle. He said, 'The state of the fridge is a symptom. Not the disease.'

Cara said, on a rising note, 'Don't give me something else to cry about. Don't tell me you're leaving Ma—'

'Of course I'm not.'

'But if—'

'Cara,' Jasper said, picking up the boiled kettle and pouring water into the teapot, 'we'd hit the buffers in this house a long time ago. Your mother doesn't really want to be here any more than I do. Life has moved on from here, you've all got your own places, I have something ahead of me for the first time in a very long time, and Susie – well, she needed a bit of a kick up the backside. You can get quite as stuck at the top of a company as you can at the bottom.' He turned to look at Cara. 'You and Dan dropping your little bombshell was exactly what was needed.'

'I'm as heartbroken as I'm excited,' Cara said. 'I'm longing to leave, and I can't bear the thought of it. I think I'd suffocate if I had to stay, but I can hardly stand the thought of not knowing everything that Gracie and Ashley know.'

Jasper held a mug of tea out to her. 'Biscuit?'

'*Are* there any?'

He smiled at her, and raised his own mug. 'Probably not.'

'I wish you hadn't suggested it then. I could kill for a chocolate Hobnob.'

'That's better,' Jasper said. 'It isn't like you to get yourself in such a state.'

Cara was opening cupboards in search of a biscuit. With her back to him, she said, 'It is, you know. I'm a car crash under a very organized exterior.'

Jasper let a beat fall, then he said, 'So is your mother.'

Cara turned round. She held something in her hand. 'Ginger nuts,' she said.

'Don't read the best-by date. It'll be prehistoric. And they'll be soft.'

Cara put the packet down on the counter and peered at it. '2009.'

'Biscuits don't go off. They get stale but they don't get maggots.'

Cara ripped the packet open. 'They look weirdly OK. Have one.'

Jasper took a biscuit and dipped it quickly into his tea. 'Delicious. I wonder who bought them? I never buy ginger nuts.'

'Ma's inner chaos is her energy,' Cara said. 'Mine too. What luck we married steady men.' She took a bite of biscuit herself and added through it, 'Has she seen this flat you've found?'

'She doesn't need to.'

'But Pa, if it's your London base—'

'*My* London base,' Jasper said. 'Where she is very welcome.'

Cara stared at him. 'Aren't you even asking her?'

'No.'

'But—' Cara began, and stopped.

'Where am I finding the money, you mean?'

'Well, yes.'

'I'm using what my parents left me, for a deposit. Followed by my share of the sale of this. It's only a studio flat.'

'But Pa—'

'Cara,' Jasper said, 'I've been the follower for years and years. I've accommodated and tolerated and compromised, and to a large extent I haven't minded any of that. In fact, for part of the time, part of me quite liked it. But I don't like it any more. I have suddenly got a small, oddly shaped but definite future. I have a studio. I have a *band*. I haven't had a band for over thirty years. The band means that I won't be doing the following, I'll be doing a bit of leading instead. Susie can join me whenever she's free to. I don't want another woman, I don't even want your mother to be much different. But I do want to do my own thing now, and I'll be pleased as Punch if sometimes she'd like to set aside her own priorities – like the company, like this ridiculous cottage – and join me.'

Cara was still staring at him, over her mug. She said wonderingly, 'What's got into you?'

He smiled at her. 'Something not a million miles from what got into you and Dan.'

'Did someone say something?'

'Maybe.'

'Who? What? Did—'

He shook his head. He was still smiling. 'Cara, you

don't need to know. It's your first lesson in not need-ing, from now on, to know everything.'

'Hard—'

'But not impossible.'

Cara turned to look down the kitchen towards the parrot cage. Polynesia was gazing almost dreamily into a little punnet of blueberries that Jasper had put there earlier. She had the air of someone who had been quietly, unobtrusively, listening.

'And her?' Cara said. 'Polly?'

'With me, of course.'

'Does Ma know?'

Jasper put his mug down. He crossed his arms. 'Sweetheart,' he said firmly, 'Ma knows *everything*.'

Morris had discovered how to use the washing machine. He had also worked out the various clips on the harnesses on Fred's buggy, Fred's high chair and Fred's car seat. He had mastered all the idiosyncrasies of the door and window locks throughout the house, and the vagaries of the pilot light on the boiler. He had had a boat on Lamu for years, a fishing boat, and looking after and operating that, as well as his precarious dwelling, had stood him in good stead as far as practical skills were concerned. He found the business of helping run a house was as little trouble to him as getting Leo to relinquish a lot of tasks had been. When it came to house-training this strange old vagrant from a tropical island, Morris thought, Leo had been pleasantly surprised to find himself pushing at an open door.

Of course, Morris told himself, it was a blessing to be needed. It was more than that, really; it was a kind of unexpected gift, to realize that one could make a contribution to a busy working household, and a marked contribution at that. Shuffling about the house in his trodden-down espadrilles, Morris knew himself to be quietly useful: changing the fuse on Ashley's hairdryer; watching Fred eat his way through his supper, pea by single pea; transferring one interminable load of washing from machine to dryer; monitoring the firm that Leo had summoned to create a garden while they unrolled lengths of turf to produce a lawn as instantly and remarkably as if it had been carpet. He couldn't remember when he had had such a sense of purpose, let alone of his own value. Perhaps, he thought with mild astonishment, he never had. Perhaps he had drifted through eight decades without ever doing more than just getting by, suspending any sense other than the immediate one of the moment. Perhaps – and this was a large and uncomfortable perhaps – that was how he had dealt with failing to be the son that his father had wanted.

But now, at an age when tradition indicated that you

should stop, he seemed to be starting. What's more, he found that not only did he like starting, but that it made him want to go on. He was agile still, he was capable, and it seemed that after several false starts he had landed in some kind of berth. Of course, the berth in Ashley's house couldn't last. He knew that. He knew it even before Ashley told him that she found it hard having him there, and before he overheard, through a bedroom door Ashley and Leo had omitted to close, that if Dan and Cara were leaving the company, then a vacancy arose which Ashley and Leo seemed certain she could fill. Morris had yet to straighten out in his own head which role in the company meant what, but as far as he could gather, Ashley was aiming to be commercial director after Dan left. And she and Leo seemed to think that Cara's old role, and her own, should be filled by people from outside the company, outside the *family*. Morris, standing on the darkened landing on his way back from the bathroom, his old feet bare and silent on the sanded planks, had almost gasped at that and given himself away.

'What about Grace?' he'd wanted to shout. 'What about Susan? What about them?'

Susan. Well, Susan was a problem that had to be tackled soon, just as the question of how he might still be useful to Ashley and Leo without actually cluttering up their spare bedroom had to be. It was, Morris thought, to use a modern phrase, a work in progress. Everything right now seemed to be in transition, and although he knew himself to be hindered by the life-time shackle of his own passivity, he also knew that there were some things he might be able to deal with himself. And one of those things was Susan.

Poor Susan. Well, not poor really – not neglected and deprived and unconfident and aimless. But poor to have had a father and mother alive, throughout her growing-up, but never in contact. Poor to have had to discover the loneliness of being isolated by your own success. Poor Susan, to be so thrown by the reappearance of your useless old parent that you were unable to react with any consistency or constructiveness. Morris had caught her looking at him once or twice on the day of the photoshoot with an expression of bewilderment and apprehension, as if she was the only person in that crowded, busy room who still had an acute problem with his very existence.

Well, as Ashley had made very plain to him, he could probably help with that. He could at least try. In fact, with Susan's London house being put on the market and her husband turning into an old rocker – such a fashion for them now, it seemed – trying to help his daughter seemed, to his surprise, to be something he urgently wanted to do. He wasn't at all sure how he should go about it – whether he should start by saying sorry, or by asking her how she was – but maybe it was better not to be sure. Maybe it was best, really, just to find a way of showing her, in a manner she could not doubt, that he had never been a father who was truly unfeeling or indifferent. He had just been a man whose emotions had been in cold storage, for all manner of reasons, some of which he was accountable for, and some of which he certainly wasn't. And now, at the age of eighty-one, they were thawing out.

CHAPTER TWENTY

Ashley and Cara were sitting at the boardroom table in the office. In front of them was an open laptop, and on the screen was Grace, slightly fuzzily holding up a huge jug in the studio at the factory.

'This is the party pitcher for the Balloons and Bunting range. Or at least, it's the prototype. I think the handle needs to be broader, and the spout less pinched.'

Ashley leant forward. 'It looks fine.'

'I think I should make the balloons bigger—'

'I can't bear it,' Cara said. 'That I won't be here to see it launched.'

Grace put the pitcher on the table beside her and looked towards her camera. She said, 'Of course you'll be there. You're not going to *Australia*, you're going a mile up the road.'

'Exactly,' Ashley said. She had had another new haircut, a sort of feathery bob.

Cara said, impatiently, 'You know what I mean.'

'Nonsense,' Grace said. Her voice sounded uncharacteristically confident. 'We'll tell you whatever you want to know. And then when we need rebranding in a few years' time, you can do it for us. For nothing.'

The others laughed.

Ashley said, 'We're inundated with applications for our jobs here.'

'I bet,' said Grace.

'People are so well qualified. Almost over-qualified.'

'What does Ma think?'

Cara and Ashley looked at each other.

'We haven't asked her,' Ashley said.

'Haven't you?'

'Of course, we will . . .'

Grace leant towards the screen. She said confidentially, 'I think she might sell the Parlour House.'

'*What?*'

'She just came out with it. She just said to me that she had had a bit of a wake-up call, partly about Pa and partly about her own need to see things a bit differently. She said all these houses and flats just suddenly looked like a metaphor for what was the matter and why she and Pa weren't doing very well together, and that what had seemed so important looked a bit daft instead.'

'But I thought it was about this creative-vision thing—'

'It was.'

'I thought she couldn't have the ideas that were so central to the company if she didn't have somewhere of her own to be, and think, and all that.'

Grace leant closer still, so that her face was distorted and her eyes grew huge as plates. 'Maybe *I'm* going to have the ideas from now on. Maybe, even if she can't quite say so yet, she sort of senses that there's going to be a bit of a change.'

The others leant forward too.

'Gracie! Have you talked to her?'

'In a roundabout way.'

'What happened? What did she say?'

'It was more what *I* said.'

'Which was?'

'I – sort of lost my temper.'

'Wow.'

'What did you say?'

Grace pushed her hair back. She said, 'I kind of told her to get a grip. I said look at what's happened – Morris arriving, Cara and Dan going, Pa finding a new lease of life – look at all that and wake *up*, stop eluding everyone and refusing to be pinned down or ever *there*, while insisting on having control of everything. You can't do it, I said, any more than you can stop Ashley wanting to do Dan's job her way, or me wanting more control up here. We are all moving on, we are all changing places. And you've got to stop wanting nothing to change unless you say so, and look at your own life, look at your marriage, take in the fact that you are actually not even going to have a *home*. You've got to be a person, not just a business obsessive. You've got to set us all *free*, like you've always been.'

There was a short, stunned silence.

Then Ashley said again, admiringly, 'Wow.'

'Ten out of ten, Gracie,' said Cara.

'Yes. Well.'

'Did she yell at you?'

'No. No, actually, she didn't. She went very quiet. Then she said Maisie had given her a painting she'd done at school. It was completely black, Ma said. All over. Maisie said it was a picture of what was under her bed. Ma said she would treasure it.'

The other two were laughing. Cara said, 'Didn't she say anything about what you'd said?'

'Not then. But this morning, she told me she was getting the Parlour House valued. Which I took as a roundabout way of letting me know she'd heard me.'

'You're very patient. I'd have asked her outright.'

'I didn't have the heart,' Grace said. 'Ash, that's cool hair.'

Ashley tossed her head slightly. She said airily, 'Commercial Director hair?'

Grace gave a little whoop.

'Will you miss me?' Cara demanded.

'Nah.'

'You must be joking—'

'Dan is so happy.'

'You will be.'

'I couldn't stand to stay. But—'

'It'll give you a chance to like Ma again,' Grace said.

'It'll free me,' Cara said. 'Agreed.'

Grace glanced at her watch. 'Gotta go, chickens.'

'Have you? Where?'

Grace pulled back slightly from the camera. She said casually, 'Oh, boots.'

'Boots?'

'Walking boots.'

'But you never walk. You're as bad as Ma.'

'I'm starting,' Grace said. 'Peak District. Saturday.'

'Not Jeff—'

'No, Car. Not Jeff. Promise. Never Jeff again.'

'Who then?'

'A friend.'

'A boyfriend?'

'A friend,' Grace said, 'who is a man. As it happens.'

'Not Neil—'

'Why not Neil?'

Ashley said, 'Could you think of Neil as a boyfriend?'

Grace had moved away from her screen to collect items from the table in the studio and was dropping them into her bag. She called, 'He's a friend I can talk to about all the things I'd like to do with the company, bounce all my ideas off – like importing bedlinen from Spain and toiletries from France—'

'Ma will have a fit.'

'About Neil?'

'About imports.'

Grace turned to the camera. She sang, 'There may be trouble ahead.'

'You mean it!'

'I do,' Grace said.

'Walking the hills of Derbyshire with Neil Dundas!'

Grace slung her bag on her shoulder. She bent towards the camera again and blew her sisters a kiss. 'I mean a lot of things,' she said. And switched off her screen.

Morris put down a thick white cup of coffee and a granola square on a blue paper napkin in front of Susie. She looked at the granola square. She said uncertainly, not wishing to sound rude, 'Thank you, but I'm not really hungry.'

He lowered himself into an adjacent chair at the café table. 'I didn't think you would be, Susan. But it'll give you something to do, I thought, breaking it into pieces.'

'Goodness,' she said, trying to laugh, 'is it going to be that awkward?'

He gave her a surprisingly level look. Then he pushed the mug of teaspoons on the table towards her. 'Sugar?'

'No, thank you.'

'No,' he said. 'I didn't think you'd take sugar, either.'

'Is this some kind of test? Or game?'

He shook his head. Then he smiled at her. 'No,' he said.

Susie picked up her coffee cup with both hands. She said, looking at it rather than at Morris, 'Do you realize that this coffee is the first thing you have ever given me in my life?'

He didn't flinch. He said gravely, 'I hope it's the first of many.'

Susie took a sip. Then she said, 'When you asked me to meet you here, I thought perhaps – perhaps you wanted to say sorry.'

Morris sighed. He said, 'Is that what you want?'

'I'd like it to be what *you* wanted.'

'Well,' he said, 'if you want the honest truth, Susan, I'd rather use my energies getting things right now, rather than weeping and wailing about a past I can't change.'

Susie felt a peculiar and unforeseen stab of affection. She said tolerantly, surprising herself, 'You're a shocker.'

'I might be. But it doesn't stop me from seeing how hard it is for you to watch those girls of yours doing exactly what you've brought them up to do, without maybe understanding the consequences of what you were doing to them all those years.'

Susie gave a little start. She opened her mouth to contradict him, and then closed it again. Morris reached out a hand, briefly gripped her nearest wrist and took his hand away again. He said, 'I've never been much of a one for running races – I don't need to tell you that – but I'd imagine that being out in front for years and years doesn't actually prepare you very well for having your own daughters drawing level. And then maybe pulling away from you.'

Susie said in a low voice, 'I am really, really proud of them.'

'I know you are.'

'*Really* proud.'

'You may not want to hear this from me,' Morris said, 'but I feel the same way about you.'

'Please don't.'

'And I can see that it's lonely.'

'It's not lonely!' Susie said with energy. 'It's liberating!'

Morris indicated the granola square. 'Why don't you eat some flapjack?'

'I don't want it.'

'I'll take it back for Freddy, then,' Morris said mildly. 'Freddy's a cookie monster.'

Susie pushed the paper napkin towards him. She said in a rush, 'You're right.'

'I don't need to be right, Susan. I just need to be allowed to make a start.'

She nodded.

'I can't change the past,' Morris said again. 'But maybe I can help you from missing out on things you can't have a second chance at, now.'

'I know.'

He gave a little chuckle. He said, 'I thought you might flare up at me there.'

She shook her head. She said sadly, 'I don't want to.'

'Drink your coffee.'

She picked her cup up again, obediently. She said, almost shyly, 'What – what was my mother like?'

Morris gave a little sigh. 'Sweet,' he said. 'Innocent.'

'Childlike?'

He nodded.

'Am I like her?'

'Well,' he said, 'Grace has got her hair.'

'You heard what I asked.'

Morris sighed. 'I see something of her in you. I see it in Cara. I see it in Maisie.'

'Why d'you say it like that?'

'The truth is, Susan,' he said, 'I don't want to see anything or anyone – even you yourself – standing in the way of your being happy. Seems to me that you've inherited some good, but a bit of bad, like we all have. But you've done something I never did – and I've suffered for it – and that's choose a good partner and have a family. I want to see you look around you. I want you to see what you've got now, instead of always what you might have. I don't want to see you wasting what you've got.'

She put her cup down again. 'Am I?'

'You don't need to be *told* a thing like that.'

Susie looked away from him across the café. She said, 'I've come so far. *So* far. You wouldn't believe how far. All those years of mistakes and negotiations, all the battles while I learned the lessons of doing business, all the recovering from bad advice, all the litigation with rivals who'd spied on me, all the training of people, the girls—'

'I don't doubt it.'

Susie gave a rueful little laugh. She said, 'I sort of feel I have to wear the scars. I feel that the company is my – validation.'

'What about the girls?'

'What about them?'

'They're your validation, Susan.'

She regarded him.

He said gently, 'They're not your rivals.'

'I never thought—'

He reached out a second time to hold her wrist, and

422

kept his hand there. She didn't take hers away. He said, 'Those girls of yours have got to learn, just as you had to learn.'

'But I've sheltered them.'

'Not any more, you shouldn't.'

She looked down at her hand in his grip. She said, half laughing again, 'I didn't think you knew anything about anything.'

Morris let go of her wrist, and wrapped the paper napkin round the granola square before he put it in his pocket. He said amiably, 'Nor did I.'

'I thought you didn't know how not to be a burden.'

Morris stood up a little stiffly. He said, 'Now that's the last thing I want to be.' He glanced down at her. 'Get up, Susan. We're starting as we mean to go on. Time to collect Maisie.'

'I don't think,' Jasper said to the estate agent, his phone in the hand not holding a vodka and tonic, 'that I'm sure enough about that flat to make an offer, after all.'

The agent, ten miles away across London, in Hoxton, did her professional best not to sound exasperated. 'I thought that the third viewing—'

'So did I,' Jasper said.

'It's a great location. And, I have to tell you, a very fair price.'

Jasper took a sip of his drink. Susie, he reflected,

would not have needed a shot of vodka before she made a difficult phone call. He said, sounding lame even to himself, 'I'm sure.'

'Well,' the agent said, gathering up her energies for a renewed assault, 'as it happens, I've got several other properties newly on the market, one-bedroom flats that meet all your specifications, even if they don't all have the view or the ceiling height of—'

'No, thank you,' Jasper said.

'Excuse me?'

'I said,' Jasper said, with elaborate courtesy, 'no, thank you. I don't think I'll be looking for a flat. Not any more.'

'But I thought,' the agent said, sounding seriously unsettled, 'that you wanted a studio flat within walking distance of your music studio.'

'I did.'

'May I ask, did the lease on the studio fall through?'

'Oh no,' Jasper said. 'Why should it?'

'I was under the impression that you—'

'So was I,' Jasper said. He smiled into the telephone. 'I read myself wrong. I'm sorry to have wasted your time.'

'Not *wasted*, I'm sure,' the agent said bravely.

Jasper took another mouthful of his drink. 'Well,' he said, 'I'm not going to be buying in your area, after all. So if that counts as wasting your time, I'm very sorry.'

The agent cleared her throat. He could tell that she was trying not to compute the hours she had spent on him which had, just now, come to nothing, nor to anticipate exactly how she would tell the vendor that his prospective buyer had just pulled out, for no reason he cared to specify.

'Perhaps,' the agent said a little tensely, and as if reading his thoughts, 'you would like to explain to me why a flat that fulfils every criteria you insisted on is suddenly no longer what you want?'

Jasper smiled into the telephone. He said warmly, 'No, I wouldn't, I'm afraid.'

'I see.'

'I wouldn't expect you to see, either. It must be maddening when people behave like I am, but there it is.'

'Is that your final word?'

'Yes,' Jasper said. 'Yes, it is. Sorry again.'

There was silence on the other end of the line.

Jasper took the phone away from his ear and looked at the screen. 'Call ended,' it said firmly. The agent had rung off without saying goodbye, without ending the weeks of their weirdly close relationship with even the anodyne platitudes of good wishes for the future. How very – peaceful.

Jasper dropped his phone into his pocket. He felt elated at having extricated himself from a complicated situation without having to ask for help to do so. It was a good feeling, strengthening. It almost merited celebrating with a second vodka and tonic, but on reflection he would save that second drink to have with Susie when she joined him, as she had promised.

'Are you working tonight?' she'd said, ringing from her office earlier that day. 'Could we perhaps have a drink together, at least? And not at home.'

No, he'd said, he wasn't working. He would be on Saturday, though, if she'd like to come to the gig?

'Yes,' she'd said.

'You don't sound very certain.'

'I'm – not very certain if you want me there.'

'Oh, I do.'

'Do you?'

'Yes,' Jasper had said.

He looked across the pub now towards the half-glazed door to the street. Susie would soon come through it, and then he could tell her about his conversation with the estate agent. In fact, he could make quite a funny story about his conversation with the estate agent. He smiled down into his glass. What was that French phrase about having a parting shot through the staircase just as you left someone you'd had – or almost had – a row with? Something about *un esprit de l'escalier*. Susie would remember. And perhaps he could then tell her what he now wished he'd said at the end of his conversation with the estate agent from

Hoxton, which was, 'The thing is, I'm not looking for a property on my own any more.' And then he would have laughed, in a jolly, we-blokes-are-so-hopeless kind of way, before adding, 'You sometimes need to go down the wrong path a bit, before you find the right one. Don't you think?'

The estate agent probably wouldn't have had a clue what he was on about. She'd have just thought that he was mad as well as being, as a potential client, bad. But it didn't matter. It didn't matter at all what the estate agent from Hoxton thought. All that mattered, really, was that Susie understood what he meant, what he was driving at. What he had determined about their future together. And she would. He was certain of that. She would.

Second Honeymoon
Joanna Trollope

BEN IS, AT LAST, leaving home. At twenty-two, he's the youngest of the family. His mother, Edie, is distraught. Her husband, on the other hand, is rather hoping to get his wife back. Meanwhile, Ben's brother is struggling in a relationship in which he achieves and earns less than his girlfriend and his sister is coping with debts and the end of a turbulent love affair.

As the children's lives become more complicated, they retreat to the simplicities of their childhood. But can you ever go home again?

Meet the Boyd family and the empty nest, twenty-first-century style.

'Trollope has perfectly caught the angst of the empty nest . . . the ebb and flow of relationships is brilliantly handled'
OBSERVER

'One of the finest chroniclers of the way we live now'
INDEPENDENT ON SUNDAY

Friday Nights
Joanna Trollope

FRIDAY NIGHTS, THE best night of the week, the night they all looked forward to more than they cared to admit – talking, drinking, laughing and crying together.

They were six female friends, different in age and circumstances, but with one common need: the warmth and support of their Friday nights. It was a time to share secrets and fears, triumphs and tragedies and, above all, to feel safe in the company of women friends. But things never stay the same forever, especially when a man is introduced into the mix . . .

'Hits a right and ringing note and keeps hitting it'
INDEPENDENT

'Many wise and accurate human observations . . . there are few writers who can understand the psyche of middle England as well as Trollope'
THE TIMES

The Other Family
Joanna Trollope

CHRISSIE, IN THE twenty-three years she's been together with Richie, had always believed that he loved her.

He loved their three daughters and their house in Highgate and their happy, lively existence. But if she really was the love of his life, why had he never given her the one thing that would have made her life perfect?

Then suddenly Richie is no longer there, and without him Chrissie's carefully constructed life is in jeopardy. The one big fact she had always tried to keep from her daughters threatens to overwhelm them all. For Richie had still been married to his first wife, the one with a son that he abandoned in Newcastle.

And now, with Richie gone and the practicalities of wills and money to be sorted out, it is finally time for the two families to face each other . . .

'Clever and thoughtful'
TATLER

'Highly recommended'
SUNDAY EXPRESS

'Beautifully crafted'
DAILY MIRROR

Daughters-in-Law
Joanna Trollope

RACHEL LOVES BEING at the centre of her large family. She has devoted herself fiercely to bringing up her three sons, but at their childhood home on the wide, bird-haunted coast of Suffolk, Rachel finds that her control begins to slip away. Other women – her daughters-in-law – are usurping her position. They have become more important to her boys than she is.

A crisis brings these subtle rifts to the surface. Can there be a way forward, if they are to survive as a family?

'Infallibly elegant . . . All this lies beneath the sparkling, well-groomed surface of a novel which could quite easily be read as a light diversion for an idle afternoon. But look more closely and something as grim as Greek tragedy is played out around the cosy family dinner table'
DAILY TELEGRAPH

'Wonderfully observed and readable'
THE TIMES

The Soldier's Wife
Joanna Trollope

THE SOLDIERS ARE COMING home – after six months in Afghanistan. Surely being reunited with their wives and girlfriends and families will be heaven, after the hell they have been through. But is it?

When Dan Riley returns to his adored wife, Alexa, and their children, his Army life still comes first. Alexa thought she was prepared to help him, and the whole family, to make the transition to normal life again – but no one had told her how lonely and near impossible the task would be. Does marrying a soldier always have to mean that you are not marrying a man, but a regiment?

'Written with all Trollope's customary skill and panache, this is an absorbing look at the modern military wife who no longer automatically follows the drum'
DAILY MAIL

'Trollope is on top form, hitting the zeitgeist with this perceptive and compassionate inside story of an army marriage'
WOMAN & HOME